THE
GOLDEN
SEASON

MADELINE KAY SNEED

THE GOLDEN SEASON

GRAYDON
HOUSE

GRAYDON
HOUSE®

Recycling programs
for this product may
not exist in your area.

ISBN-13: 978-1-525-89983-6

The Golden Season

Graydon House
22 Adelaide St. West, 41st Floor
Toronto, Ontario M5H 4E3, Canada
www.GraydonHouseBooks.com
www.BookClubbish.com

Printed in U.S.A.

To Diantha and David

For their love, which has never altered.

THE GOLDEN SEASON

I think it is safe to say that while the South is
hardly Christ-centered, it is most certainly Christ-haunted.

—Flannery O'Connor

PART ONE: Summer

You may all go to hell, and I will go to Texas.

—Davy Crockett

TEXAS SUMMERS ARE MURDEROUS.

The grass—lush, green, and filled with wildflowers only months before—withers. Boys pretending to be men wear full football pads during their two-a-day practices and pay no attention as the dry, brown grass cracks beneath their cleats.

The sun is inescapable. Temperatures rise into the one hundreds by midmorning. Heat rolls off the pavement in waves and makes the horizon ripple. By afternoon, it's hard to tell what in the distance is real and what is an illusion.

Pine needles roast on forest floors; their shade insulates the heat more than anything. The sharp scent is heavy, like too much perfume sprayed in a poorly ventilated room.

Mosquitoes thrive in the heat. Frogs, too. Cicadas come out at dusk and call to one another, their monotonous song cutting through the evening, a reminder that in summer there is no peace, there is no rest: there is only heat and noise.

Out of the city, when dusk comes around and the breeze picks up to offer some semblance of cool, folks sit out on their porches, layered with insect repellant, to survey their land, ravaged by the relentless heat. They drink iced tea, lemonade, water, or, if the summer is particularly long, beer, wine, whiskey, tequila.

It's inescapable. Man may have made box fans and central air-conditioning, but only four walls and a paid electric bill hold their manufactured air. The heat waits. It snakes into every crevice, cracked door, open space.

In West Texas, it's a dry heat. The dust rises up with the wind and blows through town like the devil, pelting rocks and sand everywhere, through car windshields, storefronts, windows. When it's over, the sun beats down with relentless precision. There is no coolness; there is no relief.

The heat breaks people. Hope for fall seems pointless. Spring is a distant memory, winter a fable told from a time long gone. By August, nothing feels real except sweat, thirst, heavy lungs, dizziness, sunburn, and the start of football season.

It's a haze, really. The need for relief outweighs the desire for anything else. It's easy at the end of summer to lose sight of what's important, to blink as it slips away.

1

EMMY

It wasn't that she didn't want to tell him. She just hadn't gotten the timing right.

Emmy's father, Steve, was not a reasonable man. He did not negotiate on matters of faith. The only issues he ever budged on were women and booze, but barely on the women and too much on the booze, and all of that only happened because Emmy's mom decided to leave him on the first cold day of the year, the first real freeze their town had seen in some time, on New Year's Day five years before. For her mom, it was the first resolution she checked off her list. For her father, it was a test from God.

"It's just my Job time," he said when Emmy had asked him how he was holding up. "Big Guy's giving me something to grapple with. Nothin' new there."

Most things stayed the same. He still coached the linebackers on the high school football team. Still taught American history to the juniors. Still lived in the same house his grandfather built, the one he grew up in with his mom and dad.

What *did* change: his house stayed empty most nights, no one waited for him after football games, and he started drinking.

It wasn't a lot, the drinking, but a couple of beers at night was a big jump for a man who had dedicated the first third of his life to teetotaling. He said he started because the coaches liked to grab beers after practice, and that could have been true, but Emmy figured the nights just got too lonely for him sometimes.

As for his stance on women, Steve used to believe their purpose in life was to become wives and mothers. But when his wife left him, he realized that marriage wasn't such a certainty after all. That even *he* could become part of the fifty percent and that everything could fall apart in an instant (though, of course, his wife would say that the instances had been accumulating for half a decade).

He never paid much attention to Emmy's education before the divorce, thinking all she had to do was get into a good-enough college that would allow her to meet a smart-enough boy who would marry her and provide her with a stable-enough life. Once he realized that no one was safe from the fallibility of marriage, though, he made sure Emmy was doing everything in her power to be financially independent.

"No, no, no," he said during her senior year of high school. "Just 'cause you're smart enough to get into those liberal artsy East Coast fancy-pants schools doesn't mean you're gonna go. You wanna pay off loans all your life for a degree in *English*? You're already fluent in the damn language! What more is there to know? No. You'll take the full ride at Walker. Stay in Texas. Major in business. You know they got one of the best business schools in the country? They're practically handing you money. I'll tell you what…"

It was a departure from the pre-divorce college discussion, which involved a couple of grunts and shrugs and a *wherever you get in is good enough for me*.

So Emmy knew her father was capable of change, of allowing

his beliefs to adapt, evolve. But she also knew that there was a limit. Every branch can bend itself a bit, but try and push it too far and it will snap.

Moments of true epiphany never come with a lightning strike or a burning bush. It's simpler than that. It's the trap of the internet, really. You can find whatever you need once you start looking.

Emmy's search began by accident, after her college roommate came back to their dorm, trembling with excitement, handing Emmy a Post-it note with a username, password, and website address.

"Free movies," she said, a little air whistling through the gap in her teeth. "Anything you can think of. Isn't that something?"

"Something illegal," Emmy, a notorious rule-follower, said, sticking the Post-it on her desk, determined to never use it.

But that weekend, her roommate went out of town, and Emmy had the dorm to herself, so she locked the door, turned off all the lights, and logged in. She searched for a movie she had seen a trailer for many years before. The website had the film— because, as her roommate had promised, it had every film—and she pressed Play.

There was a small moment at the beginning. Two women were sitting next to one another, watching a presentation. The lights were off. Their hands were close, but not touching. The women reached out their pinkies so that they lightly grazed one another. From both women, there was a sharp intake of breath, the briefest of glances, and, for Emmy, watching alone in her room, the most subtle click between her body and her brain.

Emmy had known that tension. She had felt that longing. And she couldn't deny it once she saw it played out on screen. Joy and dread flooded in her, a lethal cocktail of emotions that tightened in her abdomen, radiating anxiety in the rest of her body.

That was two years before Emmy told her dad, and in those

two years, she used every illegal site she knew of to watch every movie she could find. She was grasping at the intangibles she saw on screen. The breath of one lover behind the other. The tension of touching. The yearning, that palpable desire. She craved every connection she saw, making the truth more difficult to repress, stuff down deep. It always rose to the surface, weighing on her chest, getting caught in her throat.

Emmy kept getting sick. Colds, strep throat, and, once, a tonsil abscess that made her throat swell so badly that it blocked her airway. She went to the ER, where the nurse took one look at the back of her throat and nearly shouted, "Why the hell did you wait so long to come in?"

She was trying to wait it out until she graduated college, until she could move to some metropolitan area, blend into the masses of people, try a dating app or something. But the *waiting*, the fear—it was a virus. And if she continued lying to the people she loved, that virus might kill her.

2

On an impossibly hot day in August, after everyone left the party, Emmy finally told her father.

Steve always threw a going-away party for Emmy before she left for Walker University to start her semester. It was their little tradition. It had started three years prior, as a way for him to let the town know the family was just fine, even after the divorce. Emmy's mom came, too. He invited people from church, from school, from the board. He ushered Emmy around and made sure she spoke to everyone.

"This town is your home," he said to her when she complained about the small talk. "And these people, the ones that helped raise you, they're your family."

"You and Mom raised me."

"But they were there, too," he said. He took off his red baseball cap and rubbed his buzz cut with his massive hands, his skin slightly pink from the sun. He smashed the hat back on his head, pulling the bill far down his forehead. "They were praying for you, asking about you, watching you grow up."

"They were only watching because they cared about y'all, not me."

"Care for us bleeds into care for you," he said as he walked over to the grill. "Now, go get the burgers out of the fridge. Buns, too. Saw on TV you can grill the bread."

After that first party, Emmy realized two things: buns should be toasted in the oven, not on the grill, and her father was right. The town *did* love her. But she was right, too: it was *because* they loved him.

Though Steinbeck wasn't so small (it had around twenty thousand people), it felt claustrophobic to Emmy at times because of her father. Football coach at Steinbeck High for over twenty years. Former deacon at First Baptist Church. Little League coach, even after Emmy moved on to softball. He was everywhere. He helped with everything.

Growing up, his friends always checked in on Emmy. And he had friends all over town.

When she was a kid, it was the librarian at the public library, who bought her sodas from the vending machine while she waited for her mom to finish with her PTA meetings. In junior high, it was the owner of the diner, who gave Emmy and her friends free milkshakes with their burgers every time they came in. And in high school, it was the manager at the café, who gave Emmy free shots of espresso and helped her with algebra homework when she came in after school. Emmy knew them all and befriended them, too. It's like Steve had said: care for him bled into care for her.

It wasn't unanimous, the admiration for Emmy's father. There was Coach Derek Johnson, the offensive coordinator, who, in recent years, had become a little uneasy around Steve. He was the only Black coach on the team, and his frustration started later, after Steve got *Assistant Head Coach* added to his title. It was a purely ceremonious position—giving out titles cost less than giving out raises—but it was supposed to honor the time he had spent coaching and teaching at the school. Almost twenty years. The same as Coach Johnson. Afterward, Coach Johnson started making comments, just little jabs like, "Well, I wonder what your dad would give you up for," or "You better be careful, Emmy. As soon as that head-coaching position opens up, he'll leave you right behind like he did your mama."

His son, Jacob, was a close family friend. When Emmy asked him about the comments, he just shrugged and said, "Your dad took something that he shouldn't have."

But Coach Johnson and others like him were the exception, not the rule. For the most part, the town respected Steve's commitment to the team and saw the lack of progress in his career as loyalty to the town. And the town honored that loyalty with their own. During the divorce especially. People liked Emmy's mom just fine. But when folks around town asked Emmy about her parents, they always had a laundry list of questions about her dad: *How's the season shaping up? Any boys getting recruited this year? He sick of having to teach yet?* And of her mom, they always asked the singular *How's she holding up without you?* before they started asking Emmy about jobs and studying and the future.

Her mom, Lucy, did her best. She had grown up in Steinbeck, a cheerleader and a straight-A student. She'd gotten an academic scholarship to Walker University, just like Emmy. Lucky Lucy, they called her. Always got whatever she worked for.

Emmy's parents were high school sweethearts. They got married during college and moved back to Steinbeck after they graduated. At some point along the way, her mom went from Lucy to Coach Quinn's wife to Emmy's mom. Her identity was reduced to the people she was charged with taking care of.

After getting married, she volunteered in the community. She joined the PTA. She sang in the church choir. She went to every football game, sat next to the other wives, and chatted and chatted and chatted, but her heart was never in it.

Lucy was often bored, except for when she was with her daughter. When they were together, they liked to talk about all the lives they could live outside of Steinbeck. They both felt a sense of freedom in those conversations, released, at least in conversation, from the mundanity of West Texas life.

It was tempting for Emmy to believe that in her mother she had an ally. With their long conversations about the limitations of the town, it was easy for Emmy to forget that her mother was as firmly woven into the fabric of unquestionable belief as everyone else in Steinbeck. After all, Lucy was a West Texas girl with West Texas roots, and those could not easily be deracinated.

That summer, Emmy interned with a large marketing firm in Dallas. The eighty-hour weeks left her utterly empty at the end of every day, but thrilled, too, at the professional prospect of being very good at something she enjoyed and got paid for. At summer's end, she had a full-time offer to come back and work in the Dallas, Houston, or Austin offices after she graduated.

The internship finished the day before her father's party, two days before she was set to return to Walker to start her senior year. Emmy was to spend the night at her dad's house to help him set up for the party, but she stopped by her mom's place first for a celebratory drink and to dish about the World Beyond—what she and her mother called any place east of them.

When Emmy pulled into her driveway, her mother was already sitting on the porch, waiting, with an ice bucket chilling a bottle of champagne. Her long, dark hair bounced off her chest when she jumped up to hug her daughter.

"Emmylou," she said, pressing her face into Emmy's neck. "My fancy marketing woman! My big-city girl!"

She ushered Emmy into the living room, where a Dolly Parton record was spinning on an old turntable. Lucy bounced between the kitchen and the living room, talking about the town while she got drinks ready, pausing every now and then to grunt as she reached for various ingredients in the kitchen. She talked quickly, the almost-giddy excitement that always came when she was with Emmy spilling out as she clinked ice into a glass and popped open the champagne. Emmy sat back and listened, enjoying the warm familiarity of her mother's home: white walls, watercolors, the faint smell of jasmine and gardenias hanging in the air from her mother's perfume.

When the drinks were ready (gin and tonic for Lucy, champagne for Emmy), Lucy settled into the couch next to Emmy. They clinked glasses and took a celebratory sip. The champagne was crisp and cold, tickling Emmy's throat and flushing her cheeks, which were slightly pale from a summer spent sitting in a cubicle.

"You're gonna get out of this town, Emmy," Lucy said as a semitoast, taking another sip of her drink. "I just know it. After the summer you've had."

"Dallas is only a couple hours from Steinbeck," Emmy said, conditioned, like many Texans, to deflect any kind of compliment. "Not such a wild leap into the world."

"No," she agreed. She tucked her dark, stalk-straight hair behind her ear and pursed her full lips, which Emmy had always envied. Hers were thin, unremarkable, like her father's. "But it's a stepping stone. And it's a big company. You said they hired you full-time for next year? You could go anywhere."

"Can't imagine leaving Texas."

"Austin is in Texas, but it's…" Lucy paused to find the words "…it's *not* Texas. If you know what I mean."

"Crazy hippie weirdos," Emmy said, nodding.

"Exactly! You could become one of them," she said.

"Dad would be thrilled."

"The idea of you being anywhere farther than an hour away breaks his heart a little bit, I think."

"And yours?"

"Oh," Lucy said, smiling. She pulled a piece of lint off Emmy's shoulder. "I'm just fine wherever you end up. Seems to me like we've both been here too long."

"What? Fifty years in Steinbeck and you've maxed out? Wimp."

"Twenty-two for you, missy." She winked, then looked at her daughter and sighed. She took her hands and traced the tips of Emmy's fingers. "You look just like your father."

"But I've got your eyes," Emmy said, rolling them. They'd had this conversation before, many times.

"They're my grandmother's, you know, a tough Texas woman if there ever was one," Lucy said. "Maybe we got some of her wisdom lodged in them."

"Probably the reason I shoot skeet cross-fucked."

"Maybe," Lucy said. She looked at Emmy for a long time, seeing her ex-husband, weighing the pros and cons of his face in their daughter's.

"Does it really bother you? How much I look like him?" Emmy asked.

"You are you, and he is him," she said, hugging her, adding, as if for good measure, "that son of a bitch."

The record ended, filling the living room with temporary silence. Lucy jumped up to start it from the beginning. Dolly's familiar, famous riff played out as she sang "Jolene, Jolene..."

"It's exciting, Emmy," Lucy said when she sat back down, her cheeks flushed already from gin and vicarious possibility. "You have no idea how many opportunities this will open up. You can go *anywhere* after you graduate. And not get stuck like I did."

"You're not stuck, Mom," Emmy said, feeling all the confidence of a new opportunity. The champagne she drank had gone straight to her head. "You said before you wanted to leave. You could do it next year, move to Dallas, Houston, Austin. Work.

Or not. You got all that money from Grammy's and Grandaddy's wills. What's stopping you?"

"I guess you're right."

"Like me," Emmy said, draining her glass, feeling invincible. "Lived in Steinbeck all my life, then Walker for college. Equally small, equally conservative. But I lived in Dallas—a city! For a whole summer! And no one really knew me there. And I could do that again, somewhere else, after I graduate. I could let loose a little, you know? Take art classes. Find a girlfriend. Or—"

"What?"

"Or I don't know. Something else cool and citylike."

"Find a girlfriend?"

They both stared at each other. Lucy's jaw dropped, and then, so did Emmy's.

"I—I just," Emmy stuttered. "I mean. I…"

She had meant to tell her mother in a much more dignified way. With background information, reasonings, explanations with built-in defenses for herself so that her mother couldn't question what was being said.

"What are you saying to me?" Lucy asked. It looked like her worst fears had been confirmed. Her dark brows were raised so high they almost disappeared beneath her bangs. She set her glass down, hard, on the side table. "What are you?"

It was the first of many moments in Emmy's life where she felt separated from her mother. They'd had a few fights when Emmy went through puberty, but that had all been pent-up frustration from her changing hormones and the confusing crushes she wasn't supposed to be having on girls. During the divorce, they'd had a few fights, but Emmy had no siblings, and Lucy had no friends who didn't sympathize with her husband, so eventually, they'd had to lean on each other. All their fights before had been cracks, not fault lines.

That moment, though, felt tectonic. Her mother was devastated. She ran her hands through her hair. Her dark brown eyes, so wide, so identical to her daughter's, bugged out in disbelief until she narrowed them, glaring at Emmy. She looked furious. She looked betrayed.

She kept talking, in quick, rapid, breathless sentences, about how it wasn't right. It couldn't be right. She didn't raise that kind of daughter. And Emmy sat, silent, looking out of the window at the old cedar tree in her mother's front lawn. It stood still, no breeze moving through the boiling Texas dusk. Cicadas started buzzing, loud, relentless as always. Mourning doves cooed. The predictability of summer. All heat and noise.

"You can't tell your father," Lucy said finally.

"What?" Emmy asked, turning away from the window, almost laughing in disbelief.

"If we were still married, we'd have heard this together," Lucy said, thinking out loud. "But we're not. Maybe that's a blessing. We can protect him from this. And in the meantime, you can think on your choices. Take some real time to reconsider what you're doing with this decision."

Emmy had known her mother was conservative, but she had also always been reasonable, willing to listen, especially to Emmy. She found her daughter's *liberal leanings*, as she called them, amusing, a sign of her own independence and ability to think for herself.

But the way she looked at Emmy then—wide, horrified eyes, clenched jaw, flared nostrils, the lines on her forehead bunched together in deep trenches of disbelief—Emmy knew something had shifted in the way her mother saw her. It was strange, she thought, seeing someone who loved you suddenly have to take in the full picture of who you were, reconstructing what they had created in their mind.

"If you choose to go down this road, Emmy," Lucy said, letting her voice trail off.

Emmy closed her eyes. It wouldn't help to push back. To fight. Speaking up for herself had always been difficult, especially around her mother, who liked their conversations to stay within the bounds of her control. But it had never felt so impossible.

As if it were a choice to be in this body, Emmy thought, to have these desires. A choice to actively, knowingly rebel against *God's will for her life*, as her mother would put it, and her mother's mother, and her mother before her. They lived by the unchanging tradition set out for them so many thousands of years ago, when a boy from Nazareth decided to tell the world he was the Son of God.

"I'm going to tell Dad," Emmy said, making up her mind.

"No, you're not. You can't."

"I have to," Emmy said. "He has to know. It can't just be you. And this isn't something that's going to change."

"You don't know that."

"Yes, I do."

"It's wrong, Emmy," she said.

"It's me."

Lucy stared at Emmy, her creation gone astray in a way she had never anticipated, had never seen coming.

"He can't handle it, Emmy," she said. "It's too much."

"You don't know him like I do," Emmy snapped back.

"I know him differently than you do," she said. She grabbed Emmy's hand in hers, gently, giving her a sad smile. "And I may not know him well anymore, but I've known him since he was a boy. Emmy, some things just don't change."

"I'm going to do it," Emmy repeated, pulling her hand away. "Tomorrow. After the party."

Lucy scoffed and turned away from her. She picked up her drink and drained the whole thing in one gulp. Emmy looked at her. Half-disgusted in her mother's reaction, half-mortified that she'd told her in the first place. She got up to leave.

When Emmy got to the door, her mother shouted after her, "You're making a mistake."

3

When Emmy woke up the next day, her father was already in the kitchen, prepping for the party. Beers in the fridge, hamburger buns on the counter. He wore his old Steinbeck football T-shirt.

"Coffee's on," he said, when he heard her walk in. "Got you a mug out already."

"Thanks," she said, pouring the steaming coffee into her mug, sipping it slowly, watching her father's huge frame hunched over by the fridge as he stocked it, gently sliding each can toward the back so that they would get extra cold. His movements were so soft for a man his size. Emmy thought about what her mother had said, about him not being able to handle it, and her stomach tightened.

"You go out this morning?" Emmy asked, seeing his keys on the counter.

"Went down to the diner. Met with Dan Holcomb."

"Weather good?" Emmy asked, looking out of the window at a cloudless sky.

"Another day in paradise," Steve said, turning from the fridge to look at her, showcasing his lopsided grin and slightly crooked teeth.

It was one hundred degrees outside by midmorning. Emmy and Steve set up a couple of fans on the front porch, but they hardly made a difference. Nothing can combat the heat of West Texas in August.

Steve had a ranch-style house with a great big front porch that ran the length of it. The house was painted white, and it seemed to glow like a beacon among all the trees. He had a good bit of land on his hands. It had been in his family forever. There were live oaks, magnolias, and pines all around it.

He'd started planting the trees when Emmy was born. One magnolia right outside her bedroom window to make sure she had enough shade in the summer. It was a good tree, and the sweet smell of the flowers blooming in the springtime always reminded Emmy that school was almost out, summer was on its way. She loved climbing the branches once they grew sturdy enough to support her, but sometimes, in the middle of the night, she'd hear them scratch on her windows. It terrified her so much that she would sleep in the closet. Most kids think that's where the monsters live, but Emmy knew better: they were just on the other side of the wall, close enough to knock, begging to come inside.

Steve was proud of the magnolia tree. He felt like the flowers that bloomed in spring were his, since he had given life to the tree in the first place. He planted three more at the edge of his property, then lined his driveway with them, and then decided he wanted Texas live oaks all around the place. After the divorce, he went a little crazy and planted the pines. They shot up with alarming speed.

For the party, he had tied pink balloons to the pine trees at the front of the driveway.

"Look at my decorations!" he said to Emmy, pointing to them, delighted, when they walked out on the front porch. "Your mama called this mornin' and said she wasn't coming. So. Had to improvise in the making-things-pretty department."

"They look great," Emmy said, hugging him, trying to ignore the deep dip in her stomach at the mention of her mother. He smelled like sunscreen and leather, and Emmy kept her arms wrapped around his waist, holding him tightly, not wanting to lose him. Her fingers barely connected on the other side of him.

Everything about Steve seemed larger than life: his hands, his biceps, the bald spot that he covered with a baseball cap at all times, except in church. He had a soft, deep voice that always surprised people when they first met him. He seemed like the type of man who would project, if only to hear his own echo, but he only raised his voice out on the field when he was coaching. Mostly, he liked to listen and laugh. When he did speak, though, people were always willing to hear him out, and there was a musicality to his speech. His accent made syllables sit in his mouth and come out several seconds longer than they were supposed to, and he said things like "Don't squat on your spurs" and "They're all riding the gravy train with biscuit wheels." A Texas man through and through.

"Drier than a popcorn fart out here," Steve said, peeling Emmy's arms off of him. "Hotter, too. Hey, after everyone leaves, how about we have a beer on the porch. Somethin' I want to talk to you about."

"Okay," Emmy said, trying to keep her voice steady. She knew her mom wouldn't have told him without her, but she couldn't think of anything else in their lives that would prompt a pre-planned conversation.

Steve was not, by any stretch of the imagination, a spontaneous man. He liked routine. He liked predictability. It's why he hated it so much when quarterbacks called an audible during football games. When a play was called, he liked it seen through to the end. Let it play out like it was drawn up, don't take any chances on instinct.

But when it came to important conversations, spontaneity was all he had, like he never gave much thought to emotional matters until they were presented to him by someone else.

That's how he often got blindsided by bad news. The divorce came to him as a total shock, like he hadn't thought about the way he and Lucy had grown apart until she'd told him that she couldn't take it anymore.

The last thing Emmy wanted was to ambush him. She wanted him to be prepared. And if he was already planning on saying something important to her after the party, she thought it wouldn't be so out of place for her to say something, too. Maybe her mother was wrong. Lucy didn't know Steve like Emmy did. In her eyes, he could handle anything.

On the porch, Steve looked over at Emmy and smiled. His smile was like hers: it took up his whole face and reached his eyes so that they became squinty and crinkled with crow's feet. He had looked at his daughter like that all her life, with love and kindness and a support that felt both wholly genuine and unconditional.

Emmy remembered how her mother had reacted. How Emmy went, in an instant, from being her daughter to being someone that her mother barely knew. And the thought of that happening again, with *him*, terrified Emmy.

But there was also a relief in her mother knowing. A little light let into the secret place that Emmy had tried to keep buried for so long. She was tired of hiding herself for the comfort of others. Her body couldn't sustain the strain of it anymore. And she had to hope that love was strong enough to hold them together.

A warm breeze blew the smell of sunbaked grass over the porch. It was heavy and overwhelming. It reminded Emmy of evenings on the soccer and softball fields with her dad. *Grass is the only thing that smells good getting roasted by the sun*, he used to say after they finished playing.

"All righty, Emmy," he said, pouring her a glass of lemonade. "We better get on and get ready. Folks are fixin' to celebrate you today."

The guests showed up at three. Exactly.

The Southern Baptists were a punctual people and never came empty-handed. Gramble Grant, the pitmaster at Grant Barbeque, came with a platter full of beef ribs bigger than an arm, smoked to perfection, with sauce on the side, like real barbecue should be served. Coach Johnson and his wife, Cora, brought their famous five-cheese mac, just like they'd done for Emmy's high school graduation party and every birthday she'd ever had in Steinbeck. One of the coaches' wives brought her homemade peach cobbler and a gallon of vanilla Blue Bell ice cream. People brought homemade salsa and guacamole, queso, red beans and rice, tamales, chocolate pie, pecan pie, apple pie. They had ice-cold sodas, sweet tea, and lemonade, and Steve brought the men into the kitchen for beers and whiskey. Younger kids were running around, screeching, thrilled to have so much room to play. They used the trees as soccer goals, and Emmy played all-time quarterback for them during a pickup game of football. The speakers were on, and they blasted the country music that Emmy always pretended to hate but secretly loved because it reminded her of Steinbeck: the abundance, the people, the place.

The yard was filled with the dull roar of people talking and laughing and catching up, telling old stories over and over again to different groups of people. Emmy made the rounds in between football games. She caught up with high school acquaintances who had never left Steinbeck, former teachers, friends of her parents, and parents of her friends. She was grateful to be with the kids, who didn't care to hear about her plans after college and didn't make jokes about how she'd become corrupt in liberal cities like Austin or Houston. All the kids wanted was to see how far she could throw and if she really had mastered the perfect spiral.

"That's a good throw you got going there," Coach Johnson said to Emmy after she took a break with the kids. He looked just like his son Jacob, except his head was shaved: broad shoulders, wide smile, dark brown eyes with little flecks of gold, full of warmth and depth and light. He gave Emmy a hug and held her tight, a little longer than he normally did. She breathed in the sweet and sharp combination of cocoa butter and Old Spice. That was just like Jacob, too.

"Emmy, baby," Cora said, peeling her away from her husband and taking her in her arms, pressed Emmy's face into her chest while she squeezed her, rocking her back and forth. Emmy was a little overwhelmed at the sudden burst of affection but accepted the warmth without question.

When Cora pulled Emmy away from her, she dug her press-on nails into Emmy's shoulders, looking her up and down, like she was scanning her for any external damage. Her hair, which she wore in long braids, swung slightly as she looked back at Emmy. "Your mama told us what you said to her last night."

Emmy felt a flash of panic as she looked around for her father, for anyone in real earshot.

"It's okay, Emmy," Coach Johnson said, putting a hand on her shoulder. "We're not gonna talk about it. We just wanted to let you know we're here for you."

"And we love you," Cora added fiercely.

"And we're proud of you, too," Coach Johnson said, smiling. Cora reached out her hand to squeeze Emmy's.

Emmy looked at them, two people who had known her since she was a baby. They so earnestly returned her gaze, so genuinely held her hand, that she couldn't help but believe that she was not lost to them.

The consistency of their love felt like a miracle. And it helped

Emmy hope for a similar sort of response from her father. Emmy looked over at Steve standing on the porch, drinking beers, laughing with his friends. She wondered if he had the capacity for it: to love her without conditions.

"Your mama's gonna come around," Coach Johnson said, his face serious, filled with conviction. "It may take her some time, but just keep giving her space. She's gonna come around. I know she will."

"She's not the one I'm worried about," Emmy said, still looking at the porch as her dad opened a beer for one of his friends.

"People can surprise you," Cora said, following her gaze. "But as long as you assume the worst, you'll never know."

A couple of folks from the school came up next to them, laughing at the kids playing in the yard, fanning themselves with paper plates.

"It means a lot to me," Emmy said, lowering her voice, trying to find adequate words to express her gratitude at feeling so seen, so known. "What you said. That you came."

"We love you," Cora said. "It's all about love, baby. It always is."

The mosquito candles were lit, and spray was out on the porch, so the bugs were kept at bay, for the most part. A small miracle in the dead of summer. But Jim Salley, the head football coach, stood by himself near the porch steps and kept swatting at his neck every five seconds, like all his time battling against them out on the field in August and September had left him haunted, his untouched, slightly pink skin forever plagued with the torture of phantom bites.

Jan Oleander told anyone who would listen that Jim was a little off his rocker. She said he had a concussion back in college that never quite went away, which affected his decision-making, both on and off the field. It was hard to believe that a man could be out of sorts for such a long time without a doctor weighing in.

Even harder to believe since Jan's late husband, a member of the school board, had been organizing a whisper campaign to take down Jim as head football coach as soon as he got the job six years ago. After her husband passed away from a massive heart attack five years ago, Jan had taken up the torch.

When Emmy started mixing her iced tea and lemonade together, Jan was gunning for him, clacking her acrylic nails together, staring down Jim with her unblinking, beady gray eyes.

"Look at him, swatting at the air. Sharon should be ashamed," Jan Oleander pointed to Jim, stage-whispering to two ladies by the guacamole, loud enough for Emmy to hear. "Ashamed, I'll say, it's embarrassing to see. Swatting around at nothing. Well. He won't have to worry about gettin' bit out on the field this year."

"You mean he got fired?" one of the ladies asked. "Who are they gonna replace him with this late in the year?"

"I heard a little thing or two this morning from a real reliable source," Jan Oleander began, savoring the attention of an audience. "That this morning, they had a conversation with—"

"Emmy!" one of the ladies shouted, spotting her a few feet away by the drinks table. Emmy looked over and saw that it was Kathy Cole, the wife of their church's new pastor. "How are you, darlin'? How was the big summer in the city? We sure did miss seeing you around here."

"It was busy, but good," Emmy said, trying to discreetly wipe the sweat from her forehead.

"Oh, honey, just give yourself a good long dab," Kathy said, handing her a napkin from the food table. She took one, too, and dabbed her forehead. "Lord knows it's no secret us ladies sweat, too. Especially if you're out there playin' with those kiddos."

"Thank you," Emmy said, taking her up on the offer and, remembering where she was, quickly added, "ma'am."

"Where's your mama today?" Jan asked, raising one of her dark, penciled-in eyebrows.

"She couldn't make it," Emmy said. She remembered to smile. Her cheeks strained with the effort. "She's sick."

"That's a shame," Jan said. She pressed her lips together. "I *do* love seeing her and your daddy together. At least once a year. Miss seeing her up at church, too."

"The Methodists got to her."

"A shame," Jan repeated, "when families aren't able to keep together."

"Jan!" one of the ladies hissed.

"An observation." She shrugged. "I don't presume—"

"Ben!" Kathy waved to her husband. "Ben, come say hey to Emmy!"

Pastor Ben walked over from a group of men who were deacons at the church. He wore blue chino shorts and a pink-striped, button-down short-sleeve shirt that Emmy knew her father would hate because it was supposedly a *dandy man*'s color, not fit for a man of God.

"Hey there, Emmy," Pastor Ben said with a smile. There was something about him that made Emmy uneasy. His smile was strained and waxy, and it never met his eyes, which were cold, calculating. Judgmental. He motioned to the food spread on the picnic table. "Folks around here sure know how to put together a potluck."

Emmy nodded, grinding her teeth as she smiled, an old anxious habit she'd had since she was a kid, shy and awkward and always nervous interacting with strangers.

"And, wow, everyone's here," Pastor Ben said, looking around the yard. "Even Bob Sherman! Thought he'd left already."

Pastor Ben motioned over to the kids' table where Bob Sherman, who had been Emmy's pastor growing up, was kneeling next to one of his grandkids, cutting up his food. His puff of white hair was matted to his head with sweat, and his thick, round glasses were sliding down the end of his long nose as he focused on his task.

Emmy's heart did a small skip when she saw him. And, instinctively, she looked around for his daughter, Michaela. She wasn't there, of course, hadn't been back to Steinbeck since they had graduated high school. But still, some forgotten hope fired up inside of Emmy, forcing her to remember the days they had spent together, lying in the freshly cut grass in the field behind the church, looking up at the clouds, their hands just barely touching...

As if he could sense her thinking about his daughter, Bob Sherman caught Emmy's eye. He whispered something in his grandkid's ear and walked over.

"Emmy!" he said, stretching out his arm for a polite side hug. She slipped her arm around his waist and quickly withdrew it. He did the same. Both of their backs were drenched with sweat.

"Good to see you, Pastor Sherman."

"You can call me Bob, now," he said, beaming. "Retired! Gotta pass the torch on to Pastor Ben before I leave, and what better place than the Quinns'?"

"Leave?"

"We're movin' out to the Hill Country to be closer to Michaela," he said. His smile reached his gray-green eyes, the same shape and color as his daughter's. Lines crinkled at the edges from years of accumulated laughter. Emmy wondered if Michaela's would look like that, too, at his age. She swallowed hard. Emmy had made it a habit not to think about her. "And that little guy's parents are moving out there, too, next year. We'll probably be back in town to have Christmas with them. You remember Michaela's brother? John?"

Emmy nodded and asked, "Michaela's in Austin?"

"You know, you should give her a call. Austin's what? Handful of hours away? I'm sure she'd like to see you," he said, looking over at Steve, who had joined Coach Johnson and the other men from the team on the porch. "Y'all were so close back then and all."

He looked back at Emmy with narrowed eyes, his head tilted to the side. He started to say something, then stopped himself, rubbing his chin, as if he needed to keep himself from saying anything more.

Emmy wondered if he knew. About Michaela and her. And, despite knowing, still wanted Emmy to be close to his daughter.

"Sure, maybe," she said, feeling suddenly dizzy. She needed to sit down in the cool air.

"Emmy, Emmy, Emmy!" a chorus of small voices chirped from behind her. "Come play, come play, come play!"

"Go on," Bob said, smiling. "Seems like you're needed elsewhere."

Waving as she turned her back to him, Emmy took a deep breath, closed her eyes, and forced herself to shout enthusiastically, "Whose team am I on first?"

4

When the last of the guests left and her suitcase was packed and put in the car for her early morning drive back to Walker, Emmy sat down in one of the rocking chairs on the front porch. Storm clouds started to roll in, obscuring the sunset on the horizon. The sky looked green. The wind picked up and whistled through the trees. The cicadas started blaring, the crickets chirped. Texas was loud and alive and ready for a storm.

Steve came out with two ice-cold beers.

"Made sure the coaches didn't down all your favorites," he said.

"You sure know how to make a girl feel special." Emmy grabbed a beer and sat down on one of the red rocking chairs, patting the one next to her so that he would sit, too. "Storm's rolling in," she said, motioning to the sky.

"Seems that way." He sat down and cracked open the beer. He slurped away the foam that exploded out on the rim and grabbed the crossword he'd been working on earlier from the side table. He pulled out a pencil from the back pocket of his Levi's. He liked looking at something else when he talked to people on the porch.

"You know," he said, chewing on the end of his pencil. "Whoever the lucky son-of-a-gun is that's going to have to ask me for your hand in marriage better like my stuff, too, not just this fancy microbrew nonsense you love so much."

Emmy pretended to laugh.

"I'm serious. He better be able to drink a *man*'s beer."

"You didn't even know the difference until five years ago."

"I know it now. S'all that matters."

There was silence. Emmy's pulse raced. She needed to tell him that he wouldn't have to worry about that kind of man, that there would never be any kind of man to introduce him to. No man to take her hand in marriage. No man to disappoint him.

"Yep," he said, as if finishing his previous thought. "S'all I ask for. A man of God. And a man who likes good beer."

He took off his hat and rubbed the bald spot on top of his head. He filled in another answer on the crossword.

During Emmy's senior year of high school, she'd taken a geology class. They learned about natural disasters. As it turned out, some catastrophes cannot be prevented. They can be foreseen, like the hurricanes that come in August down by the Gulf. Galveston could build up as many storm walls as they wanted, but the storms would still rip through their beaches, the wind would tear up their homes, and the rainwaters would flood their streets. They could evacuate, save themselves, but some part of their lives would get destroyed.

That's how Emmy felt on the porch with Steve. One last moment of peace before the storm ripped them apart. Still, she hoped. Some hurricanes were downgraded to a tropical storm right before they hit land.

Thunder cracked.

"Looks like it's gonna come down," Steve said. Emmy didn't

answer. Her mouth was dry. She had lost her ability to speak. "Remember how I said I talked to Dan Holcomb this morning? Before the party?"

"Oh, yeah?" Emmy said, distracted, trying to manufacture a moment to tell him.

"Yep," he said. "He's still head of the board, you know. We had a nice long talk."

"That's good." Emmy looked over at his crossword. "Four down is *Donne*."

"Huh?"

"The clue. *Metaphysical poet*."

He looked back at the paper, crossreferencing the clue. He flipped his pencil eraser up and counted the squares needed for the answer.

"Not *Dun*. It doesn't fit."

"No, it's *Donne*. D-O-N-N-E."

He counted out the spaces, turned the pencil again, and filled in the blanks. When he finished, he looked up at Emmy with a proud smile. He took another sip of his beer.

"So anyway," he said. "Like I was saying. I talked with Dan Holcomb today."

There was another crack of thunder, but no rain. The cicadas' buzz increased to a monotonous blare, like a siren coming from the trees.

"How're his kids?" Emmy asked, wondering how anything to do with Dan could be of any importance to him or her. He did that sometimes. Beat around the bush of whatever it was he wanted to say. Talking in preludes, relaying unimportant anecdotes before he got to what mattered.

Normally, she didn't mind it. His rambling. But this night was different. She needed an opening, an opportunity to say it out loud, get it out there in the open. And he was moving too slowly through whatever it was he needed to say.

Her palms were sweating. Her mouth was dry. Thunder rumbled.

"Oh, they're fine," he said, chewing on the end of his pencil, the words spilling out of his mouth like molasses. "Growing up and moving out and all. But, you know, it was sort of a funny thing, our talk."

"Oh, interesting," Emmy said too quickly. She tapped her finger on the arm of the rocking chair, trying to play out the rhythm of what needed to be said.

"So there's going to be a change coming up," he said. He smiled, his real one, the kind he got when his defense came up big on third down or when they played a pickup game of soccer in the front yard. Emmy had just registered his excitement when he frowned and asked, "Where's your head at, Emmylou?"

"Oh, sorry, I was just thinking... The cicadas," she said, choosing the first thing she heard. "Why are they so loud?"

"They're singin'," Steve answered automatically. He always had an explanation for everything. "Just the males, though. To attract the females."

"What if the females don't like it?"

"It's not about liking or not liking," he said. "Just nature. Females hear the call, and they go runnin'."

"But what if the females sing a song, too? But only the other females hear it? And run to each other?"

"The cicadas?" he asked. He looked up at Emmy. "Doesn't work that way."

A moment. An opening. An instant. Emmy kept his gaze. She took a deep breath.

"It does for me."

He stared at her. He didn't understand. And then, suddenly, he did.

Redness flushed his face. His eyes watered. The pencil dropped to the floor.

"What are you saying to me, Emilia?"

"Dad, I'm—"

"God, no," he shouted. She'd never heard him speak so quickly. "No. Not now. Not today. Don't say it. Don't you ever say it."

He jumped out of the rocking chair, and it swung violently back and forth. The creaks were drowned out by a deafening crack of thunder.

He walked to the edge of the porch, leaned on the railing, and looked out at the yard, the expanse of land populated by so many trees that he had spent so many hours of his life planting. In that field, he and his daughter had played soccer, football, Frisbee, make-believe games where she was a knight and he was a dragon guarding a castle with a princess inside that she had to save. They had lain out in the grass on clear nights and looked at the stars, and he had shown her Orion's Belt, which Emmy loved, and he tried to point out the Big and Little Dippers, but Emmy couldn't tell the difference once the constellations got too complicated. Three stars in line, that was all she could see.

"Dad."

He wouldn't look at her. He was hunched over the railing. Even so, Emmy had never seen him look so tall.

"Daddy."

He stood up straight and turned to face her. He looked older, somehow. His face was a mask, no warmth in his eyes. He opened his mouth to speak, then shook his head. He covered his face with his enormous hands, the hands that had held her when she was a baby, picked her up when she had scraped her knees, threw her first pitch. They separated him from Emmy now.

"Dad." She stood up and walked toward him. He did not turn away from her. "Dad, I can be happy. I can love someone. Can't you be happy for me? Be happy for the life I can lead?"

Steve put his hands down from his face. Emmy wasn't sure why, but she had expected to see tears. His eyes were dry, cold, filled with resolve. Then, he said, calmly and clearly, "That road leads to hell."

He walked through the door and slammed it behind him. The sound echoed through the field. Emmy stared at the door.

"Are you fucking kidding me?" she shouted. Spit flew from her mouth. "That's your line?"

The door locked. The dead bolt, too. The TV turned on. Joe Buck's muffled voice seeped through the cracks. Someone was up by two. Probably not the Rangers.

Emmy rang the doorbell. The curtains were drawn, but she banged on the windows, anyway. She shouted. She paced back and forth on the porch, her footfalls slamming on the floorboards, which wobbled and creaked. She tried the door again. Locked. She knocked, her fists hammering on the enormous oak door. No one answered.

Her knuckles throbbed. She looked down. There was no blood.

Emmy turned, pressing her back against the door, and slid down it, letting the ridges roll down her spine. If she closed her eyes, she'd start crying. She could already feel her rage recede and warp into some twisted knot of regret and anxiety and guilt. It would sit in her chest, make it hard to breathe.

Instead, Emmy looked out at the dry, dead grass, her dad's land wilting in the heat of summer. Mixed with the sounds from the TV inside the house she was no longer allowed to enter, she heard the doves in a nearby live oak coo. The trees whipped back and forth as the wind picked up and swirled. Lightning illuminated the clouds in a purple glow. Thunder rumbled. It still hadn't rained.

It was getting close to dusk. The cicadas were out, buzzing their one blaring note from the trees, underscored by the deep-throated croaks of frogs. A bush in front of the porch shook as something rustled within. Emmy listened for a rattlesnake shake, but it never came.

Eventually, she got in her car and started the ignition. Before she reversed out of the driveway, she took one final look at the home in which she had grown up.

The porch was empty. The lights were off. She couldn't hear the TV. If she hadn't known any better, she might have thought the place was abandoned.

5

STEVE

On the day of Emmy's party, Dan Holcomb's call came as a shock.

Normally, on the Sunday before the season got going, Steve relaxed. The next four months were consumed with the team every day of the week. He had to be focused. Had to lose himself to the game.

But the Sunday before it all got started was his day to rest, to survey all that was his and be grateful. It always made it seem like the perfect day to host Emmy's party. See all the folks from around town, from the church, from the school. Have them see Emmy off, show her how much she was loved. It was a proud thing for Steve. Exciting, too, that so many people were willing to show up.

But that Sunday, Dan Holcomb asked Steve to head over to Oliver's Diner to have a chat with him early in the morning, right at dawn. Dan was head of the board, and he made most of the big decisions about the team, like hiring and firing guys. In his twenty-odd years of coaching at Steinbeck, Steve had never once met with the head of the board. With Jim doing such a half-assed job, it didn't seem like a good sign.

Football for Steve was always more than a game. It was an opportunity. It was a baptism.

Boys could be molded into men with the right direction. Guidance. Preacher men had their calling: to save folks from their own predisposition to sin. And Steve had his: to save boys from the weakness of the world.

Kids came in off junior varsity, all swagger and showmanship, ready to walk the halls with their letterman jackets, get their girls, go to parties. But it was a coach's job to make sure that they became more than that. Help disciple them into good men, in the world and on the field.

Football's not a sport often associated with empathy, but Steve believed a team couldn't win anything without it. If you didn't feel every hit, every missed catch, every inch that got lost on a big third down play, then it was hard to pull it all together and come back at the end of the game, to dig in deep, to do it for the guys next to you. Teams couldn't work without trust. Couldn't work with one guy prioritizing his stats over the good of the team.

So Steve punished selfishness. There was no joy in that outcome. It was a means to an end. Some coaches disagreed. Thought a selfish player would do whatever it took to make himself look good. They'd feed their egos and write off their bad behavior with *boys will be boys*, letting them fuck up forever, never letting them learn that no man is free from consequence.

A good head coach understood the necessity of investment— in the players' character and skill, in the game, in the program. It had to become an obsession. Had to get the boys to see that their future was tied to the game. That if they worked hard, if they died to themselves and were reborn on the gridiron, they could become more than they ever would have dreamed for themselves. A good head coach saw to it that no potential was left unmet, that every boy was challenged, pushed, and molded into a man.

That's how Steve knew they'd never be any good with Jim leading them.

They were going on their sixth season with him at the helm, and it was like he'd run out of steam. He'd been a Texas high school football legend for years. Division One State Championships. Coached top recruits. Turned programs around. Mentored the men he worked with so that they could go on and land head-coaching jobs of their own all across Texas.

But Steinbeck was the final resting place for his career, and he knew it. He'd been phoning it in. Going through the motions. Insisted on doing the play calling on offense, even though Johnson had a natural knack for it. Jim clung to past spreads and schemes that had worked at other schools, bigger schools, where you didn't have your best players playing on both sides of the ball. He wasn't willing to adapt his approach to a Division Two school. Whenever anyone questioned his judgment, though, he'd crack his knuckles so that they were forced to stare at the three State Championship rings lined up on his right hand.

Where Jim fell short, Steve had started picking up the slack. He reached out to recruiters. He sat down to dinner with kids' families, laid out their options for them, taught them how to conduct themselves during an interview. He joked with them, prayed with them, believed in them. And Jim kept on in his way, going through the motions, never taking the time to invest in anyone.

Steve knew that Johnson was mad about the assistant head coach title. But Steve was putting in the work. He was doing his damnedest to make sure Jim didn't run their program into the ground. Steve thought Johnson was a great offensive coordinator, a real genius on that side of the ball, if he was being honest, but he had Cora and Jacob and a horde of nieces and nephews that took up his time after practices and on the weekends.

But Steve? All Steve had was time. After Lucy had left him

and Emmy had gone off to college, Jim kept on as head coach, and it was clear that someone would have to put in the extra work to make sure they didn't become the laughingstock of the state. So he poured all his extra time into the program. Into the players. Into the game. He gave everything he could to the team and never asked for anything in return.

But Steve hadn't expected to be punished for it, either. So when he walked into Oliver's Diner, a light sheen of sweat trickled down the back of his neck. His stomach was rolled up in a tight knot. He tried to cough it away, but his throat was tight, and all that came out was a little wheeze.

The diner was old and smelled like the aged pages in a long-forgotten library book. The walls were painted a robin's-egg blue, and at the back of the diner, the paint had started chipping. Pictures of Texas football stars were hung up all over the walls—Earl Campbell, Bobby Lane, Raymond Clayborn—and Johnny Cash was playing on the jukebox.

Dan was already at a booth, sipping coffee, looking like he'd been sitting for some time. He looked up when Steve walked in the diner and waved him over, tipping his black cowboy hat back so he could get a good look at him.

Dan brushed a piece of lint off the navy sports jacket he wore over a white T-shirt. When Steve sat down, he took off his cowboy hat and rested it on the table.

"Howdy, Steve," he said, as the men shook hands. "Hang on, I'll get you a cup."

Dan slid out of the booth and walked behind the diner counter, grabbing a pot of coffee and a white, cracked mug. He grunted a little as he tried not to spill the overfilled cup, his wide frame swaying side to side as he made his way back to the table. He set the cup in front of Steve and ran his hand through his full head of hair. It used to be jet-black in high school, but it had salt-and-peppered over time.

"Sorry I can't make it to Emmy's shindig tonight," Dan said.

"The boys are back in town, and Cindy wants to do a family dinner. You get how it is."

"'Course," Steve said. "Family first. Y'all can swing by for leftovers tomorrow."

"Appreciate it," Dan said, shifting in the booth as he prepared to change the subject. "So y'all ready for the season?"

"Guess we'll see about that tomorrow. Two-a-days starting and all."

"Heard Jim hadn't changed any of the schemes from last season."

"Well, no, but—"

"And we didn't even make the play-offs," Dan said. "You know how easy it is to make the play-offs these days? Top four teams in every district make it in. Six teams in our district, Steve. All we had to do was not be one of the worst two teams. And we couldn't manage that. Now, what do you think of that?"

Dan was a dangerous man to let something slip in front of. He was an attorney, always building a case against something, someone. Steve had to be careful. He looked down into his coffee. The black liquid morphed his reflection into a whirlpool of nose and eyes and chin.

"Yeah, well," Steve said, letting his voice trail off.

"How would you change it?" Dan asked.

"Oh, you know, Jim's got an idea of what he wants."

"But I asked about you, Steve. You've been coaching the 'Stangs for, what? Twenty years? Never left the program. Most men shop around a bit when they don't get promoted after three with a team. So you either don't got any ideas and you really are just a history teacher who coaches on the side. Or you know exactly what to do to make this team great."

"What is greatness, anyway? They're just a bunch of kids," Steve said, trying to avoid saying anything that would make Jim look too bad. Dan's face darkened, and Steve understood the implication of what he'd said almost a second too late. He immediately started to backtrack, panicking. "Not that I don't—"

"You don't know what it means to be great in high school football?" Dan's face had turned a deep shade of red.

"No, I do. I don't know why I—"

"'Cause if you're not sure about that, Steve, I don't know if this is a conversation we need to be having."

"No, no," Steve said, knowing an ended conversation with Dan was worse than whatever it was he had to say. "No. I know. State. It's always State."

"All right," Dan said, taking a sip of his coffee, frowning at him over his mug. "Good."

Steve grabbed a napkin from the table and wiped his forehead. He couldn't stop sweating. Dan shifted in his seat and cleared his throat, the way most Texas men did when they were done beating around the bush.

"Well, here's the deal, Steve," Dan said, setting both his hands on the table like he must have done in many meetings before. "Jim's gone. He doesn't know it yet. But the board talked it over, and we're just not comfortable with the direction this program is going in."

The blood drained from Steve's face. His head throbbed with pressure. This was it. This was the end of his career. The day before two-a-days.

"We thought about looking around for another guy," Dan continued. "But it's a bit late in the game for that. All the contracts getting extended and signed and all."

Steve nodded, jaw clenched.

"So the board was thinking—well, it was my idea, really, if you want to know the truth—but we were thinking we oughta find a guy on the inside, who knows this program better than anyone. Who's committed to the team. To the community." He smiled at Steve. His capped teeth seemed to gleam in the dim light of the diner. "And who better fits that description than Steve Quinn? Former star linebacker turned coach. Previously a deacon at the church. Raised a daughter beloved by all. Divorce doesn't even matter, that's all water under the bridge now.

"It's a big responsibility, I know. You don't have to accept right away. But you're the man for the job. It's an interim position, keep in mind, so if it doesn't work out… Well, we're not there, yet. But. We can draw up the paperwork on Monday. But I guess I'm getting ahead of myself. What do you say, Steve? How would you like to be the head coach of the Steinbeck Mustangs?"

Steve inhaled deeply and looked away from Dan toward the jukebox as the album changed, and Johnny sang out, deep and strong, about love.

His first thought: *I'm not getting fired.* His second: *Holy hot shit.* Head Coach. Of the Steinbeck 'Stangs. After Steve knew he wasn't good enough to play pro, it was the only dream he'd ever had. To have the 'Stangs for himself. To not have to teach. Get to reorganize schemes, approaches, the locker room. Get the boys tough. Real tough, like they did back in Steve's day.

It took all the self-control he could muster to not cut Dan off, shout *Yes!* right away. Composure was an important part of coaching, and you never wanted to come off as too emotional when you weren't on the field. Women often got in a tizzy at the slightest bit of news, and Steve believed it was important for a man to bury deep down the instinct to react, where no one could see. So he took a deep breath, looked at the pictures hanging on the walls, and exhaled as Johnny sang about a ring of fire.

"Don't got to think about nothing. Opportunity of a lifetime," Steve said, sticking out his hand to shake Dan's. "Let's get us a State Championship."

"Now," Dan said, after shaking hands, "I know you're a no-nonsense kind of guy. But you're about to become a public figure. Reporters, interviews. The whole nine yards. And you know this town holds folks in power to the highest moral standard. As they should. So I wouldn't be doing my job if I didn't ask. Anything at all, family or finances or otherwise, that would cause us a problem? Can't afford a scandal when we're shaking things up so late in the game like this."

Steve took a moment to think it over. Did a quick scan of his life. Everyone knew about the divorce. He and Lucy were on good terms. Emmy split her time between them both. He spent some time and money at the Corral Bar, but never too often and never too much. His conduct, as far as he could tell, was pretty damn clean.

"Emmy's thinking about moving to Austin," Steve said, practicing the way he'd talk in all his future interviews. "A real shame, but not such a scandal."

"Can't control our kids' crazy choices," Dan said. "One of my boys is down in Houston. Started going to Astros games and everything."

"Well, now, that's a scandal if I've ever heard one," Steve replied, a little too quickly. With every second Dan didn't add a caveat, a light-headed giddiness started slipping into his speech.

"No kidding," Dan said, sliding out of the booth, putting his black cowboy hat back on his head. "This all sounds good to me. Gotta go get the board together. Have a tough conversation with Jim. But starting tonight, the team is yours. Good luck. And congratulations, Steve."

After he walked away, Steve sat in the booth for a moment, letting the AC vent above him blast cool air down his neck until the hair stood up.

Lucy would love this, Steve thought. If they were still together, she'd be the first one he'd tell. He'd try to stay casual about it, keep it a secret for as long as possible, but as soon as he'd see those deep brown eyes, he'd take her face in his hands, kiss her deeply, and say, "You'll never believe it, baby."

Steve thought about calling her. But they hadn't spoken in some time, and she wasn't even coming to Emmy's party, so he figured she was busy. Still, imagining what could have been made him smile.

And then Steve thought of Emmy. A lightning strike of excitement hit him when he imagined telling her. No one loved football more than her. She knew every play call, every player, every statistic for every season he'd ever coached. On Saturdays, when Steve came back from breaking down film with the team, he'd come home to Emmy sitting on the porch, her legs swinging off the rocking chair when she was little, and then firmly planted on the ground when she was in high school. She'd look up at her father and say something like, "Well, Daddy, what're we gonna do about the line, huh?" She was his favorite assistant coach. He called her his secret weapon.

When Steve told her, he knew she'd jump up and down. Maybe let out a little squeal. She'd smile her real smile, the big wide one that she didn't have to think about. She had his smile. It took over her whole face and reached her eyes and transformed her whole person into a beacon of pure joy and light.

For the first time since the divorce, Steve felt the pieces of his life coming back together. This was the beginning of a new era, the one he'd been working toward since he started his pre-season three-mile training runs when he was twelve years old.

Steve saw Oliver coming out from the kitchen and didn't reckon he'd be too pleased to see Dan had got him a cup of coffee without his permission, so Steve slipped out of the booth, the leather sticking to his jeans, and went outside.

The sun was already hot, even early in the morning. It thawed his skin, frozen from the AC in the diner. When he felt it burn his face, a delayed excitement started to simmer in his chest. He jogged to his car, feeling young again, like eighteen instead of fifty, like he had all the time in the world before him.

When he got in the car, he rolled down the windows and turned the radio up real loud. They were playing a country song with a steel guitar and a fiddle and a deep, twanged voice singing about lost love and interstate daydreams.

If Steve had known what was to come, he would have bottled

up every ounce of joy he felt in that moment. He would have stayed in the sun a couple seconds longer, would have sung along to the radio a little louder, would have marveled at the miracle of being alive—every breath a reason to give thanks.

But like anyone who's gotten everything he's ever wanted, he assumed that his Job time had ended, that he had been tested and had proven himself to be a good and faithful servant, worthy of his reward.

So instead of sitting in the moment, Steve let it catapult him into the future. He watched as it unfolded in front of him like mile markers on the state highway: a dozen seasons as head coach. Championships. A dynasty. They'd become a force to be reckoned with. No one would mark them as an easy win on their schedules. In two-a-days, before the season even started, they'd warn boys about them: *Those 'Stangs will kill us if we don't get our shit together!* They'd finally earn the respect of their opponents, of the entire state of Texas.

Other things would fall into place, too. In a couple years, Steve could imagine Emmy at the games with her husband and their little baby that he'd hold up in the stadium after they won another State Championship. She might have a little boy dressed in a tiny football uniform with little headphones covering his ears, protecting him from the noise, because the stadium would be roaring. The whole town would be there. Lucy would be back by Steve's side. He would lift up the little guy so he could see the field, the goalposts, the end zone, the fans, all of it a kingdom he could inherit.

Steve hoped that Emmy might have a girl, too, a little legacy that Lucy would dress up in too much lace that he would ruin when he took her out to play in the backyard. He'd plant another magnolia near the old one and build a treehouse where she could read and play and laugh.

He'd get offers from other programs, bigger programs, maybe

even Dallas, at Highland Park, or down in Houston, at Katy High. Permian would come calling, too, and Midland Lee.

None of it would matter. He'd turn them all down. No amount of money could buy him out of the dream. Steinbeck. A new program. A new era. No more head-coaching turnovers, no more job insecurity for the guys not teaching. A program strong as iron that he'd get to forge.

Steve turned into the driveway, wondering if Emmy was up yet. He smiled, looking at the pink balloons he'd tied to the pines the night before. He took a deep breath and got ready to tell her.

6

The day after Steve's conversation with Emmy on the porch, he
led his first practice as head coach. For him, life went, unbear-
ably, onward.

"Jesus Tap-Dancin' Christ!" Steve screamed at one of the Williams twins—Big Williams—as he dropped another interception. "Catch the goshdarn ball!"

Steve slapped him on the helmet as he ran back to the line.
Good defensive end, fine kid, Steve thought, but he had terrible
hands. Steve took a towel out of his back pocket and buried his
face in it, wiping as much sweat away as he could. The heat was
suffocating, especially in the afternoon.

During two-a-day practices, there was nothing but burn, sun,
pain. Steve looked down at his hands. There was dirt underneath
his fingernails, and a heat rash snaked up each finger. Lucy used
to tell him to be more careful about it, to slather on sunscreen
whenever he got the chance, but he always ended up sweating

the stuff off, and it got in his eyes, and there was no real way to outrun the Texas sun. No real protection, no real relief.

When Emmy was little, she'd stay out with Steve during the afternoon practices, running along the sidelines, watching the boys hit and run and pass. She screamed at them to go faster, play harder, and they listened. She high-fived every single player when practice was done. She was a staple on the team.

During a tackling drill, Steve took his eyes off the action to look at the abandoned sideline. She hadn't come to two-a-days in a decade, so he didn't know why she would have been there on that day, but he had to look. He couldn't help it.

It had to be Lucy's fault, Steve thought. That she ended up like this. The mother was supposed to teach a daughter how to be a woman. All those years of her not having a boyfriend... Lucy could have done more, *should* have done more. This all could have been prevented if she had just done her job.

"Coach Quinn, did you see that fucking tackle?" the quarterbacks' coach screamed, elated. "Woo-wee, y'all are flying off that line!"

Steve snapped back to attention, watching the boys, trying his best to bury Emmy and Lucy down deep, somewhere they wouldn't come up and distract him.

"You see the new kid?" Johnson asked, walking over, pointing downfield. "Miguel Martinez. Transferred here from El Paso."

Steve's first thought when he saw Martinez was *Now, that's a quarterback.* Tall and lean and broad-shouldered, he stood by the water coolers with his arms crossed, looking out at the linemen going through their blocking drills. Trey Maxwell, the star running back and team captain, came up beside him, said a couple words, put his hand on Miguel's shoulder, which the new player shoved off immediately, walking away.

"El Paso don't look so friendly," Steve said.

"Got a hell of an arm," Johnson said, shrugging.

"We already got a QB."

"Not like this kid," Johnson said. "I know you've been working with Little Williams for a couple years."

"Big Williams, too."

"But this kid can *throw*. And scramble. He's quick."

"Doesn't look like much of a leader," Steve said, watching
Miguel walk away from Trey. "And the guys trust Little Williams. Can't underestimate the power of trust in a huddle."

"Can't underestimate the power of an arm during a pass play,"
Johnson said as Little Williams dropped back and underthrew his
receiver on a slant route. Before he walked away, he said, "You're
a head coach now. You don't get to play favorites."

Steve had been working with the Williams twins since they'd
both made varsity their sophomore year. Big Williams was a
natural lineman on both sides of the ball, but especially the
defense—strong and quick and ruthless on a blitz. Little Williams was shorter, smaller, less naturally equipped for the game,
but no one worked harder than him. He studied the offense ob-
sessively, memorized routes, always knew his checkdowns; he
lifted and ran and put in the hours after practices. He was good
enough to start, but he lacked that ineffable quality, that natural instinct, that no one could ever achieve through work. You
were either born with it, or you weren't.

Steve watched Little Williams's drop back. Eighty percent of
his weight on his back foot, twenty on his front. He pivoted off
the ball of his back foot. Kept his chin over his toes so he didn't
fall backward. Quick step, crossover. Looked to the right for his
first read. One big step, two quick.

One step. Two steps. Three steps. Textbook perfect. But not
natural.

Steve looked away as one of the offensive linemen lifted his
helmet to vomit. The first of two-a-days, but certainly not the
last.

Two-a-day practices were an exercise in insanity. If you could
will yourself through them, wake up in the morning, push your

body to the breaking point and come back in the afternoon to do it all over again, then pouring yourself into forty-eight minutes of organized brutality under the blazing lights on Friday night felt like nothing.

After all the years, there was still wildness in it for Steve. A freedom. Removed from society, from reality, from any problems outside the stadium, they were all men united in one goal, one focus. Nothing could hold them back. They could not be reduced. They were "not a bit tamed"—that was from Walt Whitman, Steve remembered, one of those fancy writers Emmy loved.

"Okay, boys," Steve screamed, blowing his whistle. "Bring it in."

It jarred Steve at first, seeing them all surround him instead of some other man. He kept forgetting he was in charge. But they came into the huddle, dropping to their knees, their helmets planted firmly in the ground, their hands gripping their face masks, their other arms resting on their thighs. They hung their heads in exhaustion. Steve cleared his throat. He had been preparing this speech for many years, on long drives, in the shower, in his sleep.

"First day is done," he said. His voice echoed over the field, across the one hundred yards of freshly cut grass. Some of the boys lifted their heads, squinting into the sun, ready to listen. "And I don't know about you, but I think we got a lot of work to do. All of us. Coaches included."

"Damn straight!" one of them shouted. Everyone laughed. Steve exhaled a little breath of relief.

"That's right. We got work to do. But the skill is there. Your power is there. We got to mold ourselves, now. That's what this is for. All the early mornings, the baking afternoons. This is where we lock in our destiny. This is where we get good. When it's late October and we got a play-off berth on the line, you know what's gonna separate us from those other guys?" He paused to turn around in the huddle, looking as many guys in the eye as he could. They were locked-in. "This week. These moments. Every hit. Every route. Every rep. Make it perfect now. Mold it. Mold it in your bodies, your minds.

"You see, in Texas, we're pretty damn lucky. God made our practice fields hot as kilns. You know what happens to clay in a kiln? It gets hardened. Fortified. If you stick a wonky-looking thing in an oven, it'll come out wonky-looking. But if you take the time to form it, to shape it, to make it perfect, when it's kilned it'll come out that way. Hard. Perfect. Unbroken.

"Now, I don't know about you, but I'm pretty damn tired of everyone in this goddamn state underestimating us. I'm pretty damn tired of losing. I say it's our time. Our time! To take it all. State Championship. Why the hell not? Let's form ourselves now, get us ready for war, get us ready for Dallas. If you give me everything you've got this week, and the next week, and the next, I promise you, we'll be the best damn team this town has ever seen."

When Steve finished, the boys broke out in a roar. They leaped to their feet, their helmets held high over their heads. Trey swaggered to the middle, shoving on his helmet, getting Big Williams to do the same. They knocked heads in the middle of the circle, and the boys around them screamed their approval. Then Williams ripped off his helmet and roared at the sky, pounding his chest. He squatted down and looked at his teammates, saying, "All right, all right, here's what we're gonna do. 'Take State' on three, you hear me? One, two, three."

The boys devolved into a mass of screaming, of call and response—"Take!"/"State!"—of shoving, laughing, howling at the vast Texas sky, their shouts echoing across the empty field. They kept going all the way into the locker room.

"Not a bad speech, Steve," Johnson said, carrying the football bags over his shoulder. "Bit of an overpromise. But it got the boys excited."

"All right, Johnson," Steve said, waving. "See you tomorrow. Say hey to the missus for me."

He didn't respond. Just kept on walking.

It hadn't always been like that. All tension and resentment and clipped sentences. They'd been close once, Johnson and Steve. Brothers in arms. Riding the wave of incompetent head coaches, keeping their heads above water, surviving all the turnover the program had seen over the years. He taught calculus; Steve taught history. He had Jacob; Steve had Emmy.

Sometimes losing in life is inevitable. But if you can foresee it, intervene at the right time, it can be prevented. And Steve wouldn't lose Johnson.

Johnson didn't think Steve had gotten the job on his own merit. That was all right. He didn't have to convince him otherwise. Just needed to convince him to stick with Steve and the team. Not abandon them at their most crucial moment. After all, what did it take to be a good head coach? Swallow your pride and make the best decision for the team.

"Johnson," Steve shouted, jogging after him. "Wait up a minute."

"Something wrong?" Johnson asked without turning around.

"Assistant head coach," Steve said. "I want you to be my assistant."

"Assistant," he said, scoffing. "Working under you."

"Both been through it. The shit."

"Same amount of years, same amount of shit," Johnson said, finally stopping and spitting beside him. He dropped the red ball bag and tightened the strap of his beige bucket hat under his chin. "And you get the pay raise. You get the job title. You get the bonuses. You don't gotta teach. You ever wonder why that is, Steve? That a man like Dan Holcomb would come to you before me?"

"I didn't ask for this," Steve said, keeping his voice calm.

"Didn't say no to it, either," Johnson said.

"Would you have?" he asked.

Johnson hesitated and pushed up the long sleeves of his gray T-shirt. "Guess not."

"Only took three years to get *assistant* taken out of my title," Steve said. "Bet you could do it in fewer."

Johnson grinned. It was reluctant. But it was enough.

"Always been faster than you, Quinn," he said, kicking the grass, shading his eyes to look out at the practice field. "All right. Assistant head coach. I get a plaque or anything?"

"Can order you some new business cards."

"Great. I'll hand them out to the in-laws at Thanksgiving, prove them all wrong," he said. "Boys don't look horrible this year."

"Yeah," Steve said, looking toward the stadium. In no time, it would be the fall, and the stands would be packed with the band and the fans, the cheerleaders leading them in screaming chants about the offense and defense. "But we need to be good."

"Boys are excited to play for you," Johnson said, tipping off the bucket hat so the string tightened around his thick neck. His head was clean-shaven, like always, streaks of sweat coming down his dark skin, and he lifted up his arm to wipe it away, his shoulders broad and stiff, his arm barely lifting high enough to wipe at his cheek. He'd been a great linebacker once, but now his body was paying the price for all his hits.

"They're just excited to play," Steve said. "You remember how it is."

"Oh, sure. Sweat and blood and dust," Johnson said. "But you got them thinking about State. Don't think those seniors have thought about that since they started playing for Jim. Hell, I hadn't thought of it since Jim started."

"Felt good up there," Steve said. "Been practicing that speech since before I can remember."

"Sounded pretty good," Johnson said, slapping him on the

back. "You comin' to the Corral? Guys'll probably buy our drinks, first practice of the season and all."

"Not today," Steve said, looking down at the grass. "Think I'm gonna head over to Lucy's in a bit."

"Lucy's?" Johnson asked, his eyes wide in concern. "Something wrong?"

"Why would there be?"

"She wasn't at the party yesterday," Johnson said, smashing the bucket hat back on his head and pulling it down low. "Something wrong with her and Emmy or something?"

"Why?" Steve tried his best to keep his voice level, not wanting to incite any more resentment from Johnson.

"It's nothing," Johnson said, holding up his hands in a declaration of innocence. "Just...I know how hard Dan Holcomb can be on the guys in charge. Making sure everything's in order in their personal lives. Nothing's...out of the ordinary."

Johnson gave Steve a look then. His eyebrows raised, his nostrils flared. He lifted the bill of his hat and looked him directly in the eye, not blinking, not looking away, like he was trying to convey something, some crucial piece of information that he needed Steve to know.

That's when Steve figured out that he knew. Emmy must have told Lucy before she told him. And Lucy must have told Cora. And, of course, Cora would have told her husband. News never settled in one place and died in their town. It always spread. A virus. It was contained for now, but Steve knew it would only be a matter of time before it leaked to Jan Oleander, who would give the news legs, spread it all over, until it eventually reached the ear of Dan Holcomb and the board, which would put his job at risk. The dream, the vision, the hope would all die once they realized he'd raised a daughter who had committed her life to sin.

"Not so strange to visit my ex-wife," Steve said, unwilling and unable to get into the thick of it with Johnson. "Excited to have you on board. We're gonna turn this program around. Can feel it."

"Yeah," Johnson said, picking up the bag of balls with slow deliberation, looking him up and down. "I'm sure it will really be something."

Steve walked toward the stadium. When he got to the track, he saw Trey Maxwell with his little sister, who was about eight or so, tossing a football back and forth on the turf.

"Hey, Coach!" Trey yelled from the field. Steve walked along the track toward them. "You remember my little sister, Angie."

Angie ran to stand behind Trey, clutching his left leg, peering out at him from behind her brother's massive thigh. Trey could squat five hundred forty pounds on a bad day.

Steve knelt down so that he could get on Angie's eye level and said, "How're you doin', Angie? You like watching your brother play ball?"

Her hair was tied up into pigtails, two black poofs that moved back and forth when she nodded her head.

"You think I'm gonna score some touchdowns?" Trey asked, smiling down at her.

"Duh," she said, giggling. "Like, one hundred, probably."

"All right, I'll try for you, girl," he said and looked back up at Steve. "Hey, Angie, you know whose daddy this is?"

He frowned at Trey, then realized Angie must have been one of the dozens of Steinbeck kids Emmy worked with back in high school for her community service project.

"Whose?" Angie said, straining her neck to look up at her brother.

"Miss Emmy's!"

Angie gazed at him in wonder. "You're Miss Emmy's daddy?"

"I—" Steve began. His voice cracked a little. "I am."

"Is Miss Emmy gonna come to a game this year?" Angie asked, elated. "I want her to sit by *me* if she does."

"Well," he said, standing up so that he could no longer look

Angie directly in the eyes. "She's pretty busy at school. Hey, Angie, you know how to catch a football?"

Angie nodded and launched herself from behind Trey, standing with her arms wide open, waiting for a pass. Steve lobbed one over to her and whooped when she let the ball hit her chest, then fall into her hands.

"Almost as good as Emmy was back in the day," Steve said. It nearly killed him.

"Really?" Angie said, jumping up and down.

A pang of loss walloped Steve in the chest, making it hard to breathe. He grimaced and rubbed the spot where his muscles had gone tight.

"You see the new kid playing? Martinez? From El Paso?" Trey asked as Angie went out for another pass. "Hardly talks to anybody. Like he's too good for all of us."

"Looks like a good ballplayer," Steve said as he tossed the ball to Angie again.

"Wants to be quarterback," Trey said. "Told Little Williams he was gonna take his spot. Big Williams nearly clobbered him."

"Gotta keep that locker room in check, Trey," he said. "Only winning will guarantee your full ride to ACU. We can't win if y'all are fighting. And you've worked too damn hard to let a new kid from El Paso screw it all up, don't you think?"

"Doing my best," Trey said. "Just thought you should know."

"Coach Quinn?" Angie asked, running up to him, tugging on his pant leg, looking up at him with her big brown eyes. "Is Emmy gonna stay in that other town forever?"

The tightness returned to his chest again. Steve leaned over, resting his hands on his knees, breathing in as deeply as he could manage.

"You okay, Coach?" Trey asked, alarmed.

"Getting too old for this damn heat," Steve said, forcing a laugh. "Y'all keep on playin'. I'm just gonna go sit in the shade for a second. You looked good today, by the way. Let's see it in the game. Two weeks till kickoff."

"Yessir," Trey said, flashing his enormous grin. "Take State, baby!"

Steve waved goodbye to the two of them and made his way to the home stands, covered in shade. An emptiness washed over him. All the adrenaline from the practice had run its course. He walked to the top of the bleachers and looked down at the field.

It was here, more than church, that Steve felt God in the silence, his will for Steve's life stretched out so clearly across one hundred yards, his purpose lying in between two giant yellow goal posts. The turf looked perfect from up here, the lines of the field bright white, the numbers on the sidelines impeccable.

Steve could still feel the phantom heat from the sun beating down his neck, even in the shade, and knew he couldn't stay outside much longer. He needed water and a shower and time to clear his head. But he still stayed sitting, looking out at the field, before bowing his head, thinking of Emmy.

There had to be something he could do, he thought. Something he could fix. Or force Lucy to say to her.

If people were pottery and time was a kiln, Steve prayed that not every part of Emmy was fully formed. If he could just get a little more time, he could smooth this whole thing out. He could save her.

7

Steve didn't even bother showering. He got in his truck and floored it to Lucy's.

Her house was small, *a little bungalow*, she called it, with a white picket fence and a light blue door. Everything on the inside was all white and beige and flooded with natural light, which Lucy loved, since she'd started painting watercolors after the divorce. They were landscapes, mostly of the sea.

Her car was in the driveway, and Steve jogged up her walkway, knocking on her door four times in a syncopated rhythm so that she knew it was him.

"Steve," she said, throwing open the door, looking him up and down. "You look dirty."

She looked magnificent. She was wearing a bright yellow sundress, her hair down and curled in thick ringlets that blended new blond highlights with her natural, dark brown color. Her face looked bright and fresh, with little sparkles on her eyelids that glimmered in the sun. And that jawline—so sharp, even after all these years. Steve felt sixteen again, standing there looking at her, wide-eyed and struck by wonder.

"No shower after two-a-days?" she asked.

"I, uh..." he said, rubbing the back of his neck.

"Come on in, Steve," she said. "I got company coming over in thirty, but we can chat for a bit. Iced tea?"

"Sure," he said, walking into the pristine living room, everything white and clean and perfect.

"Put a little lemonade in it, just the way you like it," she said, coming in from the kitchen with two glasses. The ice clinked as she handed Steve's over and pulled out a chair for him. He thanked her, sat, and took a deep gulp of his drink. It was icecold and sweet.

"Appreciate it, Lucy."

"I guess I should say congratulations," Lucy said, sitting on the couch across from him. "Head coach. Cora told me. And starting so quick. What'd you have—two days' notice?"

"Somethin' like that," he said, looking at a framed watercolor on the wall. It was an ocean with turbulent waves and a sky filled with gray and purple and red. "You paint storms often?"

"Why are you here, Steve?" she asked, cutting straight to it like she always did with him.

"Well, Luce, it's Emmy..." he said.

Steve explained the story, what she had told him, and how she had said it. He included everything: the cicadas, the crossword, the storm.

When he finished, Lucy looked up at him, her eyes the exact shape and shade as Emmy's.

"You son of a bitch," she said, her jaw clenched.

"I know I didn't react great."

"She told you. When? And I'm not sure what to make of it, either. But hell, Steve? Really? *Hell?*"

"Am I wrong?"

"We want our daughter to get back to normal, but this... Hell?

My *word*, Steve. Do you want her to hate herself? Want her to grow old and alone like us? I told her not to tell you. I *told* her."

She buried her face in her hands. Steve thought about going over to put an arm around her. But he was dirty. And he had a mission. It wasn't the time to be soft.

"What did you do wrong, Lucy? How'd she end up this way?"

Lucy's face shot out of her hands so quick Steve thought her neck may have snapped. Her face was red, and her lips pressed together in a tight line of fury.

"Me? What did *I* do?" Lucy glared. "You've always been a selfish man, Steve, but I never took you for a stupid one."

"I didn't raise this kind of girl!"

"You *did*," Lucy said, standing up. "*We* did."

Steve balked at that, the idea that it was *their* failure. Something they both had done—or failed to do—that had led Emmy to make this choice. It softened him a little, knowing he didn't have to bear this alone.

"If the board finds out about this," Steve said, sighing, hanging his head, "I'll lose the job."

"You don't know that," Lucy said. "Dan is a reasonable man. And this town loves you."

"No love's strong enough to overlook this, Luce, you know that. How folks here react to something…different." Steve clenched his fists. "I don't know what to do. How do we change her mind?"

"Well, I've not known for much longer than you," she said, moving over to Steve, putting her hand on his shoulder. Despite everything, he felt a warmth from her touch. "But, you know, I figure it's not something we can do anything about. We just gotta wait for her to come to her senses. Realize she wants a family. And a life like ours."

"I can't accept that. Waiting around, not doing anything."

"Well," Lucy said, removing her hand, "you could talk to

someone about it. Like y'all's pastor, the one that took over after Bob Sherman."

"Ben?"

"Yeah," Lucy said. "Maybe have dinner with him. Get the opinion of a Lord's man. Find out how to get her back."

Steve thought about it. It wasn't such a bad idea. To draw her back in with faith.

Emmy had always been attracted to the church. When she was little, she loved Vacation Bible School and Christmas plays and her picture-book Bible with all its colors and simple words and miracles. She couldn't fall asleep unless she said her bedtime prayers with Steve and Lucy, and she was thrilled by the idea of heaven—that after it was all over, they could all begin again somewhere new, somewhere perfect.

When she got older, getting up to go to the morning services was a chore. But the music kept her going, especially the hymns, the old stuff that the worship band made new with their modern arrangements. She was partial to that most famous one:

Amazing grace, how sweet the sound.
That saved a wretch like me.
I once was lost, but now am found...

She'd always sing out the first verse loud and strong, faltering when she got to the word *found*. She'd close her eyes, bow her head, and lapse into silence. Every time. It never failed.

Amazing grace, how sweet the sound. Was Emmy lost in those moments of music, struggling to be seen? Or was she lost now, in the music's absence? Had she forgotten what it meant to be found?

"Luce," Steve said, unable to say anything but the truth, "I can't lose her."

"Then don't let her go," she said gently. "Talk about it with Pastor Ben. Love's a simple thing, really, Steve. It just is."

"Was never so simple with you."

He didn't know why he said it. Why he'd made it about them all of a sudden. He hadn't collapsed into that kind of talk since the divorce was finalized and he got drunk and called Lucy up every time he came home alone. To nothing. She hated those calls. Hated hearing his hurt. Whether that was impatience or empathy Steve was never sure. He expected her to yell at him. To tell him to focus on his daughter. To not fuck up the last thing in his life he was willing to love.

But she laughed.

"Well, maybe that's the point, Steve."

"Huh?"

"Get right with God. And figure out what to do about our daughter. Now, if you don't mind, I've got my book club coming over in fifteen minutes, and unless you've got something to say about *Little Fires Everywhere*, I'd recommend you get on home."

Steve wanted to ask her more, to figure out what she meant by it all, but she was ushering him out the door before he could find the right words to say.

8

The next day, Steve took Lucy's advice and called up Pastor Ben, who said he and his wife, Kathy, would be happy to have him over for dinner after practice that night, if he was free. Steve hadn't expected it to happen so soon, but he figured time was of the essence, and so he accepted. After Tuesday's afternoon practice, Steve showered and dressed in his best button-down shirt, blue jeans, and boots.

Kathy answered the door when Steve rang, and she ushered him inside, offering him sweet tea, a seat at the table, and a million questions about the football team.

"Well, I just hope Jim doesn't take it too hard," she said. She tucked a piece of her stick-straight, platinum-blond hair behind her ear and bit her bottom lip, getting red lipstick on her front teeth. "Seemed like it was all he had going for him."

"Never polite to speculate on a man's mind, Kathy," Ben said, coming in from the kitchen. He wore a short-sleeve button-down with flowers on it and those tight jeans that showed every nook and cranny of a man's legs and parts. He wore the same thing when he preached, too, Steve remembered, as if the house of God were the most casual place in the world. "And before we get sidetracked by any gossip nonsense, I figure we oughta say grace."

They bowed their heads, and Ben cleared his throat. He prayed like he was behind a pulpit: urgent, passionate, filled with meaning. His voice quavered when he asked for forgiveness for their sins, and Steve wondered what it must be like to be so close with God, to feel him so deeply in every prayer, at every moment, no matter who was around. Did it amplify his voice in God's ear? Did his prayers get priority because of his position on earth?

"Amen," Ben finished. Kathy passed Steve the meat, roasted perfectly, and he took a few slices and plopped some mashed potatoes on his plate, bypassing the salad altogether. He took a sip of iced tea, then a bite. Pepper-crusted outside, medium rare inside. It cut like butter.

"Oh, Kathy," he said. "This is too good. Thanks."

"Anything for Coach Quinn." Kathy winked. "Gotta keep you nice and strong for the season."

They talked for a while about the school, about football. Kathy tried to tell Steve how he should have taught his US history classes—she taught eighth graders at the junior high—but he told her he'd used the same syllabus for fifteen years, and it had worked out just fine for him back when he'd had to teach. It was history, after all, he said. It never changed.

When they were finished, Kathy cleared their places and waved away their attempts to help out.

"Don't you think about it, Coach Quinn," she said, as she gave his shoulder a squeeze. "Will give me somethin' to do while the coffee's making."

Ben watched his wife go into the kitchen, waiting for the swinging door to stop moving back and forth before he turned to Steve.

"So." Ben ran his hands through his overly gelled hair. "What's on your mind, Steve?"

"Guess us and the Catholics aren't too different," Steve said, suddenly nervous, forcing himself to laugh, dreading having to say it out loud.

"How's that?"

"Come to a preacher man. To talk and all."

"But Catholics don't look one another in the eyes," Ben said, maintaining eye contact. "Though, some like the confessionals. Make it a little less awkward to get it all off your chest."

"It's Emmy," Steve said with a sigh. "I think I may have done something wrong."

It all came rushing out of him like tumbleweed across the road before a big dust storm. The party. The conversation. How he hadn't let her finish. Didn't let her give life to the truth by letting it live in the air. Only took a few minutes, but before Ben could respond, Kathy came back in with the coffee. They cut the conversation and thanked her.

"So," Kathy said as she sat back down. "Amy Garrison said she saw Emmy drive through town in a hurry last night after the party."

Frozen with fear at the mention of his daughter's name, Steve held the mug to his lips, not wanting to betray any emotion. He thought, with a surge of anger, Did these damn women ever stop gossiping?

"Everything all right?" Kathy asked, leaning forward, her eyes squinted in concern, her concentration intense. Her eyelids were dark and sparkly with some kind of fancy makeup. She looked a little like a raccoon.

Steve sipped his coffee, willing himself to stay calm, ready to brush her off.

"Seems like Emmy might think she's one of those lesbians, apparently," Ben said to Kathy before Steve could respond.

"Emmy? A lesbian?"

Steve glared at Ben, but he didn't notice.

"What she says," Steve said, with some reluctance.

"But—" she frowned like she was trying to piece together a particularly difficult puzzle "—that doesn't make sense. Emmy's so pretty!"

"Ellen from TV is a pretty woman." Ben shrugged. "Guess it's possible."

"I guess she *did* play softball," Kathy said, frowning as she thought it through, collecting evidence against Emmy. "She never dated Jacob? Derek Johnson's boy?"

"No," Steve said through clenched teeth. He remembered the conversation he'd had with Emmy a couple years before about him. *He's not my type*, she'd said, laughing. Steve's face went red at the memory. Had she decided, all that time ago, to live this kind of life?

"You know, I just don't quite get these lesbians," Kathy said, folding her arms across her chest. "It just seems a bit icky to me. No man? Just two women?" She laughed a little and then looked deeply serious. "How does that even work?"

"Well, I think one of them—" Ben started to say.

"No! I don't want to know." Kathy put her hands up in front of her face and shuddered. "That's just unnatural. I can't *imagine*…"

Her voice trailed off, and her eyes glazed over. It seemed she had found the imaginational capacity for it. Steve looked at Ben, who nodded.

"Great dinner, Kathy," Steve said, placing his napkin on the table.

This snapped her out of whatever world she had conjured up in her mind, and she jumped up quickly to clear the coffee mugs from the table as the men walked toward Ben's office.

Ben motioned to his bar cart. "Gift from the Kearneys. Supposed to be for booze, but, you know, being a Baptist preacher and all, stocked it with soda pop. Got that good stuff from Waco, the original Dr Pepper. Care for a glass?"

"Sure."

"Good man."

Ben poured them both a glass of Dublin Dr Pepper. On the rocks.

Steve looked around the office. It was nice, all mahogany with a shelf filled with leather-bound books behind Ben's desk. There was a Bible and an open notebook on it.

"Nice space you got here," Steve said, to fill the silence.

"Yeah." Ben handed him the glass and went behind his desk to sit. "Always hoped we'd get to turn it into a nursery. But wasn't in God's plan for us."

"I'm sorry," Steve said, shifting in his seat.

"So. Emmy," Ben said, folding his hands in his lap. "How'd you leave things with her?"

Steve avoided his eyes, pretending to examine the ice cubes clinking around the crystal tumbler. "I went back into the house. Didn't say much. She left. Back to school, I guess."

Ben looked at him with narrowed eyes, as if he detected the lie.

"Okay," Ben said finally. "We can work with that."

Steve sat up straighter. Ready for the solution. "So how do you reckon I fix her? Give her a call? Drive down?"

"Fix?"

"Or change her mind about it all. I just—"

"Steve—"

"Lucy seems to think I may have been *wrong*."

"Steve."

"She basically said I was an ass, and I just—"

"You're not in the wrong here, Steve," Ben said, frowning. He cocked his head to the side. Then shook it. "Loving someone doesn't mean accepting them." He took a sip of soda. "Sometimes, and in your case with Emmy, we love someone deeply. But they've turned away from God in order to live their life in sin."

"But she's my daughter."

"It's unnatural, Steve. Two women together? It's simple biology. Our bodies are built for procreation. Any other use of our sexual selves is a betrayal of creation."

"Hmm," Steve grunted, not wanting to talk about anybody's sexual self, especially not his daughter's.

"Think of it like this," Ben said, sensing Steve's discomfort. "She wouldn't be able to have children. You and Lucy would lose out on grandkids. A son-in-law. The expansion of your family. It's a matter of your happiness, too, you know."

Steve thought about that. Emmy liked the simple things in life. Just like him. They liked to live in the moment. Never needed more than that to call themselves content.

But he had always hoped—not even hoped: *assumed*—that they'd add more people to their moments. Emmy in her Sunday best, one of those sundresses she liked to wear with sandals, her hair thrown up in a bun to keep it off her neck in the afternoon sun, and a baby on her lap, a little kiddo with a full head of hair, dark, just like Emmy's, with thick little legs sticking out of a Dallas Cowboys' onesie, squirming, kicking, fussing so much that Emmy would have to hand him over to her husband, a man Steve couldn't quite picture, couldn't quite imagine...

"Can't make a decision based on happiness," Steve said, pushing back. "Especially not mine. That'd be selfish."

"Right, you're right," Ben said, putting up his hands. "But you know what this sin is, Steve. Think about it. First Corinthians chapter six, verse nine. *Or do you not know that wrongdoers will not inherit the kingdom of God? Do not be deceived: Neither the sexually immoral nor idolaters nor adulterers nor men who have sex with men—*"

"Emmy's a woman."

"Homosexuality is homosexuality," Ben said, waving him off. "Romans. There's always Romans to remember. Chapter one, verses eighteen to thirty-two. All about the wrath of God, you know. Verse twenty-six, *God gave them over to shameful lusts. Even their women exchanged natural sexual relations for unnatural ones…and received in themselves the due penalty for their error."*

"Penalty?"

"Damnation. Eternal separation from God. And that's just the New Testament. There's Leviticus and Genesis. The classics on this matter."

"But don't we all deserve that damnation? Isn't that the point of forgiveness? And Jesus?"

"True." Ben set his glass down and leaned forward, sitting on the edge of his seat. His hands were clasped in front of him. The AC blew strong through the room. Steve shivered. "Consider Matthew ten."

Grabbing the Bible on his desk, Ben began flipping through it, the thin pages slapping against one another as he searched for the right passage.

When he found it, Ben cleared his throat and began to read out loud in his deep, strong preacher voice about the cost of following Jesus.

It was a passage Steve had read many times before. The sending out of the disciples. How the world would swallow you up and spit you out for following Christ. It was not safe to walk the narrow path, the righteous path, but it was the only road that led to heaven, salvation, paradise.

As a boy, the passage helped Steve understand the importance of both sacrifice and fear within Christianity, that certain persecution was to be expected. It was not a faith for the faint of heart.

As a man, it helped him see the importance of willpower. To hold on to the truth outlined in the Gospels and the letters of the Apostles. The world was filled with temptations: to cheat, to be corrupted by greed, to hate those who've wronged you; to envy, lust, gossip, steal. In Christ alone could a man conquer those most basic temptations of the flesh. In Christ alone could a man fill a once-barren life with fruit: joy, hope, peace, faith, and love, that most central tenet of Christianity.

In Christ alone. A phrase said so often in church it seemed to have lost its meaning. But it never got lost on Steve. To be of Christ, to be like Christ; to be just, fair, kind, righteously angry when necessary; to love others so much you'd risk your life for them; to love others so much you'd commit your life to helping them gain salvation. And that salvation could only come through knowing Christ alone as Lord, God, Savior.

"Steve, this is what I really want you to hear," Ben said, running his hand through his coiffed hair again, pausing extra-long like he did in the middle of his sermons before he got to his main point. "Jesus says this to the Twelve: *'Do not suppose that I have come to bring peace to the earth. I did not come to bring peace, but a sword… Anyone who loves their father or mother more than me is not worthy of me; anyone who loves their son or daughter more than me is not worthy of me.'"*

Steve sat in silence, sipping the soda. He'd never remembered the verse ending that way. With such fire and fury, such a clear-cut definition of worthiness.

"You understand what I'm saying?"

"Sure," Steve grunted. He took another sip of soda. The fizz burned the back of his throat, reminding him not to lie. "No, I mean. Not quite."

"This makes damnation and salvation very clear. Those who turn away from Christ, as Emmy has done for the time being, are damned. And those who love the damned more than they love Christ," he said, motioning to Steve, "like, say, a father and his daughter, they're damned, too. In accepting Emmy as she is now, in her current state, you're not only guaranteeing her damnation. You're solidifying your own."

Steve sat back in his chair, looking up at the ceiling, letting the words sink in.

To Steve, a life devoted to family had always seemed in keeping with a life devoted to God. Provide for the ones you love. Keep your pride in check. Lead others in spirit and in truth. Just like his father had taught him. Compassionate and kind, strong and silent, he always said the only purpose they had on earth was to keep their eyes set on heaven.

That's why Steve's mother used to tell him, "Stevie, you can be *in* the world, but you gotta make sure you're never *of* the world." *In* and *of*. To exist in a place is different than becoming a product of a place. They were not meant for this world. It was just a stop along the way to eternity.

Steve had done the work. He had surrendered his life. He had secured his salvation. And he knew that was something another man couldn't tell him he was going to lose. Like it says in 1 Corinthians, *For who knows a person's thoughts except their own spirit within them?* Who can know a man's salvation except the man who's asked to be saved?

"Think about the boys you coach," Ben said, interrupting the silence. "If they're jumping offside every play, you're going to do something about it, right?"

"Pull 'em out before they lose us another chunk of yards," Steve grunted.

"Exactly," Ben said, nodding. "It may seem strange. Hell, I don't have a kid. I don't know what it's like. That kind of love. That's something I'll never—"

His voice—usually so calm, so confident—broke. He couldn't finish his sentence. He looked down at his hands, clenching his fists. When he looked back up, there were tears in his eyes. He didn't cough them away like he was supposed to. He let them sit, let them spill over. Sniffed real loud. Ran his hands through his fancy hair. Each move seemed calculated.

Steve wanted to believe him. Wanted to feel confident that this man of God could give him answers that he'd trust. Wanted to believe that he cared about his daughter. And maybe if Ben had watched Emmy grow up, Steve would have bought it. And maybe if he were standing in the pulpit like he did on Sundays, far away from him, it wouldn't have seemed so staged.

But Pastor Sherman, not Ben, had baptized Emmy and watched her grow up alongside his own daughter. And Steve was sitting too close to Ben in his office. It was like when you sit in the front row at a play and see the pulleys and strings that make the actors fly. It takes away all the magic, getting too close.

"Weren't there moments when she was a kid?" Ben asked, pulling himself together too quickly. "And you'd have to discipline her in some way? Like, did she ever take a cookie when she wasn't supposed to? Or sneak out past curfew in high school?"

Steve thought about that. When she was a kid, Emmy used to take three cookies at once when her mother wasn't looking, but Steve laughed and took out three for himself, too. In middle school, there was the issue of her and Jacob's hair, which she kept touching even when he asked her not to. But Jacob's mom had taken care of that one. And once, when she was a senior in high school, she came back home late, well after midnight, breaking her curfew after spending time with Michaela Sherman. Steve had found her crying on the porch. Girl drama of some kind, he'd guessed. She never told him what was wrong, and he never asked. He just got beers for them out of the fridge and asked her not to tell her mother about it when she went over to her place the next day. She took a couple sips and just kept repeating, "I think I lost her."

But Ben was wrong about this. It wasn't a question of discipline. Of keeping Emmy out of the cookie jar or enforcing her curfew. Those rules, and the punishments that came from breaking them, were all about control.

Her soul, the preservation of that beautiful life force he'd helped cultivate, from the moment she took her first shrieking breath in the too-small hospital room during the early hours of that late July morning in Texas, had nothing to do with control. Steve had never wanted that with Emmy. Not even during her preteen years, the dark days when she shut herself away in her room and blasted her angst-filled punk-rock music that shook every window in the house. When it came to her, it was never a question of power; it was always a matter of love.

Ben was right about one thing, though: Steve knew what this sin was. Love was strong enough for a lot of things, but it couldn't bend the rules of morality. It couldn't make what was unnatural natural. It couldn't make wrongs suddenly become right.

If he could have, Steve would have gone up to God and asked that her soul be exchanged for his. He would have ripped the Book of Life from the Lord's hands and crossed out his name, written in hers, and thrown himself into the lake of fire that John foresaw in his Revelation. Steve would have twisted the wrought iron, pearl-encased gates with his bare hands so that he could let his daughter into heaven, into that eternal joy, so that she could sit with her creator and bask in the glory of his love, forever. He would burn, a thousand times over, for the promise of her eternal life.

Jesus said that there is no greater love than a man who's willing to lay down his life to save the people he loves.

To save someone's life, then, was the greatest act of love. But how much greater must the act be if you're saving someone's soul?

Emmy was young. There was still time for her to sort herself out. But it was like Steve told the guys on the team: if you didn't correct your mistakes in practice, you were destined to repeat them when it mattered. To let Emmy keep on going in the world, uncorrected, seemed to be an act of indulgence. And there was nothing, Steve believed, in greater opposition to love.

9

EMMY

Emmy was baptized in the First Baptist Church of Steinbeck when she was fourteen years old. Her Sunday school shifted in preparation for the event. Everything was suddenly serious: no more *Veggie Tales* or Vacation Bible School.

The horror of those classes was inevitable. Changing hormones, conversations about sex, boys liking girls, girls liking boys. It didn't help that the teacher, Mrs. Zeamora, who went by Mrs. Zee, was so desperate to be universally loved that she refused to discipline anyone in class for anything. When they started their unit on sex—or, rather, abstinence—Mrs. Zee explained that every time you did something sexual with a person who you were not married to, something inside of you was lost. She begged girls to consider Velcro. Every time you ripped a piece of Velcro, it lost a little bit of its stickiness. If you did it over and over and over again with different pieces, it would eventually lose its capacity to come together with the one piece of Velcro it was supposed to stick to for the rest of its life.

The metaphor, like most used in conversations about abstinence, was heavy-handed but effective in its way. The kids in Emmy's class discussed Velcro at great length, mocking it. Poor Maggie Ann Peterson wore a pair of Velcro sneakers the day they discussed it, and all the boys converged on her, ripping the Velcro on and off while she squealed. Mrs. Zee laughed and said, "Boys will be boys."

On the day they discussed homosexuality, the girls and the boys were out of control.

"It may seem cool to be a gay and all," Mrs. Zee explained, "but it's a sin. Don't let *Will and Grace* fool you, now!"

"That's an old-people show."

"My mama won't show that in our house. Calls it filth."

"They're all a bunch of fags, even the girls."

"Girl fags are dykes, idiot."

"Now, there's no need for ugly language," said Mrs. Zee. "But yes. You get the point."

"Mrs. Zee! Harrison just told me if I don't touch his little thing it means I'm a lesbian!"

"It's not little!"

Mrs. Zee had lost complete control of the class, and her frantic cries for order were drowned out by the angry wave of accusations flying across the room.

"Sara Beth don't have to worry. She ain't playing sports like softball. It's Emmy over there you gotta look out for."

Emmy's mouth went dry, her face hot. No response, no defense. Had they seen her YouTube search history? she frantically wondered. All the Emma Watson fan videos she had watched?

"So if you're a girl and you're strong, you're automatically gay?"

Temporary silence. Emmy strained her neck to see who had spoken. It was Michaela Sherman, the pastor's daughter.

"Why so defensive of Emmy? Is she your girlfriend, Mi-GAY-la?"

Michaela rolled her eyes, shrugged, and smiled at Emmy,

then looked down at her hands. Emmy knew she should have thanked her for stepping in, but she didn't want to draw attention to herself. Besides, Mi-gay-la was too catchy to risk another opportunity for its use.

By the time Emmy's baptism rolled around a year later, her YouTube searches had become more incriminating, and she had developed a full-fledged crush on Maggie Ann Peterson, the Velcro-shoes girl.

On the day before their baptisms, each member of the class had to meet one-on-one with Pastor Sherman. Even Michaela. There were no exceptions.

Baptisms in the Southern Baptist Church weren't anything like the little sprinkle some people get when they're babies in little lacy white dresses. Baptists have to make the decision for themselves, decide it's time for their lives to be tied to Christ and the church. When that time comes, it's full immersion in the water. Body, mind, spirit: everything is submerged.

So it's a serious decision and one they were told not to take lightly. The meeting with Pastor Sherman was meant to reassure them about their choice, but it made Emmy anxious.

It was in part due to Maggie Ann. On the way up to Pastor Sherman's office, their whole class crammed into the elevator. All twenty of them. Maggie Ann stood in front of Emmy, squished against her. Maggie Ann noticed this and pressed her butt into Emmy's crotch. She grabbed Emmy's hands and pulled them around her waist, joking that they were in the perfect position for a prom pose. Everyone laughed, someone took a picture, and Emmy, horrified, felt something stirring inside her, down south.

The telltale tingle.

Emmy knew what was going on down there because of the abstinence videos she'd watched in her class. *If you feel a tingle, don't stop to mingle!*

Painfully aware of how turned-on she was by a girl, Emmy walked into the pastor's office, closing the door behind her. It was a small room with posters of Christian rock bands lining the walls above a small minifridge, from which Pastor Sherman offered her a Coke. She declined, took a seat, and placed her hands on her lap in an unconscious attempt to hide any signs of what she felt. He sat behind his desk and smiled at her. They stayed like that for several moments. Emmy wondered if she was supposed to talk first, but she didn't have anything to say, so she just smiled right back at him.

Finally, he spoke.

"You're one of the good ones, Emmy."

"Excuse me?"

"All these girls, distracted by boys. Boys, boys, boys. It's all they can think about, talk about. Sing about, too. No time for anything else. Michaela tells me all about it. But you, you're different."

"What do you mean?" she asked too quickly, panicking.

"You're just pure, you know? Going after God, school. Focused on your family. You've really got your priorities straight for someone your age."

"Uh..."

"I think you're one of the only young people in your confirmation group who understands the importance, the *weight*, of a baptism."

"Weight?"

"Tremendous weight. Giving up your old self, breathing life into a new one dedicated to Christ. Washing away your sin. Coming up clean, pure, perfect, as you were intended to be."

"Oh."

"It's a great step forward in your faith. You'll be a great woman of God. A Proverbs Thirty-one type. *Eishet Chayil.* A woman of valor."

He looked at Emmy over his thin, wire-framed glasses and smiled, all the warmth and hope and expectation in the world for her creased in the laugh lines around his eyes. A woman of *valor*? Emmy thought. She was hardly a woman at all yet.

"Well," he said, breaking eye contact to look down at his desk and shuffle some papers, "you seem ready as ever to me. I'll see you out there for the dunk!"

With that, he ushered her out of his office, calling in Maggie Ann after her, who brushed her hand against Emmy's shoulder as they passed each other. Emmy shuddered.

In the chapel, during the baptism, the house lights were down. Shades had been pulled over the windows. The spotlight was on Emmy. The congregation sat in darkness, hidden behind the blazing stage lights.

Pastor Sherman spoke into a microphone, the echo of his voice booming throughout the silent, packed room.

"Emilia, please repeat after me the words of the Good Confession. I invite your church family to repeat them with you."

She obeyed, and so did the church. Disembodied voices spoke with her, like she was surrounded by ghosts. She squinted into the audience, but the darkness was too dense: she couldn't see a single face.

After her recitation, Pastor Sherman led Emmy up the three steps into the marble baptismal pool, big enough for them to step in together, the water waist-high. Emmy's youth group T-shirt clung to her, and her mesh shorts billowed in the water. She wondered, briefly, if she should have worn the Nike shorts the rest of the girls were wearing.

"Deep breath in," Pastor Sherman whispered before placing a supporting hand on her back. He placed his other hand on her forehead and dipped her back into the water.

He held her down for what couldn't have been more than a couple of seconds. But Emmy could have sworn she was drowning.

She kept thinking about Maggie Ann, the tingle. The way she felt pressed against her. The smell of her perfume. How she wanted more than anything for her to turn around, get closer.

Emmy felt heavy. Like something deep inside of her might weigh her down to the bottom, keep her there forever. She couldn't breathe. She was panicking. Pastor Sherman was keeping her under too long, way too long, trying to get her to fess up, to purge herself of all her feelings, to change, to be better, purer.

Finally, he lifted Emmy out of the water, and the darkness exploded with applause, cheers, *amens*, and whoops of joy. The stage lights were blinding.

Emmy took a deep gulp of air, thankful to have it fill her lungs, and recited a prayer that would never be fulfilled.

If I'm going to keep getting these tingles, please, God, let it be for boys.

Three years after Emmy was baptized, her parents got divorced. It was around then, when she was seventeen, that she started spending most of her time with Michaela Sherman. It was a haze, the quick burn of it all, a jumbled memory of hope and fear.

A text. That's how it started. Checking in on how Emmy was handling her parents' divorce.

How did you know?

Sara Beth told me during free period today, don't get mad at her, my cousin's parents divorced, too, and I know how hard it can get, do you want to get coffee sometime and talk?

Mocha caramel bullshit lattes. Foam stuck on the top of her lip. So embarrassing! No, so cute. Knees touching underneath the coffee table. Mirrored body language, hands underneath chins, hands flat on the table, strong, long fingers, short nails. Emmy dreamed about their hands intertwined. A fire started in her blood.

Mandatory Sunday school every week. Michaela listened with rapt attention. Emmy watched her listen, flipping through her

Bible, bored, hitching her breath when she read, *You have stolen my heart, my sister, my bride; you have stolen my heart with one glance of your eyes, with one jewel of your necklace. How delightful is your love, my sister, my bride!* Song of Songs, split between He and She. Emmy thought, I am He, she is She, then slammed the book shut, terrified at her own daring.

After school, walks, because it was too expensive to keep going to the coffee shop every day. They sweated in August, then danced on the sidewalks during the first cool day of fall, the sky a crisp, clear, deep blue, the horizon massive, never-ending. Michaela looked up, her hands outstretched. *Texas's gift! Her apology for the punishing heat!* she'd proclaimed in her singsong voice. *How do you know Texas is a woman?* Emmy had asked. She rolled her eyes. *Because everything worth a damn is a woman, soft and strong and cruel and life-giving and willing to say I'm sorry,* she'd said, as she traced Emmy's bicep and gave it a squeeze. *Like my dear friend Emmy.* Emmy laughed and pulled her in close, smelling her lavender shampoo, and screamed at the sky, *We forgive you!*

Abandoned fields with weeds everywhere. They would become wildflowers in spring, a blue and coral wave that rippled with the wind, but in those moments with Michaela, they were just tangled hues of green, wilting as winter crept in. It was their favorite time, nighttime, all darkness, except for the stars splattered across the sky like a Jackson Pollock painting. Blankets and pillows, the back of her dad's old pickup truck. No need to sneak out, no rules being broken. Except the stolen cabernet sauvignon from Emmy's mom's not-so-secret secret stash in the back of the coat closet. They both pretended to like it as they took swigs straight from the bottle, letting it burn the back of their throats, coating their tongues with a bitter, velvet aftertaste they had not yet grown used to. They pressed next to each other, lying down in the bed of the pickup, staring up at the stars, trying to read their future, their past, any secrets the universe may have folded into the fabric of the Texas sky they both loved so much. Michaela offered gum. Their arms at their sides. Every shift she made sent a jolt through Emmy. Racing heart, racing mind. What if she moved her hand just an inch...? And then her pinky was wrapped around Emmy's pinky, and she started seeing little black spots that blotted out the stars. If her heart went any faster, Emmy thought, she would have blacked out, but there was no time for that: she needed to be brave. Their hands were intertwined. Their foreheads pressed together. Michaela's eyes were locked on Emmy's: gray-green, warm and wide, what Emmy fell in love with first. The next part was natural, like breathing. Emmy leaned in and kissed her, eyes closed. And, unbelievably, she kissed back. She buried her hands in Emmy's hair. Spearmint gum, honey ChapStick, lavender shampoo. Emmy's senses were overwhelmed with her.

Emmy moved to Michaela's neck, her hands going everywhere, she gave them free rein, there was no more control, worry, context for what they were doing. Michaela breathed "Emmy," and she never knew how much meaning her name could have, like it finally was given purpose, rhythm, music coming from her lips. Michaela's eyes were closed, her mouth was open, no thought, just feeling etched across her face, like a Bernini statue brought to life. Kissing her was timeless; Emmy wanted it to last forever.

But then it stopped.

Michaela pulled away with a gasp, like she had saved herself from suffocation. Her eyes were wide, wider than Emmy had ever seen them. Filled with a fear so deep Emmy thought she might drown in it if she stared too long.

"What are we doing?" Michaela shouted. "Oh my God! I'm so sorry, I'm so sorry. Let's pray, let's pray, let's pray."

She closed her eyes and turned away from Emmy, shouting out, *We've sinned!* and *Forgive us!* Emmy reached out to hold her, then thought better of it, looking down at her own hands and clasping them together in prayer.

On Sundays, Emmy now liked to sleep in instead of going to church services. And she preferred *East of Eden* to Genesis. Bible study groups stressed her out. The theological debates about whether or not *homosexuals*—said with an emphasizing distaste and fear—could be accepted in the church made her feel erased, like a ghost hanging around their group they could never see. She didn't listen to worship songs in her free time; she didn't read morning devotional books; she didn't spend much time in prayer.

So Emmy wasn't, by the definition of her church, a very good Christian. But she still liked Christ and the idea of love as power, and she was pretty sure that she believed in God, even if those who also did refused to acknowledge her belief as legitimate because of who she was attracted to.

They could be right. Her capacity for love, her inability to love the so-called *correct* way, could keep God from hearing her. But as Emmy sat beside Michaela, who shouted at the sky, she wanted to help. To say something. To be heard.

So she tilted her head toward the stars, closed her eyes, and tried to pray. She didn't know what to ask for, what to say. She knew that God may have already tuned her out.

But she had to try. So she just thought, *Please don't let me lose her.*

10

Emmy had been back in Walker for two weeks when Jacob called her, asking her to meet him at the Grizzly, a dimly lit graduate student bar where he worked as a bartender. He said he wanted to meet for a beer and to ostensibly catch up about their summers, but Emmy knew that Cora had called him and told him to make plans, wanting to make sure Emmy had at least one friendly face to see after everything that had happened with her parents.

When Steve and Coach Johnson were still close, their families had spent a lot of time together. Cookouts in the backyard, road trips to away games, pool days in the summer. Jacob and Emmy were both only children, and they both played sports, so they became fast friends as kids. When they were teenagers, they became embarrassed by their closeness, at having such a good friend outside of their cliques at school. They came back together, though, in the second half of high school, when they bonded by stealing beer from their parents' fridges and drinking it out in the backyard while the adults talked in the living room until late at night. On one of those nights, after half a dozen beers each, they decided to kiss, just to see what it was like, but burst out laughing after it was through. It was too weird, they decided. Like kissing a cousin.

"So that's why you didn't like kissing me, huh?" Jacob teased at the Grizzly after Emmy finished telling him everything—about Michaela, about her parents. Jacob had listened intently the whole time, running his hand over his temple fade, the edges of his hairline at a sharp ninety-degree angle. It accentuated the tight curls he was growing out. When they were in seventh grade, he'd yelled at Emmy for touching his hair. When Emmy had told Cora about it, she nodded and said, "You heard him. Don't touch it." Emmy knew better than to disobey her.

"If that makes you feel better," Emmy said. "What is it they always say? *It's not you, it's me.*"

"It's us," Jacob said, rubbing his palm on his right temple where he had a small scar from when he took a line drive to the forehead during Little League. "I'll tell you one thing, though, after hearing all that."

"What's that?"

"Sounds like you were in love with that Michaela, huh?"

"I don't know about that," Emmy said, embarrassed by the intensity of the word, even more so because it was true.

"And she broke your heart."

"That's a little dramatic."

"Fucked up, what that is. Where's she at now?"

"No clue."

"How do you not know?" Jacob asked. "Information's everywhere. Has been since high school."

"She blocked me on everything." Emmy paused for a moment and then said, "Her dad says she's still in Austin."

"You sure she didn't unblock you?"

"Maybe she forgot."

"I could look her up."

"I don't want to see her."

"Well, that's just depressing as hell."

Emmy took a sip of her beer and avoided his gaze.

"Michaela Sherman." Jacob shook his head. "How'd I miss that one?"

"Not like we were hanging out without our families during high school."

"Still, I usually gotta good eye for these things."

"Well, no one really saw me. Or could see me. I had to make myself small."

"Jesus, that's even more depressing," Jacob said as he drained his beer. "You gotta loosen up. Let go."

"Easy for you to say. You got together with Kiera your first week at Walker."

"Yeah, 'cause I *tried.*"

"Don't I get a little time to wallow in the wake of my father's rejection?"

"That motherfucker doesn't get to keep you from living anymore."

"Well, where does Walker keep their lesbians? Not exactly a hot spot for my kind of girls."

"You don't even know your type of girls," Jacob said. "Besides, you've heard stories, right? Rumors. There's all kinds of people in Walker outside that little sorority bubble of yours, Em."

"Okay, *Jake,*" Emmy shot back, knowing he hated his name being shortened almost as much as she did. He held up his hands in apology. "But, I mean, of course I've heard rumors. Right before we came to Walker, two girls in Theta Omega got caught making out at a fraternity party."

"Very *Girls Gone Wild* of them."

"Right," Emmy said, biting her bottom lip. She had asked to hear the story again and again during rush and afterward, fruitlessly waiting to hear it told with the empathy and understanding she so craved, instead of the disgust it seemed to elicit in all the girls. "That wasn't the supposedly bad part. People do stupid shit when they're drunk, and the boys thought it was hot. But then..."

It happened again in the coat closet at the house, in the middle of the day, in complete sobriety, and the leadership board of the sorority had to investigate and found it had been a pattern of behavior, one that could damage their reputation on campus. Rather than suffer the humiliation of getting kicked out, both girls transferred and were never heard from again.

"But that's not everyone," Jacob said. "There's gotta be others, you know, maybe even in different departments, graduate schools..."

Jacob trailed off, looking at David, the bartender, who glanced at his watch and gave him a small nod.

"What was that?" Emmy asked, looking from David to Jacob. "You don't work today, do you?"

"What? Oh. Nothing," Jacob said, pressing his palm to his temple once more. "So, you hear about your dad?"

"Slamming the door in my face?" Emmy said, trying to get him to laugh. "I just told you about that."

Jacob didn't look at Emmy, keeping his hand to his temple, his eyes focused on the bar in front of him. "My dad told me about it. Must have been right after your party. I'm surprised you haven't heard."

"It *was* after the party, Jacob. Are you even listening to me?" Emmy punched his arm playfully. Jacob cracked his knuckles. A knot started to twist in Emmy's stomach. Her mouth got dry, so she took a sip of beer.

"And, of course, my dad was pissed it wasn't him," Jacob said, clearing his throat. "Think it may be the last straw for him at Steinbeck. He always wanted to be head coach."

Emmy nearly choked on her drink. Beer went up her nose. She coughed it away, and it burned in her nostrils. "Head coach?"

"Steve. Your dad, I mean. He's pretty good, apparently. Pisses my dad off even more."

"I can't believe he didn't…" Emmy left the sentence unfinished. Of course he hadn't told her. They weren't speaking.

It was their collective dream. For him to have the job, take her advice on Saturdays after games. To look beyond the present—the games, the season—and figure out how to build a program, a legacy. At Steinbeck, no coach ever seemed to think that far ahead. They were too worried about getting fired. They thought about themselves, the short-term contracts, how to stay alive, keep good faith with the board. But Steve and Emmy knew the key was planting seeds. Waiting. Trusting the process.

Emmy wondered if he remembered the whistle she'd bought him five years ago, when Jim got hired. It wasn't fancy—black string, silver whistle—but she'd told him he could only use it once he got The Job. She said that the first season he wore it, he'd take the boys all the way to State.

"Well, we gonna win if I wear it?" Steve asked, rolling the whistle around in his massive palm, smudging the shine with the tips of his fingers as he put it to his lips.

"I'm not a soothsayer, Dad. I can't predict everything," Emmy had said. "But State. That much I can promise. That you'll get there. And I'll be right behind y'alls bench, on the fifty-yard line."

"Emmy?" Jacob asked, finally looking over at her. "You good?"

"Oh, yeah," she said, rubbing her eyes. "It's just… I'm sure he's so happy."

"Bet he misses you," he said, putting his arm around her.

"Not *me*," Emmy said with a hollow laugh, leaning into his shoulder. "I'm just a sinner, remember?"

"Well, I don't know about that," Jacob said, giving her shoulder a squeeze. Before he could say anything else, his phone buzzed. "Shit, it's Kiera. Mind if I take it?"

"Go ahead," Emmy said. "Tell her I say hi."

When Jacob walked away, Emmy looked down at her reflection in the beer and drained the rest of it. Pulling out her phone, she typed a text message to her mom.

Heard Steinbeck has a new coach.

She looked it over for a few seconds, her fingertip hovering over the Delete key. She set her phone down on the slightly sticky bar, trying to make herself look busy. She studied the different beers on tap, looked around at the mostly empty booths, tapped out the bass line of the song blasting over the speakers with her fingers. Her eyes kept going back to the glowing screen, the unsent message. Finally, she took a deep breath, hit Send, then looked anywhere else but the screen. Seconds later, three dots popped up in the text conversation. Her mom was typing. And then they went away. Nothing was sent.

It felt strange to Emmy—to be so disappointed by the pixelation of a screen. But it was the ghost of her mother on the other line, sitting in her living room, maybe looking out the window, then back at her phone, holding it far out in front of her so that she could read the message, her eyes squinted as she grabbed her reading glasses to make sure it was really her daughter. She may have accidentally hit a letter with her finger. When she realized her mistake, she would delete it, then place her phone facedown on the side table and walk into the kitchen to make herself a glass of sweet tea, leaving Emmy behind.

Emmy looked straight ahead, accidentally catching the eye of David, who had been staring straight at her. He was a burly, mountain-man type with a beard down to his chest. As if to recover from being caught in his covert stare, he asked if Jacob and Emmy wanted another round.

Before Emmy answered, he looked over her shoulder, muttered "Finally," and shouted in a booming baritone, "Well, I'll be damned! Captain Cameron, back from the east!"

"David!" A deep, feminine voice, made for radio, came from behind Emmy. "Still doing God's work, I see."

The leather jacket was the first thing Emmy saw, a whirl of black that enveloped the woman who waltzed into the bar, a broad-shouldered, wide-hipped wonder with all the confidence in the world, her hair thrown up into a messy bun, dark but streaked with gold, which leaned to the left side of her head, as if it shifted from the middle by the sheer force of her movement as she hurtled toward the bar, leaning over it to grab David by the beard, yanking his enormous body toward hers and kissing his cheek.

"All right, now," David said, pushing her off him, smiling. "Got a Belgian Wheat you might like."

"Pour away, my friend." She plopped down in the stool next to Emmy's. "How have the ladies been treating you lately?"

"Like a friend," David boomed back, pouring her pint. "You?"

"Well, I'm back in Walker," Cameron said, holding out her hands like a weighted scale, dipping her right hand down. "So, like a sister in Christ."

"Aren't you Jewish?"

"Catholic, Davey," she said. "The confidence is misleading. Need a good dose of guilt to bring me down."

"What'd I tell you about calling me Davey, Boston?"

"Yeah, yeah, Sir David, I apologize." She pulled a laptop out of her backpack and an old, worn-out paperback. David placed the pint in front of her. He shook her hand. Emmy looked at them. Her nails were short and clean, her fingers strong and long.

"Let me know when you're ready for another. Got a good IPA from Austin today."

"I'd probably get my thesis done a lot faster if I worked at a library instead of a bar, huh?"

"You'd get kicked out with that mouth of yours."

"Research librarians already hate me, too. I keep asking about lesbian literature," she said, sighing dramatically. "An inappropriate subject at such an esteemed Christian institution as our beloved Walker University. I will wait out my exile here!"

"Long as you're payin'," David said with a grin, taking a tray of dirty glasses and walking toward the back.

Emmy sat frozen, starstruck by the sheer coincidence of the situation. She tried her best not to look at Cameron, not to seem overeager or too curious, but she found that it was not possible to avert her eyes. She was magnetic, this stranger at the bar, opening her laptop, her unruly dark brows coming together in the center, a line of concentration forming just above the bridge of her slightly crooked nose, the tip of which she tapped with her index finger as she waited for her computer to boot up.

Emmy felt breathless and was grateful for the return of David, who had two beers for her and Jacob. She thanked him.

"No problem, Emmy," he said, looking from her to Cameron to the front window, where Jacob stood on the phone, laughing as he talked with Kiera. "Hey, have y'all two met?"

He pointed between Emmy and Cameron, who was deeply focused on the Word document she had opened, already furiously typing. She hadn't looked over at Emmy once.

"No," Emmy said slowly, the covert looks and silent communication between David and Jacob finally starting to make sense. "But I don't want to—"

"Hey, East Coast," David boomed, ignoring Emmy. Cameron looked up from the laptop, her eyes slightly out of focus, as if she'd just come up for air. "You met Emmy yet? I think y'all'd get along *real* good."

He winked at Cameron as he nodded toward Emmy, his eyebrows raised in some secret language between the two of them. Cameron narrowed her eyes. Then, as if in slow motion, she turned toward Emmy.

A leap of excitement shot through her when she met Cameron's eyes, which were golden, deep, with the sort of perpetually sleepy, downturned corners that emphasized the dark circles beneath them. It was that same shock of electricity Emmy had felt while she watched those countless, secret movies in the years before. She was surprised to find that the shadow of desire she'd felt in watching it play out on-screen mimicked the real thing so well.

Cameron's lips—full on the bottom, but thin, almost imperceptible on the top—pulled upward in a slightly crooked smile that emphasized the dimple on her right cheek.

"Do you know anything about dyke literature?" she asked Emmy.

Emmy had just taken a sip of her beer and coughed after hearing the question, choking slightly.

"No? Pulp fiction? *The Price of Salt*—they made that one into a movie. Cate Blanchett, Rooney Mara. Called it *Carol*. Nothing?"

Emmy nodded. She had loved *Carol*. At Emmy's slight recognition of the film, Cameron swiveled her stool toward Emmy, leaning forward to touch her wrist. Her hands were cold. Emmy shivered.

"It's good, isn't it? I think everyone in the universe needs to see it. And it's on Netflix. No excuse for anyone!"

"Ha, yeah," Emmy said, lamely. Her tongue suddenly felt too big for her mouth.

There was something about Cameron that rendered Emmy—who was always a little shy, but a master of small talk—suddenly incapacitated. It was how Cameron carried herself. Her shoulders eased back, her arms waved about when she talked, tan skin, bright eyes. Confidence. She exuded it. And she talked quickly. The terse efficiency of the East Coast, no dawdling drawl of Texas in her speech.

"The sex scene in that movie made my ex realize she was a lesbian," Cameron added, like it was a fact as uncharged as a sports statistic. "Didn't stop her from being a bitch, though."

"How fast you think I can drink this?" Jacob asked, coming

up behind Emmy with a beer in hand, making her jump. She hadn't heard him return. He slid back into his stool, looking over at Cameron, giving her a small wave.

"Finish that thesis yet?" he asked her. Of course he knew Cameron, Emmy thought. He poured beers for just about every graduate student at Walker.

"Closer every day," she said, raising her pint to him in a silent *Cheers*.

After giving Emmy another look, her lips still upturned in that wry smile, she started typing again, a little more slowly this time.

"What? You're leaving?" Emmy asked Jacob, who had started chugging his pint. "Isn't Kiera still out of town? In nursing school? In Dallas?"

"Yeah, but I'm gonna go," he said, finishing the beer in less than thirty seconds, burping with gusto and patting his stomach after he set the empty glass down.

"But we haven't even talked about you yet!" Emmy said, protesting.

"Dad's good, coaches with your dad. Mom's good, got lunch with your mom. Kiera's good, still want to marry that girl. There. Caught up."

"But—"

"And I'll leave you to it," Jacob said.

"To what?" Emmy asked, exasperated.

Jacob ignored her. "David, you can put these two on my tab, yeah?"

"Actually, Davey," Cameron cut in, her eyes shining with withheld laughter as she looked from Emmy to Jacob, "put them on mine. Least I can do after all the pints you've poured for me, Jacob."

"Thank you kindly, Cameron," Jacob said with a little fake bow as he got up to leave. He leaned toward Emmy and stage-whispered, "Don't fuck it up, Em."

"It's Emmy!" she shouted after him, swiveling her stool just far enough so that he had a clear view of her giving him the finger.

"What's Emmy short for?" Cameron asked. She had stopped typing.

"What?" Emmy swiveled back toward the bar.

"You lost your shit there about your name."

"Oh. Emilia. You can't shorten a name *twice*. It's too much."

"David's can go down to Davey and then down to Dave." She winked at the bartender.

"Well, Emilia goes down to Emmy. End of evolutionary chain."

"Evolutionary Emmy." She had thought Cameron's eyes were golden, but Emmy realized, in dimmer light, that they were hazel, a little amber, with flecks of gold.

Cameron bopped her hand on her bun before running it through the undercut at the base of her neck. "So, looks like we've been set up, huh? Didn't realize I was going on a date today. I probably would have worn…" She looked down at what she was wearing—an old Ramones T-shirt underneath her leather jacket and black, slightly ripped jeans—then shrugged. "Actually, I probably would have worn this. Fate smiles upon me every now and then."

"Set up?"

"David and Jacob," Cameron said, shooting David a quick wink before he held up his hands and retreated to the other side of the bar. "Bartenders extraordinaire."

Emmy sent a silent curse toward Jacob for putting her in this situation. It was too soon to date, too soon to try. She'd dreamed of it, of course, the freedom to find someone who she was attracted to, someone who shared that same attraction for her with no shame, no question. But there would always be a question, wouldn't there? When she lived in places like Walker? Like Steinbeck?

But David and Jacob had not been afraid of them coming together. Had even made it happen. Could it be possible, Emmy dared to wonder, that she could do what every person she'd grown up with had done since they were thirteen, full of new hormones, their faces acne pocked as they sweat too much and yearned too much and tried too hard to emulate love?

"Are you scared or something?" Cameron asked when Emmy didn't respond. She put her hand down on the bar, close to Emmy's.

"Oh, no, I mean…" Emmy had no control of her words, but she also found herself incapable of lying to Cameron. What was the feeling—her elevated pulse, sweating palms, and slight nausea—if not fear?

"Just tell me you're not one of those evangelical crazies," Cameron said. "You know the ones. They post up at every coffee shop and bar to try and convert people or whatever."

"Oh, no, I'm not—"

"I swear, I've gotten numbers from like, five girls thinking they were interested. Turns out they just wanted to take me to The Well. A fucking Bible study. I almost went the first time. Thought it was a bar."

"What tipped you off?" Emmy asked.

"She asked if I needed a Bible. Said she had an extra I could borrow."

Emmy laughed at that, and she felt an ease start to overtake her, understanding why Jacob had wanted them to meet. Emmy rarely met someone who made her actually laugh. But Cameron had caused a swell of excitement to overtake Emmy, which burst into the air in her unselfconscious giggle. Cameron smiled, her lips upturned and slightly parted, seemingly delighted by Emmy's laughter.

"You wanna go out sometime?" Cameron asked. She looked down at her hands. "It seems like you're into this—girls, I mean. And the boys obviously want us to try it out. So."

Emmy nodded. She was afraid if she said something, the spell would be broken and Cameron would remember that two women together was wrong, a sin. Emmy imagined her slamming her computer shut, jumping out of her seat, and sprinting far away from her like Michaela had done.

Instead, she asked, "How about now?"

"Today?" Emmy asked, taken aback.

"Better than texting each other, waiting twenty-four hours. Lesbians move fast, you know. U-Haul, all that."

"Oh, I…" Emmy looked down at her hands. Her fingernails were chipped and too long. She had read an article that said lesbians' nails were supposed to be short and clean.

"Just dinner," Cameron said, clasping Emmy's hands, her voice filled with a tender sort of understanding. "I promise."

Emmy looked at Cameron. Later, she would wonder if there was something she should have seen, some telling glint, like an oracle's orb or a Magic 8-Ball, that could have tipped her off. A hint hidden right in front of her that could have saved her from it all.

If there was, Emmy missed it. All she saw: amber mixed with gold, laugh lines, a clump of mascara, and warmth. Emmy didn't give it a second thought. She trusted Cameron right away.

The heavy door of the Grizzly slammed behind them. Cameron walked in front of Emmy, who, still slightly shell-shocked, followed behind, trying to remember how to breathe.

"We'll just pop in here," Cameron said, walking briskly into the gas station next to the bar. "They have pretty good tacos, too, if you're hungry."

"Uh…" Emmy said, her stomach squirming.

"Or not," Cameron said, slowing down to match her pace with Emmy's. "We can get wine. Or beer. Or both."

"I like wine," Emmy said. The words rang back in her ears and sounded so unbelievably stupid that she was sure Cameron would turn around on the spot, go back to the Grizzly, and never speak to her again.

Instead, she smiled. "All right, beautiful. Wine it is."

Emmy and Cameron walked through the rows of the gas station, the fluorescent lights buzzing, saying nothing. Emmy kept shooting glances over at Cameron, who happily hummed along to the country song playing on the radio. She took her time as she looked through the cheap bottles of white wine, finally deciding on two. She paid at the register and walked outside, Emmy following along behind her.

"You keep staring at me," Cameron said, stopping suddenly on the sidewalk and turning to Emmy.

"Oh," Emmy said, caught. The August sun beat down relentlessly on her neck. "I just... I'm just..."

"Nervous?" Cameron asked.

"Is that embarrassing?"

"Not at all," Cameron said, setting the wine bottles down on the ground and stepping toward her. "We just need to shake it out of you. Do you mind if I...?"

Emmy allowed Cameron to wrap her arms around her waist. And then, without warning, she picked Emmy up off the ground, twirled her around, and shouted, "Fly away, nerves, fly away!" forcing Emmy into a fit of giggles that seemed to expel all the anxiety and tension that had held her spellbound for the last half hour.

When Emmy was back on the ground, Cameron still held her hips. Their faces were close together, and Emmy felt a magnetic pull, her entire body drawn in by Cameron's. It was a crackling sort of chemistry that dizzied her on the spot.

Just as Emmy leaned in, Cameron pulled away.

"Come on," Cameron said. "I want to show you my favorite place."

They hopped into Cameron's car and drove fifteen minutes west of town. They passed a group of fraternity brothers playing beer pong so loudly that it forced Cameron to crank up the song she was playing so that the bass shook the car windows.

Emmy didn't know the song, but she instantly loved it, as if she'd been waiting to hear that music for her entire life. It was a pop song with a complex drum pattern and swelling chorus sung by a woman with a voice so good it seemed to hit Emmy right in the ribs as she sang about being alive and in love and burning.

Cameron parked outside of an old, abandoned firehouse, a brick building with vines snaking up the sides. Surrounded by weeds and poison ivy, the ladder up to the roof was rusted and shaking, as if one great gust of wind could send it toppling to the ground.

"Well, this is it," Cameron said, putting the wine in her backpack, looking out at the building with a reverential sort of awe.

"That ladder," Emmy said, eyeing it, "doesn't seem very stable."

"It's not!" Cameron said, putting on her backpack and tightening the straps. "Do you want to be brave?"

Emmy nodded, not hesitating, knowing, as she put her first foot on the bottom rung of the ladder, that she'd go anywhere Cameron asked her to.

Once they were at the top, they sat on the edge of the roof, their feet swinging off the ledge. Cameron opened the wine, took a swig straight from the bottle, and handed it to Emmy, who brought it to her lips, relishing the crisp, cool liquid, refreshing on such a scalding summer evening.

As she drank, Emmy looked out at the dying fields of West Texas, which seemed to sprawl out for miles and miles, the windmills turning slowly on the horizon as the lights from the interstate twinkled in the distance.

"So," Cameron said after Emmy passed back the bottle, "tell me about yourself, Emmy Quinn. Or should I call you EQ?"

"It's just Emmy, remember?"

"Just Emmy," Cameron repeated, smiling, interlocking her leg with Emmy's so that they swung together.

"Well," Emmy began, relishing Cameron's closeness, and

wanting more of it, rested her hand on Cameron's thigh. "I was born in Texas, at the end of July…"

Once she started, she couldn't stop. Emmy talked for hours. Everything she had ever felt, thought, done, came spilling out in the air that night, the memories like building blocks she tried to put together so that Cameron could see the shape of her, feel the texture of her life, understand all that made up the foundation of who she was. The moon had fully risen by the time she'd run out of things to say.

"I just talked for like, seven hours," Emmy said, pulling out her phone to look at the time.

"You're remarkable. You're beautiful," Cameron said, in complete earnest, looking Emmy directly in the eyes, grabbing her hand. "I feel like I've been waiting to meet you my whole life."

Something in Emmy's chest swelled and burst so quickly that it nearly took her breath away. She didn't know what to say. But words couldn't contain that moment. So, instead, she leaned into Cameron, who did not pull away.

They kissed. There was no shame in it. There was no halting, no sudden proclamation of faith. They came together, and it was good. It was right.

Emmy allowed herself to get lost in Cameron completely. In that relinquishing of control, Emmy felt, for the first time in her life, finally, fully alive.

11

Emmy woke up in her room the next morning, the night after the firehouse, and felt as if she were living in a dream. Sunlight slipped in through her half-open blinds, and she watched the dust particles float in the light, dancing. Though they looked almost alive to Emmy, they seemed to lack substance. She wondered why they couldn't cast a shadow on her periwinkle wall.

Her room had been decorated, furnished, and designed by her roommate Annie's mother, who was a good family friend of the Quinns with horrible taste, about which she was very particular. When she had first moved in, Emmy had tried to hang a framed poster of Bruce Springsteen at Madison Square Garden on the wall, above the overstuffed, lime-green armchair in the corner of the room, but Annie's mom had heard Emmy's hammering and nearly had a heart attack when she saw a sleeveless Bruce shredding his guitar, thrusting out his hips, leaning back on Clarence Clemons Jr., who stared straight ahead into the crowd, his sax at his side, a headband stretched across his forehead, biting his lower lip, taking a breath before he started to play.

"This is a place of peace!" Annie's mom had shrieked. "You can't usher in that kind of evil!"

Cameron would hate it here, Emmy thought, looking around, seeing no trace of herself in the room she'd lived in for nearly three years. The only things she owned were her clothes in the closet, which all fit into the small suitcase she kept underneath her bed. She imagined what Cameron would make of it, what kind of comment she'd have about the lace duvet that was spread at the end of the twin bed or the ruby-red bookshelf filled with all of Annie's mom's favorites: *Redeeming Love*, C. S. Lewis books, and three different translations of the Holy Bible.

Emmy sat up and stretched, feeling the stiffness leave her body, jolting her awake. She traced her lips with the tip of her finger, remembering the night before, reminding herself that it had not been a dream.

She could feel the shift in her life the way she could smell the rain in the air before a storm: everything around her had become denser, heavier. Even time seemed to move through the viscosity of her newfound freedom.

Was this normal? Emmy wondered. For life to shift in an instant?

She wanted to ask someone about it, but who was there? The girls in her sorority talked about love in the same scripted, rehearsed way: they were waiting for a man to come and lead them in their spiritual walk with Christ. They were waiting for a man to date them with the intention of marriage. And once they found that man, all they talked about was how much he loved the Lord, how he walked with Christ, and how he guided them to be stronger in their faith. Any talk of love with them was always devoid of desire or fire or fate.

There was Jacob, who had been dating Kiera for nearly four years. But Emmy had tried to talk to him about love before, and he'd just shrugged and said, "I mean, have you seen her?" Kiera was beautiful, it was true—long legs, perfect skin, a wide, warm smile that made everyone feel at ease—but Emmy wanted to dig deeper, to crack the code, which made Jacob roll his eyes and say, "You're so fucking annoying, Em."

She had talked about almost every major event in her life with her parents, but they weren't speaking to her. She imagined their faces if she told them about Cameron, an atheist lesbian from Boston who hated football. It wouldn't matter to them that Jacob had set them up, that he approved. Cameron was a woman. That was all it would take for them to turn them away.

But even if Emmy could talk to any of them about it, she wasn't sure they would understand. There was something about her and Cameron that felt distinctly different. The sudden, instant attachment, the ease with which she could talk with Cameron about everything that had ever happened to her. Emmy didn't have the language for what she was feeling. Without the context of community, she felt isolated. An island of too-sudden, too-intense feeling. And because she didn't understand it, this instantaneous connection made her afraid.

As she got dressed for the day, Cameron texted her.

Last night was fun. Let's break the law again tonight?

Emmy smiled as she read the text. A jolt of excitement flooded through her that was almost instantly doused by dread.

The night before, as they were kissing, Cameron had whispered in Emmy's ear, "Let's go back to my place." It was an offer, said kindly, not a demand. It was the sort of thing you said on first dates, Emmy thought, when they were going well.

But Emmy had freaked out. She made up a lie—one of her sorority friends was in crisis over a boy and needed Emmy right away—and Cameron had driven her home without complaint, seeming to believe her. When they parked in front of Emmy's condo, she'd sprinted out of the car, forgetting to kiss Cameron goodbye.

Emmy wasn't sure what she was supposed to do, how she was supposed to have sex with a girl. She had slept with one boy during her freshman year at Walker, in an attempt to prove to herself that what had happened with Michaela was a fluke, not a pattern. (This was, of course, before she'd seen all the movies that solidified what she'd known since her baptism.) The boy Emmy slept with was in a fraternity, and he was surprisingly sweet and gentle and very drunk. He cried after he came and then cried again when Emmy said she hadn't come, too, at the exact same time as him. *But they do in the movies!* He'd sobbed, and then, what seemed like seconds later, he was snoring, still on top of her.

Emmy had wanted to go back with Cameron to her apartment. But she had felt frozen with the possibility of everything before her. Even then, at the beginning, she could feel that slow-motion fall into love, which was propelled by the quick succession of obsession that folded Cameron into the fabric of everything she did, every thought she had. The longing for love had taken up so much space in Emmy's brain for so many years that when it finally fell in her lap, she wasn't sure what to do with it.

Emmy remembered how she'd felt the night before. Free, yes, for the first time in her life, but also terrified. Emmy had held her breath when Cameron got near her. She had tripped over her words. Cameron was dizzying to Emmy, both in her presence and experience.

West Texas had never felt smaller to Emmy than when she was listening to Cameron list all the places she'd been, and all the women she'd dated, and all the films she'd seen, and books she'd read. The world of her mind was so layered and so vast. Emmy was just a speck on the map. How could she keep up? How could she compare?

The dread she had felt at the end of the date returned, streaming through her as the sun filled the room with morning light. It wasn't the sort of thing someone wanted, Emmy reasoned to herself, someone so afraid.

So she dealt with her fear as she had for many years: she buried it. She ignored Cameron's texts. She tried to forget her altogether. It had been like that with Michaela, hadn't it? One night of passion interrupted by the reality of their love's impossibility. Maybe that was the way it would always go for Emmy. Always just a taste, never the whole thing. It was better for them both if she just stayed away.

Two days later, though, on a Friday night, Emmy answered a knock at the door.

"You don't get to ghost me," Cameron said, leaning against the porch, wearing a patterned button-down maroon shirt with white-washed jeans and white sneakers. "I feel like Italian. Let's go to Johnny's."

She turned around and led the way, her hair in a bun on top of her head that bobbed side to side as she made her way down the front steps, onto the sidewalk. Emmy hesitated for a moment, frozen with disbelief, and then bounded toward her, as if pulled by her magnetic force.

They walked down the street in silence, and Cameron held Emmy's hand, and she felt something surge and come close to bursting in her chest.

Then, a huge black pickup truck roared by them, blasting music too loudly with the windows rolled down. A boy screamed, "Dykes!" out of the window before revving up the engine and speeding off, leaving a black cloud of exhaust smoke for them to walk through. Cameron laughed. Emmy clenched her jaw and dropped Cameron's hand.

Cameron's smile faltered for a moment as she looked from her hand back to Emmy. It could have been a trick of the evening light, but Emmy thought she saw Cameron's lip tremble. She recovered her smile almost instantly, so Emmy convinced herself she'd made it up. It was confident Cameron after all, Emmy thought. She was immune to trembling.

Johnny's was packed, but Cameron, always prepared, had made a reservation before she picked Emmy up, and they sat in the back of the restaurant, in a little corner by the window, where the crystal candlestick on the white tablecloth made light dazzle into rainbows before them.

"The table is gay!" Cameron squealed, delighted, grabbing Emmy's hand in her excitement, which Emmy squeezed once before dropping, giving the room a quick, nervous scan.

Throughout dinner, Emmy moved any part of her body Cameron tried to touch. It was an instinct she didn't know she had, some sense of self-preservation. *Don't let them see, don't give yourself away. Stay safe, hidden, in the shadows.* If they exposed themselves to too much light, Emmy thought, like the crystal, the reality of who they were would blind everyone around them. And in their blindness, Emmy knew they would attack.

The *they* was evasive but ever-present in Emmy's mind, an audience she always looked around for. They had the faces of her father and her mother and every person in Steinbeck who surrounded her family—Jan Oleander, Dan Holcomb, Pastor Ben, Pastor Sherman. Homogenous in their whiteness, in their rightness, in their systems of belief that rendered Cameron and Emmy and everyone like them invalid.

After Emmy snatched her hand away for the third time, Cameron frowned.

"You don't have to be so afraid anymore," she said, taking Emmy's hand in hers, kissing it for emphasis. "You're safe. We're safe."

An older couple next to them glared. Cameron gave them a sidelong glance, grinned, and leaned across the table to kiss

Emmy, lightly, on the lips. Cutlery clattered on plates. A harsh *Good God!* was aggressively whispered by the woman at the table.

"All they have is outrage," Cameron said. "But no balls to act on it. The beauty of Texas: they can try to shame you into submission, but when you have no shame, you can always be free."

"When'd you move here, again?" Emmy asked.

"Year and a half ago."

"You don't know anything, yet," she said.

But Emmy wanted to believe her. Even more so, she wanted to take away the power of those people who hated her. Emmy's longing for that freedom Cameron spoke of was so desperate, so wild, that she almost forgot where they were and believed Cameron could be right.

"Of course I do," Cameron said, stretching across the table to steal a bite of Emmy's pasta. "I know everything."

Their waiter came over from the older couple's table.

"Hello, ladies," he said. "How is everything?"

"Great!"

"Wonderful."

"Excellent," the waiter said. He looked back at the couple and cleared his throat. "Just a reminder that we ask that our guests respect the…the *environment* while they dine with us."

Cameron and Emmy looked at one other. A flicker of rage ran through Cameron's eyes. Her jaw clenched, and her eyebrows knit together tightly. She turned to the waiter.

"We didn't use plastic straws," Cameron answered. "And we walked here, even though it's hotter than hell outside. Not sure how else we can respect the environment."

"The restaurant, ma'am." The waiter gave her a strained smile. He placed his hands behind his back. "It's a family-friendly restaurant with family-friendly values."

"And stale-ass bread with subpar Bolognese."

Emmy glanced at the waiter, who was no longer smiling, and then at the couple behind him. The husband was focused on his linguine. His eyes were downcast, and his thick, round glasses fogged from the piping hot pasta. But his wife stared. Not at Cameron, not at the waiter. At Emmy.

Her small faded blue eyes were narrowed and watery. Her lips were taut, forming one stern, red-tinted line. Her wrinkled and liver-spotted hands were clasped in front of her as if in prayer.

She hated Emmy.

It took a second for that truth to register, but Emmy couldn't deny it once she had seen it.

The woman didn't break her stare. Bussers swooped in to grab her salad plate, fill her water glass, and still she stared, her distaste radiating across the aisle between them. Her judgment and disgust were so strong, Emmy imagined they could permeate any aisle, any road, any border—even the banks of the mighty Rio Grande.

Emmy imagined what it must be like to hate someone you've never met so deeply. She wanted to believe that it made the woman the weaker of the two of them, but her disdain invaded every part of Emmy with such strength that Emmy couldn't help but think of it as power.

"So you're telling me—" Cameron said on a roll and building steam "—when I come in here, pay you money, tip you *well*, drink your overpriced, cheap Chianti that will give me a roaring headache twenty minutes after I leave this shitty, knockoff Olive Garden, that if I kiss my girlfriend on a *date*, I'm going to have to leave?"

"Children dine with us, ma'am," the waiter reasoned, slowly backing away from the table with little shuffle-steps as Cameron's rage increased. She inhaled deeply.

Emmy wanted two things in that moment: to box up her tortellini, and to force herself to snap out of whatever delusion had made her think she would ever be free enough to date a woman, to be so public with her affection in a place like Walker, which was just as small and conservative as Steinbeck.

Emmy knew they needed to leave.

"Let's just go," she said, fishing cash from her wallet and slapping it on the table. Emmy stood up. The older woman was still looking. Emmy didn't have to glance over to know her pleasure at seeing them go.

"Emmy!" Cameron was indignant. "We can't just—"

"Thank you, sir," Emmy said to the waiter with a smile, unable to purge the politeness so instilled in her since she was young. She prayed that Cameron would follow her.

Emmy threw open the door of the restaurant, and the hot air thawed the chill from the overly air-conditioned room.

"Emmy, what the hell!" Cameron yelled from behind. Emmy felt freer outside, safe from the older woman's oppressive gaze. "We were getting somewhere with those antiquated, homophobic—"

Emmy turned around, suddenly freed from all her reservations once she was back outside in the West Texas heat. She took Cameron's face in her hands. Kissed her deeply. Emmy had never dreamed she would ever kiss anyone in public. Cameron shut up, then kissed back. Emmy felt her relax.

"You don't know Texas very well," Emmy whispered to her after she pulled away. "And you told the waiter I was your girlfriend."

"Heat of the moment. Didn't have time for a define-the-relationship talk."

"Sure."

"*My girlfriend* sounds better than *this girl that I'm seeing that I think is really cute but I'm not really sure what her deal is yet.*"

"*Deal?*"

"Fucking homophobic pricks!"

"But what deal?"

"We're never eating here again."

"Cameron."

"What?"

"What deal? You said you don't know what my deal is."

"Oh," Cameron looked disoriented for a moment, her mind still in the restaurant, fighting with the waiter. "I mean, you ran off last week. And you tense up any time I hold your hand when we're walking."

"I'm just…"

"And the whole thing with your dad hating gay people and the small-Texas-town thing… I don't know, you don't know what you want, I don't think."

"My dad has nothing to do with this."

"And I don't want to be the bitch who pressures you into something you're not ready for."

"What do you want?"

"It's not about me. I just don't know if you're ready."

"Ready for what?"

"Me," she said, opening up her arms. "This." She pointed to herself and then Emmy.

Cameron pulled at her thumb, looked down at the ground, and kicked the concrete with her high-top sneakers, doing her best to avoid Emmy's eyes, looking, for the first time since Emmy had known her, self-conscious, vulnerable, afraid.

"I was going to stay in Boston, you know," she said, her voice soft and shaking. "Go to law school. I got into Harvard Law. Did you know that?"

"Like Elle Woods," Emmy said, trying to make her laugh, the smallness of Cameron's voice so broken it terrified her. She let out a sharp, loud bark of a laugh.

"Yes," Cameron said, her confidence returning, steadying the tremble in her voice. She motioned forward, and they started walking. "But instead of pink, everything would be draped in flannel and cut-off denim."

"So," Emmy asked, "why are you in Walker?"

"My parents are lawyers, you know, big-time ones, with their own practice. Defense attorneys. The sort that makes money, so all their clients are assholes who embezzled their company's money or some shit like that. I was supposed to graduate from Harvard—their alma mater, where they met—clerk for a Massachusetts judge for a year, then come to the practice, work as an associate, until my parents were ready to let me into *The Fold*, as they call it. Both of my brothers did it. They're in the associate stage now. I was on board. All set to follow the master plan. But then..."

Everything changed. She majored in English literature at Yale and fell in love. It was supposed to prepare her to read well, to analyze texts, a useful skill for any lawyer to have. But as soon as she had her first seminar, she was hooked. The discussions, the energy, the arguments: she wanted that for the rest of her life. A PhD, a classroom, an institution that would fund her research questions until she was satisfied. But she knew, deep down, that there was no way she'd ever be satisfied, and she'd keep asking her questions until the end of time.

Her parents refused to pay for her master's in something so useless, as they called it, when she had a lifetime of financial security guaranteed by the master plan they'd set up. So instead of taking out student loans, she had gone to the only program that offered her a full ride. Her parents never thought she'd move to the middle of Nowhere, Texas, to do it. They were impressed at her determination, if not furious at where that determination was channeled.

"So anyway, all that to say..." she said, taking a deep breath in "...I'm glad I'm here. It's worth it. Even though half the professors hate me. Because of the whole lesbian thing. But I've found some good ones, like, you know, Dr. Cunningham, who let me research whatever I want.

"But, Emmy, it's been lonely," she said, kicking a fallen pine cone on the sidewalk. They watched it bounce in front of them and land in an overgrown lawn, lost among the weeds. "And when I met you at the Grizzly, I thought, Yes! I don't have to be alone in this! Someone else like me!"

"You aren't alone!" Emmy said, her head heavy with the weight of her story, of her loneliness. That Cameron could feel that same fear, that same loneliness, was mind-blowing to Emmy, who thought her an impenetrable wall of confidence.

"Aren't I?" Cameron shot back, fiercely. "You're so afraid of everyone around us that you can't *be* with me. Emmy, I can't come out with you. I've already done that. Ten years ago. I can't go backward. And if you're not ready—"

Emmy pulled her in again and kissed her deeply, holding her face in her hands, pressing herself against her, trying to convey the full weight of herself, how willing she was to thrust herself into Cameron's world, into her life. Emmy wanted to make herself ready. She wanted Cameron to know that she could be there, that Emmy wanted *her*, not the fear that had enveloped every inch of her life.

"You're everything I've ever dreamed of," Emmy whispered, still holding Cameron's face.

"I'm not a dream," Cameron said, but her eyes were still closed from the kiss. She took her time opening them. When she finally did, she looked down at Emmy's lips, then up at her eyes. She hesitated when she met them, like she had found something she wasn't expecting. It froze her for a moment. She ran her hand through her undercut, her bun bobbing.

"Can't you just, I don't know," Emmy said, trying to find the words to keep her, "let me try? To be with you?"

Cameron stayed still for a long time, closing her eyes again, breathing through her mouth as her brows came together in concentration.

"Okay," Cameron said, as if resolving something in herself. She leaned her forehead on Emmy's. "Let's try."

When they got to Cameron's apartment, Emmy tried to strip away every ounce of insecurity she could from her consciousness. She was determined to show Cameron that she was serious. That she could try.

Cameron led Emmy into her room, and she knew it was going to happen. Her heart was hammering, but she let desire lead her. No questions, no doubts. That fear had held Emmy back for too long.

Cameron's room was small. White walls, four lamps scattered throughout, a framed Arcade Fire poster hanging over her bed. They were kissing. Cameron was on top of Emmy. She was lost in her.

"Emmy," Cameron whispered. It was like with Michaela, Emmy thought. Her name made music on Cameron's lips. "Are you sure?"

Emmy felt the significance of the moment. Everything was heightened. Cameron's hair tickled her face; her breath hitched in Emmy's ear; the smell of Cameron's shampoo, something floral like rose petals, filled her up when she inhaled.

"Are you sure?" Cameron asked again.

Her body was soft, so much softer than the clumsy, hairy body of the man Emmy had had on top of her before, his beard itching as he kissed her mouth, neck, breasts. He'd felt like rug burn. Cameron felt like silk. Her lips, eager but delicate, made their way down Emmy's body, noticing it, taking her time, not just squeezing and yanking her breasts like the boys before her had done. She traced Emmy's nipples with the tip of her tongue to tease her, forcing her hips upward in longing for more.

More. More. More.

More softness. More pressure. More of her.

"I need to hear you say yes or no," Cameron said.

Emmy didn't want it to end. She thought of Michaela, the momentum suddenly halted by faith. The demonization of her desire.

Cameron's face hovered over Emmy's, her bun flopping forward against her forehead. She stared at Emmy's lips, and Emmy could tell that she wanted her, could tell there was no shame in that desire, no stopping her once she started.

When Emmy realized it was okay to want her back, she gave in. She stopped thinking. She grabbed Cameron's face and kissed her.

"Yes," Emmy said.

Cameron let herself loose. She made her way down Emmy's body. She was between her legs, and all she felt was pleasure. She was blinded by it. She closed her eyes, and colors burst, unbidden, in the back of them with every flick of Cameron's tongue: red, pink, orange, then, finally, a pure white light.

Emmy looked down at Cameron, who looked up at her and smiled.

"Trying is fun," Cameron said. She kissed the inside of Emmy's thighs and made her way up to her lips. Emmy didn't move. She hardly breathed.

"Hey," Cameron said, nudging her with her forehead. "Are you okay?"

Emmy nodded. Cameron's head was resting on her chest. Her bun was lopsided and falling out, the ombré of dark and blond hair sprawling across her breasts. Emmy looked at her profile: high cheekbones, dark brows, jawline so sharp it could cut glass. She traced it with her finger, delicately, as if it could cut her, too, if she got too close.

Cameron kissed Emmy's fingertip and asked, "What are you thinking?"

"I want to do that to you," Emmy said, the honesty springing out of her before she could filter it.

"Oh, God, yes, please."

"But I don't know what I'm doing."

"None of us do."

"No, I mean," Emmy said, suddenly embarrassed, "I've never done it before."

Cameron pushed herself up and straddled Emmy. Kissed her neck.

"You don't have to do anything you don't want."

"I want. I just don't know how."

She rolled onto her back.

"Just listen to my voice, I'll guide you," Cameron said. "All you need to do is listen."

Emmy hesitated.

"Start," Cameron said, smiling, "by kissing me."

12

Emmy's days with Cameron rolled into one another like the heat from August clinging to the first few weeks of September. Emmy spent every day with her; every night, too. She went to class. She skipped her sorority meetings. She blew off her friends. Emmy's world narrowed down to the size of Cameron, the shape of her, the feel of her lips against her own.

During Labor Day weekend, while Cameron was working on her thesis at the Grizzly, Emmy went for one of her usual walks around the three-mile, gravel-paved track that looped around Walker's campus. The first stretch ran parallel to the interstate, where the whoosh of cars zooming and horns honking made it difficult to think. All Emmy could do, really, was keep walking, enduring the noise, trying to piece together some semblance of an uninterrupted thought.

Emmy couldn't believe she'd only known Cameron for three weeks. What had life looked like before her? Emmy tried to remember. She had been happy enough, she thought, spending her weeks studying, staying on track, volunteering at her sorority's philanthropy events. The weekends were an exercise in numbness. Going from one fraternity party to the next, each house as filthy as the last: sticky floors, too-strong punch, the pungent air filled with stale sweat and urine and liquor on the breath of close-talking Republicans who wanted to share about their summer internships with the senator's office. Emmy always ended up cornered by these boys. They were all the same, really: khaki pants and white polos made see-through with sweat, eyes glossy, their words slurred as they talked about taxation and the economy with reverential fervor. After their third or fourth pull of the tequila handle they kept gripped in their ironclad fists, they would start philosophizing about love and life and whether or not it was a sin that they let their girlfriends go to third base with them.

"I don't know," they would say, their eyes nearly closed. "What's love, anyway, Emma?"

Emmy turned the corner down by the math building, and the highway fell away; the buildings did, too. To the east was campus, but the west was all Texas, field and sky and telephone wires stretching for miles and miles. The clouds separated and came together in enormous cotton-candy puffs of white and gray, thinning out into wisps on the edge of the horizon, like a careless stroke on an impressionist painting. In the distance, an old oil pumping jack dipped up and down. Behind it, windmills moved slowly with the breeze, turning into towering silhouettes as the sun set.

The emptiness, the silence, the sheer vastness of space, always made Emmy feel small. That smallness humbled her into stillness. And in the stillness, she could feel something rise and settle inside her chest, a turbulent sort of joy that she had felt since she was a child, overwhelmed with all the room she had to run as she screamed with laughter, imagining her voice could echo into the infinite. The echo, Emmy thought, was God laughing along with her.

She told this to Steve, once, that she and God had been laughing outside. He got a real kick out of that.

"Oh, yeah?" he asked, squatting down to get eye level with her. "He tell any good jokes?"

Laughter was what Emmy most associated with her father. The silliness of childhood never quite died away when he was around. It was brimming, waiting just under the surface, to be released in a chorus of giggles and shouts and side stitches. She wondered if that well of joy was only accessible with him around. Had he cut off her greatest source of light when he shut her out of his life?

Emmy looked out at the field by campus. No one else was around. Too hot, probably. But it was a dry heat, and the burn from the sun felt nice on her skin, a pain she had endured since she was young, as her father had done, and his father's father. Emmy had been born in the heat, at the end of July. She had grown up in it.

There was always a point, though, when the heat became too much.

A breeze from the north swept through the fields, the dry, dead grass unmoving. The back of Emmy's neck was covered in sweat. The wind was almost cool enough to be a relief, but the sun was stronger, more powerful. It was oppressive and claustrophobic. She swatted a mosquito on her thigh and felt the familiar itch of irritation creep up. Summer had stuck around too long.

Emmy's mom liked to make Arnold Palmers in the afternoon when it got to this point, when the heat felt like an infringement, a guest who'd overstayed their welcome. They'd sit in her living room, the AC on full blast, and listen to one of her records, always Dolly Parton, and they'd dance while singing along to "Jolene." Sometimes her dad would be over for Sunday supper after church, and he'd say, "Ain't no woman trying to take your man, is she, Emmylou?" And they'd all laugh, and

Emmy's cheeks would burn at the thought of a woman paying her enough attention to take anything of hers.

By the field, as Emmy wiped the sweat from her forehead again, she had the sudden urge to scream. To shout so loudly her throat would crack and shake and burn with the force of it, the sheer volume of fear and loss and grief resounding through the fields, the interstate, the back roads behind campus. She wanted to be heard, to be seen, to let herself know that she hadn't started to disappear, that she was still substantial, even though the creators of her life had ceased to acknowledge her existence once they realized their creation had gone astray. She was banished from her loved ones because of their perception of her love as sin. And so, her home had become an Eden she was no longer allowed to enter.

"I don't understand why you insist on walking in this goddamn *heat*," Cameron said, coming up behind Emmy. Her black leather backpack was slung across one shoulder while she fished through it to find a water bottle. When she did, she twisted off the top and drank greedily, dramatically, letting out a loud "That's the stuff" when she'd drained the whole thing.

Emmy smiled. She may not have been allowed to enter the garden, but she was given the whole world with Cameron. Everything in Emmy relaxed as she watched Cameron wipe the top of her lip with the back of her hand.

"Why are you looking at me like that?" she asked. "You know I don't share water."

"Just happy to see you," Emmy said.

"Yeah, well, you should've seen me at the Grizzly. I was a woman on a mission. Lesbian literature has never seen a more dedicated scholar. You know, I was researching Elizabeth Bishop today, and I read..."

They walked off the track while Cameron talked, into the field in the west. The sun was starting to set, and the grass— always so destitute in the day—started to shimmer with gold in the waning light. Cameron waved her hands emphatically as she talked about her thesis, and her shadow mimicked her, long and dark and larger than life.

Those were the golden hours. Emmy's hand in Cameron's, the wind warm, the sun brutally hot, but never too much to keep Emmy from holding Cameron in her arms, which she did when Cameron finished ranting about the professor who refused to chair her thesis.

"Okay, okay," Cameron said, peeling out of the embrace. "You're sticky."

"A little heat never hurt anyone," Emmy said, laughing, kissing her until she spun out into the open.

"Air-conditioning," Cameron demanded.

"It's only ninety-five!" Emmy said, wiping the sweat from her forehead, leaning in to hug her before Cameron could spin away from her.

"Emmy!" a voice shouted from behind them. Emmy whirled around. It was Mary Kate Franklin, the president of Theta Omega, Emmy's sorority.

Emmy looked from Cameron to MK, panicked, wondering if she could have seen them before, kissing and hugging and laughing. She seemed normal, though, unreactive.

"MK!" Emmy said, her voice high and strained. She looked over at Cameron, willing her to disappear, become invisible, protected from whatever consequence would come from MK seeing them together.

Cameron, though, cocked her head to the side as she took in MK. Big blond hair pulled up in a ponytail, toned body, spray-tanned and slightly orange skin, hot pink leggings, a black crop top, and bright white tennis shoes the exact shade of her blinding veneers.

"I thought Southern sorority girls were a myth," Cameron whispered to Emmy in awe as MK walked up. She shot Cameron a look to shut her up and walked into MK's outstretched arms.

"Where have you *been,* Emmy?" she asked, giving her a big squeeze. "Not one meeting this semester?"

"Yeah, well," Emmy said, smiling. The smiling was key. Every interaction, every word, every sentence had to begin and end with an enormous, cheek-numbing grin. "Busy semester, you know. Gotta keep up the GPA to start my job in May."

"And, who's this?" MK asked, looking behind Emmy at Cameron, who was still gawking at MK. Her *this* was extended, strained, an interrogation. The more syllables a Texas woman put in a word, the more trouble you were in.

"Cameron, this is MK. MK, Cameron," Emmy said, stepping aside, with some reluctance, so that Cameron could be fully seen.

"Nice to meet you, Cameron. Have I seen you around campus before? With the Kappas?"

"I don't think so," Cameron said, trying hard not to laugh. "I'm a graduate student in the English department. You may have seen me around that building. I basically live there."

"English! You know, I love to read. And I used to want to be a writer back when I was a little girl, but, you know, there's never any time for that stuff anymore, and besides, I don't think I'd have anything anyone'd like to read, really."

"Don't say that!" Cameron said, adding a slight inflection in her voice to match MK's.

"No, no, I'm sure about that much. So how do you know our Emmy?"

"She's my girlfriend."

The slight twinge of pleasure Emmy felt in hearing that was paired instantly with fear. Emmy hadn't thought through how she was going to tell people at Walker. How she would explain herself. It was a delicate matter, one she wasn't entirely convinced Cameron knew the intricacies of. Everything, for Cameron, was posited within the lens of what she herself had experienced.

Where she had come from, people understood, inherently, that love could be any number of things. In West Texas, though, everything was smaller: the towns, the ideologies, the tolerance for difference. White, straight, Christian. Those were the people in power. Those were the lives that could be easily understood.

Emmy watched, holding her breath, as MK frowned, then smiled.

"Well, she's my girlfriend, too, you know. We met in Theta Omega, during rush, actually. And y'all met...?"

Cameron frowned at her. She looked at Emmy, who tried to tell her with her eyes that it was too complicated to explain, that MK wouldn't understand, that it would be different telling people here, in Walker, than it could ever be up north, in Boston, where people's frame of reference for love wasn't dominated by the belief that love had limitations: a man and a woman, a holy union, right love and wrong love.

Cameron opened her mouth and then closed it. She turned from Emmy back to MK, her head held high, her sharp chin sticking out defiantly, her shoulders set with resolve.

"We met at the Grizzly three weeks ago, and I took her on a date that night, and we kissed, and now she's my girlfriend." She walked up beside Emmy and held her hand. "My *actual* girl-friend."

If she was shocked, MK showed no sign of it. Her eyes flickered between Emmy and Cameron and narrowed as understanding dawned on her. She nodded and smiled again.

"Well," she said, her ponytail moving back and forth behind her as she looked between the two of them. "I'll see you soon, Emmy. It was so nice to meet *you*."

Her last word seemed to draw out even as she walked away. So many syllables, Emmy thought. Never a good sign.

"She was a *delight*," Cameron said, mocking MK, smiling at Emmy as if nothing had happened.

Emmy stared at Cameron, who swam before her as a strong dose of dizziness that had nothing to do with the heat overtook her vision. It was like a rug she hadn't known she was standing on had been yanked out from under her.

It wasn't quite feeling betrayal; it wasn't quite anger. It was something in between. The fundamental feeling of being unseen, invisible to Cameron in the face of her need to be right. Cameron was passionate and smart and kind, but she lacked patience for those who did not share her thinking. And in that way, Emmy thought, Cameron was similar to her father. Slamming the door in the face of difference.

Emmy admired Cameron's ability to proclaim who she was with confidence. She envied it, too, still so uncomfortable in her own body, in unveiling the parts of herself that she'd kept hidden for so long. But it was *her* truth to unveil. Even then, when Emmy wanted Cameron to have every inch of her, she knew that was a place Cameron could never touch. It was hers alone.

"I have to get home," Emmy said, turning away from Cameron. She had always been prone to avoidance in the presence of conflict.

"Stay," Cameron said, tugging at her hand. "I just got here."

"I've been out here a while. It's hot."

"You love the heat."

"Only at first."

"Always talking about how Texas hardens you to the heat."

"Yeah, well," Emmy snapped, pulling her hand away, "there's always a breaking point."

It was like Emmy had slapped Cameron. She stood, frozen, her mouth slightly open, her brows coming together in confusion. Her eyes—hazel but golden in the light of the sun—darted between Emmy's clenched fists and her face. Emmy could tell her brain was whirring, trying to piece together what had happened. When she figured it out, Cameron closed her eyes. She put her face in her hands. Her whole body seemed to slump. Emmy realized, for the first time, that she was taller than Cameron.

Emmy wondered later whether her response was out of love

or a fear of loss, of being alone. Maybe there wasn't a difference. But in that moment, all Emmy saw was her softness, her vulnerability, her ability to recognize wrong. Everything Emmy felt for her collected in her chest and sank down deeper, richer, more fully.

"I don't always think before I do stuff," Cameron finally said. "And sometimes I say things I shouldn't."

"I just haven't figured it all out," Emmy said quickly, cutting her off, taking her hand, squeezing her forgiveness into Cameron's palm. She couldn't handle any fracture in their closeness. "It's complicated. Or, I guess not complicated, it's just hard to bring up."

"MK going to send a hit job after you?" Cameron asked.

"Maybe," Emmy said, laughing. "If I know her, she'll send something."

As Emmy walked back to her condo after saying goodbye to Cameron, preparing for whatever MK would send her, she felt a short fuse of fury rise up again at Cameron's inconsideration. She tried to beat it down, force herself to remember that she was lucky to even have someone like Cameron in her life. Not threatened by any faith, not shamed by any family members for her personal life.

But she couldn't help but feel as if Cameron's need to tell MK stemmed from some part of her that was compelled to see Emmy as a statement. Just as Cameron saw Walker's graduate school as a way to send a statement to her parents. And the statements seemed to be, across the board, a resounding *Fuck you*.

Could someone fall for an idea? Emmy wondered. She shuddered at the thought, which was made more terrifying by its possibility. She thought of the way Cameron had plowed ahead with MK, despite Emmy's silent pleading for her to stop. It was as if, for a moment, she had been rendered invisible once more. A ghost.

It was exhausting, Emmy thought, cracking her knuckles as

she approached her condo. To move through life unnoticed, to never be truly seen, to be propped up for other people's purposes, her true self cast aside as if it were an inconvenience. She wondered if it would be like this forever, if she would always be stuck haunting.

13

Emmy had to hand it to MK: she knew how to work quickly.

When Emmy got home, her roommate, Annie, a small, red-headed mousy girl who had grown up with her in Steinbeck, was waiting in the living room.

"One of your sorority friends..." Annie said, her voice dipping off at the end of her sentence, as it often did when she was delivering bad news.

"Was it MK?" Emmy asked, already knowing the answer.

"The blonde one? Who'll probably run for president someday?"

"That's her."

"She said to meet her at the house as soon as you get home," Annie said. She cleared her throat and looked down at the ground. "I really need to talk to you about something... important."

"Okay. Let me shower and go deal with these girls first. We'll talk when I'm back."

"It's just that—"

"Just hold on a minute, Annie," Emmy said, heading to the shower. "I have to get ready to get kicked out of my sorority."

"You...what?" Annie called after Emmy, her voice reaching an operatic octave in her confusion.

After Emmy showered and got dressed, she slammed the door behind her, walking with purpose toward the Theta Omega house, only two blocks from the condo she shared with Annie. They had lived together in a dorm their freshman year and found that they functioned well in the same space. Emmy had her sorority, Annie had her book club, and they had their shared history in Steinbeck that allowed them to sit in silence without any pressure to fill it. Annie's mom, always looking for investments in West Texas, decided to buy a condo near campus to rent out to students after Annie graduated. The rent was unbelievably cheap. Emmy got a family-and-friends discount that had made Steve uncomfortable, but Lucy had waved away his concern over coffee and cake the summer before Emmy's sophomore year.

"Steve, don't be such a hard-ass," Lucy said.

"She's not making Emmy sign a lease," Steve said, pouring a touch of Kahlua in his coffee, the way he always did to dull the edge of his frustration. "And she's getting discounted rent? That's bad business."

"We've known Annie's family for years. Her mom is a friend of mine," she said. "Do you not trust my judgment?"

"Never served me too well, that judgment of yours."

"Emmy, don't listen to your daddy. He doesn't know what he's talking about. It's sweet of Annie to even offer. Go ahead with it."

"It's a mistake, Emmy."

"Better than living in that sorority house. Lord Almighty, I could tell you stories about that place."

Lucy had been a Theta Omega at Walker in the eighties when

it was all big hair, bright eyeliner, and women paying thousands of dollars to get their so-called MRS degrees. When she found out Emmy was going to Walker, Lucy had tried to play it cool, but she kept dropping hints like, "Oh, you know, when I was a Theta O…" or "The real benefit of Theta O for me…" or, more heavy-handedly, "You know, if you decided to rush Theta O, you'd be a shoo-in because you're a legacy, and it's a great way to form connections in the business world."

The notion of a sorority had seemed silly to Emmy: girls taking boys to different events, walking around in matching T-shirts, chanting and clapping in cultlike unison to recruit new members into their group. But it was an easy way to make friends, and being in a group like that provided a certain amount of anonymity that Emmy craved: to sink into the background of a monochromatic group, allowing the privilege of her appearance—white, feminine—to protect her from the scrutiny of her interior life.

The Theta Omega house was a two-story redbrick building with the two large gold Greek letters hanging above the front door. The landscaping was impeccable: the grass was green despite the heat due to sprinklers that watered the lawn in the early morning and late evening. Trimmed boxwoods ran across the perimeter of the house. Inside the hedges, there was a small garden with pansies, violet sprigs, and caladiums, their leaves oval, the pink inside of them shaped like hearts; they grew over the boxwoods and tickled the back of Emmy's legs as she walked through the large oak door.

MK was waiting in the hallway. She had changed into black slacks and a blazer. Ready for business.

"We're meeting in the office," MK said, walking ahead of Emmy. The click-clack of her kitten heels echoed through the empty entryway.

"Where is everyone?" Emmy asked, looking around at the abandoned common room. There were two overstuffed brown leather chairs and an enormous beige sectional that pointed toward a large flat-screen television.

"Philanthropy event," she said without turning around.

MK's efficiency and blind dedication to the rule of law made her an excellent sorority president. She could not be swayed by girls' stories about financial stress, emotional upheaval, or trauma of any kind. There were dues to pay, events to attend, and a protocol to follow. Anything that fell outside the bounds of these firmly established mandates of behavior had to be addressed, quickly, lest that leniency spread and upend the fragile balance she had managed to find following Theta Omega's embarrassing record of behavior that had gotten them kicked off campus for two years.

There had been several incidents involving hazing. A pledge filmed them on her smartphone and sent it to the university's office of student affairs: older members forcing other pledges to sit on running washing machines, circling parts of their bodies that jiggled with permanent marker; older members forcing pledges to strip and sit on paper towels while they watched clips of lesbian porn, checking afterward to see if anyone's paper towel had gotten wet; forcing any pledge that *had* gotten the paper towel wet to pick one boy from their brother fraternity, Tau Kappa, and give him a blow job, to make sure she would be what they considered normal enough to stay in the sorority.

The videos forced the university's hand. The sorority was punished, then put on probation. Their academic adviser, Dr. Sara Cunningham, a professor in the English department, had been brought on to oversee the reintegration of their chapter on campus.

When they turned the corner from the living room to the office, Emmy saw Dr. Cunningham standing outside the office doors, looking exhausted, as she often did when she attended meetings. Her bright red pantsuit was wrinkled, and there was a coffee stain on the white button-up shirt she wore. Her short jet-black pixie cut was all over the place, like she had been running her hands through it, exasperated, for several hours.

"Emmy," Dr. Cunningham said. Her voice was low yet loud, with all the confidence and command of a tenured professor. She ran her left hand through her hair, and Emmy noticed it was ringless. She had assumed Dr. Cunningham was married. "Before we start, I just want to say—"

"Dr. Cunningham," MK interrupted, "we really need to get started. The other girls are waiting inside."

"Oh, oh, okay. I don't want to hold anything up," Dr. Cunningham said, shrinking back.

MK charged through the office door. It was a small room, just big enough for an old round oak table, a printer, and several file cabinets. MK took her seat at the far side of the room while Dr. Cunningham pulled a chair away from the table to sit against the wall, a notepad resting on her leg. She fished out a pen from her purse and started scribbling. There were two other girls at the table, sorority officers who looked to MK without saying a word to Emmy.

"Thank you for meeting with us on such short notice, Emmy," MK began, briskly. "But this couldn't wait. As you know, Emmy, we ran into each other earlier today."

"Yeah," Emmy said, her voice shaking slightly, not so much from nerves but from the formality of the meeting. "Two hours ago."

"And in that encounter, I found out some troubling news about the way you have chosen to conduct your personal life."

"Define *troubling*," Emmy said.

"Your decision to embark on the lesbian lifestyle," MK said. She looked resolved and steady, almost bored. Business as usual.

"We just need confirmation," Dr. Cunningham said, shooting MK a look, "that all of this is true."

Emmy didn't know what to say. Her throat expanded as the silence remained.

"Emmy," MK asked, "is it true?"

They all stared. Emmy was on display. The tension in the room was so palpable it started to suffocate her. Emmy closed her eyes, inhaled deeply, and thought of Cameron.

That night, they were going to watch the sunset while they drank wine by the railroad tracks, on the roof of an abandoned grain silo. Cameron would explain the plot of the book she was researching, and they would rate the author's level of gayness, on a scale of Nancy Reagan to Eleanor Roosevelt. Emmy might come up with some kind of counterargument to whatever Cameron said, just to see her get worked up, and then Emmy would stay quiet, listening to her, tracing the lines of her palms, trying to read herself in Cameron's future. They would stay like that until the stars came out, and then they would start kissing, and they would never want it to stop, and they wouldn't have to. They would be alone. They would be free.

As Emmy thought about the expansion of her life that had happened once Cameron had entered it, she realized that nothing else mattered. Not these girls, not this club, not even the approval of her parents, her home. She could lose them all, and it would be worth it to have Cameron with her.

Emmy thought about earlier, about her anger at Cameron for putting her in this position in the first place. The sorority, for three years, had been all Emmy had needed. A place to not be lonely. Nice-enough friends who didn't ask for much, who didn't give much, who took Emmy in because she paid her dues and played intramural softball and helped keep up their average GPA. But Cameron filled up all those missing spaces, flooded Emmy's life with meaning and hope and light. Did it matter that Cameron had violated Emmy's trust if, in the end, it had ushered the truth into the light? And perhaps, the more pressing question, would Emmy have ever been brave enough to come out without Cameron's small push?

No, Emmy thought. She looked around the room at the girls,

who were still staring at her, their faces blank, with slightly narrowed eyes. How could Emmy hope to move forward in her life if she spent any more time catering to the people who'd always held her back?

She remembered what her mother had said for many years: grief is the price people pay for love. But what was the price someone paid when they denied themselves love? Surely that cost was equally great.

"You can imagine what people on campus would say if we didn't take action," MK said, glancing down at a stack of papers in front of her. "So we just need you to confirm. Wouldn't want to throw around any false accusations or—"

"It's all true," Emmy said, cutting her off. "I'm dating a girl. You know her, I think, Dr. Cunningham. Cameron Rovers, in the graduate program."

Dr. Cunningham looked surprised to have been acknowledged. She had been nervously scribbling in her notebook, biting her bottom lip during the meeting, her only real role making sure the bylaws were upheld with strength and dignity.

"Oh, Cameron," Dr. Cunningham said. "Of course. Her research is fascinating, you know. I've never had a student here dive so deeply into the erotic—"

"Dr. Cunningham," MK said sharply. "We have to take action here. Our bylaws are very clear. *In accordance with the biblical understanding of love and marriage, no member of the Iota Chapter at Walker University may deviate, in any way, shape, or form, from the biblical expectations of a woman, whether in homosexual relations or sex outside of marriage.*"

Emmy snorted. Every girl at the table had had sex with at least one fraternity guy. They all ignored her.

Dr. Cunningham looked from MK to Emmy to the binder that held the sacred bylaws. She bit her lip again.

"I want you to know," Dr. Cunningham said, looking at

Emmy, "that these are outdated policies. But the university insists on—"

"Scripture is never outdated," MK said. "Even after two thousand years. It never changes."

"It's the rules, Emmy," one of the other girls said. "You'll have to..."

Her voice trailed off, like what was to come was too unspeakably horrible to voice. Dr. Cunningham shook her head. MK checked her watch, her face stoic.

Emmy had to bite her cheek to keep from laughing. It was too ridiculous. The makeup, the severity, the insistence upon being right; a jury of twentysomethings sentencing her to...what? Not waste money on a group of friends who had to disown her as soon as they knew the truth of who she was?

Out of all that Emmy lost in that first year of coming out, this was the easiest to stomach.

"You'll have to depledge, Emmy," MK said, finishing the other girl's sentence. "If this is the sort of lifestyle you're choosing to lead."

"Well," Emmy said, smiling, "it was fun while it lasted."

MK nodded and stood up abruptly, stacking her papers together. She walked over to Emmy, shook her hand like they had just closed on a long-negotiated deal, and said, "Good luck," before rounding up the other girls and heading to their philanthropy event, leaving Dr. Cunningham and Emmy alone in the room.

"Emmy, this whole thing is ridiculous, really," she said, wringing her hands. "But, you know, I have my hands tied with the bylaws, and I'm only really in this role for another year or I'd try harder to change it, and... Well, I guess every excuse is bullshit. But I just wanted you to know that I'm here for you, still, despite all of that."

Emmy nodded slowly, unsure whether to trust her. Her acceptance by someone in West Texas wasn't impossible, she knew, remembering the Johnsons. But it didn't seem likely.

"But I'd really love to get coffee with you sometime. Just to show…to show that all of us aren't so bad, I guess."

"All of us?"

"Texans, Christians, women," she said, counting them off on her fingers. "I guess *Texan Christian women*."

Emmy laughed, still wary of her, but pleased with the prospect of an ally, an adult unlost in the wake of Emmy's truth coming to surface.

"Okay," Emmy said, walking toward the door to leave. She felt impatient to get back to Cameron. "Thanks, Dr. Cunningham."

"Oh, call me Sara, please," she said, too eagerly. "Really. I think it's just…a shame. The way we treat people."

After Emmy said goodbye, she looked back at Dr. Cunningham one more time. She sat at the table, the bylaws opened up to the section MK had referenced, the Human Sexuality clause, and was biting her bottom lip, running her hand haphazardly through her hair, lost to some other world or memory. Emmy closed the door gently so as not to break the spell.

After the meeting, Emmy felt good. Really good. Better than she had in weeks. As more and more people found out about her, she felt herself grow more confident, sure of herself. Like she had finally become visible after spending the first part of her life in the shadows.

Emmy threw open the door of her condo and saw that Annie was waiting on the couch in the living room, staring at her.

"Emmy," she said. "This can't wait."

Her voice was loud, clear, and confident. Emmy had never known a surer sign of despair from Annie. The necessity of what had to be done could not have come from her, Emmy thought. She was under orders.

"Okay," Emmy said. "Just tell me."

"Well," Annie said, looking at her hands, "you know I love you."

"Sure."

"And you know my mom *loves* you."

"Okay."

"And this doesn't change that love at all."

"But..." Emmy said, feeling ice form in her veins. Her pulse started hammering in her ears, a sixth sense that something was about to go horribly wrong.

"You see, word has been spreading across town, in Steinbeck, you know, about, well...you."

Emmy stayed silent. She barely moved. Dread crept up her spine, replacing all the joy she had felt just moments before.

"It's just... It's hard to trust this sort of thing. The deviant stuff, you know."

"Deviant?"

"Homosexuality, Emmy. My mom doesn't want it to spread to me."

Emmy stared at her, dumbfounded, then laughed, a harsh, loud echo of noise without any depth of feeling.

"Spread?"

"Right. My mom doesn't feel comfortable having you in this home anymore. With me."

"Being gay isn't contagious."

"I know that," Annie said quickly. "Really, I do know that. It's stupid. But...she owns the condo."

The girls stared at one another. Emmy wanted to scream, to yell, but her voice had disappeared somewhere deep inside of her. She suddenly felt small, ashamed, diseased.

"I can buy a week, I think, so you can find a new place," Annie said. "But my mom's coming down next weekend, and, well..."

"She won't want to see me here," Emmy said, nodding. "Got it."

"Emmy, I'm sorry."

"Don't," Emmy said. She was horrified to find her voice quavering, tears welling in her eyes. "It's not your fault. It was stupid of me to think I could…"

She lapsed into silence. That she could what? Get away with it? Live her life? Fall in love?

"Is there anything I can do?" Annie asked.

"Not kick me out," Emmy said, letting out a little laugh-cry. "No, I know. It's your mom. I guess this is why people like leases."

Lucy had told her. Annie's mom. About Emmy. There had been no malicious intent in it, of that Emmy was sure. She could not, would not, believe that in her heart her mom would have ever done something that would have left her homeless.

Emmy could understand the reasoning. Sort of. An unknown presence in the space of your beloved. Annie's mom was afraid Emmy was diseased and that the disease might spread to her innocent, impressionable, shy daughter. Emmy might plant ideas in her head. About lifestyle choices. About what it could mean to love.

Emmy called Cameron in a daze, and she came over. Annie had gone out for ice cream to give her space.

"Jesus Christ," Cameron said when Emmy told her. "Is that legal?"

"I never signed a lease," Emmy said, miserable. "The whole agreement was made under the assumption that we were all—" she made air quotes "—good people."

"God."

"He's really been a pain in my ass recently."

"No shit," Cameron said, rubbing her undercut with tensed fingers. "Where will you go?"

Emmy shrugged. "If my mom would fucking speak to me, I could move back in with her, but she's not answering her phone, even though this whole thing is her fault."

"And your dad's a no."

"The biggest no."

"Well," Cameron said, smiling, "move in with me!"

"Excuse me?"

"Move in with me."

"It's been a month. Has it even been a month?"

"Almost. Just about."

"That's insane."

"Maybe. But it's cheap."

"Cheap?"

"Sure. The rent was unbelievable already, but with two people, we'll pay almost nothing."

"Don't you think it's a little fast?"

"Yeah, I do," Cameron said. "But that's what lesbians do. Welcome to the club."

"It seems like a bad idea."

"You could always see if you could move in with Jacob," Cameron suggested.

"He doesn't have enough room."

"You know who has enough room?"

"I know."

"And who would sleep with you?"

"I know."

"*And* who would culture you and screen an endless playlist of amazing films that you have yet to see?"

"Jacob?"

"Move in with me, Emmy. I want you there. I want you all mine."

Emmy's autonomy had always been sacred to her before she met Cameron. She could not be possessed by another person. She was her own. But, with the rejection of her family, some core part of Emmy had cracked. She didn't know what it meant to be her own after disownment. And Cameron felt to her like coming home, felt like hope and possibility and everything Emmy had ever wanted. It felt like, with Cameron, Emmy could find herself again. With Cameron, she could mend herself back together.

There was the smallest part of Emmy that pushed back. A voice that said, *You're not ready for this!* It was the voice of her father. A low, strong, rumbling voice of dissent. *Don't do it, Emmy*, the voice warned, *don't do it.*

Emmy clenched her jaw. His voice, the one she had always considered reasonable, her North Star, could not be right. If he was Reason, then his reaction to her coming out was measured. If she listened to him now, then she would have to entertain the possibility that the very existence of her love was poison, sin, hell.

That was not a road Emmy could go down any longer. She was free. Even if that freedom had consequences.

In her freedom, Emmy buried her father's voice away, down into her depths, which could only be accessed in dreams, nightmares, spaces outside her consciousness.

Emmy smiled at Cameron. Wrapped her arms around her neck. Ran her fingers through her undercut.

"Okay," Emmy said. "I'm all yours."

PART TWO: FALL

Sectional football games have the glory and the
despair of war, and when a Texas team takes the field
against a foreign state, it is an army with banners.

—John Steinbeck

IT TAKES A WHILE for the cool to come, but when it does, all of Texas sighs in relief. It can be felt in the first fall breeze—the crisp, cool wind cutting through the humidity and the heat, making it possible to stay outside for more than five minutes without sweating.

Texans break out their blue jeans and flannel shirts, their cardigans and corduroys, tucking them into their well-worn cowboy boots, taking every opportunity they can to be outside: patio brunches, backyard barbecues, tailgates before high school football games on Fridays, college games on Saturdays, the NFL on Sundays. Everyone is grateful for the respite from the heat. They thank God, they thank the wind, they thank one another for inviting them out.

That first weekend without the heat is extraordinary. No one needs anything other than a deep inhalation of the fall, the lightness of the air rushing straight to their lungs, the revitalizing sting of cold reawakening a part of themselves that took shelter during the brutalizing, never-ending months of summer.

It is nothing short of a miracle, Texas fall. More than spring, it is a time for rebirth, renewal. Around the country, the fall is a time to slow down, to hibernate. But in Texas, it is an invitation to begin.

14

STEVE

When Jim was head coach, he used to say he was the King and the team was his Kingdom. The players and coaches were subjects who were expected to bend to his will without question. It wasn't such a bad idea back when he was able to coach with a strong hand, a sharp mind, a willingness to risk everything for the win.

But in his later years at Steinbeck, he got lazy. Stopped paying attention. Cut down on his hours watching film. Then got furious when Steve or Johnson tried to implement changes they'd thought of while watching film from college teams or reading books by other successful coaches. They were punished for innovation. When they tried to get the guys going, shake things up on offense and defense, they'd get twenty minutes in Jim's office, trying to avoid the spit flying from his mouth as he screamed at them about loyalty, about knowing when to sit down and shut up.

Steve dismantled that order in his first week of coaching. His first move was making Johnson his assistant head coach, giving him free rein on offense. Let him try out different formations, incorporate more bubble screens into the mix, get Trey going on pass plays, too.

Steve changed around some packages on defense. Last season, they were terrible guarding the pass, so he had the boys practice in a nickel package, which Jim had always hated because he said it was "too damn confusing" for the boys to understand. But Steve knew that the boys wanted to be challenged, that they wanted to learn. They were capable of more than Jim ever gave them credit for. He treated them like boys when they were willing to step up and be men.

That's why Steve created the Leadership Council. A group of twelve players voted on by the whole team, coaches included. He got the number twelve because he had the disciples on his mind, from his talk with Pastor Ben. It helped him keep that conversation fresh at all times, thinking of the disciples, the ones that Jesus sent out into the world to spread his word, the ones who were willing to sacrifice their lives, their families, for a life lived with purpose.

The Council was simple. Four team captains, eight other players. They helped in the decision-making process with the coaches, got a say in how the ship ran. When a coach gave the players power in the locker room, Steve believed, they started stepping up on the field, started taking ownership of how they played, how they worked, how they acted on and off the field. In order for it to be successful, though, the whole team had to buy in.

That's why Steve was so worried about Miguel Martinez.

He'd been practicing with the team for almost a month— summer workouts and two-a-days—and he'd barely spoken to anyone. He took his reps, worked hard, put his all into the game, there was no question about that. But he refused to connect with any of the guys.

Now, Steve knew there was nothing wrong with a strong-

and-silent kind of guy. He believed there was honor in a kid who knew how to hold his tongue. But that's not how Miguel was. He didn't *like* anyone. And he wanted everyone to know it. Especially Trey.

Players always liked Trey. It was part of what made him such a good captain and an even better recruit. He'd been on varsity since first year, and Steve had never seen such raw talent in a running back before—determination, too. Trey was one of those guys who just got it. Kept his head down, kept his legs moving. He ran angry, spoke kind. Two-star recruit well on his way to a full ride at Abilene Christian. He was a coachable kid. Always willing to hear what he needed to do to get better. He had an ego, any good player worth his salt did, but he knew the importance of building a cohesive team, a brotherhood. He was their offensive lifeline. Little Williams got better every year, but he still struggled with pass completions under pressure. The 'Stangs' most reliable play was to hand it off to Trey, let him find the hole, and watch him fly down the field.

Trey was a hard guy not to like. But Miguel managed to find a way. Found a way to not like every single guy on the team, every single place in town. None of it was good enough for him. When Trey asked how he was liking Steinbeck, he just shrugged and said, "Everything here's flat. No hills, no rivers, no nothing. Even your girls are flat as fuck, no ass to hold onto."

Steve normally wouldn't have had to worry about it, but as it turned out, they needed Miguel. He was so good Steve felt like it was a gift from God that Miguel's mama finally decided to leave his good-for-nothing dad in El Paso and move back home to Steinbeck with her mom and sister. Miguel certainly didn't see it that way. But Steve knew that sometimes gifts came before you were ready to receive them.

Steve believed that quarterbacks were special. You couldn't put a guy in just because he had an arm. He had to lead the team. Settle them down in a crisis. Get them to trust him in a huddle.

The team would have run through a brick wall for Little Williams. They weren't good last season—didn't even make the play-offs, a difficult thing to do in this day and age when the best four teams from every district made it in—but Little Williams managed to make them believe that every game was one they could win. Impressive sort of thing to do since they almost never did. Little Williams had the heart, the voice, the confidence of a starting quarterback. But he threw at least two interceptions a game and was never quick enough to scramble out of the pocket to avoid a sack. Every game they lost the past season was a close one. Could have gone either way. Especially if they'd had a quarterback who didn't make mistakes.

Put next to Miguel, Little Williams looked like a pee-wee player. He had the right mechanics, the drop backs, the reads, but everything was a second slower than Miguel. Johnson had them take their snaps side by side, see how they sized up. Miguel was quick, sharp, accurate. His throws had tight spirals, and they zipped out of his hand. Little Williams looked over after he threw another incomplete pass and saw Miguel's throw soar into the open arms of a wide receiver on a corner route. Little Williams tugged on his face mask and looked over again at Miguel, who was already back in the shotgun formation, ready for another snap.

"Little Williams isn't looking as sharp as he should," Johnson said to Steve during practice, watching the two boys throw. "His drop back is sloppy. Panics in the pocket. He's slow, too. Like he spent his whole summer slacking off."

"He spent all off-season training," Steve said. "Season hasn't started yet. Time for him to get in shape."

"Miguel's in shape," Johnson said. "Fast. And smart. He can read a defense. You see film of him in El Paso?"

Steve had. The guy was sharp. Seemed to gel with all his receivers. Steve even gave his coach at El Paso a call to see if attitude had always been such a problem for him, but the coach said there was no kinder kid. Loved his mama and his brothers and his teammates and his coaches all the same; treated everyone like family.

"Can't put that guy in a huddle, Johnson, you know that."

"He's new, just needs to get comfortable," Johnson said. "We can split time between the two of them for now, see how they do in the scrimmage. But, Steve, if you're serious about State..."

"Of course I am."

"Then, you gotta find a way to get Miguel to buy in," Johnson said, squinting, watching Little Williams's throw soar over the head of his intended receiver. "Because we're not gonna win with that."

Steve knew that Johnson was right, but he hoped that Little Williams would prove him wrong. Find a way to dig down deep and show up, blow everyone away.

But, in their last preseason game, an away one on a Thursday, Little Williams bombed.

It was like he'd forgotten every route, all his check downs, how to scramble in the pocket when it collapsed. He fumbled a handoff to Trey, threw two interceptions, and dropped a perfectly good snap when he was in shotgun.

"Get Martinez in there," Steve said to Johnson when they went down 14–0. "See what he can do."

He was amazing. Threw a fifty-yard bomb for their first touchdown, then called an audible for a QB draw, and ran it in for the second. Johnson gave him a little shit for the audible—he liked the guys to stick to the game plan—but other than that, it was a sight to behold. Steve saw their future unfold before him, the path to State so clearly resting in the hands of Miguel Martinez, the kid from El Paso.

But then, everything changed.

In the third quarter, Miguel was on the line of scrimmage,

lined up in the shotgun formation. He looked around, his helmet shifting left and right, and he was screaming something.

"What the hell is he doing?" Steve asked.

"Audible," Little Williams said, his fists clenched around his face mask.

"Second time tonight he's done that," Steve said. "Johnson, what play's he calling?"

"Fuck if I know," Johnson said, waving his arms at the line of scrimmage, trying to get Miguel's attention. "I called a draw play to Trey, wanna get him through that A-gap."

Miguel moved out of the shotgun and under center. Trey looked over at the sideline, toward Johnson, and shook his head, putting his hands on his thighs, squaring up at the line of scrimmage, getting ready for the play Miguel had called.

The play clock was winding down, but they got the snap off with one second left. Miguel dropped back, faked a handoff to Trey, and rolled out to his right. He looked like he was going to tuck the ball and take it himself, but a linebacker was bearing down on him. The crowd was roaring, ready for a sack, but Miguel planted his right foot. Cocked his arm. And launched the ball downfield.

It was a gorgeous throw. A perfect spiral. The ball got lost in the lights for a moment. The wide receiver was downfield, his arms extended, nothing but the end zone in front of him. The crowd held its breath as the ball came down, right on target, into…

A safety came from out of nowhere and jumped up, intercepting the ball before it ever got near the receiver's hands. The crowd exploded. The other team leaped up in celebration, sprinting down the sidelines. The safety kept on running, juking out four guys, stiff-arming Miguel at the forty before taking it all the way to the end zone.

"Son of a bitch!" Johnson screamed, slamming his clipboard on the ground. "I called a fucking draw for a reason!"

The brass from their band played out loud and strong. The drum line kept their chaotic beat. Their cheerleaders tumbled down the track. And the scoreboard updated, 20–14.

"We ain't gonna win any games if we don't take no risks!" Miguel shouted at Johnson when he was back on the sideline. "You can't keep giving it to Trey. You gotta give me a shot!"

"Get your ass on the fucking bench now, Martinez!" Johnson said, pulling Miguel's face mask and dragging him over to the benches, forcing him to sit down. "Might as well take off your helmet. You're dreaming if you think you're going in again."

"Fuck!" Miguel grunted, throwing his helmet on the ground.

The game got away from them after the interception. They'd lost all their momentum, and Little Williams couldn't complete a pass to save his life. Trey had a few good runs, but no big breaks. They lost 36–14.

"He's trying to take my spot," Little Williams said, coming up to Steve after the game was over. He ripped off his playbook wristband and waved it in Steve's face. "He don't even know these plays. He can't run this offense. You can't let him do this, Coach. We've worked too fucking hard!"

"You care about you?" Steve asked, shouting in his face. "Or you care about the team?"

Little Williams shrunk down a little. His blond, too-long hair was slicked back with sweat, and his cheeks and crooked nose—broken in some kind of fight a couple years ago—were covered in acne. It reminded Steve that he was still just a kid. That it was Steve's job to turn him into a man.

"You don't want Martinez to take your spot?" Steve asked, still shouting. "Then, make sure you're the best goddamn quarterback on that field every day. And don't bitch about it to me."

"Tattling to Daddy?" Miguel whispered loudly behind Little Williams, on his way to the locker room.

"Man, do you ever shut the hell up?" Trey asked, walking close behind him.

"When I got the lights off and I'm fucking your girl," Miguel said, turning around to give Trey a little shove. "I like to keep quiet, so I can hear her scream my name real loud."

"Motherfucker!" Trey screamed, launching himself at Miguel, tackling him to the ground. The two rolled around on the turf just before the track, trying to get in jabs, punches, any kind of contact, screaming expletives and threats.

"Jesus Christ." Steve sprinted over to them, grabbing the back of their shoulder pads and throwing them off one another, stepping in the space between so they wouldn't launch at each other again. Both of them stood up, heaving, sweat running down their faces. Trey had a cut on his lip and blood ran down his chin, dripping onto his white uniform. Miguel angrily pushed his long, dark hair out of his face, curling his lip up in a snarl, revealing his slightly gapped teeth.

"Fucking pussy," he spat at Trey, trying to get another rise out of him.

"This is some grade A schoolyard bullshit," Steve screamed at them, shoving Miguel in the chest so hard he stumbled back a little.

"Sorry, Coach," Trey said, hanging his head, looking down at his helmet.

"I don't want sorry, I want solutions," Steve said. Other coaches and players had surrounded them in the process. A reporter from the paper watched by the stands on the other side of the track, his phone up, the flash on, recording the whole scene. Steve grabbed Trey and Miguel by the shoulder pads and pulled them in close, keeping his voice low, close to a whisper. "You boys want to win State?"

"Yessir," Trey said. Miguel nodded but stayed silent.

"Then, you're gonna have to figure out how to play on the same team without killing each other on the sidelines," Steve said. "Sunshine Club tomorrow morning. Both of y'all. Four o'clock sharp. On the practice field. If you're one second late,"

Steve said, looking at Miguel, who'd rolled his eyes, "then you're off the team. I don't care who you are, how good you think you are, you don't show up tomorrow morning right on time, you're done. Understand me?"

"Yessir," they both said in unison, their heads hanging, their eyes downcast. They looked so young. Just kids, Steve thought.

"Now get your asses ready for the bus," Steve said, shoving them back toward the field and the locker room.

As he watched Trey and Miguel and the rest of the guys jog into the locker room, Dan Holcomb walked onto the field from the stands, headed straight for Steve.

"Doing okay, Steve?" Dan asked, reaching out his hand to shake. He was wearing his standard outfit: white T-shirt, navy sports jacket, dark denim jeans, and black cowboy hat. "Now, I know I'm no coach, but shouldn't they be saving that kind of hitting for the field?"

"Just on edge is all," Steve said, fidgeting with his hat. "No one likes losing."

"I sure as hell don't," Dan said, crossing his arms. "Don't like being lied to, neither."

"Lied?" Steve asked. "What are you—"

"You know, it was the funniest thing," Dan interrupted him. "I was down there at Margaritas having me a drink with the missus, when Jan Oleander came up to us and asked us how we were doing and all, if we were going to the game today. And you know what she asked me next?"

"Look, Dan—"

"She asked me if I'd heard about Emmy Quinn."

"Dan, here's the thing—"

"And I sat there thinking, Emmy Quinn must have found herself a man! And I said as much! Out loud!"

"Emmy is just—"

"And you know what Jan did? She laughed right in my face, Steve. Like I'd told the funniest joke in the world."

Dan's face was a deep shade of red. His cowboy hat was tipped down low, but Steve could still see his eyes, narrowed and dark. The scar on the right edge of his mouth showed up clear and strong as he clenched his jaw and pressed his lips together, a white line of rage.

"Dan, I can explain."

"I asked if you had any baggage," Dan said. "You looked me in the eye and *lied*."

"I didn't know," Steve said, the truth tumbling out. "I found out after our conversation. I would have never... Look, Emmy's not even living in town anymore. What does it matter? Walker's forty miles away."

"But she's yours. Distance don't make her any less yours."

"She's not..." Steve couldn't bring himself to say it out loud. *Not mine.*

"Steve, I want you to see this season through to the end," he said, taking off his cowboy hat and twirling it in his hand. His long salt-and-pepper hair, flattened by the hat, curled out like wings around his ears. "But I'm gonna need some answers. Need to know where your head's at. This is too big a lump to sweep under the rug. This is the kind of stuff that makes parents nervous. A parent of a kid like Emmy in such close contact with so many young men? Well, you get it, Steve, don't you?"

Steve looked down at his hands. Dirt had collected underneath his fingernails. He picked at them, trying to get them clean.

Dan was right. Steve knew he was right. If it were another man, he'd say, *Get your house in order. It's your own damn fault you didn't raise your kid right.* But it was Emmy. And it was Steve.

When she was a kid, she used to run up and down the field with a football that was half her size, tripping over her feet, picking herself up, not stopping until she got into the end zone. She'd been to every game when she lived in town, and at least two games a season when she was away at school. Steve talked to her about all the personnel changes, all the havoc, all the triumphs. She was part of all of this. This was hers as much as Steve's.

But an inheritance, like salvation, could only come from commitment: to family, to morality, to a race well run. Pastor Ben had made that clear in their conversation. There was no room for compromise.

"Well, Dan, the truth," Steve said, grasping for it, remembering what Ben had said to him about the cost of following Jesus, "is that...I think she means it. I really think she believes she's that way." Steve felt a lump shoot up through his throat and get stuck there. "She's forgotten herself."

Dan's eyes were shining. For a second, Steve thought they might have been tears, and a relief that felt like hope came into Steve's chest, seeing that kind of empathy from a man like Dan. But he realized, quickly, that it was just the reflection from the lights of the stadium.

"A shame," Dan said, shaking his head. "It's this whole damn country, not your fault, Steve. Kids these days think they can do whatever the hell they want, call themselves whatever they hell they want. You know what Jesus would do if he came back right now? He'd look at all we've become, and he'd just weep."

"I had myself a sit-down with Pastor Ben a couple weeks ago," Steve added. "Talked up a plan on how to get her back to the right path. After the season, of course. You know the team has my full focus."

"Pastor Ben?" Dan asked, nodding, twirling his cowboy hat in his hands. "Well, that's something. I think I can sell that to the board. They'll like to know you've been sticking strong with your faith in all this. Lord knows you need it. But Steve, this is real important. You can't have Emmy coming around here. Not to games, practices, potlucks, tailgates, nothing. She's gotta stay away. You gotta make sure she does. Can't come close to this stadium until she straightens her act out."

"'Course, Dan," Steve said. "Whatever it takes. For the team."

"It's just better for everyone. That kind of gossip is fine and all when it feels far away. But get that sort of stuff in close, around town, people start getting nervous. We all like a good cautionary tale, but no one wants to see it hang around at the diner, sipping coffee and eating flapjacks like the most real thing in the world."

"Sure," Steve said, nodding, trying to ignore that Dan had called his daughter *it*.

"Ha!" Dan laughed, putting his hat back on. "Didn't even realize I said it. But '*straightens* her act out.' That's pretty good, don't you think?"

Steve forced himself to smile, sticking out his hand, wanting more than anything for the conversation to end. Dan shook it and walked away, still laughing.

As Steve made his way toward the bus, he got a phone call from Lucy.

"What's up?" he answered, checking his watch. They needed to leave in ten.

"Just checking in," Lucy said, breathing heavily into the phone.

"Luce? You okay?"

"Just went for a run," Lucy said, still panting. "Get the blood flowing, you know."

"You hate running at night."

"Yeah, well."

"Said it makes you nervous."

"Little nerves never hurt nobody."

"All right," Steve said, frowning, watching the guys file onto the bus.

"So," Lucy said. Steve heard the slam of her front door and the click of her television remote as the theme song to one of the shows she and Emmy liked to watch started to play softly in the background. "How'd the scrimmage go?"

"Like shit," Steve said. He hesitated, wanting to tell her about Dan Holcomb. What he'd said about their daughter. How isolated he felt in all this. How he just wanted to see his daughter, get her take on this whole Miguel situation. But there would be no situation to speak of if he did talk with Emmy. The dream would disappear as soon as he made contact. And he wasn't willing to risk that. No need to bring Lucy in on a decision that'd already been made. "But we'll get it together before the opener next week. Since when do you watch TV after nine?"

"Just a little quiet around here these days."

"Look, Luce," Steve said as Johnson waved him toward the bus, "I gotta get going. We're fixing to leave here pretty soon."

"Want to get breakfast on Saturday? At Oliver's?"

"What?" Steve asked, confused. They hadn't gone to breakfast since they got divorced. "I gotta watch film all day."

"Just a coffee?"

"Fine, sure, Lucy. I'll see you then, but I really gotta go."

Before she could say anything else, Steve hung up.

On the bus headed home, Johnson came up to the front and sat beside Steve. The bench seat, with its stuffing spilling out of the worn, green leather, was too small for two grown men.

"You seen Lucy lately?" Steve asked, looking up from the film he was watching on his tablet. "She called me earlier. After she got home from a run."

"Lucy doesn't run at night," Johnson said.

"That's what I thought."

"Been a few weeks since we've seen her," Johnson said, looking down at the play Steve was watching.

"Wants me to get breakfast with her Saturday," Steve said.

"Huh."

"Yep."

"Everything okay, Quinn?" Johnson asked, putting a hand on his shoulder. His enormous emerald and gold State Championship ring reflected in the window. "Saw Dan Holcomb come up to you after that fight."

"Still got my job, Johnson," Steve said, shrugging off his hand, looking back at the tablet. "Don't get your hopes up."

"Dan knows about Emmy."

Steve glanced up at Johnson. His eyes were wide with concern. He rubbed the back of his neck, his stiff, broad shoulders seeming to strain with the effort. "Cora told me. And Emmy told Jacob. What'd Dan say?"

"Keep her away from town," Steve said, rewinding the footage, trying to take a better look at their pass rush. "During the season especially."

"You tell him to go shove it?" Johnson asked.

"This pass coverage. We gotta fix it in practice."

"Did you at least tell him to go to hell?"

"How do you feel about our blocking on the O-line? Big Williams has good protection on the left side, but everything else…" Steve said, trying to find a good clip to show him. Johnson took the tablet out of his hands so that he was forced to look at him. He still had on his bucket hat, and his long-sleeve gray T-shirt was darkened with sweat.

"Steve, come on," he said, locking the tablet and putting it in his lap. "It's Emmy."

"I told Dan the truth," Steve said, eyeing the tablet. "That Emmy was making a choice I didn't support. Couldn't support. That I'd make sure she didn't show up to games."

"Told him what he wanted to hear," Johnson said, nodding. "Tough position to be in. I get it."

"Told the truth," Steve said. "I don't lie."

"Oh," Johnson said, frowning.

"What?"

"Guess I had just expected…" Johnson's face fell, and he turned back to look at the boys on the bus to make sure none of them were eavesdropping. Most of them were sleeping or listening to music with their headphones on, paying their coaches no mind. He turned back to Steve, sighing, rubbing his eyes in exhaustion. "I mean…it's just that… Damn, you love that girl, Steve."

"I know."

"I never seen you love someone so deep."

"Still do," Steve said.

"So can't love win?"

"Isn't that one of those gay-pride slogans?"

"Doesn't change the question."

"Didn't take you for such a friend of the dandy man, Johnson."

"Steve."

"The only thing I got for Emmy is love. Always been that way. You know that. And I love her too much to let this go on. It's a loveless life she's choosing."

"Don't know if I should say this," Johnson said, tipping his bucket hat back so that the string tightened around his neck. His head was freshly shaved. "She's got a girl, Emmy does. Real pretty one, from what Jacob told us."

Steve felt like he'd gotten the wind knocked out of him. He dug his fingernails into his palm and asked, "That right?"

"Isn't that something to celebrate? That she found somebody to love?"

"When Jesus sent out the disciples..." Steve began, trying to summarize everything Ben had told him.

"Disciples? We're talking about your daughter, Steve."

"Look," Steve said. "Dan doesn't want Emmy coming to the games this season. Says it's bad for business. Now, when we're all through, when we've won State, done our jobs, I'll get the Emmy situation figured out. You don't gotta worry about me. She's my girl, remember?"

"Okay," Johnson said, nodding slowly, looking Steve up and down with squinted eyes, not quite convinced. "Well, after State, then. When Emmy's home for Christmas?"

"Sure," Steve said. "After State."

Johnson gave him back his tablet, slapped him on the back, and headed back to his seat. Steve tried to look at more film, but his eyes were tired, so he put it away and looked out of the window, watching the lit-up billboards for churches and radio stations and restaurants whip by, the only things visible in an otherwise all-consuming darkness.

What had Johnson expected from him? A defense? *Pride?* And why had he looked so disappointed? Jacob was going to marry Kiera someday, like he was supposed to. How'd he respond if his son came up to him and said, *Sorry about your dreams, Dad, but here's who I am now.*

Dreams. It wasn't even dreams so much as how it oughta be. Dreams were rooted in silliness and hope; *how it oughta be*, that was something ordained by God. Nothing more real than that.

"How do you know what's real for you is real for everyone else?" Emmy had asked once, when they were camping out in Big Bend before she went off to college. They were sitting on logs, looking into the fire. The night was clear as it ever got, and the wind had died down so the fire stayed alive and crackling. Steve looked up. The line of the Milky Way stretched across the sky like a great gash of fire and light.

"Well, that's real for everyone," Steve said, pointing up to the sky. "No one sees it different."

Emmy looked up and winced, like the stars had some painful memory folded into them. She looked back at the fire and lapsed into silence.

"But what about the other stuff?" she finally said. "The stuff you can't see?"

"Stuff is stuff. It's not invisible."

"But the parts inside you," she said, struggling for words, "the parts that are all uncertain. And. And stuff. All uncertain and stuff."

Steve thought about that. There was stuff he didn't know. What lived at the bottom of the ocean. How many stars there were in the sky. But that was the stuff for God to know. Not a man like him.

"Ain't that faith? Covering up all the stuff you can't know?"

"But that!" Emmy said. She was excited. "What if your faith

is different? So you view things differently? Because of what you believe, what you've seen and not seen?"

Steve felt they were getting into territory that flirted with blasphemy. He said as much.

"Emmylou, remember, Jesus said, *'I am the way, the truth, and the life. No one comes to the Father except through me.'* Seems pretty straightforward."

"But what is *the way*? What *truth*? And *life*? What if there are different roads along the way, different ways of seeking truth? Finding life?" She'd found her voice somewhere in the conversation. She was becoming alarmingly articulate.

It was strange that a person he had helped create could have a mind so different from his own. It usually made him proud. But when it came to matters of faith, he had to draw the line.

"What is *chickenshit*? *Horseshit*? *Bullshit*? What if it's all just shit at the end of the day?" Steve said, laughing, wanting to get out of the murky waters of subjective truth.

Emmy looked at him straight on. The fire danced in her eyes.

"You're so afraid of what you don't understand, aren't you?" she'd asked, sighing. She looked back up at the stars. "It's okay. I am, too."

Steve wondered, as they turned down Main Street in Steinbeck, if Emmy was still afraid. If she still knew how much she didn't understand. *There is no fear in love. But perfect love drives out fear*, it said in First John. But if she'd turned away from that perfect love, then her whole life was destined to be ruled by fear. A nameless, faceless sort of fear that would creep into every crevice of her life, like the heat outside an air-conditioned room in the dog days of August.

Emmy was always afraid of the dark. She hated scary movies, haunted houses, Halloween; anything dedicated to dread she wanted no part of.

If she could just let him lead her, Steve thought as he walked off the bus into the parking lot, they'd find a way to the light.

15

The stars were still out when Steve got to the practice field at three forty-five, waiting for Miguel and Trey.

He got the lights going. The buzz from them was the only sound in the otherwise-silent morning, still hours away from the sunrise. He jogged over to the field house, the not-quite cool air filling his lungs, and dragged two tackle dummies out on the field, his shoes wet with morning dew.

At the fifty-yard line, Steve stopped to catch his breath. He put his hands on his hips and looked up at the sky, where his eyes went straight to the belt of Orion. *Three stars in a line*, Emmy used to say. *You can never not see it.*

"Coach Quinn!" Trey said, jogging over. He was in his gray sweats, with his black cleats on. When he got to Steve, he apologized for the fight, for not keeping his cool. "And I'll talk to Miguel, too, see what I can do."

"I figure I oughta do that," Steve said, looking down at his watch. Five minutes to four.

"He gonna show?" Trey asked, looking over to the sidelines. There was still no sign of him.

"You just worry about you, Trey," Steve said, not sure of the answer. "And not losing your cookies here in about five minutes."

Sunshine Club was a tradition Steve kept from Jim's days as head coach. Whenever a kid screwed up—got suspended, mouthed off to a teacher, got caught cheating—they were sent to Sunshine Club.

Jim called it a baptism. Boys came to the field before the sun rose, submerged themselves in pain, sweat, and blood, and when it was finished, they walked off the field, pulses racing, lungs heaving, ready to face the day as men.

The template was simple. Four exercises with the tackling dummy. Up and down the length of the field. Two hundred yards. Sounded easy enough, but by the time the boys got to the last exercise where they had to roll with the dummy up and down the field, they usually vomited all over the grass beside them.

"An hour in hell," Trey said, jumping up and down, getting his legs warm. "Don't blame him for skipping."

"There he is," Steve said, pointing to the sidelines.

Miguel was wearing all-black sweats and a long-sleeve T-shirt with a bright orange Astros snapback hat. He jogged over, slow and deliberate, letting his long legs take the shortest possible strides.

"Almost late," Steve said, looking down at his watch. One minute to four. "You're gonna want to take off that hat. Just gonna fall when you start."

Miguel scrunched up his long, thick nose, straight as an arrowhead, his silent protest before taking off the hat, putting it gently down on the grass.

"You ready?" Trey asked, lining up his dummy on the goal line.

"Let's just do it," Miguel said, giving his dummy a little shove.

Steve blew his whistle, and they were off, tossing and hitting and carrying and rolling with their dummies in the darkness before dawn.

Trey threw up on the last hundred yards. Miguel held it together until the last forty. When they were done, Trey put an arm around Miguel and said, "Welcome to the Club."

"Never want to do that again," Miguel said, heaving, his hands on his knees, his head hanging.

"Amen," Trey said, walking toward the locker rooms. "See you Monday, Coach."

"Miguel," Steve said to him as he grabbed his hat, putting it on his sweat-drenched head. "Come to my office. Let's talk."

They walked from the field to the building in silence, Miguel occasionally pausing to cough something up and spit it out beside him.

"That sucked," Miguel said when they got to Steve's office, sitting in a chair in front of his desk. "Seems illegal."

"Takes hard work, becoming a man," Steve said, taking his seat behind the desk.

"*Tuh.*" Miguel rolled his eyes. He flattened out the bill of his hat and then stretched out his arm.

"You know, I know a thing or two about how to help boys like you become men," Steve said, getting ready to start his standard speech, the one he used to rally boys when they were feeling down or defeated.

"Oh, yeah?" Miguel cut him off. The mole above the left side of his lip twitched as his mouth twisted up in a grin. "That how you managed to raise a dyke instead of a daughter?"

Steve's stomach twisted, his eyes watered like he'd been punched in the nose. He swiveled away from Miguel, toward the wall where the old, chipped bookshelf stood, tilted slightly to one side. It'd been in the office since the forties, at least, but it was strong enough to house what he had lined up on the shelves. Coaching books, leadership manifestos, and an old, tattered copy of *Leaves of Grass*. Emmy had given it to him for Christmas three years ago.

Steve wanted Miguel out. Of his office, the team. He wanted to let the wave of fury that rose out from the pain of those words crash down on Miguel with a force so punishing it would drown him.

Instead, he closed his eyes. Cracked his knuckles. Took in three deep breaths.

A good coach knew how to rise above his instincts. Control all those first feelings. It was an act of defiance as much as one of self-control. Emotions could lead him wrong. Get him into all sorts of hot water.

Steve had to breathe through it. Just close his eyes and breathe it all away. Or inhale it down deep. Bury it. Hardly let it see the light of day.

"Look," Steve said, taking off his cap and slapping it into his palm a little too hard. "You can get angry. You can get mean. You can hate me. That's fine. I can't make you feel something that ain't natural. But we're all brothers out here. And families fight sometimes, right?"

"Shit," he said, nodding.

"But just because you fight," Steve said, "doesn't mean you're gonna give up on each other."

"Unless it gets too bad," Miguel said, tugging the bill of his baseball cap farther down. "And you pick up and move away to the middle of nowhere."

"Home's hard?" Steve asked, putting his cap back on, leaning forward, clasping his hands together in front of him. Guys came in every now and then to talk with him about what was going on with their families, their houses, all their different situations: money, custody, neglect. It was one of the great incentives of the game: get good enough and you can get out of—or give back to—the place that raised you.

"I don't got space here," Miguel said, sniffing loudly, brushing his thumb across his nose in an act of feigned nonchalance. "Share a room with my two little brothers, live with my mom and her sister and my abuela. People everywhere, no space inside that house. And then I go outside and space is all I got. No mountains. No rivers. Just dead grass. Flat. There's like, five streets here. And more windmills than people, swear to God. Depressing as hell."

"Steinbeck's not so bad," Steve said. "It grows on you."

"And my tia's all up in my shit, always asking if I knocked some girl up, if I'm gonna be like my pop... Look, I'm not a fucking sob story," Miguel said, cutting himself off, pursing out his lips and shaking his head. "I can take care of myself."

"I know that," Steve said, nodding. "But you want to go to college?"

"Wanna play college ball," he said, turning his hat around backward so that his dark hair poked through the hole in the back, the snapback closure pressing into his acne-pocked forehead.

"Gonna be hard if you can't find a way to start on your high school team, don't you think?"

"I'm better than that punk-ass Little Williams or whatever y'all call him," Miguel said, scrunching up his nose to look tough, but with his lineless face, he just looked like a little kid on the brink of a tantrum.

"You are better," Steve agreed. "But better don't mean nothing if you don't got the trust of those guys in the huddle. Quarterback's different that way. You know that."

"Look, I know the plays, I can read a defense. Those audibles could've worked."

"Miguel, here's the deal," Steve said, putting his hands flat on the desk. "You're good. And you're young—a junior, right? If we could have you start for two seasons... I think you can help me make this program great."

"No shit," Miguel said, airing out his sweat-drenched shirt from his neck.

"But sometimes you gotta sacrifice something to be great."

"Oh, yeah? What'd you sacrifice to get this gig?"

"Plenty," Steve said, forcing himself to not look down at the framed photo of him and Emmy on his desk. "Don't worry about me."

"So, what do I need to do?" Miguel asked, shifting in his seat, looking down at his feet. "I just wanna play."

There are moments in a coach's career when momentum suddenly halts. The pendulum waits to swing one way or the other. An entire program, season, game, defined in a moment, with one decision.

Football was like religion: success came from a strong foundation of belief. If players and coaches and staff could come together to conquer a common enemy in pursuit of one goal, then they could become virtually unstoppable.

If Miguel kept up with his attitude, though, he'd derail everything. He didn't believe in the program, in any of the players, in Steve.

But Steve saw the spark of it. The kind of player he could be if he'd put away his pride and his own baggage and bought in. A kid can't command that kind of audible if he's not a leader. So Steve knew he had it in him. That he could be great—that *they* could be great. He just needed to get him to believe.

Steve tried to paint a picture: what it would look like, sound like, feel like, with him as the starter, leading their team to the town's first ever State Championship. What he could gain from settling into the locker room, getting a rhythm going with the guys. How he didn't have to be friends with everyone, but when he stepped onto the field, he needed to be their brother in arms, ready to fight, battle, win. Why it didn't matter what he had going on at home. When he played for Steve, he was a part of his family. And with them, he'd have plenty of space—to run, to hit, to lose himself to the game.

Steve didn't mention her, but he thought of Emmy. How she used to say that a field could change a person. Soccer, softball, football, any sport, really. When you stepped out on the grass, you shed some part of yourself. Became a body and a brain blended in motion. It was sacred, she used to say. Giving yourself up for the team.

Miguel was silent when Steve finished talking. Steve let him sit. Let the words seep in. Miguel turned his Astros cap forward, pulling the bill down on his forehead so that it almost hid his eyes.

"It's all I've ever wanted," Miguel said, his voice cracking slightly. He leaned forward, hunching over, looking down at his hands. "Taking a team all the way."

"Me, too," Steve said. "But I can't do it without you. And you can't do it without me."

They sat in silence again. Miguel brought his thumb to his mouth and started biting. The sound of teeth gnawing on nails made Steve's skin crawl, but he stayed completely still.

"Okay," Miguel said, nodding. "For State."

"For State," Steve agreed.

"Sorry, by the way," Miguel said. He sat up straight in his chair and looked just beyond Steve's shoulder at the framed posters he had hanging up. Bruce Springsteen playing back-to-back with The Big Man; the Great Coach, Tom Landry, standing on the Cowboys sideline in his black fedora and gray tailored suit; and a topographic map of the state of Texas, the Guadalupe Mountains raised and contoured on the edge of West Texas.

"Make sure you look a man in the eye when you apologize," Steve said, waiting for him to look away from the map and back at Steve. "But I don't want sorry, I want solutions. You can hate every inch of this town, except for that football field out there and those guys in the locker room with you."

"Yes, sir, Coach. I got you. I'm all in. I want to play," Miguel said, frowning. "But that's not why I said it. Meant sorry about what I said. About your daughter. Not really such a bad thing, being a dyke. I mean, there are worse things your kid could be, I guess."

Steve tried to smile. Make his response nice and easy to expel all the heaviness he felt inside himself. But it wouldn't come. And he didn't force it.

"No need for all that. Can't say sorry for what's true," Steve said, standing up. Miguel did the same. "So. No more fights. No more bullshit."

"No more fights," Miguel said, nodding, his thick dark brows knitting together in seriousness. "No more bullshit."

"Good. Now go hit the showers. I know you've got plenty of time before class, but still, be fast about it. Ever since I left the history department so quick, they've been trying to find a way to get me back. And any of my guys showing up late is a good enough excuse for them."

Miguel gave Steve a salute and a gapped-tooth smile, bounding out of the office and down the hall.

After he was sure Miguel had gone into the locker room, Steve poked his head out of the doorway to make sure no one was walking down the chipped-tile hallway. The fluorescent lights buzzed and flickered. A couple of girls on the volleyball team burst through the door by the track, out of breath and squealing about some boy named Tom before disappearing into their locker room. After that, everything was silent. Steve was alone.

He went back into his office and closed the door. Pressed the lock on the knob. Went to his desk. Took off his cap and put it in his lap, like his mama had taught him to do in church.

On the right side of his desk, there was a framed picture of Steve and Emmy, back when she was young, maybe eight or nine, taken after a football game. A district game they needed to win to make play-offs. They'd lost by a field goal. After the game,

Steve had headed for the stands to find his girls, like he did after every game, and Emmy shot out onto the track, running up to him, talking so quick he could barely make out what she was saying, but it was something about the other team jumping offside and the good-for-nothing referee being too blind to call it, and then she wrapped her arms around him, pressing her face into his stomach, letting out a frustrated scream that was muffled by his body. Lucy was up in the stands. She got out her camera and yelled at them, telling them to smile, before taking the picture.

Emmy had brown hair like her mother. Eyes, too. Button nose. Deep dimples like Steve. Backward red hat and a white Steinbeck football T-shirt. Her head came up to Steve's rib cage. Her arms were wrapped around his waist. He was looking up at Lucy taking the picture. Emmy was looking up at him. Behind them, everything was in motion: people walking through the stands, players jogging past them, the floodlights of the stadium a great orb of light in an otherwise-dark sky. But Steve and Emmy were in focus. Lucy'd snapped it just right.

Steve opened the right drawer of his desk and took out a silver whistle on a black string. Emmy had given it to him for Christmas the first season he coached with Jim. *Can't wear it until you're head coach,* she'd said. *But when you do, that first season, this will take you all the way to State.*

He picked up the framed photo and tucked it away in the drawer, facedown, before putting the whistle around his neck, tucking it beneath his shirt. He gave it a small pat, then got started breaking down film from Granary High.

Never knew when they might come in handy. Those old talismans of belief.

16

On Saturday morning, Steve showed up at Oliver's Diner around eight. Lucy was already sitting in a booth at the back, picking at a bowl of fresh fruit as she sipped her coffee and flipped through a worn paperback that she'd propped up against a glass ketchup bottle. When she saw Steve, she quickly closed the book and stored it in her purse.

"Coach Quinn," she said, reaching out her hand to squeeze his as he scooted into the other side of the booth. "Hope you didn't lose too much sleep over the loss."

"Always do," Steve said. He ordered a coffee when the waitress came around. "What were you reading?"

"Oh," Lucy said, taking a blueberry from the bowl and popping it in her mouth, "this book Cora gave me a few weeks back. By a Franciscan father."

"Catholic?" Steve said, frowning. "Why'd she give you that?"

"It's been helping me," Lucy said simply. "Don't got a lot of time this morning, huh? You're trying your best not to look at your watch. But I can tell you want to."

"It's not personal," Steve said, looking down at his wrist, unable to help himself. "You know how it gets in the fall."

"Yeah, I know," Lucy said, twisting her mother's signet ring that she wore on her middle finger. "When do you think you'll have time for other things, Steve? Before, it was all about becoming head coach. Now…"

"What?" Steve asked, teasing her. "You lonely or something, Luce?"

"Of course not," she said quickly, taking a long sip of her coffee, avoiding his eyes. "Just forgot. How busy you'll always be."

"Busier than ever," Steve said, leaning back in the booth, crossing his arms. "Head coach now. Lots of responsibility."

"Real big man," Lucy said, smiling, still not meeting his gaze.

"Everything okay?" Steve asked, clearing his throat, always a little uncomfortable getting deeper than the standard small talk. "Anything you wanna, I don't know, talk about?"

"I just…" Lucy said, looking around to make sure no one was eavesdropping. She took a deep breath in. Steadying herself. "I miss Emmy. So much. I can't…"

"There's nothing you can do right now," Steve said, suddenly alert, sitting up, resting his elbows on the table as he leaned close to Lucy, trying to keep her from saying something she might regret. "We gotta just stay the course. Especially during the season. The whole job depends on it."

"But, I really want—"

"No *but*s, Lucy. Dan Holcomb said it's nonnegotiable. No contact."

"I understand that for you, but I'm—"

"Lucy, no. You have to follow my lead here. You have to trust me."

Lucy closed her eyes and let her head drop into her hands. She stayed like that for a while. Steve was worried she'd started crying. When she lifted her head up, though, her eyes were filled with fury.

"So that's how we're gonna do this," Lucy said, clenching her jaw. "Not talk about it until *you're* ready to deal with it. Not reach out to her because it might threaten *your* job."

"It's the team, Lucy. I can't just—"

"It's your *family*, Steve. But I guess it's always been the team, really," Lucy said, nodding, as an odd sort of clarity washed over her face. "The team was what mattered. And we mattered, too, when we were on the team. When we could fall into line. But now..."

"But what? Lucy, this is our dream. *Ours*."

"Don't you see? You're alone in this. You've gotten everything you've ever wanted. But the rest of us, we're..."

"What?" Steve asked, frightened by the calm precision of her words, the faraway look in her eyes, like she was no longer in this with him.

"After the divorce," Lucy said, speaking slowly, as if every word were carefully chosen, "everyone took your side. You do realize that, right?"

"Well," Steve said, shifting in his seat, uncomfortable with the territory they were tiptoeing around, "I didn't want the divorce, did I? Suppose people just felt sorry for me is all."

"Do you ever wonder if you're wrong?" Lucy asked, her tone now detached, with a look on her face Steve had never seen before. It was somehow both blank and resolved.

"This is ridiculous," Steve said, leaning to grab his wallet out of his back pocket. He fished out a ten and placed it on the table.

"Your words are always ironclad, you know?" Lucy said, unfazed by Steve's attempt to leave. "Your faith... I always thought I should follow your faith. That I should follow your lead."

"I don't got time for this," Steve said, sliding out of the booth. "I'll see you after the game on Friday."

"I'm not going," Lucy said, looking down into her coffee, that same odd expression plastered across her face. "Without Emmy, who am I going to talk to?"

"Make new friends, Lucy," Steve said, towering over her as he stood beside the booth. "It's not that hard."

Without looking back at her, he rushed out of the diner, walking into the hot September sun, full of rage and a strange disquiet that he buried down deep within himself, into all the secret, faraway places he never saw again. By the time he got in his truck, he was already thinking of the game next week, making a plan for how he was going to get the linemen to blitz the hell out of the Granary High quarterback when they had them on a third and long. It was, for Steve, almost as if the conversation with Lucy had never happened.

17

On the Friday morning of their first game of the season, Miguel invited the Leadership Council and the coaching staff over to his grandma's place for breakfast tacos and coffee. Steve was still slightly shaken by his conversation with Lucy, but there was no time to lose focus now. The season was about to begin. He had to give the team everything he had.

Pastor Ben was at the breakfast. The quarterbacks coach had invited him to come so that he could bless the food and the season. They needed him to sanctify their road to State.

"And above all…" Pastor Ben said in the middle of his prayer, right as Steve opened his eyes to look around the room. The men made eye contact, and Ben gave him a little smile. "Bless and keep Coach Quinn on this road. May he never waver in his sense of righteousness. May he keep his eyes fixed on glory and not let the world dissuade him from it. Amen."

"Amen!" the men shouted, digging into their plates, a dull

roar of conversation rising up after everyone had taken their first few bites.

"You keeping tabs on me, Pastor?" Steve asked when Ben walked over to him after the prayer.

"Just doin' my job," Ben said, sipping his coffee. "Dan said y'all had a talk last week."

"Right."

"So," Ben said, "just wanted to make sure we were still on the same page. From our conversation last month."

"I understand what needs to be done." Steve had no desire to talk about it any further. Especially not here, with the boys and coaches everywhere. He had made his decision. There wasn't any reason to talk about anything other than football.

"Well, if at any point you feel yourself…faltering," Ben said, his voice drowned out by the booming laugh of Big Williams, "find me, won't you? There's no shame in asking for help."

"All righty," Steve said, giving him a curt nod, walking toward the rest of the team so that he wouldn't get cornered again. *Pushy people, those pastors*, Steve thought, as he bit into his taco.

All twelve guys on the Leadership Council had showed up, even Little Williams, though he stood in the corner of the packed living room, sipping black coffee and sulking, shooting looks at Miguel every time he made one of the guys laugh, especially when it was his brother, who had stuffed himself on the couch in between Trey and Miguel, cracking jokes, his mouth filled with food.

Big Williams had seven tacos piled on his plate, each one stuffed with scrambled eggs, skillet potatoes, pico de gallo, beans, and a side of carnitas that Miguel's grandmother insisted on plopping on his plate, delighted that there was no empty space, even more thrilled when Big Williams cleared his plate and came back for more.

"These are the best tacos I've ever had," Big Williams said to

Miguel, making his way through his ninth taco. "I wanna marry your grandma, Martinez."

"Way she's looking at you, you might have to," Miguel said, pointing to her in the kitchen, already putting together a third plate for Big Williams. "Didn't think she liked white boys, but I don't know if she's ever met one who can eat as much as you."

"Gotta eat, man, keep that pocket protected for you," Big Williams said, slapping Miguel on the back. "You think you can scramble against Granary?"

"Shit, what do you think?" Miguel said, grinning. "Pass on 'em, run on 'em, flex on 'em."

"Amen," Big Williams said before stuffing an entire taco in his mouth.

"Coach!" Trey said, barreling through the crowd of people to get to Steve. "Look what I just got. Those Texas magazine people sent it over. Look at these!"

He had a high-quality picture blown up on his phone screen. Him in a Steinbeck uniform, their red home jersey, flexing his arms, grinning from ear to ear.

"Good-lookin' pictures," Steve said, squinting, taking out his glasses to get a better look. Trey looked like a real pro, his smile wide, his teeth white, his uniform just tight enough to show how much time he'd been putting in the weight room. It was good for them to have a face of the program. And good-looking guys starting on the field always added incentive for girls at the high school to come and fill up the seats on Friday nights. "Not the point of all this, all this glitzy-glam stuff, but it'll be good for ACU to see."

"We don't do it for Instagram, though?" Trey asked, smiling, giving Miguel, who had walked over to see the pictures, a little shoulder shove. "Don't get any DM slides if we're not thinking a little bit about the 'gram. Come on, now."

"No shit. Girls see a thousand likes," Miguel said, scrolling through his phone and showing it to Trey, "and their pussies turn to puddles, swear to fucking God."

"Oh, shit, she from El Paso?" Trey said, zooming in on a picture.

Steve took their distraction as his cue to leave, wanting no part in their extracurriculars off the field. Besides, their phones had them speaking seven different languages he didn't come close to understanding.

"See y'all this afternoon," Steve said, slapping them on their shoulders. "Miguel, where's your mama? Want to thank her for having us."

"In the kitchen with Abuela," Miguel said without looking up from his phone, showing Trey another girl he'd found on the internet. Before Steve got to the kitchen, he looked back at Trey and Miguel. They were standing shoulder to shoulder, showing each other stuff on their phones—DMs or profile pictures or whatever kind of nonsense—reveling in the universal truth of the game: the best players always got the girls.

When Steve left Miguel's, he had an armful of tamales that Abuela wouldn't let him leave without plus a strange feeling. He'd never had one like it before. He felt light, and he walked toward his truck with an extra bounce in his step. His heart was racing, but in a good way. Like adrenaline. It felt *good*.

It wasn't just his body. It was everything in him. Body, mind, soul, all filled up, like he was doing something he'd been born to do. And he was doing it well. Jim would have let the quarterback showdown drag on, using non-district games as a way to have Little Williams and Miguel compete, when it wasn't a question of skill. It was a question of heart. And Steve knew Miguel had it. He knew if he could snap his head out of his own ass and look around him, he'd see he was on a team worth playing for.

Seeing him with Trey, joking around, having guys over, making an effort, Steve realized that Miguel meant it. That he was all in. Focused. Getting the right guys on his side, starting to gel with the team, building rapport, buying in.

Little Williams would be pissed, of course, losing his starting position. But this game was never about one person's individual happiness. It was about sacrifice. It was about heart. And, more than anything, it was about doing whatever it took to win.

Their first game was at home against Granary High. It was the first of five non-district games, which didn't count toward play-offs. Only district games mattered for that. But they wanted to win every one they could. Show the rest of the district they were something to watch out for. Show them they needed to be afraid.

On the night of that first game, Mustang Stadium was *alive*, electric. It was early September, so still unreasonably hot. But the edge of fall was in the wind, making it a little crisper, and the sun felt farther away every day. The cheerleaders held up their pom-poms and cartwheeled their way down the track, wearing their new, one-piece uniforms they'd switched to after a group of ladies from the PTA complained that the two pieces distracted their husbands from the game. The band played "The Imperial March" from *Star Wars* and drowned out the visiting team's band. Every seat was filled—the home side and the visitors' side—and Kyle Yates, who had spent the last fifteen years as the announcer at games, boomed, "We're moments away from kickoff on another Steinbeck High football season!"

Around his neck, tucked inside the Dri-Fit polo shirt he wore, Steve had on the whistle Emmy had given him. It felt cool against his skin. He pressed it with his index finger, closed his eyes, and said a little prayer. Not for anything in particular. Maybe just to feel her close.

Wear this, and you'll take them all the way to State, you just watch, he could almost hear her say. Steve looked for her up in the stands. She always sat on the fifty-yard line in the first row on the season opener. It was stupid to look for her. Steve knew the only reason he got the gig was on the guarantee that she wouldn't show up. But still. A little hope lingered that she'd found her way back home.

Five minutes to kick off, Johnson walked up to Steve.

"Ready, Coach?" he asked, grinning, pointing to his bucket hat. "Got on lucky beige. Can't lose."

"If we do, you gotta burn that thing," he said, watching the captains walk out on the field for the coin toss.

There was nothing like the start of the season. Everyone's record was 0–0. The slate was clean. Anything could happen.

The 'Stangs won the toss and elected to start with the ball. The crowd was on their feet. They were screaming. Pounding their feet into the metal bleachers. Clanging clappers, cowbells, anything they could get their hands on.

"Are you ready for some football?" the voice of Kyle Yates echoed through the stadium, and the crowd roared in response.

The boys lined up on the field in their return formation. Trey was back to receive. He jumped up a few times, making sure his legs were loose, and raised his hands up to keep the crowd roaring, yelling, hoping.

Steve's town, his home, his team: in that first moment before the first whistle blew, when anything was possible, he felt the wave of their collective hope, an entire stadium filled with unshakable belief.

"All righty, Coach Quinn," Johnson said, coming up beside Steve, slapping him on the back. "Let's make ourselves a case for State."

18

EMMY

For all of Emmy's life, fall had been dedicated to football.

There was something about it—the shorter days, the cooler wind, the harvest moon rising over the visitors' stands, huge and red and filled with fire. Everyone huddled together, hot coffee clutched in gloved hands, Kyle Yates's voice booming through the speakers as the game clock ticked down to zero. Stores shut down, and life halted in anticipation for those buzzing, blazing lights on Friday night.

It was her father's time. His conquests on the field were their shared obsession. Emmy watched film with him in the living room when she was growing up, and she'd help point out the blocks that got missed, the coverage that was misread, the guard that couldn't keep himself from jumping offside.

"You got an eye for this, kiddo," he'd said one afternoon. "Maybe you should play for me."

Emmy laughed, wishing he were serious, and went back to taking notes, making sure she didn't miss a thing.

It was a cozy and predictable rhythm that they cultivated for themselves. To keep the game on the forefront of their minds while autumn crept into West Texas, the trees' leaves remaining green until the last vestiges of the season when they'd finally turn brown and drop. No color in their transition. Life and death; green and brown. Fall colors in Texas were closer to camouflage than the abundance of fiery reds and oranges and yellows seen in other parts of the country.

Before Cameron, Emmy's life had always felt regulated. Time clipped by at a fixed rate, like the twelve-minute quarters in a high school football game. Moments were just moments, few more significant than the rest. There was the night in the back of the pickup with Michaela, and her parents' divorce, but besides that, all periods of her life had been measured, predictable, split into equal parts.

But that fall, with Cameron, everything changed. The rhythm of Emmy's life halted. Everything shifted its orbit around her.

Sundays were their best days. Lazy mornings in bed, the sun streaming through Cameron's never-quite-closed curtains, lilac comforter, white walls covered in framed posters from concerts she'd gone to in Boston—Arcade Fire and Alabama Shakes and Fleetwood Mac. Cameron would hum along to her favorite songs while they lay next to each other, their legs intertwined, their eyes on their phones, putting off all the work they had to do for the week ahead. It was a quiet cohabitation rooted in routine spontaneity.

In those first two months of dating, every week was different. There were some weeks when they stayed home all day long, singing along to their favorite songs, Emmy trying to teach Cameron how to two-step to country music, Cameron trying to teach Emmy the waltz she'd learned in her cotillion class in Boston, both of them trying to learn to salsa as they watched instructional videos and tripped over their feet, their hips swaying a few beats behind the music. Sometimes Cameron would plan a picnic or find a new taco stand she'd heard about from someone in her cohort. Once, Cameron invited her classmates along on one of their adventures, and Emmy had to sit through three hours of insufferable debates and gossip about who was the most obnoxious person in their program, often forgetting that Emmy was with them. When they realized she was, they asked half-hearted questions about her future job at the marketing firm, then scoffed at how corporate she would become, beginning a new slew of arguments about the evils of capitalism, while Emmy sat back, suddenly self-conscious of the four-dollar cappuccino she was sipping. When Emmy and Cameron got back to the apartment, Cameron pulled her in close, kissed her neck, and whispered, "We're a bunch of assholes, aren't we?" then vowed to never waste a Sunday on them again. And she never did. Instead, that next weekend, she took Emmy to the caves.

It was the first Sunday they lived together. Emmy woke up to Cameron sitting on the edge of their bed, clutching two cups of coffee, extending one to Emmy when she sat up, groggy, looking out of the window to see a still-dark sky.

"What time is it?" Emmy asked, rubbing the sleep from her eyes. She took the coffee from Cameron and sipped it slowly. It was black and strong and piping hot. Just like Emmy liked it.

"We're going on an adventure," Cameron said, grinning. "The car's gassed up. Time to get dressed."

"But it's Sunday."

"Exactly," Cameron said. The circles under her eyes were dark as ever, but her face was awake and alive, with a bright smile and red cheeks, her eyes wide with impatience and wonder at what was to come. "Wear something you can walk around in. And bring a jacket. It gets cold."

The open road in Texas had always been heaven for Emmy, but she had no idea had much more glorious it could become with Cameron beside her, navigating the two-lane highways, cursing under her breath every time she saw a cop car on the horizon, slowing down fifteen miles-per-hour, convinced every state trooper in Texas was out to get her because of her Massachusetts plates. She grabbed Emmy's hand and shouted "Hallelujah!" whenever she saw no cop lights flashing behind her. They kept on holding hands because the road was flat and straight and held nothing before them except the horizon and telephone wires and overly religious and political billboards about the sanctity of life and the perils of hell, which made Cameron roll down her windows and scream "Booo!" Her voice was drowned out by the whipping wind, but she didn't care. She just needed to scream.

Cameron didn't believe in pit stops on road trips, but when they saw a billboard for a gas station selling Krispy Kreme doughnuts, she looked over at Emmy, who was failing to hide her excitement by biting down on her lower lip and sitting on her hands. Cameron rolled her eyes and took the next exit, buying them half a dozen for the road.

"I'm usually such a hard-ass about not stopping," Cameron said between bites of a plain glazed doughnut, little flecks of sugar sticking to the edges of her lips. "But you make me weak, Emmy Quinn."

The sun rose behind them as they drove west, and Emmy tried to guess their destination, but every time she asked, Cameron just turned the music up louder, throwing her head back and laughing at Emmy's feeble protests filled with fake indignation.

Emmy had never felt so light, so filled to the brim with giddiness at the simple pleasure of being in someone's presence. She snuck as many glances as she could at Cameron when they entered into silent stretches, when Cameron's eyes narrowed on the road ahead. Her dark brows were furrowed in concentration. Emmy noticed the soft way Cameron rubbed her chin when she sang along to the chorus of a song she'd always play when she was working on her thesis, and Emmy knew her mind was miles away, in some imagined world. The sunlight poured through the back window, just enough to illuminate Cameron's profile, her smooth olive skin, her slightly drooping eyes, her bottom lip dry and chapped, but full and hypnotizing to Emmy.

"Are you ready for magic?" Cameron asked when they drove under the state-line sign of New Mexico. The land of enchantment.

They arrived at the Carlsbad Caverns by midmorning, checked in at the visitors' center, and made their way down a decline of switchbacks toward the natural opening of the cave. Cameron shoved Emmy's shoulder a little and said, "Hope you're not afraid of the dark."

Emmy laughed nervously, pulling at her thumb, a tightness entering her chest. There was nothing she feared more. But she wanted to have fun, to be adventurous, and she'd promised Cameron on that first night they spent together that she would be brave. So when they got to the entrance, Emmy took in a deep breath and followed Cameron into the cavern.

The mouth of the cave was more like an eye, Emmy thought, looking back at the small opening of blue sky they were leaving behind. It was cool inside, slightly damp, and had the musty smell of mold, with the occasional whiff of something pungent and foul. A ranger told them later that it was batshit.

The temperature had dropped at least twenty degrees, and they were almost a mile inside of the earth when they entered the Big Room. It was a cathedral of darkness, Emmy thought, looking around. There were some lights on the pathway and others illuminating the cave formations. Sulfuric acid had eroded the limestone to create the strange, almost porous, stalagmites rising from the floor. They were grotesque and beautiful beyond imagination, almost like a coral reef had jumped out from the ocean and into the earth. An otherworldly configuration of stalactites jutted from the cave's ceiling, sharp and long, like fangs.

They reminded Emmy of the mouth of a whale, which made her think of Jonah, swallowed whole.

Cameron had bought them tickets for a guided tour, which was hosted by a ranger, and he took them deeper into the cave, beyond the Big Room, down a path that narrowed and became increasingly dark, almost punishingly quiet. Emmy's pulse pounded in her ears. She tried to focus on her feet in front of her. Whenever she looked around, into the cavern's depths, she felt dizzy, like she'd lost her center.

The ranger prattled on about the various geological phenomena of the cave and pointed out the burn marks from the lanterns of explorers who'd traversed the cave first. Emmy couldn't help but wonder if they'd ever found their way out or if they'd been lost, consumed by the darkness, their bones eroding in some tunnel, never to be seen again.

"And this is the real special part," the guide said in a whisper. Sound carried far in the caverns. It was almost like he was in Emmy's ear. "It feels sort of dark, doesn't it? Even with the lights we've got on here? Well, the caves have some of the most impenetrable darkness in the world. And I'm going to—for just a minute, don't worry—I'm going to, in three, two, one…"

Turn off the lights.

It was as if the oxygen had been sucked from her. Like she was floating, untethered, in outer space.

Emmy waved her hand in front of her face, but she couldn't see it. She couldn't see anything. She was submerged into a nightmare, into everything she had feared, and she wondered if this was hell, if this was where she would be sentenced to go if her father were right, and Pastor Ben, and Mrs. Zee, and everyone else who had ever damned her soul for the love she could not control. She thought of her baptism, of the suffocation she'd felt, the guilt and pain and shame pressing in on her from all sides.

She couldn't breathe. She knew that she should be able to, that she was not drowning, that she was on dry land, but she felt her whole body betray her, refuse to work, protest against the darkness that squeezed her with such violence. It was all ending in New Mexico, and she marveled at the real cruelty here: that she wouldn't be able to die in Texas.

Cameron grabbed Emmy's hand and whispered, "Don't be afraid." Her voice seemed to ground Emmy, bringing her back to the surface, just as Pastor Sherman had done when he'd lifted her out of the water. When the ranger turned the lights back on, Emmy was face-to-face with Cameron. Emmy could barely see her expression in the dim light of the cavern, but even the shadow of her was a comfort. She squeezed her hand, and Cameron whispered, "You made it, Emmylou."

It was a tenderness Emmy had never known but had longed for all her life. It filled Emmy up, carried her through the other two tours in the darkness and then out of the cavern, back into the light, where she sat with Cameron at the end of the day, waiting for the bats to emerge from the cavern. They found a spot in the amphitheater above the mouth of the cave as the sun started to set. The flat land yielded to the curvature of the horizon, which the sun dipped into, an orb of fire, leaving the sky beyond it pink and periwinkle, the last threads of light as the darkness closed in from the east.

Emmy felt free outside, released from the darkness. She let herself succumb to the giddy peals of laughter that bubbled up from the receding fear she'd felt within the caverns. Cameron listened to Emmy giggle and smiled, taking her by the shoulders, looking her up and down.

"Your laugh is my favorite sound in the world," Cameron said. "How did a person like you come from a place like Texas?"

"Luck," Emmy said, looking at Cameron, her face cast in the sunset's golden light. Emmy traced the arch of her dark, full brows with the back of her palm.

"It's not luck," Cameron said, resting her forehead on Emmy's. "It's something else."

"God?" Emmy asked, half-joking. "Fate?"

"I don't believe in that stuff," she said. "Or maybe I do. If that's what made you."

"My parents made me, technically."

"I think I'm in love with you," Cameron said in a rush, looking up at Emmy. In the fading sunlight, she was cascaded in a magnificent light, and her eyes looked like honey, gold and viscous and deep.

Before Emmy could respond, the sun disappeared from the horizon, and a black cloud shot from the cave, a mass of bats collecting and spreading out into the open air. It was like a plague. One flapped above Emmy, forcing her to duck, and Cameron cackled, wrapping her arms around Emmy, rocking her back and forth, managing to say in between peals of laughter, "It's okay, Emmy. You don't have to worry, I'm going to protect you. I'm here to save you now."

As she leaned her head into Cameron's chest, watching the moving black cloud fade away, she felt Cameron's heart hammer in her ears, and Emmy finally understood the fanaticism of the faith in which she'd been brought up. What else mattered in the world, Emmy thought, if you had someone there to save you?

19

It was always a surprise—and a delight—when the first cool front came to Texas. That year, it was later than usual. So much later, in fact, that Emmy was afraid the heat would stay forever. She said as much to Cameron, who said, "Global warming is going to get us all. Even West Texas can't avoid the inevitable."

But on the first night of October, a storm rolled in, and when the morning came, the clouds had disappeared and left behind a clear, deep blue sky. Emmy walked outside, and goose bumps shot up her arm, the air cool and crisp and dry. She inhaled and felt the air sting in her lungs, her breath coming out in a cloud of vapor as she exhaled, savoring the pleasure of it as she walked to the local coffee shop to meet with Dr. Cunningham, who had invited Emmy for coffee after the scandal of her disciplinary meeting with the Theta Omegas had died down.

"We should have gotten beers," Dr. Cunningham said, letting out a nervous laugh and stirring her piping-hot cappuccino. Her hands were shaking a little, and the cuticles were bitten down, raw and red. "Perfect day for it. Fall always begs for kegs. My brother used to say that."

"Are we allowed to do that?" Emmy asked, pulling at her thumbs. It felt awkward for her to be somewhere without Cameron. She'd not done anything alone, outside of classes, for two months.

"Sure. You're not *my* student. We can be friends." Dr. Cunningham rubbed the back of her neck and ran her hand through her dark hair, the pixie cut parted to the side and smoothed down with mousse. It was getting a little long at the back. It had started to curl up like a duck's tail. "Just... I love this weather."

"Try growing up here, Dr. Cunningham," Emmy said. "Stays summer for six months a year. Then you get a day like today. And it's like heaven."

"Please, call me Sara," she said. "And I did grow up here. Just outside of Amarillo."

"And you stayed?" Emmy asked, genuinely surprised. With her pantsuits and articulate, polished speech, she'd assumed Dr. Cunningham—*Sara*, Emmy thought, correcting herself—was from the northeast or had at least spent some time there before ending up in Walker. "Jesus. I can't wait to get out."

"Well, it's complicated."

"Couldn't pay me enough money to stay in West Texas," Emmy said.

"Was in Austin for a bit."

"Only reason I went to school here was because my dad..."

"For undergrad. But I came back."

"You should have stayed put."

"I didn't have a choice, Emmy," Sara snapped, her blue eyes wide in earnest, with overdone, too-dark eyeshadow giving them a sunken, hollow look. She looked down at her coffee, forcing herself to laugh. When she looked up again, she was smiling, a strained grimace, to make up for her outburst.

Texas women learned this skill at a young age, the act of arranging the face into a mask. They knew how to make themselves palatable to everyone. It was almost formulaic: show your teeth, bare your teeth, hide your anger behind your teeth, always making sure your mouth was turned up in a smile.

"Sorry," Sara said, her smile fading a little. "There's always a choice. I don't know why... I love my job. I'm grateful to be here."

"What didn't you choose?" Emmy asked, noticing her clenched fist around her coffee mug, remembering how she'd looked when she'd left the office in the sorority house, eyes intense and downcast, entranced by the bylaws section on homosexuality.

"It was a different time," she said, slowly, looking around the coffee shop. When she was sure the coast was clear, she leaned in close and started speaking, quickly and clearly, like she'd been asked to hold her breath for too long and was finally allowed to exhale.

It was the same story that they all had, in one form or another: her father was a preacher at a small Baptist church in the Panhandle, just outside of Amarillo. Her mother was a first-grade teacher at the public school. Her brother was the high school quarterback, her sister the head cheerleader. Her siblings had both moved back to town after they graduated college, got married to their college sweethearts, and started their families, going to church every Sunday, where they listened to their father's sermons on the justice of Jesus, his favorite topic.

Sara had been the smart one. Went to the University of Texas, where she studied English and smoked weed with her friends in Austin and got swept away in new age, hippie bullshit, as her father called it, like past lives and tarot cards and astrology. She fell in love with the wrong people, specifically a butch Gemini who played bass in a punk-rock band.

It was the kind of love, she said, that cut her up from the inside. Everything she had ever known got flipped upside down. She was disoriented. If she had been more aware, if she had been paying closer attention, she would have realized that the Gemini's roommate's boyfriend's best friend, who came to a house party at their apartment one night, was the son of Gary Masterson, the youth pastor at their hometown church.

He saw Sara making out with the Gemini. It took a couple times asking around the room to confirm that the girl kissing the dyke was, indeed, Sara Cunningham, the daughter of his pastor.

Sara didn't say how long it took him to make the call home, but Emmy imagined it must have been the next day, in the afternoon, after church was done so he was sure to get a hold of his mother. It would have had to be his mother—women were always in charge of the gossip. You couldn't trust a man to spread that kind of news around town with any kind of efficiency. And Emmy imagined it spread real quick, within the day, if not the hour. Word always found its way around in towns like theirs. It was inescapable. To be haunted by a home was the eternal promise of the South.

It didn't take long once news got to Sara's parents. A preacher had resources, connections, ways of solving problems with an added expediency. There was a list of numbers he'd collected over the years for other families with kids like her. It was easy to get her in. All it took was a phone call.

They called it *conversion therapy* in some places, *sexual rehabilitation* in others. It was in vogue, sending your kids away to camps to get them back on track. Math camp, fat camp, cheer camp. A month away from home in the trusted care of good people. A place to get away and get connected to God.

And even though Sara thought it was all bullshit, if you got told enough nights in row that something in you was disgusting, demented, damned by all that was good in the world, it started getting harder and harder to stand your ground. Everyone gave in eventually, she said. She submitted herself to their will, which they equated with God's.

There was also the matter of her parents, not wanting to disappoint them. They had always had expectations for their children. There was a preset mold that they all had to fill. And if something didn't quite fit, it was never an issue with the mold.

Sara tried to make herself fit into their expectations of what a daughter should be. She went back to UT to finish her degree and joined Theta Omega, too, just like her mother had always wanted. Her parents rewarded her obedience with funding for her education. She went to grad school and then got a PhD from Walker, where she landed a tenure-track job soon after graduating, which almost never happened. The rarity of the opportunity made her believe it was her reward. When she accepted the position, she had to sign the Statement of Faith in order to keep teaching there. It was a contract that all faculty had to sign, assuring the university that they were a Christian and a member of a church and willing to comply with all their standards of morality. Adultery and homosexuality and sex outside of marriage were not tolerated in those staff associated with the school.

"I know that it's all bullshit," Sara continued, her voice slightly hoarse from all the talking. "I guess I was afraid of hurting my family. And then I got this job and thought, maybe, even if it was too late for me, I could help the kids who ended up here. Who were in my class. Or even colleagues in the same boat..."

Sara fidgeted with the sleeve of her blazer that tapered off just above her wrist. Emmy watched her, breathless, her mind reeling at the story, at once so familiar and so uniquely her own.

"Honestly, though," Sara said, "those were just excuses. Truth is I found something that I was good at. Something that I loved. Funded research, designing my own courses, working with really smart, interesting colleagues. The school has its restrictions, but the department gives me a lot of freedom. It's rare, you know, the chance to do meaningful work."

"So you're just...alone?" Emmy asked, trying to wrap her head around the concept.

"I have my friends and my family. An army of nieces and

nephews I'd have never gotten to meet if—" She broke off, leaning her head back, rubbing her hand along the back of her long, thin neck. "Look. I can't say that it's been easy. It was a sacrifice. And those are always painful. Think about Jesus—voluntarily on the cross, dying for all of humanity. He signed up for that pain. And still, while he was hanging there, bleeding, he looked up at the sky, screaming, asking God why he had been forsaken."

"You really think your family would have cut you off forever?" Emmy asked, thinking about sacrifice. She had forgotten that Jesus had been ready to give up. That, at the end, it all became too much.

"It threatened my dad's job," she said, nodding. "You know how it is. Men in power in places like West Texas, ruled by the Southern Baptists. Personal life has to be spotless. Cut out the blemishes if they can't get washed clean."

Emmy looked away from Sara, toward the back of the coffee shop, where a man with a thick beard was tuning an old acoustic guitar, plucking at the strings, one by one, the sounds sharpening into clear, strong notes that rang throughout the room.

"Do you ever regret it?" Emmy asked, looking back at Sara, who was taking a long sip of her cappuccino. It left a line of milk above her lips. "Leaving Austin? Leaving her? That life you could have had?"

Sara tugged at the collar of her button-down shirt and bit her bottom lip, her dark, penciled-in eyebrows coming together to form a straight line between her bright blue eyes.

"It's not about regret, really," she said, slowly, like she was thinking out loud. "It's more... I didn't want to lose them. My family. So I made a choice. That's all."

A choice. A sacrifice. Maybe it was that simple. Letting something go in the name of love.

"You know, if you ever need anything..." Sara started. "I mean, I know you can't have too many people around here supporting you. And, well, one of the reasons I'm here, in this job, in this place, is to help."

"Thanks," Emmy said, touched by the warmth of her acceptance.

"I know the circumstances suck." She cracked her knuckles and looked down at her hands, avoiding Emmy's eyes. The gesture made her look younger somehow. "But it's sort of nice. Having someone to talk to. About all of this."

It was more instinct than thought. Emmy reached out her hand and grabbed Sara's. She gave it a firm squeeze and felt the spark of connection when Sara squeezed back, her mouth open in a small oval of surprise. Full lips, chapped. Emmy couldn't help but look at them, notice the sharp indentation of her upper lip, like the top of a Valentine's Day heart. Her face flushed, a rouge running up her high cheekbones.

"Meet again next week?" Emmy asked, still holding Sara's hand. It wouldn't be such a big deal, Emmy thought, to invite Sara along on her and Cameron's adventures on Sundays.

"I can't wait," Sara said, pressing her lips together in a small smile, pulling her hand away from Emmy's slowly, with some reluctance, before lifting her cup to her lips and draining the last of her cappuccino.

While Emmy was walking home, she thought about Sara's story, which, of course, made her think of her own parents. She thought about her mom and what she'd said about Emmy's dad. About how he hadn't changed. *Couldn't* change. And Emmy thought of how he'd looked on the porch, red-faced, clear-eyed, his voice filled with such finality it felt like a declaration of law, the permanence of their separation.

But Emmy also remembered all the ways he'd been willing to change. She had always been the exception to the rule. Before her, he'd had no interest in things like women's sports, or poetry, or national parks. After her, they had Women's World

Cup–watch parties, a Walt Whitman poster in the hallway, annual trips to Big Bend. Something shifted in him when it came to Emmy. His convictions softened around the edges, made pliable by love.

"Oh, gee, I don't know, Emmylou," Steve had said when he got passed over for the head-coaching job six years ago, when the board decided to hire Jim. He'd spent the entire season trying to prove he had what it took to take the team into his own hands, putting in extra hours with recruiters, staying up at the school on weekends, staying late after practice to work with players or help talk them through something going on at home. It was the final straw for Lucy, his never being around. But that was a sacrifice he'd been willing to make. "Hope you never know it. That feeling. Not being enough for what you love."

Steve was *good* at a lot of things: planting trees, fixing flat tires, performing scripture readings at weddings, cooking the perfect steak, throwing a beautiful spiral, calling the perfect play for a goal-line stand.

But there were very few things that he *loved*. Emmy could only think of three. Her mom, herself, and the Steinbeck football team. He'd already been willing to give up his marriage for the game. It wasn't so unlikely that he'd given up on her, too, for a chance at his dream.

A head coach wasn't a preacher, but it was close enough. That kind of influence, power, in a town like Steinbeck, with a game like football, was not taken lightly.

Emmy hadn't considered how telling her dad would jeopardize his job. Or maybe she had always known the risk and had been willing to take it. Maybe she could have waited until the season was done to say something. Then, at least, she would have gotten to see the boys play.

But was there ever a good time for those sorts of truths? Emmy wondered. If everything went according to his plan, her dad would stay coaching at Steinbeck well into his sixties. And

Emmy couldn't imagine Jan Oleander or Dan Holcomb suddenly shifting their thinking, opening their minds to a different interpretation of the right and wrong ways of living a life.

Emmy could have listened to her mother. Never told him. Stayed quiet about that part of her life for another decade or two or three. Was that what it meant to love someone? Lying to protect them, to keep them around, when you knew they couldn't handle the truth?

Maybe love could be allowing her dad to believe what he wanted about her life, letting him in just close enough to have her, but never close enough to know her. He could fill in the blanks that were left unsaid with his own imagination, his own vision for her life that was palatable to him and the church and the board and the rest of Steinbeck.

Love could be holidays spent apart, Emmy with Cameron, him with Lucy or with his friends, and birthdays spent together, just the two of them. Emmy could drive from whatever city she ended up in and cook him something with vegetables, make sure he wasn't all steak and beer.

Love could be never letting him know her future children, never letting him know the impossibility of having those children without federal forms and test tubes and donors and money, money, money—it would take so much money, another price she would pay for the love she would never let him see.

Love could be a second baptism, a new life, a chance; love could keep Steve with Emmy and Cameron with her, but never together, always separate. Love could erase that moment on the porch, take it in its old, aging, liver-spotted hands, and wash it clean with hard lye.

But was all that love? Emmy wondered. Or was it a performance?

When Emmy got home, she grabbed her laptop. She knew that Cameron wasn't back yet from the Grizzly, but she still looked around the room a couple of times, just to be safe. She wanted to be alone for this. She decided to turn off the lights, to hide, before opening her laptop and going to the website of the Steinbeck newspaper.

He was there, on the home page. A blown-up picture of him and Coach Johnson laughing after a game. Coach Johnson had on his beige bucket hat and his gray long-sleeved T-shirt. His arm was draped around Steve's shoulders. The bucket hat covered most of his face, but Emmy would have recognized that smile anywhere: it was just like Jacob's.

And Steve. Soft jawline. Long, thin nose. Red Steinbeck baseball cap pushed up on his forehead. A little white stubble on his cheeks, more than Emmy had ever seen him with. He'd always been clean-shaven. She could almost smell the sharp, acidic aftershave he used to slap on his cheeks. His eyes were closed, his mouth open midlaugh, all the creases of his face turned up with his smile, glowing from the camera flashes and stadium lights.

Emmy clicked on the article. Before it began, there was a video interview. A still image of her father standing next to a short, well-dressed woman. His hands were on his hips. She hesitated and then pressed Play.

"Oh, hell no. We keep on winning, I'm not shaving," he said, his deep voice booming over the noise from the team behind him. All his vowels elongated, sunk down in his speech. That familiar twang of home. "Hope to look like Santa by Christmastime."

"Coming down the chimney with a State Championship?"

"Well, Mary, we're a long way out from that," he said, laughing, two sharp exhales, a performative noise. "But that's the goal."

Emmy shut the laptop. Squeezed her eyes shut. Cursed the internet for making it impossible to forget anyone. She could almost feel him there with her, flipping on the lights in the room, saying in his low, soft twang, *You don't gotta be scared of the dark, Emmylou, when you got all that light inside of you.*

Emmy missed him in a way that made itself known in everything she did. All the things she wanted to say to him, all the words she wanted to hear back, got all clogged in her, lodged in her throat. It was hard to breathe.

How could this be love? Slamming the door in the face of truth? Emmy wanted to scream at him, to get in her car and drive all the way to Steinbeck, to pull up in his gravel driveway, making sure her headlights flooded the front porch. She would see his silhouette in the window as he peeked through the blinds, not used to anyone coming to see him, especially that late at night when he usually was left alone. She wanted to remind him of who she was. *His daughter.* And who cared who she dated? That was a title she had locked in for life.

But then she thought about the cost of her return. This wasn't the story of the Prodigal Son, Emmy's favorite parable from Jesus. A son makes one wrong choice, realizes his mistake, and is welcomed home with open arms, back into his father's house, where he was clothed and fed and treated like a lord.

No feast would await her return. Only pain. Nothing had changed.

Emmy couldn't ask her dad to choose. He'd been working toward becoming a head coach for longer than he'd been a father. To make him choose felt selfish. Like she'd be asking too much. Maybe it was her turn to sacrifice something. To stay away from him while he lived out his dream.

Her dad had given her so much of her life, her confidence, her sense of self. He'd given up so much of his time to teach her, spend time with her, love her.

The only way she could come to terms with who she was, who she needed to be, was because of the lessons Steve had taught Emmy when she was young: always be honest, always be yourself, never let anyone make you afraid to say who you are.

So Emmy flipped on the lamp in the living room, took a deep breath, and tried not to be afraid.

20

Every Saturday morning, before Cameron woke up, Emmy looked up the scores for the high school football games that were played the night before. Cameron had caught Emmy checking it one Saturday afternoon and slammed her laptop shut.

"It's not healthy for you to look at that stuff," Cameron said. "You've got to put him—I mean it—out of your mind."

Cameron *hated* football. More than anything. She said it was the worst part of Texas. She couldn't quite fathom the state's infatuation with the sport. The way they used it to measure power and success. How it excluded women. How it was allergic to activism. She believed that to be a fan of football, especially at the professional level, was to sell your soul to everything that was wrong with the United States: capitalism and misogyny and inequality across the board.

"It's just stupid," she said when she caught Emmy checking the scores again. "I don't see how you can enjoy it."

"I know, I know," Emmy said, wearing her favorite Cowboys T-shirt. It had an old coffee stain on the right sleeve from when her dad had jumped up in a rage and spilled it after Tony Romo's botched field-goal hold in 2007. "But I grew up with it."

"And I grew up with Catholicism, but you don't see me tithing to the church," Cameron said, eyeing Emmy's T-shirt with distaste before pulling out her laptop and sprawling on her stomach on the bed.

But Emmy couldn't help it. She had to keep up with the season. Things were always changing at the high school level. Week to week, the play-off landscape became clearer and more surprising. And Emmy didn't want to miss a thing.

According to Texas high school-football experts, that year was an unprecedented one. Division One giants were losing left and right, every other division a tight race for the play-offs. And Division Two saw its fair share of surprises. Sweetwater and Perryton and Mexia, all making their cases for State after getting shut out of the play-offs for nearly a decade.

The biggest shock, though, were the Mustangs from Steinbeck, the formerly underwhelming retirement project of Jim Salley. They dominated their division, wiping the floor with their opponents with the help of Derek Johnson's offense, starring running back Trey Maxwell and surprise El Paso acquisition, quarterback Miguel Martinez. The whole operation was spearheaded by longtime defensive coordinator turned head coach, Steve Quinn.

"Sure, in some places life is bigger than football," the coach told reporters. "But in Texas, football is bigger than life."

21

In Emmy's sorority, there had been a great schism: the conservative Baptists who partied, and the conservative Baptists who judged the partiers. *Partied*, Emmy would later learn, was not quite the right word for what they did. They had a few drinks at someone's apartment (usually an almost-undrinkable, cheap, light beer) and then—if they weren't yet twenty-one—went on to either the backyard of a fraternity house or, if they were legal, a shitty, sticky Irish pub called Burly Murphy's, where they served two-dollar shots of Jameson and free Irish car bombs for the ladies (who never wanted them) after eleven. Emmy got dared to drink the car bomb once after having four margaritas with dinner at El Fuego, and then, after finishing it (she never turned down a dare when she'd had tequila) promptly sprinted to the bar's back patio, leaned over the railing, and vomited everywhere. The next morning, hungover, in desperate need of food, Emmy went to the greasy burger shack down the street from her condo and ran into a group of Theta Omegas who fell on the judging side of drinking. They were in their church clothes and insisted on sitting with Emmy while she waited for her to-go order, talking in almost violently high-pitched, loud voices about the sermon they'd heard that morning, which had, of course, been about the value of temperance.

She didn't miss the lectures, but Emmy did miss the wildness of it. It felt distinctly college, the random nights, the parties, the bars. With her graduation coming up in May, she knew the months left for recklessness were ticking down, and she wanted to take advantage of them.

Emmy couldn't go to any of the old spots, not since MK and the girls had effectively ostracized her from them, but she did crave something. Some kind of group. So she tried to socially merge the only three people who would talk with her. Jacob, Sara, and, of course, Cameron.

It had been difficult for Emmy to get Cameron and Sara together. When Emmy first told Cameron about Sara's story— being closeted, having a pastor father—Cameron had been delighted. Not at the pain she'd experienced, of course, but at the prospect of someone in her department who could really understand the research work she was doing. The English department at Walker was one of the more progressive ones on campus, but it was still West Texas, and some of the older, tenured professors (mostly the men) were downright appalled at Cameron's desire to study texts through the critical lens of queer theory. Two of the professors, during two separate semesters, had asked Cameron to meet them during their office hours, closing the door behind her as she entered, making her sit for half an hour while they lectured her on the proper use of research, on which topics were *appropriate* and which were an *abominable* waste of time. Cameron brushed them off. She had expected as much when she chose a school like Walker. But to know there was someone in her department who could not only support her work (which several of the professors did with great enthusiasm) but truly grasp its significance was momentarily thrilling to Cameron.

She asked Emmy to set up a time for them to all get together, and Emmy, jumping at the opportunity to create a small community during her final year at Walker, told Cameron that she and Sara had made plans to meet up that next weekend and that Cameron should join them.

Cameron's elation deflated. The spark of excitement that had been building in her eyes dimmed, and a dark sort of suspicion replaced it.

"You know you shouldn't hang out with other people when I'm not there," Cameron said. "That's not how relationships work, Emmy. We're supposed to do everything together."

And Emmy, who had never been in a relationship before, profusely apologized for the misstep, promising her it would never happen again.

But by coincidence, that Sunday Emmy went into the Grizzly to watch the Cowboys play and ran into Sara, who was also there for the game. Both Emmy and Sara had grown up with—and been unable to rid themselves of—an unshaking devotion to the Dallas Cowboys. Sara had grown up in the age of glory. The tail end of Tom Landry's reign, the beginning of Jimmy Johnson's. Troy Aikman and Emmitt Smith and Michael Irvin. Subpar seasons and Super Bowls and so many blown plays it was a miracle she could still watch the games with any kind of faith.

So on that Sunday, they sat together at the bar, and Emmy texted Cameron, asking her to join them, hoping that they could all have a friendship, form some kind of core group Emmy could hold on to in that last year of undergrad.

But, as soon as Cameron walked in, Emmy knew that would never be possible.

It was an unfortunate moment. Just bad timing. The Grizzly kept the television volume blaring during game days, and Sara had to lean in to catch something Emmy said. In the process, she slid slightly out of her stool, falling into Emmy's shoulder, her cheek buried there for less than a second, but long enough for Cameron, who had walked in at that exact moment, to see.

She stood dumbstruck in the doorway, staring at Emmy, who, after spotting Cameron, quickly leaned as far away from Sara as she could.

"Cameron!" Sara said enthusiastically, turning around to see who Emmy was looking at. "Pull up a stool. The game just started."

"Dr. Cunningham," Cameron said, nodding. She turned toward Emmy, pointing at the screen. "You still watch this stuff?"

"How's your thesis coming along?" Sara asked as Cameron sat down to Emmy's right. "We haven't gotten a chance to talk about it since the seminar last year."

"It's fine," Cameron said without looking at her.

"We missed you at Dr. Williams's shindig last night," Sara said, trying again, her earnestness almost unbearable in the face of Cameron's indifference. "He brought out the good scotch, and your cohort had no problem drinking half the bottle."

"Emmy," Cameron said, as if Sara hadn't spoken to her. "How much longer is the game?"

"Couple hours," Emmy said, glancing at the time remaining in the second quarter. "It's only just getting going."

"God," Cameron said, pulling out her phone and scrolling.

They sat at the bar in a line of silence. Sara kept opening her mouth to say something, then stopped herself. Emmy had never seen Cameron so icy, and she wasn't sure how to respond. Cameron kept checking her phone, shooting narrow-eyed glances at Emmy, then Sara, then the television screen, rolling her eyes every time someone made a tackle.

"Fuck football. This is a waste of time," Cameron said, bursting out of her barstool after only five minutes. "You coming, Emmy?"

"It's only the second quarter," Emmy said, clutching her still-full pint. "I'll see you at home. Maybe you can make some good headway on that paper you've got to turn in this week. You know, without me bothering you."

"Oh!" Sara said, her face lighting up, desperate for connection. "Is this the one for Dr. Burns's postmodern class? Have you looked into Anzaldúa? Her work would add so much to your thesis project."

"I've already got that covered, Dr. Cunningham," Cameron said, barely looking at Sara. "And, Emmy, you never bother me. I work better with you around."

It was an awkward moment. Emmy pulled at her thumbs, trying to bridge the gap between Cameron's rudeness and Sara's eagerness to connect. She knew she needed to say something, but she couldn't find the words, so she picked up her pint and chugged, staring at the ceiling, hoping the tension would resolve itself once she put the glass down.

It did not.

"Well," Cameron said, her lips a taut line, "if I can't convince you to come, can you at least pick up dinner on your way home?"

"Sure," Emmy said, relieved the moment had passed. "I'll pick up a pizza."

Then, Cameron swooped down and kissed Emmy, a big kiss, the kind that should have been housed by four walls, intimate, belonging to only them, not broadcast in public with Joe Buck's play-by-play blaring in the background. It was not sweet or kind or filled with love; it was a territorial move.

It embarrassed Emmy, who pulled away quickly, giving Cameron a quick pat on the shoulder, thankful that Sara was looking away from them, her eyes fixed, unblinking, on the football game, her cheeks slightly pink. She didn't look away until Cameron had left with a self-satisfied smile.

"So," Sara said, finally looking over at Emmy, but barely able to meet her eyes, "things are going well with y'all?"

"Sorry about that. She's not usually—"

"It's fine," Sara said, waving her apology away before cracking her knuckles. "It's like they always say. *If you've got it...*"

After that, Cameron had blatantly resisted any sort of gathering with Sara. Emmy wasn't sure she really wanted them around one another. But her impending graduation date was approaching, and every day that passed reminded her that this was her last chance for freedom before she was tethered to her corporate job in the real world, which she envisioned as a never-ending cycle of long days with short weekends that wouldn't quite replenish the energy required for feeling carefree.

So she barreled ahead in her determined effort to establish some kind of community. And because she didn't want to think about what the real problem was, she convinced herself that the issues with Cameron and Sara were rooted in their number. Three people was a trio, not really a group. It was too small. All they needed was to add one more person, Emmy thought, and the tension would dissolve.

On weekends, Jacob was either in Dallas visiting Kiera or working at the Grizzly. But on one Friday in mid-October, Kiera had clinicals and he was off from work, so Emmy convinced him to come to dinner with them before he met up with his fraternity brothers for cigars.

"Fine," Jacob said. "But only because Cameron's going. Also, you're driving and buying."

Emmy agreed to buy his dinner, but they settled for a rideshare, since Friday nights meant Tex-Mex, and Emmy couldn't say no to a frozen margarita.

Puebla's had been in Walker since Emmy's parents were in college, and they were known for their lime-green walls, mariachi music, enchiladas verdes, and margaritas, which were made with tequila, triple sec, fresh lime juice, and the deadly, secret ingredient, Everclear.

Sara was sitting at the bar, nursing a tequila on the rocks, when Emmy, Jacob, and Cameron walked into the restaurant. Cameron whispered something to Jacob when they saw her, and he cackled, shoved Cameron, and whispered something in response.

"Thanks for meeting here," Sara said when Emmy walked up to her. "All the other places are filled with undergrads. No offense."

"You know," Cameron said, still smiling at the joke Jacob had whispered. "I sometimes forget Emmy's an undergrad, don't you, Dr. Cunningham?"

"She's very mature," Sara said with a strained smile, her eyes narrowed. She flagged down the hostess. "Our table's ready."

"Y'all two go ahead," Jacob said, smirking. "Cameron and I got some, uh, business to attend to at the bar real quick."

"Shots," Emmy explained as she and Sara walked to the table. "Cameron always buys him one at the end of his shift at the Grizzly."

"Hopefully it makes them a little friendlier," Sara said, taking a long, final sip of her tequila and looking back toward the bar.

"They're just—"

"It's okay, Emmy," Sara said, gently grabbing her hand and giving it a reassuring squeeze. "I'm here for you, not them."

It was like that moment at the café, the slight spark of connection. A comfortable warmth that Emmy had felt before, many years ago, flooded through her. She looked from her hand back up to Sara, who dropped it quickly before they sat down at their table, a waiter coming over almost instantly to ask if they wanted one of Puebla's famous frozen margaritas.

"Two," Emmy said, still a little breathless from the moment before. Then, remembering Cameron and Jacob, added, "I mean four."

Jacob and Cameron were more friendly when they returned to the table, which meant they had both taken two tequila shots each (Patrón, Emmy knew; Cameron never went below top-shelf). But Emmy didn't care. She was just happy to have everyone around her at the same time, sitting at a table, about to eat enchiladas and drink too much tequila, like people were supposed to do in college. She could pretend, for a moment, that nothing had changed.

"Dr. Cunningham," Cameron said after dunking several chips into the queso. "I never thanked you enough for talking Dr. Zonia into letting me do my thesis on…" Cameron's face cracked open into her molten, warm smile "…such unsavory topics. Queer theory's my shit."

"No problem," Sara said, beaming. "Students don't have to sign a statement of faith, so I don't see any reason why their research should be restricted. Though, I assume you're looking elsewhere for PhD programs."

"Just turned in about twenty applications last week," Cameron said. "So competitive, you know, can't take a chance on fate."

"I didn't know you finished them," Emmy said, a little shocked. Cameron had talked about applying to places on the East Coast, and Emmy had tried to convince her to look in Texas—UT, University of Houston, Rice—and she had seemed receptive-enough to the idea. But Emmy wasn't sure if they had made the final cut.

"I got your top choices in there, don't worry, Em," Cameron said, winking at Jacob, who raised his glass to her, then leaned in to ask a question about one of the programs. Emmy couldn't hear the last bit because a roaring plate of sizzling fajitas had just been brought out for the twelve-person party to their right, who let out a raucous, drunken cheer when it was set down in front of them.

"Is there anything more West Texas?" Sara asked, leaning over to Emmy, getting close enough so she could be heard. Emmy felt her breath tickle the back of her neck. Goose bumps rose on her skin.

"No," Emmy answered, trying to shake off the feeling, pointing to the table. The cheering had ceased, and they were all holding hands, their heads bowed, as one of the men stood up, his voice gravelly and deep, leading the group in a presupper prayer.

"Did your mama ever lead a prayer at a church dinner?" Sara asked, taking a long sip of her frozen margarita.

"Of course not," Emmy said, turning from the table to look back at Sara, whose eyes were wide, slightly panicked, from brain freeze after drinking her margarita too quickly. Emmy laughed and said, "Here, do this."

Emmy stuck her thumb underneath the top row of her teeth and pressed them into one another, the surefire cure for ice-cream headache that her father had taught her. Sara looked confused and still in pain, so Emmy grabbed Sara's thumb, brought it up to her mouth, and pressed it up against the bottom of Sara's front teeth. Emmy's hands briefly grazed Sara's lips before she pulled them away, but not before Cameron, who had turned to ask Sara another question, saw.

Emmy expected her to yell. Her face was so warped with shock and rage, her fury seemed inevitable. But when Jacob shoved her shoulder and asked, "What's your deal?" she shook off whatever it was she had felt and turned back to him, all the lightness of before returning in a rush.

Emmy was very careful not to get too near Sara for the rest of the dinner. She didn't want to risk anything that would force her to lose someone, either Cameron or Sara. At first, she thought she had pulled it off. Cameron was perfectly polite, cracking jokes, asking questions, but her smile, Emmy noticed, was strained. It didn't turn up to the right in that carefree grin Emmy loved so much. Her jaw was clenched, and her laugh was forced, harsh, empty.

Sara's rideshare got there first, and she said goodbye to everyone, no hugs, just a small wave before she got in the car. After she had driven away, Cameron looked at Jacob and Emmy and said, "So can we all agree we're never doing that again?"

Jacob laughed and shouted out the affirmative before ducking into his rideshare, eager to meet up with his friends. But Emmy felt a bit crushed. She had wanted, for one moment, to feel as if her life from before could return.

"You're so different from my last ex," Cameron said in bed that night, her voice slightly hoarse, as it always was after she'd had too much tequila.

The space between consciousness and sleep opened Cameron up like nothing else. Emmy would run her hands through her hair while she talked about everything, her eyes closed, the words slowly dying down to a whisper, then silence, as she fell asleep midsentence.

"She was so insatiable, unpredictable," Cameron mumbled, wrapping her leg around Emmy's. "You're the opposite."

"So," Emmy said, brushing a strand of hair off her forehead, "satiable?"

"She came from out of nowhere, crashed into my life. You know how that feels?"

"I've got a good idea, yeah."

"And she just—" Cameron broke off. Emmy thought she might have fallen asleep, but her breath was shallow, almost held.

"Why did y'all break up?" Emmy asked in a whisper. Cameron rarely talked about the last girl she dated, the only one who had broken her heart.

"Cheated on me," she said, sighing. "With her best friend. So cliché."

"I'm sorry."

"Brought me here," she said, burying her face in Emmy's shoulder. "To the middle of nowhere, to you."

"I thought the scholarship did that."

"Decision was solidified by heartbreak, let's just say that."

She rolled over on her back, her dark brows coming together, her eyes still closed. Emmy put her hand over Cameron's heart.

"Does it still hurt?" Emmy asked.

She opened her eyes. Stared at the ceiling. Then smiled, kissed Emmy's hand. Turned toward her.

"You'd never do that to me," Cameron said.

"Of course not," Emmy said, turning on her side so that their foreheads pressed against one another. "Besides, the only people I talk to are you, Jacob, and Sara. And you're the only one of them I'd sleep with."

"Sara," Cameron asked, her eyes narrowing.

"Dr. Cunningham."

"Yeah, I know."

"My dad always used to say that—"

"Your dad is an asshole."

"I know, but he used to say—"

"How often are you alone with Dr. Cunningham?"

"Sara," Emmy corrected her. "Whenever you don't want to come watch the Cowboys with me. You know we walk to the Grizzly together to watch the games. But Jacob's always there on Sundays, working."

"Right," Cameron said, closing her eyes, turning onto her back, laughing a little. "Jacob. Duh. I don't know why..."

"Sara's been through a lot," Emmy said, trying to reassure her, which felt bizarre. She never thought that was something she would have to do with Cameron.

"I know, you told me," she said, exhaling slowly, centering herself. "You're a good friend."

"You can try and watch the game with us again."

"I'd rather die," she said, wrapping her arms around Emmy's waist and resting her head on Emmy's chest.

"Emmy," she whispered after a long while, her breathing slow and measured, almost drifting into sleep. "I'm glad that I have you. That you're all mine."

Emmy looked down at her, savoring the vision, the unprecedented access. Olive skin, smooth, except for the scar on the right side of her forehead, the one that, when she was a kid, made her believe that she was secretly an orphan with magical powers, which would be explained once she turned eleven. Her dark brows were unplucked and wild, with a line of smudged mascara smeared in the middle of them. Her lips, like a pale heart, were parted in sleep as her exhales whistled softly between her teeth.

That Emmy marveled at Cameron was not new. But the slight twinge of discomfort she felt in that moment *was*. It rose up that night for the first time, seeing Cameron so close, holding Emmy so tightly.

Her suspicion scared Emmy. The faintest sliver of trust felt stripped away in that moment, replaced with possession, control.

It would pass. That's what Emmy told herself. That she could breathe through it. Pretend the closeness that she craved came without consequence. That she could find freedom in the bounds of Cameron's control.

22

October melted into November with an unnerving ease. It was timeless in the way that happiness always was for Emmy: the days were short, but the hours were long, spent between Cameron and Sara, settled within herself for the first time in her life.

Emmy tried hard not to think about the holidays coming up, what they would look like without her family. Cameron told her not to worry about it. They would spend them together and be happy. Whenever Emmy tried to talk about her parents, Cameron would interrupt her with a kiss and tell Emmy to forget about them.

But Emmy couldn't. And she needed to talk to someone about it. So, when they walked to the Grizzly to catch a Cowboys game, Emmy talked to Sara about everything Cameron didn't want to hear. In that way, they built a closeness, an intimacy Emmy hadn't expected to find outside of Cameron. There was trust between them. They could talk about anything.

"Have you ever been in love?" Sara asked Emmy as they

walked to the bar on a mild November afternoon, two weeks before Thanksgiving.

"Now," Emmy said, kicking a rock off the sidewalk. It rolled into the grass and got lost among the fallen leaves.

"I meant before," she said. "*Had* you ever been in love?"

"Sort of," Emmy said, tracing her jaw with her thumb. "I'm not sure you'd call it love, though."

She told her about Michaela Sherman and the months they had spent together in high school, how it all ended in the back of the pickup truck, with a scream and a prayer. Sara listened with great attention, letting out a low *hmmm* every so often, never interrupting or interjecting, just nodding slightly, her eyebrows knitted together in concentration, much in the same way that Michaela had looked as she listened to Emmy back in high school.

Sara had a serious face. Emmy thought it would change as she got to know her, soften with familiarity. But it stayed the same. It wasn't unkind, but it did demand distance. Severe cheekbones, soft jawline, slightly pointed chin, a scar underneath her bottom lip from a long-gone labret piercing. Her eyebrows were dark and groomed and always coming together, creating a permanent line in between them. Her short, dark hair was soft and sheer and perfectly swept across her forehead. Everything about her was in such contrast with Cameron, whose hair was always pulled up in a messy bun with flyaways framing her face like a halo, who looked for any excuse in a conversation to laugh, smile, let out some of the exuberance within her that seemed to bubble over and spread to whoever she was with, as if through osmosis.

"It's weird," Emmy said, trying to stop herself from comparing the two of them, a habit she had picked up since she started spending more time with Sara. "I can still remember how it felt with Michaela. Her sitting next to me at high school football games, hanging onto me. Noticing me."

"You're allowed to miss her, you know," Sara said, checking

the slim silver watch on her wrist. "We gotta pick up the pace. Kickoff's in ten."

"I have Cameron now," Emmy said. "It shouldn't even matter. Maybe I'm broken."

"Memory doesn't make you broken," she said.

"It doesn't make me whole, either."

"*Healed* and *whole* are two different things," Sara said as they turned the corner, walking up to the Grizzly. "Now stop being such a sad sack. It's bad luck."

The door was a heavy, solid wood that Emmy had to push in with her shoulder. Jacob said that the man who owned the bar liked it that way, hard to open. Kept the place filled with regulars and scared off most of the undergrads, kids with fake IDs who never knew what to order except PBRs and shots of cheap whiskey.

When Emmy finally pushed through the door, she was met with the familiar, artificial glow of neon signs with logos for Bud Light and Miller Lite and Coors Light. The whole place smelled like stale beer and cigarette smoke, and her shoes stuck to the floor as she made her way over to the bar.

"Cameron mad you're here?" Sara asked as they settled into the two stools at the end of the bar, their lucky seats on game days.

"More mad that football exists," Emmy said, flagging Jacob down for two pints.

"Well, let's hope she didn't curse us," Sara said, crossing her arms across her chest, watching the kickoff. "We need this one."

"All right, ladies," Jacob said, turning his Cowboys hat around backward as he pushed their pints in front of them. He turned toward the screen, leaning back on the bar. "We gonna win this one? Or the Birds gonna get us again?"

"Never count out the 'Boys," Sara said, taking an enormous swig of her beer as the opening kickoff sailed through the end zone for a touchback.

"Hope you're right, Doctor," Jacob said, giving Emmy a fist

bump before hustling down to the other end of the bar to grab another round for the PhD students in the corner.

"Is your dad more of a Jimmy Johnson or Tom Landry kind of coach?" Sara asked, keeping her eyes on the game.

"A little mix," Emmy said, smiling, remembering the Tom Landry poster he kept framed in the spare bedroom at his house, the one he always said he'd hang in his office if he ever got the head-coaching gig. She wondered, briefly, if it was there now.

Sara liked to hear about Steve. Just the football facts, for the most part. When Jacob was working, he'd throw in old stories about his dad and Steve, the old days when they were assistants on offense and defense. How their families would get together afterward, cook up something on the grill in one of their back-yards. Jacob and Emmy would play, running around the freshly cut grass in their bare feet, the ground getting harder as winter approached, shocking them numb as they hit the ground after making their various diving catches in their invisible end zones.

When Emmy mentioned her dad to Cameron, she just rolled her eyes, gave Emmy's arm a little squeeze, and said, *You're safe from that motherfucker now.*

What Cameron didn't seem to understand, though, was that it was a form of grief, Emmy losing him like this. She tried to explain it to Cameron, the complexities and the contradictions of her family and faith. She listened. But she always ended up saying some version of "Every day I'm with you, I'm more and more grateful that I didn't grow up in Texas."

Comfort can't be given without empathy. And that wasn't something Cameron seemed capable of when it came to Emmy's home, her family.

But Sara was born into it. The contradictions. They were folded into her life, her history. With her, Emmy didn't have to defend or explain. She could just talk. Laugh. Remember.

Sara also taught Emmy about the varying facets of her beliefs. It turned out that she'd never given up astrology after she broke it off with her butch Gemini. She still kept her eyes on the stars, on the movements of the various constellations. Found purpose and hope tucked away in the sky, where no one could take it away from her.

"Sara says I'm a Leo sun with a Gemini moon," Emmy told Cameron one Sunday evening at their favorite taco truck in town.

"Figures she would like astrology," Cameron said, dunking her taco al pastor into a bowl of tomatillo salsa. "Lonely ladies always look to the stars for meaning."

"What are you?" Emmy asked, ignoring her comment, trying, as always, to forge some kind of connection between Cameron and Sara.

"Hungry," she said, taking the rest of Emmy's uneaten taco and wolfing it down in two bites.

"Goddammit," Sara said, slamming her fist down on the sticky, wooden bar as the referee blew the final whistle. The game was a nail-biter. Momentum shifted back and forth the whole game, the Cowboys going up by three every other quarter, until finally, in the last five minutes, they put together a four-minute ninety-nine-yard drive that ended with the quarterback diving headfirst into the end zone for a touchdown. It looked like the Cowboys were going to close it out, but the Eagles managed to make their way down the field, scoring a touchdown in the game's final seconds.

"We'll get 'em next time," Jacob said, shaking his head, changing the channel to the other game that was still going on.

"You heading out?" Emmy asked Sara, who was putting on her jacket and grabbing her purse.

"Gotta grade," Sara said as she drained her beer. She wiped her mouth with the back of her hand. "By the way, full moon in Aries tonight."

"Am I gonna to turn into some kind of pumpkin or something at midnight?" Emmy asked.

"Transformation is a component, yes," she said, standing up after slapping cash down on the bar.

"If you could put in a good word with the stars," Emmy said, tugging on Sara's jacket in a faux plea of earnestness, "I'd love to wake up tomorrow and be able to speak French."

"*Je verrai ce que je peux faire,*" Sara said as she pushed her stool into the bar, smirking when she saw Emmy's jaw dropped in surprise.

"Are you fluent?" Emmy asked.

"*Oui.*"

"Since when does a girl from the Panhandle know French?" Emmy asked.

"*Violon d'Ingres,*" Sara said, winking. "*Au revoir,* Emilia."

Emmy gawked at her as she walked out of the bar and pushed the door open in a dramatic flourish, disappearing into the evening.

"She's really something, huh?" Emmy asked Jacob when she swiveled forward on her stool.

"You sure got a type," Jacob said, nodding, collecting the cash and placing it in the register. "Never would have guessed."

"What?"

"Older nerds."

"Sara's not a type," Emmy said, feeling her cheeks flush. "She's just a friend."

"Cameron doesn't like her too much," Jacob said, pulling a rag out from under the bar and wiping the counter in small circles. "She gets all tense and weird whenever she's around. Less loose. Less fun."

"Sara's a professor in her department," Emmy said. "Cameron's just being professional."

"Don't lie. You've noticed," Jacob said, pushing back from

the bar, grinning. "You love that attention, two ladies fighting over you."

"No one's fighting," Emmy said, pushing her pint away from her.

"Not even out of the closet six months," Jacob said cackling, "and you're already stuck in a love triangle. Shit, Emmy, never knew you'd have game."

"There's no triangle!" Emmy shouted. She hadn't meant to. The bar got silent as everyone turned to look at her and Jacob before returning to their conversations.

"I'm just messing with you. Calm down," Jacob said, his eyes wide with surprise at her outburst. He looked down at the counter and shook his head, smiling a little bit. "I just thought of something."

"What?"

"You know who'd love Cameron?"

"Who?"

"Steve," he said, slapping the rag over his shoulder and rubbing his chin with the bottom of his palm. "Was thinking about how she stormed out of here that one Sunday. And then it just clicked."

"You realized my dad would like her," Emmy asked slowly, "because she refused to watch a football game?"

"Think about it," Jacob said, taking off his hat and pulling at his curls. "You and she would be posted up in the living room, right? Cowboys on, y'all drinking beer, eating chips. The usual spread. And your dad's talking about the Nickel package and the blitz and all that good stuff, and then out of nowhere, Cameron just starts going *off* about the NFL and brain injuries and how the whole thing is just a colossal waste of time."

Emmy stared at him, mouth agape, waiting for him to go on— because *surely* he must go on. He knew Steve better than that.

"And then," he said, noting her skepticism, always able to read her face better than anyone, "your dad would push back. Argue with her. But not in that mean, stubborn way he gets sometimes. I think he'd love it. The spirit of the argument. The passion. The intelligence!"

"That's so…" Emmy started to dismiss him.

But then she realized, with a gut-punching level of certainty, that he was *right*. And the wave of hope and grief that flooded her nearly took her breath away. The hope for that kind of life for them, that they could have a normal, unassuming Sunday with predictable arguments and comfortable silences, their presence accepted without a second thought, and the grief of knowing that kind of life would not come to them soon, if it could ever come at all.

"All I know," Jacob said when Emmy didn't respond, "is he wouldn't take to the professor that quick. She's too stuffy. And that astrology stuff would drive Steve bonkers."

"True."

"And she doesn't laugh very often," he said, putting his hat back on, flattening out the bill. "You know who laughs all the damn time?"

"I get it," Emmy said, reaching across the bar to give his arm a little shove. "No triangles. I promise."

"Good," he said, pushing himself away from the bar. "First gay setup I do better stick. Or I'll be pissed."

"Shut up," Emmy said, gathering up her backpack.

"What're y'all doing for Thanksgiving, by the way?" Jacob asked before she headed toward the door. "My mama could save you a plate at Thanksgiving if you don't have a place to go. Gonna have that corn bread you love and The Mac—and you know we always smoke that bird."

"Your grandma banned me when I didn't try her sweet potato pie that one year, remember?"

"And don't forget the yams. Auntie Nene still does an impression of you taking your little nibble, asking why it was so sweet, your face all pinched and pale and all. 'That little girl didn't know what the hell was happening in her mouth.' Ha! Always gets a laugh."

"Sounds like a blast," Emmy said, rolling her eyes, remembering the shock of sweetness from the candied yams, maple syrup and brown sugar and the tang of orange coating the tender, baked yam, sliced into thick circles.

"For real though," he said. "You're family. Mama and Dad and me, you know. We love you like that."

"Your grandma would have to ban me all over again if I brought Cameron," Emmy said, letting out a sharp, empty laugh. "Besides, can't imagine my mom would be too pleased with Cora if she found out y'all'd had me over."

"Yeah," he said sighing and shaking his head. "Granny might have a heart attack if y'all came around. Guess you're right."

"We would if we could," Emmy said, putting on her jacket. "We'll probably just eat shitty frozen pizza and watch the game."

"She gonna watch it with you?"

"Says it's her Christmas present to me," Emmy said, looking at her watch and heading toward the door. "See you next week?"

"Be careful walking out there," Jacob shouted from the bar, squinting toward the window. "Kiera said it's supposed to storm tonight. Cold front coming through."

"Can't hold off winter forever, I guess," Emmy said, looking through the door at the dark sky.

When she walked outside, she was slapped in the face by a freezing gust of wind. Leaves rose up and swirled, a minitornado on the cracked sidewalk. Clouds collected, a mass of purple, moving quickly across the sky. The change of weather came from out of nowhere. Emmy picked up her pace as she walked home, the wind whistling through the trees like something haunted. It started to rain, then turned into something more solid, ice swirling and floating in the wind.

Her phone rang. Thinking it was Cameron, she took it out of her pocket to answer. She almost didn't register the name. She had to double-check to make sure it was real, not an illusion, a trick of the light.

The sleet came down faster, getting in her eyes, freezing on her hands. She brought the phone up to her ear. Nearly shouting over the wind, she said, "Mom?"

23

On Thanksgiving morning, Cameron and Emmy were cleaning every inch of the apartment, making sure it was spotless for her mother.

Emmy had been tempted to hang up on her almost as soon as she answered the call outside of the Grizzly. She wanted to punish Lucy for her absence. For not being there when her father had slammed the door in her face. For being right about him. She wanted her to feel that sting of loss, the pain born from absence, a connection severed too soon.

But she also wanted to feel her mother's cheek against hers. Lucy's face would be cooler than Emmy's, it always was, and her mom would check her forehead for a fever before telling her that she had always run hot, that as a baby she had screamed and kicked and sweat until Lucy took off her wool socks. That she was just like her father, hot and impatient and itching to be on the move.

When her mom said she wanted to spend Thanksgiving with

them, Emmy couldn't help but want to watch her move around the kitchen, her hands always busy, chopping or stirring or opening a bottle of wine. Lucy said they could order pizza instead of cook, but Emmy still wanted to see her over the skillet, the crackling of sautéed onions and garlic filling the air with a heavy, sweet smell that always made her mouth water.

If Cameron was surprised at Lucy's desire to meet her, to have Thanksgiving dinner with them in Walker, she didn't show it. When Emmy told her, Cameron took one look around the apartment, smiled, and said, "We have to clean the shit out of this place. It's been a mess since you've gotten here."

Emmy invited Sara, too, because she knew she was staying in town for the holiday to catch up on grading. It was hard to sell to Cameron.

"Remember when Sundays were our days?" Cameron had asked Emmy. "Now you spend them with Sara. And you want her to meet your mom? At the same time as me? Don't you think that's weird, Emmy?"

Emmy brushed her off, reasoning that Sara would be spending Thanksgiving alone if they didn't invite her. But Emmy also had a secret, strategic reason for inviting Sara. She thought they needed a fourth person. A buffer just in case her mom decided to start preaching the Gospel, trying to save Emmy and Cameron as her form of small talk. Emmy knew that Lucy had joined the Methodist church, and they seemed less pushy about those sorts of things. But still. Once an evangelical, always an evangelical.

Sara got to the apartment about an hour before Lucy was set to arrive. She was wearing one of her black pantsuits and had a tote bag filled with bottles of red wine.

"You know," she said, lifting up the bag, "just in case."

The blinds were open, and sunlight streamed through the living room, dust particles dancing in the rays of light. The room was silent except for the quiet click of kitten heels as Sara walked across the room, her hands behind her back like she was at a museum, looking at the various knickknacks on the shelves, the books that were organized by color.

Emmy tried to see the apartment through her eyes. So much of it was Cameron. Her books, her pictures, her collection of old movies, her furniture and television and stereo. Everything that was Emmy's could fit into the old suitcase her dad had lent her before she'd moved into Annie's fully furnished condo her sophomore year.

There was a small part of Emmy in the living room, though. A framed picture she'd taken from her mom's house before her junior year. Emmy, around five or so, grinning in a red Steinbeck High hat, holding onto a football that was almost half her size, out in the yard of her father's house, right by the old magnolia tree by her bedroom window. Sara picked up the frame, clutching it with both her hands, running her thumb along it, her eyes crinkling at their edges as her lips tugged up in a small smile.

"So you've always been cute," Sara said, holding up the frame to compare Emmy with her younger self. "Not fair."

"The Lord hath blessed me," Emmy said, extending her arms and bending down in a performative bow.

Emmy looked back at Cameron, expecting her to laugh, crack a joke. But she stood completely still by the table, a dinner plate in her hand, hovering just above the placemat, staring at Sara.

"You okay?" Emmy asked when Cameron started rubbing the back of her neck in a slow, compulsive rhythm.

"Fine," she said, forcing a smile and putting the plate down. "Just nervous. I'm not great with moms."

They all started getting tense twenty minutes before Lucy's arrival. Cameron kept fidgeting with the table setting. Sara kept asking if she should run out and get more wine. And Emmy kept pacing back and forth in the living room, checking out of the window, convinced her mom would cancel at the last minute, deciding Emmy wasn't worthy of a visit or that it would be too weird meeting Cameron or that it would be too great a betrayal to Steve, reopening the line of communication that he had so definitively slammed shut.

But, at five o'clock exactly, Emmy heard a car door close and the familiar, quick click-clack of her mother's heels on the sidewalk as she made her way to the front door.

Emmy wanted to wait for her to knock. To play it calm and cool. But it was her mom, who she hadn't seen in over half a year, and as soon as she was close enough, Emmy threw open the door and ran into her arms, almost knocking her over in the process.

Lucy was shorter than Emmy by several inches, but Emmy squatted down so that she could bury her face into her mother's chest like she had done as a child, coming home from a long weekend away at church camp. She squeezed her mother as tight as she could, breathing in the warm, overwhelming scent of her perfume, like gardenias in spring, light and sweet and clean.

"Whoa there, Emmylou," Lucy said, extracting her from her chest. She had tears in her eyes. "You can't just barrel into me like a bull. I'm no spring chicken, you know."

"I've *missed* you," Emmy said, her voice cracking, almost unable to believe she was real. Emmy took a moment to look Lucy over, drink in the full picture of her, three-dimensional, no longer warped in the fragmentation of memory.

Lucy had cut her hair short. Long was her signature look, had been since Emmy was born. But now it was bobbed, a sharp line that started at her chin and rose a little behind her head, straight like silk, dark brown, highlighted with caramels and auburns. Her face looked sharper, more angular. Her jawline seemed accentuated, the skin slightly looser around her chin than it had been when she was younger, but it was lineless, soft. The beauty products she'd always spent so much time hunting down seemed to be paying off. Her eyes—*my eyes*, Emmy couldn't help but recognize with delight—dark brown like Tootsie Rolls, were wet with the first wave of tears.

"You look different," Emmy said, still eyeing her new haircut.

"Good different?" Lucy asked, flattening the front of her red velvet dress, the veins in her hands popping out, blue and strong. Just like Emmy's.

"I didn't know your hair could get that short."

"But good," Lucy said, tucking a piece of her hair behind her ear, "right?"

"It's nice. It's very…" *different* Emmy had meant to say before she saw them: dangling from both of her ears were two enormous plastic rainbow earrings.

"What are those?" Emmy asked, trying not to laugh.

"You like them? They're my gay-pride earrings! Found them at Al's Antiques."

"They're…" Emmy started, still trying to keep a straight face. She looked at them again, the ridiculous rainbows hanging from her mother's ears, and was touched by the gesture. "They're perfect," she finally said, giving her another hug. "I love them."

"I *thought* you would!"

"It's good to see you," Emmy said, holding Lucy's shoulders, keeping a tight grip. "You're doing well?"

"Just fine," she said, taking Emmy's hands off her shoulders and holding them in hers. "We got all the time in the world to get you all caught up."

"And Dad?" Emmy asked. "His boys can't seem to lose."

"He's the same as always," Lucy said, looking down at Emmy's hands, holding them in hers, shaking her head. The smile that had been stretched across her face sagged a little. "We all have to live with our choices."

"This isn't a choice, Mom," Emmy said fiercely, ready for a fight.

"I know," she said, cocking her head to the side in confusion, her rainbow earrings banging against her neck with the motion. "I wasn't talking about you."

A breeze from the north picked up, cold and strong. Lucy

shivered a little but otherwise didn't move. Just stood firm on the porch. Looking at Emmy like she had done for so many years before Emmy had left the house to go on trips or back to school. Lucy used to say she was memorizing her, making sure she got every detail in before she went away. She didn't want to forget a thing.

"This isn't easy for me, Emmy," Lucy whispered, looking past her shoulder toward the door where Cameron and Sara were waiting inside to meet her. "But I don't think I'd forgive myself if I spent another second of my life without you in it."

"Maybe it'll get easier with time," Emmy said, slightly stung.

"Everything does, darlin'," she said, giving Emmy a little wink. "All righty, now or never, as they say."

"Mrs. Quinn!" Cameron said as soon as Emmy opened the door. Her hand was extended, her smile wide. "I'm Cameron. It's so nice to meet you."

"Call me Lucy, Cameron," she said, swatting her hand away and going in for the hug. "Thank you for giving my daughter a home."

Emmy didn't know what she'd expected when they hugged. Some cataclysmic, earth-shattering force of energy fracturing the pain of the past year. Or a well of feeling, rising up, unstoppable and strong, confirming that Cameron was *the one*, her destiny, an olive branch from the Almighty to cover the price of what had been lost.

But as she watched Cameron bend down a little to wrap her arms around her mom, who gave her two quick pats on the back before pulling away, Emmy felt nothing except the slight twinge of awkwardness in watching two people trying very hard to be nice.

"And you must be the friend," Lucy said, moving around Cameron to get to Sara, giving her a hug, insisting that Sara call her Lucy, too, doing the dance she'd been trained to do all her life—charm everyone she met, make them feel safe, at home.

After the introductions, Lucy took the glass of wine that Cameron offered her and walked around the apartment. She took her time around the living room, running her fingers over every surface, checking for dust, nodding her head in approval when she found none. Cameron gave Emmy a wink and mouthed, *I told you so*, when Lucy turned toward the window.

"Not much of a view," Lucy said without looking back.

"It's Walker," Emmy said. "Not much to see."

Lucy didn't respond. Just kept staring out into the light, one arm across her chest, using the other to bring her glass up to her lips, taking a long sip of wine. She leaned back on her right leg, tapping out an erratic rhythm with her left foot. Cameron and Sara looked at Emmy, both their eyebrows raised in confusion.

Emmy ignored them. This happened sometimes with her mother when she was overwhelmed. She sank into herself.

It was simple, really, getting her back. Emmy walked toward the stereo. Plugged the auxiliary cord into her phone. Scrolled through her playlist until she found what she was looking for. And pressed Play.

A piano hammered out a bassline. A typewriter came in underneath it. A horn blasted one note. And then, Dolly Parton started to sing.

"You sure you know what you're doin'?" Lucy asked, turning from the window, her foot adjusting its rhythm to match the beat. "You know this is my dancin' song."

"Dare you," Emmy said, holding out her hand.

Emmy didn't know what it was about that year. But for all the moments that made her feel like she was dying, she sure did do a lot of dancing.

Lucy took Emmy's hand, and it was just like they were back in Steinbeck, in her father's living room, the afternoon sun streaming in, the music playing loud, no thought, just the feeling in their feet as the band came in with the chorus. Lucy threw her head back in laughter, and her absurd rainbow earrings went haywire, moving every which way, bouncing off her neck and chin, and Emmy couldn't get over the miracle of her there, reunited after months of rejection.

When Emmy twirled Lucy, she saw Cameron and Sara looking at them, some blend of laughter and horror mixed in both their faces, but when Emmy shrugged at Cameron, they settled on laughter and clapped along with the rhythm, hooting out, never getting in close enough to dance because they both knew that it was a moment just for them, Emmy and her mom.

As the song faded out, Lucy inhaled deeply. She closed her eyes and nodded. Then, as if resolving something in herself, she turned toward Cameron and Sara.

"I hear you're a Cowboys fan," Lucy said, pointing to Sara. Her nails were painted a deep ruby-red.

"Yes, ma'am," Sara said, beaming, the smile immediate, seeming to come from out of nowhere. Emmy had never seen it before. It reminded her of Michaela. That spontaneity, the lightness. Cameron looked from Sara to Emmy, her smile faltering.

"Well, what are we waiting for, Emmylou?" Lucy asked, pointing toward the television. "We gonna just *imagine* the game?"

The Cowboys were winning by a landslide, so they were able to keep their attention on one another, the pizza, and the wine.

Lucy was good with people. Always had been. She knew how to ask the right questions, get people interested in conversations. *All people ever want is to talk about themselves*, she said. *The easiest thing to do is ask.*

And that's exactly what she did with Cameron and Sara. Rapid-fire questions about where they were from, who their parents were, what they did. It turned out that Sara's aunt, from the Panhandle, was in the same amateur bowling league as Lucy's best friend.

"You ever heard of Smooth Sailin' Sally Mills?" Lucy asked,

tapping her nails on her teeth like she did before she delved into a long string of gossip.

"Have I ever!" Sara responded, an eager audience.

"Well, let me tell you about the time..." Lucy began, her wineglass gripped firmly in her hand as she swished it around before diving into her story.

That's all it took for them to collapse into the flow of small-town gossip, making connections in the strangest places. Sara's mom knew Lucy's cousin because they'd gone to summer camp together as girls. Emmy knew Sara's brother because she and his girlfriend had played in a competitive softball league together. It went on like that, as small-town gossip always did, the connections seemingly endless. Lucy was in her element. Nothing could keep her talking like a scandal, though she avoided discussing the scandal of Steinbeck sitting across from her.

"And your parents?" Lucy asked, turning to Cameron after howling at a story Sara told about some mutual friend. "What are they up to?"

"Lawyers," Cameron said before taking a huge gulp of wine, looking from Lucy to Emmy, her eyes open wide with panic. She hated talking about her family.

"Surely they must do more than work," Lucy said, pressing in like she did when someone didn't give her enough information to go on.

"Not really," Cameron said. She grabbed the wine bottle and poured.

"Oh, well, you must miss them, being so far away and all. Especially on the holidays."

"Sure," Cameron said, shooting Emmy a look, trying to get the conversation to stop.

"East Coast folks, Mom," Emmy said, knowing it was safe to blame any social construct Lucy didn't understand on one of the coasts.

"Boston," Cameron cut in before she could ask. "Suburbs."

"Now, tell me," Lucy started, gearing up for her next question, loosened by the wine, pointing between Emmy and Cameron. "Which one is the boy and which one is the girl?"

Sara nearly spit out her wine. Cameron's eyes widened in disbelief, looking between Emmy and, remarkably, Sara, for help.

"God, *Mom*!" Emmy said, her voice rising an octave, extending her vowels so that she sounded distinctly Texan, always a side effect of her indignation.

"Am I not supposed to ask that?" Lucy asked, genuinely confused, her thin eyebrows raised in concern.

"It's okay," Cameron said, her face softening. She had such an easy laugh in situations like that. Always willing to lighten the mood, put everyone at ease. "I'm me, and Emmy's Emmy. That's all."

After that, everyone relaxed, especially Lucy, freed up after making her first mistake. They talked and laughed and drank until Lucy, looking down at her watch, jumped a little at the time. She gave Sara and Cameron hugs and rushed goodbyes and promised to see them around soon, maybe at her place in Steinbeck next time.

Emmy led the way out of the apartment, holding open the door while Lucy fished for her keys in her purse. When they were outside, she cleared her throat.

"So you've thought about what office you'll be in next year? With that company you interned with?" Lucy asked, roping her arm in Emmy's as a northern breeze picked up, the slightest bite of chill cutting through their thin sweaters.

"Was thinking Austin," Emmy said. "Why?"

"May come as a surprise to you," Lucy said, smiling, crow's feet crinkling around her eyes, "but I decided to do it. Move. To Houston, where my friend Jeanie lives, the one who owns that craft shop in the middle of town. Said she could use a little help in the store, if I was ever looking for an excuse to start over new in the big city."

"Oh, Mom," Emmy said, pulling her into a hug. Lucy had been talking for years about leaving Steinbeck, about doing something different with her life. Emmy never thought she'd actually have the courage to do it. "That's amazing."

"And, well, I know you have your own life and your own plans, but you said that company had offices in Houston…"

"I'll have to talk with Cameron," Emmy said, genuinely excited about the idea, thinking she could convince Cameron to look at one of the schools in Houston for her PhD. "But that could be good. To be near you."

"You know I'm not one hundred percent about all of this," Lucy said, looking up at the apartment where Cameron stood, her back facing the window. Emmy could tell from outside she was standing with her arms crossed, probably glaring at Sara, giving her one-word answers. "But she seems good for you."

"She is."

"And your friend, too," she said. "You've crafted a little community here, haven't you? Without us."

"There's always room for you," Emmy said.

"And your father?" Lucy asked, tugging at the ends of her newly cut hair, biting her lower lip. "Do you have any room left for him?"

Emmy opened her mouth to respond and was surprised by the flood of emotion that rushed up in her.

"Always," she said, knowing it to be true. "An abundance."

"Oh, darlin'," Lucy said, pulling her in for a bone-crushing hug. "He'll come around."

As Emmy watched her drive away, she could feel the phantom pressure of her mother's arms around her. Emmy wanted to believe her. That he could change, like Lucy. And the force of that wanting surged so strong through Emmy it felt like hope.

But deep down, she knew something truer. That same sentiment of old. Her father was not a reasonable man. He did not negotiate on matters of faith.

★ ★ ★

"So," Emmy said to Cameron after Sara left. "What'd you think of her?"

"I think she's in love with you."

"My mom?"

"Oh," Cameron said, pausing as she picked up the empty wineglasses from the table. She shook her head a bit, as if suddenly coming out of a deep dream. "She was great. Less weird than I thought she'd be."

Emmy waited for more, but Cameron moved into the kitchen without expanding.

Emmy wasn't sure what she wanted from Cameron. Probably everything. Some balm or antidote to heal her wounds, cut the poison out of her. To make her unafraid like Cameron. Invincible like Cameron. Unflinching like Cameron, who never needed anything. She didn't miss anyone. She took life in stride. When the world was an ocean of fear, she'd managed to maintain some sense of buoyancy. And Emmy wanted to learn how to keep herself afloat.

"You gotta love someone strong, Emmylou," Steve had said to her one night when they were looking up at the stars. "Like the Big Dipper there. You see those three stars at the top there? The handle? They're anchored by the other four stars, the bowl. You shoot out like the handle, with all your daydreams. You need someone to hold you down. Keep you from floating too far off in space."

"I wish you could have met my dad, too," Emmy said, following her into the kitchen with the rest of the dishes. "I think y'all'd get along."

"How'd we end up using so many plates for pizza?"

"He's not all football, you know."

"Is it weird that we didn't serve pie on Thanksgiving?"

"Sort of," Emmy said, shrugging. "But not really. Pizza pie instead."

"I don't see why you're so willing to forgive him."

"Who?"

"Your dad."

"He's my family."

"*I'm* your family."

"You're my girlfriend."

"Can't that be the same thing?"

"It's different."

"How?"

"My mom was nice," Emmy said, walking toward the kitchen, pouring herself another glass of wine. "She liked you."

"I gave you a home."

"My dad would like you, too, if he ever comes around, was all I was saying."

"What else is family? If not a home?"

"It's just an adjustment for him, you know? All of this."

"Love always adjusts," Cameron said, looking down at her feet. "Is Sara family?"

"What?"

"She knew half of your mom's friends," she said, cracking her knuckles.

"My mom knows half of Texas."

"Why was she here?"

"I told you," Emmy said. "She didn't have anywhere to go." Emmy paused, then told her the truth. "Also. To help. With my mom. With the awkwardness."

"You think I'm awkward."

"That's not what I meant."

"Or that your mom wouldn't like me."

"I think it's a *good thing* that I've managed to make one friend here despite all of this," Emmy said, gesturing between the two of them.

"*Friend,*" Cameron scoffed. "You're not stupid, Emmy. You've never been stupid. Don't start now."

"Look," Emmy said slowly, setting her wineglass down on the dining-room table. "I didn't mean to get us into all of this. All I was trying to say was that I think you'd get along well with my dad."

"Enough with your fucking dad, Emmy!" Cameron snapped, balling up her fists and shutting her eyes. "He's a conservative asshole. He chose a *game* over his *daughter*."

"It's not that simple."

"Then, break it down for me."

"It's hard to understand if you're not from here," Emmy said. "What it's like. To be steeped in his kind of belief."

"Oh, but Sara knows, doesn't she? Texas Panhandle. Conversion therapy. She just *gets* all those broken parts of you, doesn't she?"

"Stop," Emmy said. "Just calm down."

"Why is a thirty-three-year-old woman hanging out with a twenty-two-year-old undergrad, anyway?"

"She says I'm mature for my age."

"God, I can smell the horseshit from here."

"Okay," Emmy said, putting up her hands in surrender. She could feel Cameron's steam building and knew better than to be on the opposing side of her once she got started. "What do you want me to do?"

It was a strange moment. Cameron's face, normally so flushed with color, went pale. She walked in front of the lamp, holding her head in her hands like she did when she was trying to focus. Her whole body was set in silhouette. An eclipse. Emmy wondered, briefly, if she would go blind looking at her.

"Emmy," Cameron said, her voice cracking as she stepped out from the light. "Please, understand."

Emmy hadn't expected to fall in love with so much of Cameron. The little parts. The way she looked around a room before she entered it, trying to see if she knew anyone before they saw her—"Never know when you'll have to turn it on," she whispered when Emmy asked about it, "the dazzle." The way she managed to say *ostensibly* in almost every conversation. The baby hair that curled behind her ear when her hair was tied up. How her hair was always tied up. How she tried to tie Emmy up one time in bed and got so worried that she'd hurt her that she spent the fifteen minutes after her hands were free kissing the inside of her wrists and putting them up to her ear so that she could hear her pulse. "Just checking," she'd said.

When Emmy looked at her, she saw lifetimes in her eyes. All the worlds they could build together. A family. Careers. Visits with her mom, a bridge to her past, and trips all around the world to all the places Emmy had only dreamed of seeing when she learned about them in the back of her history classrooms, the barred windows letting in so little light from outside, where the miles and miles of brown, dead, beautiful West Texas seemed to stretch on until the ends of the earth.

Sara had helped Emmy heal, she couldn't deny that. But Cameron was her future. Her present. The justification of everything that had happened in her past. Without her, Emmy felt she had no one.

"Emmy," Cameron breathed. "Please."

Emmy wanted to keep Sara in her life. But she *needed* Cameron. And if it came down to a choice... Well, there never really was one to begin with.

24

"She doesn't want me to see you anymore," Emmy said, watching her breath roll out in front of her as she spoke. It was an overcast day, chilly enough for sweaters and scarves. Winter was rolling in quick. It was early evening, but the light was already starting to fade fast from the sky. Shorter days, longer nights. The leaves were falling from the trees, littering the ground, crunching underneath their feet as they walked.

"I wondered when this would happen," Sara said, blowing into her fist to warm it up. "Should have expected as much."

"She doesn't understand."

"What?"

"How you help me."

"Help?"

They stopped at a bench and sat down to watch the sunset.

"It's just," Emmy said, letting the frustration tumble out, "she doesn't get it. Texas. It's not even that. You can't understand a whole place if you've only seen a slice of it for less than two years. So I get it. But…"

"But what?" Sara asked, leaning forward on the bench, barely breathing, not blinking, her eyes locked on Emmy's. Sara's were a different color, but the same size and shape, Emmy realized for the first time, as Michaela Sherman's.

"But," Emmy said, trying to shake away their resemblance and the slight twinge of desire that sparked once she'd noticed it, "sometimes I think it's more than Texas. It's me. She doesn't get something…fundamental? Is that the right word?"

"It could be," she said, still unblinking. "If it's some core part of you."

"*Fundamental*, then," Emmy said, nodding. "She doesn't get something fundamental about me."

"First loves don't have to be forever loves."

"And sometimes I wonder if she even tries to understand it, where I've come from."

"But what do I know about love?" Sara asked.

"Or even my dad. And all I've been through with that. She just keeps saying *Fuck him*. Like that will solve everything."

"I've never really been in love."

"But *you* understand me," Emmy said, turning toward her, as if realizing it for the first time.

"I do?"

"Because you understand this place."

"I do."

"And you know what it's like. To love a place that hates you."

"Just a part of you."

"Right. But you see, don't you?"

"I see you, Emmy," Sara said, meeting Emmy's eyes so intensely that she had to look away, up toward Sara's forehead. Her hair was parted to the left, a straight line sprinkled with strands of silver, reminding Emmy of their age gap, of all the years she'd lived before she'd met Emmy.

The air was cold. Emmy shivered in the darkness, no longer protected by the warmth of the sun. Sara scooted closer to her. Their thighs pressed against one another's. Emmy's heart started racing. But it wasn't like with Cameron or Michaela, the pounding in her chest going so quickly it muted her senses, blurred vision, a deafening thrum in her ears. It was more subtle, manageable. It was strange to notice. The different decibels of desire.

Sara brushed her hand against Emmy's.

Emmy could have pulled it away.

Sara moved closer.

Emmy could have stood up.

Sara leaned in.

Emmy could have turned.

But she stayed. Frozen.

Hand on Emmy's thigh. Lightest brush of lips. Did Emmy kiss back? So short, sweet, delicate, it almost seemed innocent.

"Oh," Emmy said, pulling away.

It was an ethereal sort of silence. Not quite real. A kind of limbo.

"I had to," Sara said finally, her face red, eyes wide. "Try."

Her head was tilted to the left, waiting for Emmy to speak. Hanging between the balance of what she'd done and the aftermath. It made her look so young, the hope in her eyes: blue like a deep sea, dark bags underneath them, purple half-moons of exhaustion. Emmy wondered when she had kissed someone last.

"Your job," Emmy said, remembering, not quite sure what to say.

What Emmy wanted to tell her: get out of Walker and every place like it that had forced her to contort and shrink herself in order to fit in. She wanted to tell her to find someplace new, with room for her to grow and stretch and fall in love without fear of consequence. She wanted to say something that mattered, that made a difference. And there was also the smallest part of

Emmy that wanted to be that person for her. The one who could save her. Who could change everything.

But they had come to each other too late. Emmy was already in love. And Emmy knew there was no such thing as destiny. Only choice and timing, the good and bad.

Veins popped out of Sara's long neck. Half her face was cast in shadow, the other bathed in the waning light of the sun. It washed out the blue of her wide eyes, leaving only the gray.

"I keep losing people," Emmy said, looking away from her toward the windmills, which were slowly turning out on the horizon.

"I can't keep you," Sara said, rubbing her temples with both hands. "Not like this."

"We can help you find someone else."

"Emmy..."

"Cameron can invite people from Boston."

"Emmy." Sara took her hand and squeezed it twice. The calluses at the edge of her palm scratched against Emmy's. She shut her eyes tight as she shook her head, and Emmy understood.

It was odd seeing it in someone else. Unrequited affection. Emmy wondered how often Sara had looked out toward the world like that. How often she'd wanted what she could never have. Her face was calm, almost expressionless. It must have taken practice, maintaining such composure in the face of rejection.

Before Emmy could say anything else, Sara stood up. Brushed the leaves off her finely pressed slacks. Took a deep breath in. And walked away.

As Emmy watched her disappear into the darkness, she felt something small inside of her crack.

As soon as Emmy got home, she told Cameron about the kiss. Cameron laughed at first. Then, realizing she was serious, collapsed on the couch, her head cradled in her hands. It seemed like it should have been a moment of clarity, this reckoning. But it all whirled past Emmy in a blur.

There were a lot of words, some whispered, some screamed so close to Emmy's face that little flecks of spit flew all over it. Words like *bitch* and *dumbass* and *how dare you*. The truths Emmy couldn't deny: *I gave you a home* and *I warned you about her* and *You have no one else without me.*

"Fuck, Emilia," Cameron said, using her full name for the first time. "I asked you to do *one thing*."

"I don't know what happened," Emmy said, fumbling. "I was talking to her about you—"

"About *me*?"

"And she just sort of leaned in—"

"Why are you talking about me to someone else?"

"And it all happened so fast that I—"

"Do you want to fuck her?"

"I... What?" Emmy asked, taken aback. Something had come over Cameron. The shadow Emmy had seen before, after Thanksgiving. All the lightness gone in a flash, an instant. Because of Emmy. What she'd done.

"Answer my question."

Emmy thought about how the people who she loved were able to love Cameron. How her mom and Jacob had embraced her, accepted her, and delighted in their connection. For so many years, that had seemed like a pipe dream, that she might be able to love someone and have that love accepted and encouraged by the people closest to her.

Emmy remembered the loneliness of those years. How, for so long, she had believed that was her lot in life. To always love and never feel it returned. Emmy feared, more than anything, the replication of that, the isolation, the despair.

"It's you," Emmy said, knowing that it was true but wishing love could, for once, go without sacrifice. "But you have to know. I'm not your ex. I'm not that girl."

"Prove it to me," Cameron said, grabbing her hand, pulling her into their room.

Emmy wanted to show Cameron the depths of her love. That she wouldn't let her slip away. That she would never choose someone else because there was no one else but her. Emmy was an island; Cameron was the ocean that surrounded her.

Emmy let Cameron lead her into the bedroom. She turned off the lights.

When Cameron was inside of her, Emmy looked up. Eyes shut, hips thrusting, hand between her thighs; Cameron knew her body well enough to work it with limited senses: just touch and taste and sound.

With her eyes still closed, Cameron buried her face in Emmy's neck with so much force it nearly took her breath away. Filled with desperation. Like she was trying to disappear into her.

25

STEVE

Steve was always a little afraid of greatness. He didn't quite trust it. It seemed to him that anyone who got remembered as one of the greats had to lose something. A big sort of something. Hamilton lost his mother, then his son, too young. Grant resigned from the military and failed for a decade before he became Lieutenant General. Reagan tore down the Wall and then lost his memory.

Steve believed greatness and sacrifice went hand in hand. The road to the top, he knew, was paved in the ashes of what was lost. Steve had never liked losing. But that first season as head coach, it seemed like everything he had ever loved was taken from him.

So Steve was left with nothing. And then he became great.

That season, the Steinbeck 'Stangs were an unstoppable force of will. In the papers, they were called "The Quinn Machine," but Steve knew that wasn't right. They were no machine. They were fully human. Made enough mistakes each game to prove it. But the guys had heart, and they showed up to practice every single week ready to get better. Ready to fight.

Steve made a deal with the guys at the beginning of the season. For every game they won, he'd take the number of points they got on offense and do that many push-ups in the film room at practice on Saturday mornings. He got the idea after their first game against Granary High, when Johnson had Miguel and Trey pull back on the offense after they were up by twenty. Steve plopped down right in front of them during the film session that next morning, cranking out twenty quick push-ups.

"You wanna see me do more?" Steve asked the guys, who had their phones out, filming him do that first twenty.

"Hell yeah!" they screamed back.

"Then, torch up the scoreboard every game, never take your foot off the gas, and see if you can make me sweat," Steve said, bouncing to his feet like a much younger man, the stabbing pain in his knees telling him otherwise. "Only way to get the attention of teams in Texas is to obliterate everyone we leave behind."

"You countin' up there, Coach?" Trey said after he scored his fourth touchdown late in the fourth quarter of their first district game.

"Forty-three ain't nothing. You boys won't even see me sweat," Steve said, slapping Trey's hand as the player danced by, throwing his head back in laughter, consumed with the joy of a landslide victory.

Steve started growing out his beard, too, when they won their third game in a row, refusing to shave until they lost. The guys loved it. They called him Coach Claus because his stubble had thickened to a bushy white beard as time went on.

The team let the wave take them—that focus, joy, ambition. Everyone's obsession was one common goal: stay undefeated to take the State Championship home to Steinbeck for the first time in history.

They had a few close games that season, but that's when Miguel shone. He stayed calm in the pocket. Never panicked. Always managed to read the defense. Knew when to pitch the ball to Trey when they ran the option. Learned to trust all his receivers so he always had options. Even Little Williams, who moved to strong safety and tight end after Miguel took his starting position, worked with Miguel during practice, even staying late so he could get the timing of the slant route perfect.

They were more than a team. They were a band of brothers. Every game was a battle they had to win. They played every game like their backs were against the wall, scrappy and quick, never willing to back down from anyone, no matter who they were, how they'd played against them in the past.

Every season before had been the foundation for what they were able to finally achieve when they had all the pieces in place: perfection.

Steve's life bled into the field, every ounce of his attention on the game, every interaction centered on the season: how they were doing, what he thought about the upcoming game, if he hadn't considered this or that play on defense. People were always trying to get a piece of his mind, figure out what he had planned next, see if he had what it took to sustain the team, get them to where they needed to be.

For Steve, time was a blur of all the practices and games and film breakdowns; the static sounds of play calls shouted through headsets by the staff at the top of the press box, seeing something he couldn't; the countless interview questions that all effectively asked the same thing: *Do y'all have what it takes to make it to State?*

The cool came. Chilly games on Friday nights where Steve's screams on the field came out in great gusts of vapor. The harvest moon rose over the visitors' side, the width of it almost half the size of the stands. Like another planet coming in too close, too fast. A great orb of fire.

Kids dressed up for the game on Halloween. Most went as Miguel and Trey, but a couple had their video-game headsets and khaki pants and red polo shirts with a whistle tucked underneath it. A couple dozen Coach Quinns running through the stands.

Thanksgiving came and went. Steve ate with the Holcombs, who also invited Jan Oleander and her sons, and they talked about football and the church and avoided any mention of Emmy, everyone going to great lengths to change the subject when anyone mentioned daughters or scandals or kids who hadn't turned out quite right.

The season consumed Steve. He watched film when he got home every night. Made notes on Miguel's drop back, Trey's ball protection, Big Williams's bull rush. There was always something to fix, one more adjustment to be made. Never knew which one could be the difference.

Emmy used to warn Steve about her friends' dads who got lost in their work. Said even Bob Sherman got sucked into preaching so much he barely saw his daughter during his heyday. "Don't disappear on me," she said in sixth grade after a sleepover at Michaela's. "All the other girls, their dads never show up."

But that was a long time ago. Emmy wasn't around anymore. And Steve had a mission to complete.

The play-offs were grueling: they had to win five games to get to the 4A Division 2 State Championship. A month-long march. Middle of November to the week before Christmas. High school football played fall out until the very end.

Steve thought it was ridiculous that there were so many teams in the play-offs. All a team had to do was beat the two worst teams in the district. Participation-trophy culture had finally made its way to Texas high school football, which Steve thought was a damn shame. Back in his day, a team had to win their district to make the play-offs. Six teams battling it out during the season for one spot, for one chance at glory. If you lost one, it could ruin everything. You had to be perfect. There was no room for redemption.

But all those extra teams weren't a wash. You couldn't sleep on any of them. Anything could happen once you made it to the show.

Nothing ever worth working toward was easy. The play-offs were proof of that. By the time they rolled around, the 'Stangs lost one of their top receivers to an ACL tear, and their kicker slipped into a postseason slump so bad he missed nearly everything he attempted, even extra points.

But they marched on, vanquishing every opponent. It wasn't easy, but it was definite. The road to State was clear as day. Until they got to the semifinals.

By halftime, Steinbeck was down 14–0.

The other team had gone up by two touchdowns in the first half, and the 'Stangs couldn't get a single play going. Miguel got sacked three times. Threw an interception. Only got two first downs. The defense was playing on their heels. Slow to the ball. Soft on their coverage. They were getting outplayed. Steve was getting outcoached.

The stadium was roaring. Two marching bands trying to drown the other out. Calls kept going the other team's way. Rubber pellets of turf exploded on the ground after each of Miguel's incomplete passes. Trey's forearm got ripped up from turf burn. It felt like everything, even the ground, was against them.

In the locker room, at halftime, Steve did his best to rouse the troops. Talk to them about honor. About what it meant to play with heart. About how they needed to *want* it more than they'd ever wanted anything in their lives. Steve looked at each and every one of them—players, coaches, staff—and said, "We've come too far. We've left too much behind. For our season to end in freaking Frisco tonight. Now, let's go out there and take what's ours!"

And the men responded the only way they knew how: with perfection.

Miguel threw a seventy-yard bomb to Little Williams for a touchdown, and the kicker made the extra point. Trey ran for a fifty-yard touchdown. And Big Williams showed up on defense, sacking the quarterback in the end zone for a safety. By the time the ref blew the final whistle, Steinbeck was winning by two touchdowns.

That's how it all came together for Steve. It was a blur. It almost seemed impossible to him. Even when Dan Holcomb found him after the game, waiting for him by the bus, shoving a bottle of overpriced scotch into Steve's hands, telling anyone who would listen that he was the future of their program, Steve couldn't quite believe it. That, during his first season as head coach, the Steinbeck 'Stangs were going to State.

On the bus ride home, Johnson came up from the back to sit beside Steve like he sometimes did, the sleeves of his gray shirt pushed up to his elbows. His beige bucket hat was stuffed into his back pocket, and he wore a red Steinbeck beanie instead.

"Freezing back there," Johnson said, pushing the beanie down over his ears.

They liked to break down the game after the guys had settled and started drifting off to sleep or sinking themselves into the invisible worlds inside their phones.

"Never thought they'd get tired after that one," Johnson said, pulling out his tablet and scrolling through the game film. "Still feels like a miracle that we can see all this so quick after the game."

"Remember the film reels? The VHS cassettes?"

"I remember when Emmy yanked the ribbon out of all your cassettes before that Granary High game twenty years ago."

"Jesus," Steve said, putting down the tablet and looking at him. "Was it that long ago?"

"That was her menace phase," Johnson said, his bright white teeth gleaming in the darkness. "Little monster tore everything apart."

"And I couldn't stay mad at her, that little face. Those pig-tails, remember?"

"She'd rip out the bows Lucy loved to make her wear."

"Never could force her to do something she didn't wanna do."

Steve turned from Johnson back to the tablet. Preparation for a game as big as State could never start too soon.

"You know, Steve…" Johnson started. Steve glanced over at him. He was staring straight ahead, toward the windshield, watching the bus hurtle down the road, the light from the interstate gleaming off his dark skin, highlighting his strong jaw, which he clenched before speaking again. "You've gotten us this far."

Steve waited for him to go on. A hit of anxiety clenched in his chest.

"No one would blame you if, after next week, you chose your family."

"What are you goin' on about, Johnson?" Steve asked, tugging at the end of his beard.

"It's just…" Johnson began, then, remembering something, shifted slightly to his left to pull his phone out of his back pocket. He unlocked it, scrolled, and said, "Here. This. Look. Jacob sent it to me. Look at her. How happy she is."

When Johnson turned the screen toward him, Steve felt a brief, blinding elation at the sight of his daughter—full pink cheeks, dark hair braided down her shoulder, a wide, illuminating smile, his dimples, Lucy's eyes—and then a drop in his stomach that almost took his breath away.

Next to Emmy, holding her hand, was a woman. She looked straight at Emmy, her face in profile, her hair pulled up in a bun on top of her head. She looked like she was talking, saying something to Emmy, and Steve realized that she must have made Emmy laugh. He could see it in his daughter's eyes, the crinkled corners, the head slightly tilted back. He could almost hear it, those loud, sharp three notes that she'd bellow out in her belly laugh that came from deep down inside her, the same laugh she'd had when she was just four months old, barely able to move but perfectly capable of sound. Steve had never loved a noise so much in his life, and he'd prayed, way back then, to never go a day without hearing that sound if he could help it.

"No one would blame you, is all I'm saying, if you choose your family," Johnson said, putting his phone back in his pocket. He didn't blink. He sat straight up. His eyes were wide and still set on the road in front of them. "If you let all of this go for her. After it's all said and done."

It was almost tempting. To drop it all. To believe him. To return to Emmy, arms open wide, willing to accept whatever it was she threw his way.

But he couldn't even entertain that thought. He remembered Pastor Ben. And Dan. And everyone else in Steinbeck who knew the truth. His conversation with Ben had never really been necessary. Steve had been taught the rules of the road since he was a little kid. The Bible, that ironclad word of God, had been very specific on what kind of behavior got you to the good place and what kind damned you for eternity.

"Told you," Steve said to Johnson, shoring up his mind, trying to bury the image he'd seen of his daughter, happier than he'd ever seen her, "I'd wait 'til the end of the season."

"And then what?"

"Let's just get through next week, all right?" Steve turned his tablet back on, ready to drown himself in the footage and schemes and plans for State.

"Steve." Johnson took the tablet. Held it in his massive hands. He turned toward Steve, looked him right in the eye. "I can keep this program going. It's your legacy. I know that."

"Keep it going?"

"So you can take Emmy back."

"It's not that simple."

"Isn't it?" Johnson asked, his eyes wide.

Steve wanted to believe Johnson's intentions were good. That he was looking out for Emmy, for their family. But Steve also knew that Johnson wanted his job. Always had. And it was easier for Steve to doubt Johnson than to take him at his word.

"I'm gonna be coaching this team for a long time, Johnson," Steve said, grabbing the tablet back from him. "Not going anywhere anytime soon. This is the dream, remember? You and me taking a team all the way. Forever."

"The dream?" Johnson asked. He turned away from Steve again, toward the front of the bus, his gaze toward the windshield, the darkness dense. It was impossible to make out anything farther than the three feet of headlight in front of them, but it seemed to Steve that Johnson had seen something. His eyes were unblinking, his mouth slightly open, his hands pushing the beanie back off his head so that he could absentmindedly rub his scalp. He nodded, coming to some kind of decision, turning back toward Steve. "Pull up that first drive we had on offense. Want to see why the pocket was collapsing on Miguel so quick."

For the rest of the ride, they studied film, taking notes, making jokes. The normal routine. But something was off. Steve couldn't be sure if it was exhaustion or a trick of the darkness. But it felt to him that, between them, something had changed.

26

They got back to Steinbeck late that night, and when Steve pulled up in his driveway, he saw Lucy's car parked there. She was sitting on the porch, reading, bundled in one of the quilts Steve's mama had made and that he always kept out by the rocking chairs when it got cool enough.

"Lucy," Steve said, walking up to her. She gave him a small wave and set down her book. Steve held out the bottle of scotch. "Want a glass? Dan Holcomb gave it to me. Won the semifinals. We're going to State, Luce! Can you believe it?"

Her hair was different. Short. Sharper somehow. More angled. Darker, too. She looked like a new woman. She cocked her head to the side, glancing at the bottle of scotch, then back to Steve. She smiled. That, Steve thought, was the same.

"That looks fancy," she said. "Don't waste a glass on me."

"Can't let me celebrate alone."

"You have champagne?"

"Only bubbles I got are beer," Steve said. "Care for a can?"

"For State? Sure."

"Wanna come inside?"

"Porch is good. Feels nice."

It was that early December cool that felt like fall. No hint of heat in the wind, yet without that unbearable bite of winter that they got every now and then. Lucy loved having talks out on the porch. It was where she and Steve had sat for hours during their senior year of high school, talking and laughing and kissing for the first time, trying not to get caught by Steve's mama, who was peeking out of the window. It was where Steve had first said *I love you*. It was where Lucy told him she was pregnant with Emmy. Somehow, those conversations on the porch produced magic, every time.

Steve came back out with the beers, cracking them open and plopping himself down in a rocking chair next to her.

"To Steinbeck and Steve," Lucy said, taking her can from him and lifting it. "And the impossible dream."

"Cheers," Steve said, taking a long sip. "So. One in the morning. You on my porch. Seems familiar."

"Just popping by."

"Never known you to pop."

"Couldn't sleep."

"Not man troubles, is it?"

"What?"

"Don't know if I'm the best person to talk to for that."

"It's not about a man."

"Know we're friendly and all, but that'd just about kill me."

"I haven't had a man in…" She trailed off, then shook her head. "It's not about a man. It's about Emmy."

It was like all the air got sucked out of Steve. The panic was so immediate, the instinct to fear for the safety of his kid embedded in him so deep that it took a moment for him to breathe through that first wave of anxiety, knowing that Lucy would have already said if something truly terrible had happened.

"You see, it's just…" she started, then looked out at the land, the trees lining the driveway. "Remember when you planted the magnolia? Right outside her window? And I told you not to because what if a big storm came in and one of the branches went crashing into her room?"

Steve nodded.

"And you told me, 'Emilia deserves to see life growing every time she looks outside.'"

"I remember," Steve said.

"From the time she was a baby, all fresh and new, you wanted her to see beautiful things. You wanted her life to be…well, alive. And filled with growth. Continued growth. That's why y'all spent all that time playing soccer and softball in the yard. Getting better. Why you brought her in to watch film with you some Saturdays. So she could learn how to pinpoint weakness. How to grow."

Steve didn't respond. He leaned back in the rocking chair, looking out into the darkness.

"She's trying to do what you taught her, Steve. To live. To not be stagnant. To grow."

"This isn't growth," Steve said, clasping his hands in front of him. "This is sin."

Lucy sighed and shook her head.

"She always liked you more," Lucy said, tucking a piece of her hair behind her ear. "Loved us the same. But liked you more. I hated you for that. That you two just *got* each other. And I was on the outside. Always left out. How could I compete? With my dresses and paintings and arts and crafts? You had sports and the stars."

"So you're saying it *is* my fault."

"I saw her, Steve," she said. "Over Thanksgiving. She's got a girlfriend."

"Johnson mentioned something about that," Steve mumbled, his mind reeling, remembering the girl in the picture, and imagined Lucy with Emmy and her, sharing a table with them, breaking bread, indulging in pleasantries, avoiding the truth of the matter, the only truth that needed to be said, pushing her further away, into the abyss.

"She seemed happy," Lucy said. "She really loves that girl. And that girl loves our girl back. Isn't that something to celebrate?"

"Why would we celebrate that kind of sin?"

"You love her, Steve."

"I do," Steve said, tugging on the end of his beard. "But I can't reconcile this with my faith. I can't. It's wrong. I talked to Pastor Ben about it like you said I should. And he agreed. If we let her keep up this life, if we let her continue this choice, the consequence is clear. An eternity in hell."

"And if you're wrong?"

"The Bible says I'm right."

"Stephen," Lucy said with all the gentleness in the world. She rarely used his full name. She was the only person who ever did. Maybe the only one who remembered what it was. "Don't do this. Don't make your life this small."

"Nothing bigger than State, Luce. You and I both know that."

"But there are things bigger than football."

"I know that," Steve snapped. "Faith. And family. I'm still the same man you married. I haven't changed."

"You are," she said, nodding. She reached out her hand and stroked his cheek, the way she used to when they were young and it was late and they weren't quite ready to go to sleep. There was a tenderness to her touch, in a gesture so deeply buried in the past. She lifted his chin so that he was forced to meet her eyes. "Every day you don't talk to her, she gets further away."

"She won't get gone," Steve said, pulling away from her. "I've got a plan."

"You keep saying that, but she's not some play call you can draw up to get her to be who you want."

"What *I* want? Don't you want it, too?"

"I just want her, Steve. One hundred percent."

The gulf between him and Lucy had always felt crossable to Steve. There was always some bridge of mutual understanding that kept them together, united in some way, even after the divorce. Steve supposed it was love—of their shared past, of their daughter, of one another.

But this, Steve knew, was an impasse.

"You take her back now," Steve said, clenching his fists, "and you'll lose her in the long run."

"Long run? Steve, this is it. This is the run."

"You know what I mean."

"You think you'll get rewarded for this? Shutting out your daughter? Cutting off love in favor of your own glory?"

"Now, that's just nonsense."

"Did you cut off Emmy for her sake? Really? Saving her soul—from what? Her desire to be loved? Happy? Or did you do it because you were afraid? Of Jan Oleander. Of Dan Holcomb. Of having to give up your dream."

"You ask anyone in this town if what I did was right. They'll set you straight."

"Of course they would," Lucy said. "They're on your side. Always on your side. And they got to have you as a coach because of it. And they may just get a State Championship out of it. But they're not your family. They're not a part of you."

Steve chugged his beer, crushing the can in his hand, all the magic of the semifinals gone. "What do you want me to say, Lucy?"

"I want you to listen."

"Oh, I've heard plenty from you."

"I'm moving to Houston, Steve," she said in a rush, making sure he didn't cut her off. "In the spring."

"Houston? That's—" Steve said, his voice dipping away before he could finish saying *far away*.

Lucy had never been one for the big city. She liked the little world they'd created in Steinbeck, the one they'd had since they were kids. Knew every inch of the town. Memories on every street. The past woven comfortably into everyday life, making it impossible to forget.

"She'll never come back here once I'm gone," she said, looking toward the magnolia tree by Emmy's old room. "If you don't make things right."

"Johnson and Cora are still here."

"You think Johnson's gonna stick around after the season y'all have had?" she asked, laughing. "He's gonna get a head-coaching job so quick it'll make your head spin."

"Why Houston?" Steve asked, remembering the moment on the bus, not wanting to picture what a season without Johnson would look like. "That's far."

"I don't know if she wants to see you," she said, ignoring Steve, still looking toward that old tree. "But she's coming here for Christmas. Just a couple days. But I reckon that's your chance."

"Chance?"

Lucy got up, and the red rocking chair slammed against the white wood paneling of the house. She ran her hand through her short hair, brushing past her shoulder, like she was grasping for the phantom strands of what it had been, long and thick and stiff with hairspray.

"Good luck at State," she said. "Bet you'll cook up something good."

"You're not going?" Steve asked, frowning. "First State game Steinbeck has ever had."

"Good luck," Lucy said again, a little more softly, leaning down to kiss his cheek, a light brush of her lips against his skin. "And don't forget our daughter."

She handed Steve her still-full beer can and walked down the steps of the porch toward her car. The headlights nearly blinded Steve as she started up her engine and backed out of the driveway, light spilling over the empty back roads once she'd gone.

Steve grabbed his tablet from the inside hall and brought it back outside, pulling up the film from the semifinal game. He sipped Lucy's unfinished beer, trying to make it last.

It was late, and he was tired, but the house was too empty, too dark, too stale. He wasn't ready to go in alone.

27

The week leading up to State was a blur of banners and dinners and pep rallies: hand-shaking, baby-kissing, hands laid all over Steve in pregame prayers. The mayor, the board, Pastor Ben, they all wanted a piece of him before they left for the great pilgrimage, the four-hour bus trek to Arlington, where they'd arrive at AT&T Stadium, that great mecca of football, the multimillion-dollar house that Jerry Jones built for America's team.

"This is just a slice of the reward," Pastor Ben said to Steve, shaking his hand before he stepped on the bus to head to State. "For being a steadfast disciple. There's so much more to come."

"All right, now," Steve said, wrenching his hand away as politely as possible, giving the crowd a big wave before he stepped onto the bus, the boys inside raucous, hanging out of rolled-down windows, banging on the exterior, drinking in the love from the crowd, the devotion of a town, accepting all their hopes and dreams as they drove off toward Main Street to hit the highway.

The boys were quiet once they'd been on the bus for an hour or so. They had their headphones on. Music blasting. Some slept. Most had their eyes locked on the windows. Watching the world pass by. Ranches and farms and windmills and great stretches of brown plains, every ounce of the ground harvested, prepared for the impending, lifeless winter.

Steve watched a little bit of film on the bus, making some last-minute notes. But there wasn't much new to see. They'd been obsessing over the opposing team for a week, and he'd seen just about every inch of them. They were playing a team from Athens, Texas, the black-eyed pea capital of the world. Steinbeck vs. Athens, Steve thought. Two towns that could never quite live up to the mythology of their names.

Athens was the last team in their district to get into the play-offs, but once they got in, they created a hell storm. Took every game to overtime. Took down every powerhouse, storming ahead to the semifinals, where they won their first game in regular time by thirty-five points. They'd found their mojo. Momentum was on their side. It was like they always said: anything could happen once you make it to the Show.

They were the underdogs. The Cinderella story. The team of Davids. The 'Stangs were the undefeated guys with a Division One–caliber quarterback. They were Goliath.

That was just fine for Steve. Magic never got anyone very far. It was hard work, strength, determination, and destiny that prepared men for glory.

In the locker room before the game, Steve took his place up front, by the whiteboard, after the other coaches had had their say. The boys were quiet. Serious. Every face locked in on Steve. Big Williams had one foot on his helmet, bouncing his knee incessantly, nodding his head up and down, psyching himself up. Little Williams sat beside him, clasping his gloved hands together, his eyes on the whiteboard behind Steve, on the play he'd drawn up, 27 Mustang, making sure he got it right. Trey was hunched over, his head between his legs, looking up every now and then, waiting for Steve to speak. Miguel was sitting front and center, his helmet resting on his knee, his lucky orange Astros snapback on backward. He looked right at Steve, smiled, and gave a little nod. An invitation to begin.

"Well," Steve said, his voice deep and a little hoarse, seeming to echo in the plush, carpeted locker room of the Dallas Cowboys. "We made it. This is what we've worked for."

The guys were silent, locked-in. The energy in the room was palpable, fueled by every single beating heart, the adrenaline coursing through every pore in the room.

"But this is not the end. We still got forty-eight minutes of football left. Forty-eight minutes. That's all you get. The last time some of y'all will play football. The first time all of y'all will play on a stage this big.

"Now, all of y'all were chosen to be here. By me, by the other coaches. By God. But you made the choice to show up. To work. To go the extra mile.

"In Second Timothy, it talks about reaching the end of something you've worked toward. It says, 'I have fought the good fight, I have finished the race, I have kept the faith.'

"Y'all have fought tooth and nail, all season long. Every single one of you. You have fought the good fight. You have kept the faith. Now, let's go out there and finish the race. Let's take what's ours."

The locker room exploded in shouts. Foot stomps. Hands banging against plastic as they beat their chests.

"Say a little prayer, men," Steve said before the captains got up and took over, taking off his red cap and putting it in his back pocket. "And if y'all ain't the praying sort, you might as well start now. Only reason we're here is by the grace of God."

Steve wasn't the sort for fancy words. Never had much new to say to God that the Big Guy didn't already know. So when he bowed his head, Steve ran those old, sacred words through his mind, savoring each one, letting them run over him, fill him up, stay in his mind, and lead him forward throughout the game.

Our Father, who art in heaven, hallowed be thy name...

Steve had been to games at the stadium before, but he never got used to how massive it was. The sheer magnitude, the *audacity* of it. He ran through the tunnel after the guys barreled through the paper banner made by the cheerleaders, and he looked up at the enormous screen overhead. It took up over three-quarters of the length of the field. Cameras were everywhere, and Steve saw his face stretched across the screen. Red cheeks, furrowed brows. He looked just like his father. The Steinbeck fans roared at the sight of him. Already on their feet. Stomping and clapping and screaming. Ready for the game of their lives.

The drum line dictated the rhythm of Steve's heart. A scattered, militaristic cadence. He tried to breathe deep, shaking out his shoulders, trying to get a little loose. But he figured it wasn't a tension that'd leave his body until it was all finished. So he went over the game plan with the other coaches, talked to the guys, made sure they were focused, and got ready for the first whistle.

They won the coin toss and chose to get the ball first. The entire stadium was electric before kickoff. Flashes from cameras, chants from the cheerleaders, everyone clanging and clapping and screaming along to the marching band, playing the chorus of "Sweet Caroline" as the players took the field for the opening kick.

"Showtime," Johnson said, pulling out the laminated offensive play-call sheets.

"Let's get it," Steve said, fist bumping him and moving down the sideline.

The other team's kicker booted the ball into the end zone, and the 'Stangs started on their own twenty-five-yard line. Miguel lined up in the shotgun. Trey was on his right. He looked over to the sidelines for the play call. Wiped his hands on the front of his thighs. Then, in a loud, commanding voice, shouted, "Hut, hut!"

The first quarter was an explosion of offense. Miguel was playing out of his mind. Didn't have a single incomplete pass in that first twelve minutes and threw for two touchdowns. The 'Stangs were up 14–0. Would have been 17–0, but their kicker missed a field goal from the seventeen-yard line at the end of the first quarter.

But the second quarter was all Athens. They gained a little momentum, scored a touchdown on a punt return with coverage so weak Steve thought his guys must have fallen asleep on the play, forgotten where they were. At the end of the second half, Athens marched down the field. The 'Stangs held them on third and long—their defense was almost perfect on long third downs—and Athens kicked a field goal as time ran out in the half.

14–10.

Halftime speeches from Trey, from Miguel, from Big and Little Williams. The coaches went over different plays. Told the guys to toughen up. Have some heart. Keep their eyes on the prize. Steve let them take over. He'd already had his say.

Third quarter was more of the same. Three and outs, a defensive showdown, each one of the teams tightening coverage, playing smarter, safer.

The 'Stangs' kicker missed his second field goal at the end of the third quarter. The snap was perfect. The hold by Little Williams was, too. He just shanked it to the left, and the score remained unchanged. A defensive stalemate since the second quarter.

Eventually, Steve knew, one of them had to break.

The clock was winding down in the fourth quarter. The 'Stangs were still up 14–10. The dream was so close Steve could almost taste it. But you never got too excited in a game like that.

Three minutes was a long time. A lifetime, in football: anything could happen. Everything could change.

Athens had the ball on their own fifteen. Steve called a safety blitz. Little Williams was creeping up from the secondary, getting ready to launch himself toward the line of scrimmage from the right side. Big Williams would bull-rush from the left. They called it the Twin Stack. It was their favorite play.

They were on the quarterback almost as soon as they snapped the ball. Big Williams got a good swipe at him from the blind-side, nearly causing a fumble, but the quarterback was a quick kid, always able to stay on his feet and hold onto the ball. He tripped a little but stayed upright, spinning away from them, taking it for twenty yards before he was run out of bounds. Athens's fan base was on their feet, back in the game. All it took was one big break to change everything.

Athens got theirs on the twenty, on fourth and long. Steinbeck had managed to stop their momentum, getting to the quarterback, forcing him to throw it away on the first two downs. Nearly got an interception on the third, but it slipped through Little Williams's fingers before he could reel it in.

"Hit him in the fucking hands!" Johnson screamed. He was drowned out by the collective groans of 'Stangs fans in the stands behind them.

One minute left on the clock.

Steve signaled the call for the defense. Fourth and ten on the twenty was easy. Preventive defense. Make sure you mark your man. Don't get sucked into the run. There's no way they're not passing.

It was a simple mistake. Buying into what wasn't real.

Athens lined up under center. Tried to get Steinbeck offside on a hard count, but the guys stayed firm, disciplined. And then, after the snap, the Athens quarterback gave a fake handoff so good even the cameras got fooled, following the running back on the big screen, when the ball was still in the quarterback's hands as he rolled out to the right. Steinbeck realized their mistake too late. By the time the safety scrambled back toward the end zone, the ball was already in the hands of the wide-open receiver.

Forty-five seconds left.

The extra point sailed through the uprights. Athens fans roared in approval, the marching band exploding into their fight song, the cheerleaders tumbling through the end zone as Steve's guys ran back to the sideline, some hanging their heads in disbelief. The Steinbeck fan base went silent.

With forty-five seconds left in the fourth quarter of the State Championship, the Steinbeck 'Stangs were, for the first time in the game, losing. 17–14.

"Just get in field-goal range," Steve said to the offense on the sideline before they ran out to start on the twenty-five. "Get into field-goal range, we'll kick one through, and send it to overtime. They can't outlast us all night."

"Coach," Little Williams said, looking over his shoulder at the kicker, who was doing his warm-up drills into the practice net. "He doesn't have it tonight. Let Miguel just rip one down the field, Hail Mary that shit."

"Trust the process," Steve said, giving his shoulder pads a good slap. "And we'll give 'em hell."

Little Williams nodded and jogged onto the field, following Miguel, who led the way. Like a good soldier, he had learned when to fall in line.

Steinbeck lined up on the twenty-five. The Athens fans were loud. Deafening. Steve could almost feel the Steinbeck fans holding their breath. Praying. Hoping. Willing their silence to wrap around the field, keep their boys calm, their heads in the game.

Miguel lined up in the shotgun. He stood up tall. Strong. In complete control. No man could lead a charge better than him.

Forty-five seconds left on the clock.

"Red 57," Miguel shouted, his voice strong, deep, clear. "Hut, hut!"

And the line collapsed into movement with the snap. Miguel looked downfield, trying to launch one to a receiver running a corner route, but the coverage was tight. He dumped the ball off to Trey before the pocket fell in around him. A little bubble screen at the line. It looked like Trey was going to get stood up by their huge defensive end, but he managed to spin away, cutting up the right side, taking off at full speed down the sideline before he tiptoed out of bounds as the free safety was bearing down on him.

The clock stopped. A chunk of time was gone. Thirty-three seconds left. Steinbeck was on the fifty.

Next play was a twenty-two-yard slant to Little Williams at tight end. He got himself out of bounds, just barely. Twenty-five seconds left. They were at the Athens twenty-eight-yard line.

Miguel got a great block from Big Williams on the next play and took it himself for eight yards, ending up at their twenty-yard line. Eighteen seconds on the clock. It was second and two.

Next two plays were incomplete passes. Ten seconds left on the clock. Fourth and short. Steve called their last time-out.

A field goal from the twenty was easy on any other day. But Little Williams was right. The kicker had already missed from a shorter range today. Do you go for it, or take the points? Send the game to overtime? Game plan was always to take whatever points they could get, to not risk what they couldn't guarantee.

"Do you trust me?" Steve asked Johnson as the boys jogged over from the field. They didn't have much time.

Johnson put the laminated play-call sheets he'd been looking at under his arm. He tugged at the string of his bucket hat, Lucky Beige, and smiled, a wide one, free from any of the tension or nerves that kept Steve locking his jaw, grinding his teeth, barely able to breathe.

"After all these years?" Johnson said, giving him a little shove. "Shit, 'course I do, Quinn."

"Okay," Steve said, nodding, getting the guys to gather. He

looked at Miguel and Little Williams. "27 Mustang, men. You remember it?"

"Yessir!" they shouted in unison. Steve could almost see the pressure slide off the kicker's shoulders and pool at his feet. It was out of his hands.

"All righty, then," Steve said, slapping their helmets. "Let's go win us a State Championship."

Miguel and Little Williams knocked their helmets together before they went on the field. They had started the season as enemies. They would end it as brothers in arms.

"Say a little prayer, Steve," Johnson said, when the guys lined up in field-goal formation. "We need all the help we can get."

Little Williams was the holder. Miguel lined up at tight end, getting into his three-point stance. Little Williams looked back at the kicker, gave him a little nod, then looked front toward the center. He took a knee and got ready for the snap.

The Athens half of the stadium was screaming, trying to get Steinbeck to jump offside, get in the kicker's head; the Steinbeck half was silent, holding their breath, waiting for a kick that would never come.

The snap was perfect. The kicker took his steps, cocking his leg back. But before he finished his follow-through, Little Williams was up and running, rolling out to the left, the ball tucked under his arm like he was going to take it all the way.

The defense bought it. Miguel broke away from the line on a corner route. He was wide open, twenty yards of open field before the end zone.

Little Williams brought the ball up in his right hand, ready to pass. He looked like a shortstop turning a double play, his chest facing forward, all the torque in his body taken away. He had to do it with the strength of his arm, nothing else. He had to be perfect.

Little Williams got the throw off and then was clobbered by their biggest guys.

The spiral was tight. The throw was a little lobbed. It hung in the air. A thousand pairs of eyes watched it, a thousand whispered prayers floated through the air.

It was overthrown.

But Miguel stretched out for it, diving forward, catching it over his left shoulder and tucking it into his chest. He landed, untouched, in the end zone, the ball secure, as the clock hit zero.

Steve didn't even see the referee signal the touchdown. He was instantly doused in a bucket of ice-cold, blue Gatorade, engulfed in a mob of screaming coaches and players, bodies collected around him. Johnson grabbed the scruff of Steve's beard and screamed, "Time to shave this ugly-ass thing!"

The players moved from Steve, storming the field, dogpiling on Little Williams and Miguel, their heroes. Everything was all limbs and plastic pads slapping against one another. Big Williams took off his helmet and screamed, a triumphant yawp. All of Steinbeck rushed the field. Security tried to stop them, but the force of their will was too strong. They'd been denied glory such as this for far too long. They all wanted a taste of it.

Thousands of people surrounded Steve. Hundreds of them hugged him. He was drowned in balloons and confetti, and he felt the sweet cold metal and the heavy weight of the State Championship trophy as he lifted it over his head to a deafening roar of approval.

Steve looked around at the sea of people in front of him, chanting, crying, laughing, consumed in the hysterical joy that could only come from the devout, fanatical loyalty of long-suffering fans. And he closed his eyes in prayer and in gratitude, and completed his words of prayer.

For thine is the kingdom, the power, and the glory, forever and ever.

When Steve got back, after more than a few beers at the Corral, he was met with the staggering emptiness of home. It was a dense silence, heightened by the echo of the constant noise he'd been surrounded by all week, all season really. Nonstop talking, planning, breaking down film, drawing up new plays, drilling them into each player until he executed it perfectly in practice.

He poured himself a glass of scotch, Macallan 25, from the bottle Dan Holcomb had got him when they won the semifinals. Steve wondered what he'd get now that they had won it all.

He took the glass outside on the porch, swirling the amber liquid around the crystal lowball tumbler. It was a windless, cloudless night. New moon blanketing the night in complete darkness, giving the stars room to shine, constellations spread out, unobstructed by light. The trees stood completely still, their leaves falling steadily from their branches, almost barren now as winter crept in, only days away.

Steve took in a deep breath. The December air was almost warm. Just like Texas to pull back, revert to summer temperatures right before a new season began. He tugged on his beard. He'd have to wait to shave it until the next day, at the parade, in the back of Dan Holcomb's pickup truck. The crowd always loved a bit of fanfare.

The scotch was smooth. Easy going down. It didn't make a big deal of itself like the other stuff Steve drank, which burned and coated his tongue in a bitter aftertaste. It was meant to be sipped and enjoyed and not thought too much about. Maybe that's why people paid so much for it. For that sense of peace.

Steve tried to summon it. The joy of before. The raucous chants of his name at the Corral. The constant, overwhelming support, gratitude, assurance that he had done something right, that he had found a way to win, something that had seemed impossible to everyone in town this time last year.

But he just felt empty. He couldn't see much beyond the pine trees lining his driveway. It was dark, a void.

"We did it," Steve said out loud.

Silence.

"I did it." As if the individualization could collect more meaning.

Silence.

"I won a State Championship."

Nothing.

He wasn't sure what he was waiting for. Some divine sign. Some validation from the infinite. Or something more simple. Like the crunch of gravel underneath car tires and headlights flooding his driveway. The slamming of the driver's side door. The shifting stones underneath feet sprinting up to see him. The squeal of laughter. The warmth of return. A sense of home.

He didn't think about what he was doing. He just got his phone out and dialed.

"Hello?" asked the voice on the other end.

"Hey there, Emmy." His voice cracked a little when he heard her. "How'd you like to come on home?"

PART THREE: Winter

Texas is rich in unredeemed dreams.

—Larry McMurtry

MORE THAN THE WEATHER, it's the trees that indicate winter has crept into Texas. Their branches transform from an abundance of brown leaves to skeletal in the blink of an eye. One day the leaves are there; the next, they're gone. It is the only consistent marker of the season. Temperatures drop and rise, the humidity comes and goes. One day it feels like spring, and the next, the roads ice over.

The trees remain, barren limbs clacking together as the winds rise and fall, whistling through the interstate. A grayness comes over the sky. Though the snows are few and far between across the state, the universal silence of winter is not lost on Texas. Fewer birds, fewer football games; the opulent joy of autumn quiets to a whisper.

In the darkness, Advent candles and menorahs are lit in living rooms. Folks are filled with expectant waiting, that holy-holiday sanctity. Church bells ring out through the streets, carols are sung, and Christmas trees are lit and hung with ornaments.

The days are short, and the nights are long. Folks search for warmth, for light, in the scarce winter months. Bonfires are built on beaches by the coast and out on the lakeshores and in backyard firepits across the state. The smell of burning wood from oak, mesquite, and pecan trees fills the air, the smoke chimneying up into the constellation-filled sky.

In Texas, winter is a hybrid season. Some say it doesn't exist at all. The shifts are subtle. It's hard to detect when fall ends or spring begins. But there is an undeniable emptiness that enters the state in the in-between. Life snuffed out, making way for solitude.

28

EMMY

Emmy was not good at love. That's what her high school friends told her once, in the middle of a home football game.

They were sitting in a homogeneous line on the bleachers, with their Daisy Dukes riding up so high that the backs of their thighs—all varying shades of beige—stuck to the steel stands and peeled away with great reluctance whenever they stood up to cheer after a big play. They all had aggressively teased hair, curled and made immovable with hairspray. Each strand crunched when Emmy tried to run her hands through it, and a nauseating chemical scent wafted around them wherever they went.

"Why do we do this to ourselves?" Michaela Sherman asked, trying to comb through Emmy's hair with her fingers to get her attention. Emmy was never much fun at games. She took them seriously. Studied the offense as much as possible so that she could try and predict her dad's next play call. He was always pacing up and down the sidelines, muttering into his headset, looking down at his play sheet, screaming at the boys on the field. No fixed focal point. A blur of constant motion.

"Because our mothers taught us how," Emmy responded without looking at her. "Gotta blitz 'em, now or never."

"I forgot," Michaela said, looping her arm through Emmy's and pressing her cheek into her shoulder. "There are two Coach Quinns."

"Yes!" Emmy screamed, standing up, ignoring the sting as the skin of her thighs ripped from the metal. The blitz worked. A sack on third down. Nothing better.

When they all settled down for the punt, Emmy noticed one of the girls from her church staring at her down the line. She was sucking a Peppy Turkey (Dr Pepper mixed with Wild Turkey whiskey, a Steinbeck staple) through a straw, squinting at Emmy, cocking her head to the side.

"Real creepy vibe down there," Emmy shouted to her.

"Hold up, I'll come to you," she said with her thick West Texas accent, hiking up her too-long bootleg jeans as she stood up. "Scooch on down, y'all. I gotta ask Emmy somethin'."

She squeezed herself into the tiny slot of space to Emmy's left while Michaela continued to hang onto her right arm. Emmy tried to ignore the pleasure she felt at the sustained weight of her, the warmth of her skin pressed against hers.

"Here, have a sip," said the girl from church, holding out the foam cup, shoving the straw to Emmy's lips. She took a small one and let the shock of sweet syrup coat her tongue before swallowing down the burn of whiskey.

"I was talking to Tommy from church," the girl said, pushing her blond, side-swept, box-dyed bangs out of her eyes. "And he said you hadn't said one thing to him since I told you about his little crush on you."

Michaela tightened her grip around Emmy's arm. Emmy could almost feel her holding her breath.

"It's nothing, really," Emmy said, shrugging. "It just doesn't feel like love."

"Are you broken?" the girl asked, rooting around for the straw with her tongue, not taking her wide amber eyes off Emmy. They were filled with disbelief. "A boy likes you."

"I'm not broken," Emmy said defensively, feeling the heat from Michaela's body on hers, trying to convince herself that the goose bumps creeping up the back of her neck were from the whiskey.

"You can't just wait for love to happen to you, Emmy," the girl said. "That's not how it works. My mama told me you gotta go out there and get your man before he gets got by some other girl. You don't wait for a feeling. You go get it."

"It's a feeling," Emmy said. "Love isn't an action."

"Oh, Emmy," the girl said, pushing the straw back to Emmy's lips. "Take some more of this, and then go on down there and talk to Tommy. Trust me, you're gonna need it. You're no good at love. If you don't figure it out now, you'll always end up choosing the wrong person."

"I don't know," Michaela said, giving Emmy's thigh a little squeeze. "When the time comes, I'm sure she'll choose just right."

29

The duplicity of feeling trapped in love—that it helps you breathe but somehow also suffocates—was something Emmy had never known. Love, to her, was something she had seen in the movies, heard about in songs, and, for a brief period, observed between her parents.

She thought it must be like champagne, that great first burst of love. Bubbling and sweet and easy going down. Tipsy giggling, easy-going conversation, nothing too out of control.

But Cameron. Her sudden shift. The darkness overtaking what had months before been only good. It was like whiskey—the strength of the burn too strong, the intoxication too immediate.

It felt a little like drowning.

Emmy hadn't spoken to Sara since the night it happened. Missing her wasn't an option for Emmy. It seemed like Cameron could sense if even her mind wandered toward anyone else. And Emmy couldn't risk it.

It shouldn't have been so surprising. That nothing was the

same. What can love become when the trust has been breached? No longer an act of freedom but of possession.

Emmy kept it all to herself, not telling Jacob or her mom about the shift. It was hard to see from the outside. They still went to the Grizzly, drank beers, joked with Jacob. Their life seemed the same. Untouched by jealousy, untainted by guilt. There was a part of Emmy that hoped that the external normalcy could seep into their internal lives, which helped her justify not telling anyone about how bad it had gotten. "Grin and bear it," her father used to say. "It'll turn out fine in the end."

So Emmy waited for the *fine* to come, all the while enduring the close watch Cameron kept on her. Tracking her phone, checking her texts, making sure she didn't see anyone else without Cameron present. Not that there was anyone else to see. Their world had shrunk down to the two of them in their apartment since that late November evening.

That's why, when her father called, it felt like salvation.

Cameron started screening Emmy's calls after she stopped seeing Sara, convinced she would try to get into contact with her. So when Emmy saw Cameron's face when she read the name on the screen, she assumed it must have been Sara.

"It's your dad," Cameron said, her brows raised in involuntary surprise.

Emmy had always been quick, and she had always been strong. So before Cameron could make up her mind about whether or not she'd let her answer, Emmy snatched the phone out of her hands.

It was a quick call. Phone conversations with her dad always were. But it was enough.

In the afternoon on Christmas Eve, Emmy got ready to return to Steinbeck.

Before she left, Emmy sat on the couch in the living room, holding Cameron as she rested her head on her lap. Emmy ran her fingers through Cameron's hair, an act of habit rather than tenderness. It was strange how much weight a head could hold. Had it always been like that? Emmy wondered. So heavy?

"Don't leave me," Cameron whispered into Emmy's thigh. Her voice was muffled and small. "You said we'd have Christmas together."

"I'll only be gone a few days."

"Do you have to go?"

"He called me."

"Fuck him."

Emmy wanted to fast-forward through all of that. The suspicion and the impatience and the *need*, for control, for her autonomy. Emmy wanted to get back to that place where they were good. Where they could be two people living separate lives with separate hearts that they willingly gave to one another when they came together. Emmy wanted it to be like spring, everything new, all wildflowers and freedom and drives down two-lane highways with the windows rolled down, the music blasting, hurtling toward the horizon, the sky so blue, so deep, that it might seem like the atmosphere had cracked open and given them a sneak peek of heaven, because maybe that's all heaven really was: an open highway in Texas.

But it was winter. And the sky was overcast, the air was bitter and cold. And Cameron kept clutching her. Everywhere she went, Emmy could feel her. It wasn't like before, when they were light, when they were golden. Everything about them had become dense with need. Cameron's demands for all of Emmy, Emmy's inability to keep anything for herself.

"Are you sure you have to see him?" Cameron asked, her face still buried in Emmy's lap. Her voice distant, barely audible.

"I *need* to see him," Emmy said, brushing the hair out of her eyes before lifting her head so she could stand up. "It's getting late. Need to hit the road."

Emmy got up quickly, relieved to be rid of Cameron's weight.

She walked toward the counter where she left her keys, eager to get going. But Cameron tugged on her arm.

"Emmy," Cameron said.

It was the only true form of time travel, that kiss. It sent Emmy back to the early days, before the screened phone calls and prolonged hugs and tracked locations. It was like summer in the middle of the cold, barren winter; it was those three good months distilled into one moment.

When Cameron pulled away, she looked at Emmy, her eyes golden in the light of the sun, the thin line of her nose crinkled as she smiled, her right dimple deep and wide. She held Emmy's face in her hands and just looked at her, like she was trying to memorize her face, keep it preserved perfectly in her mind.

She traced Emmy's cheekbones with the back of her hand and tucked a stray piece of hair behind her ear. She kissed Emmy's forehead and then wrapped her arms around her waist, holding her, pressing her head into Emmy's chest, listening for her heartbeat, tapping out its rhythm on her back.

Bum-bum, bum-bum, bum-bum. Steady, strong, consistent. Everything Emmy wanted.

"Let's take a trip together when you get back," she said, pulling away from Emmy, rubbing her shoulders. "Like we did with the cavern. Get out of here, get some space. You can show me the *real* Texas."

"This is the real Texas," Emmy said.

"I just want to go somewhere I can breathe," Cameron said. "It's just so small here, you know?"

"I want you to breathe."

"Not enough *space*," Cameron said.

"We'll go to Big Bend," Emmy said, remembering all the camping trips she'd taken with her dad. If things went well at Christmas, she might be able to ask him if they could use their old tent.

"And see the stars?"

"And see the stars."

Cameron grabbed Emmy by the hands and spun them around in a circle. They spun faster and faster until the room started to tilt and sway and they collapsed on the couch. Their arms tangled around one another, she leaned into Emmy's ear and whispered, "You're all I've ever wanted, Emilia."

If Emmy could have found a way to keep them like that, all dizzy eyes and tangled limbs, she would have bottled up the joy and saved it for the rest of their lives like some eternal elixir, a fountain of their youth.

But moments were lived through, and then they were gone. Ensconced in memory, but erased from the physical world. Unable to be preserved.

30

The drive into Steinbeck was the same as always: sun shining in Emmy's face, the football stadium a silhouette on the horizon, the familiarity of it all rising like waves of heat on the pavement in the middle of summer. As Emmy got closer, she saw a banner draped across the front of the football stadium: *Steinbeck 'Stangs, State Champs!* And underneath that: *Thank You, Coach Quinn!*

Emmy thought about her dad, what he must have looked like when they unveiled it. She could see him standing in the parking lot, looking up at it with Coach Johnson by his side. His red baseball cap would be pulled far down his face, so Johnson would flip the bill to make sure he was looking. His white polo would be drenched in sweat at the back, even in the winter, and his shoulders would stretch the material, the collar closing in too tight around his thick neck. His face would be red, and his eyes would be closed as he enjoyed the moment.

Emmy imagined her mom there, too, by his side. Even though they weren't together, she thought Lucy ought to be a part of it, his crowning achievement, what they'd all waited their whole lives to see. Lucy would have gone to the salon beforehand, gotten her hair and nails done and maybe even asked one of the girls to help her with her makeup. Her dress would be yellow, like the sun, and she would beam in bright red lipstick, with her arms wrapped around Steve. They would all look up and marvel. The Steinbeck 'Stangs, State Champions. Head Coach Steve Quinn had taken them all the way.

Emmy had missed it. The season, going to games. She hadn't even gone to a game at Walker because Cameron thought it was too commercial and that football was "a conservative institution that perpetuated the ideology of toxic masculinity and violence instead of free expression and love and emotion and reasonable discourse."

Maybe she was right. But still. It felt like Emmy had missed all of autumn, all the cookouts and tailgates. Oliver from the diner, his face painted red, his outfit all black, grilling burgers for everyone. Cora Johnson mixing up her famous Mustang Punch in her red cooler, limiting everyone to just one cup because the stuff was so strong. Dan Holcomb and his family blasting country music out of the speakers of his monstrous, souped-up truck, the sounds of fiddles and acoustic guitars blasting across the parking lot. You could always hear them from a mile away.

It was like Emmy had missed a pivotal ritual. A skipped pilgrimage back to some sacred place. And as she drove by the stadium and Oliver's Diner and the general store and the church, all the places she had grown up around, she was overwhelmed with a flood of gratitude. The joy of return.

Emmy pulled into her mom's driveway. Lucy was on the porch, waiting, like she'd always done.

"Welcome home, Emmy," her mom said, engulfing Emmy in a bone-crushing hug. Before they were even inside, Lucy asked, "Are you sure you want to go tonight? There's still time to back out. We can go to my church. They don't have candles, but they sing all the good songs."

"I have to go there," Emmy said, knowing it was true. She gave her mom's shoulder a squeeze. "It's part of my home."

The sanctuary of the First Baptist Church had sterile, off-white walls. The pews were black, wooden, and cushionless. It smelled like pine needles from the enormous, decorated Douglas fir tree at the back of the church. A cross hung at the front, in between the metal organ pipes. The aisle was covered in an emerald carpet. The pulpit and baptismal pool at the front were lined with a pine garland that had little lights strung around it.

"More festive than usual," Emmy remarked to Lucy, as they settled into their empty pew. They were the first ones there. Emmy liked to settle in before a service began. It was strange for her to see the lights and trees: the sanctuary usually remained undecorated, plain, even during Christmas.

"Someone complained that it made the service too grim," Lucy said. "At least that's what your father—"

"Lucy, Emmy," Jan Oleander interrupted from the pew behind them. She had just walked in from the back. She put one of her hands around Emmy's shoulders, pressing her acrylic nails into her skin. "What a surprise."

Lucy and Emmy both took a simultaneous deep breath in before they stood up and turned around, smiling.

"Mrs. Oleander," Emmy said, her cheeks numb with the effort.

"Jan," Lucy said, reaching out a hand to touch her shoulder. "It's been so long."

"Too long," Jan said, her voice high-pitched and saccharine, as she extended each word with deliberate precision. "We *must* get lunch sometime. Bless your heart, it must be so hard to stay connected going to church all the way across town."

"I make it work," Lucy said, her voice equally high, sweet, strained—Texan. "But it's so *sweet* of you to think of me."

They both stared at each other, smiling, neither saying a word, like they were trying to get the other to submit to their will through their overwhelming politeness.

Jan broke eye contact first, turning to Emmy.

"Now, I know it's Christmas Eve and all," Jan said, grinning, showcasing her gray teeth, "but I was up there at the front talking to Kathy—you know, Pastor Ben's wife—and we saw y'all come in."

Kathy was at the front, talking to Pastor Ben, who had just walked in. He was nodding, serious. He looked over at Emmy, his brow furrowed, his head cocked to the side, as if he were looking at a museum exhibit.

"Hard to be missed when you're the first ones to walk in, I guess," Emmy said, slightly nervous, trying to shake off the intense discomfort she'd felt at the pastor's gaze. The sanctuary had started to fill up. Several people were taking their seats, gawking at the decorations, delighted in the church's commitment to festivity.

"Well, you did always like to get your pick of the pews, Emmy," Jan said, still smiling. "But we think there may be a little bit of a problem here with y'all."

"Oh?" Lucy asked, her jaw tightening.

"I think we may need to ask y'all to leave," Jan said, pressing her lips together. She got up from her pew to stand in the aisle, ushering them forward. "You understand."

"We will not leave," Lucy said, sitting down, crossing her arms. "This is a church. Anyone should be welcome."

"Normally," Jan said, nodding. "But it's Christmas Eve. You understand."

"I don't," Lucy said, dropping any false pleasantries, her eyes narrowed, her jaw set. The tough Texas woman coming out from underneath the faux sweetness.

"Y'all need to get on," Jan said, lowering her voice to a whisper, dropping her smile, too. "This isn't your day, Emmy, this is the Lord's day. And we can't have you in here, in the house of the Lord, living the life you are choosing to live, and not expect people to get distracted, ask questions."

A group of people were collecting in the aisle, blocked off by Jan, straining their necks to see what the holdup was. Emmy looked over and saw Dan Holcomb and his family whispering to one another. And coming up right behind them was Steve.

Emmy felt a jolt of shock at the sight of him, even though she knew he would be there. It almost didn't seem real, seeing him before her, not a figment of her imagination, after all this time.

He was wearing his navy sport coat with a white button-down oxford shirt, khaki pants, and cowboy boots. It took him a second to spot Emmy, but when he did, his eyes widened in surprise. He opened his mouth as if he were going to say something, then closed it, then opened it again. But he didn't look away.

He stared at Emmy. Dan Holcomb turned around and put a hand on his shoulder, preemptively holding him back. But Steve didn't budge. Just stood, his head cocked to the side, his cheeks flushed red, his mouth open just wide enough to see his slightly crooked teeth. He raised his right hand, and Emmy thought, for a moment, that he was going to reach out for her, pull her into him, let her rest in his protection and power, safe and home once again, returned to the arms of her father in Steinbeck's most holy house.

But he just brushed Dan's hand away. He held Emmy's gaze for a second. His thin wisps of eyebrows rose slightly, as if in defeat, before he bowed his head, looking at his shoes.

"Let's just go," Lucy said, noticing Emmy looking at Steve. She stood up and shoved Emmy toward the aisle, brushing past Jan, pushing her toward the door, away from him.

"Be a *father*," Emmy heard Lucy whisper. It seemed to echo through the silent sanctuary. Like it came from a ghost.

The heavy wooden doors slammed behind them. A cold, dry breeze blew through the trees, drooped and barren without their leaves.

"He just let me leave," Emmy said, breathless, staring into the darkness. "He didn't say anything."

"Let's go home," Lucy said, grabbing Emmy's hand. "We'll have church there."

She pulled on Emmy's hand, but she didn't budge. Emmy stood, frozen. In front of the door she'd opened with such joy for so many years, welcomed into a community, into a home, thrilled by the invitation to be a part of something bigger than herself. The rush of warmth during worship when they played the hymns, those centuries-old odes to the infinite. How grounded it had made her feel. How worthy of love.

As she stood out in the darkness, in the cold, Emmy wondered if people had the power to pull something like that away from you. Strip you of that holy assurance and leave you bare.

When they were in the living room of Lucy's house, Lucy led Emmy to the plush armchair she'd had since Emmy was a baby. The fabric was white linen, worn from years of use. Emmy collapsed onto it and buried her face into one of the arms, breathing in the light, floral scent of her mother's perfume. It calmed her, that old sense of home.

Lucy came back in from the kitchen with a tin tub of soapy water and a fresh, white towel thrown across one shoulder and an old teal washcloth on the other. The water sloshed as she set it down, gently, in front of Emmy. Lucy kneeled at her daughter's feet and took off Emmy's shoes.

"Mom, what—"

"Let me wash your feet," she said, taking off the other shoe, placing both of Emmy's feet into the warm water. "I said we'd have church here. Well, this is how I imagine Jesus might like to celebrate his birth. Washing the feet of someone dearly beloved."

Emmy stayed silent, watching Lucy's dark hair hang in front

of her face like silk curtains as she dipped her hands in the water, making sure both feet were completely submerged. She took the teal washcloth and dipped it down. It was heavy with water when she lifted it up, wringing it out with tender hands, the water trickling into the tub like the most subtle summer rain.

Lucy hummed a hymn as she worked, taking Emmy's right foot out of the water, running the washcloth up and down it, working in between her toes, wrapping it around the arch of her foot, giving it a firm squeeze, relieving the pressure. The low, soft notes she hummed were accompanied by the slosh of water, the scrubbing of cloth across skin, the washing away of dirt in warm, clean water. It was miraculous, Emmy thought, watching her mother. All that love and light finding its way through, despite the darkness in between.

"The Apostle Paul says to love one another with genuine affection," Lucy said, placing Emmy's right foot back into the water, grabbing her left one. "And to take delight in honoring one another."

Her hands were blue-veined and strong. Her nails were painted with a deep cranberry-red polish. Her sleeves were pushed up to her elbows, her navy blouse darkened in spots across her chest where the water had splashed out.

"And it is a delight to honor you, Emmylou," she said, her voice full with the lyric twang of Texas, "as you love whoever you love—*her* and others—with genuine affection."

She placed both of Emmy's feet at the rim of the tin tub, and plunged her hands into the water, scooping it out and pouring it over her feet, one final rinse.

"No one can steal your faith from you," Lucy said, wrapping Emmy's feet in a warm towel. "Your heart is wholly yours. Even when you're in love. You control what goes into it. Whatever beliefs you hold that give you hope. Let those fill you up. Not words from folks like them."

"Dad's one of them," Emmy breathed, her chest heavy with hurt and hope and love, all at once.

"No one can steal your faith from you," Lucy repeated, placing her daughter's dry, clean feet onto the carpet, kissing both of them before standing up. Her face was relaxed, calm. "Not even your father."

Emmy sat in the chair. Dug her toes into the carpet, let the softness wrap around them like a promise. Breathed in the smell of gardenias and spring. Her mother's home.

"Here," Lucy said, taking Emmy's hands, pulling her from the chair so that she was kneeling with her, facing her. Lucy took two votive candles and a matchbox from the side table. She struck a match, letting the flame flare up on the tip before she dipped it onto the blackened wicks. "I know how much you love the lights."

They each held a votive. The slightest warmth in the palm of their hands. Emmy swayed a little, humming that old hymn. Lucy picked up the melody and sang, softly, "Come thou fount of every blessing, tune my heart to sing thy praise."

They stayed kneeling until the candles burned through and the flames were snuffed out, the light no longer sustainable.

31

STEVE

No one ever really thinks of winter when they talk about dove-hunting, but Dan Holcomb and a few of his friends—big important men around town and one hardcore hunter who acted as their guide—went on a hunt, every year, on Christmas Day.

Steve wasn't a big hunter. Never had been. Every few years he'd go with guys around town in the fall, before the football season really revved up. The temperatures were blistering, and the doves were abundant, and they sat on lawn chairs, cracking open beers, swapping horror stories about all the hardcore high school football coaches they'd had back in their day. They sweated and shot and made sure the dogs had plenty of water, hot as it got in those early September days, as they bagged birds, trying to reach the daily limit of fifteen.

But winter dove hunts were different. Quieter. Cooler. Overcast skies. Fewer folks out. It was sort of nice, sitting in the field, camouflaged, the only noise the wind making its way through the empty field, turning the windmills over out in the distant horizon, and Sparky, the hunter's black Labrador retriever, who sniffed around the field, barking every now and then, bounding from his owner to the wide-open field, eager to start retrieving the fallen birds.

"Scouted this spot for the past week," the hunter said, a wad of tobacco tucked in his cheek, giving him an artificial sort of lisp. "Birds keep coming back here. Once I get the decoys up and running, I'm sure they'll come on in."

While he set up the fake, plastic doves—some were stationary, some had motorized wings—around their shooting range, Steve sat back in his folding chair, opening his thermos and taking a slow sip of steaming-hot coffee, which steamed in the chilly morning air.

The sky had that pale gray-gold glow of dawn, a hazy, slow sort of light that was muted by the overcast sky. The open field was filled with dead grass, but the ground was soft and wet with morning dew. No hills, no trees in the distance. Only flat, endless space, as far as the eye could see.

"Usually they'll flock in from the north, fly out in the southeast direction," the hunter said, after the decoys were posted into the ground, pointing toward the sun as it rose steadily out of the horizon. "They're more concentrated around this time, on account of all the crops already being harvested and they got limited food resources. I guess they like something out in this field here. So I reckon we wait a bit, but they'll come flying in eventually."

The doves came in and out. Everyone was getting good shots off. Except for Steve. He couldn't aim right. Kept overshooting, going directly over the birds, into the sky. Dan and Pastor Ben and the guys were bagging birds like no one's business. They were getting pretty close to the daily allowance. But around the second hour of sitting out in the cold, something shifted for Steve. He settled down. Took in a deep breath of the cold morning air. And the field suddenly came into focus.

It all happened fast. A flock flew up from the field. Steve had the shotgun pressed into his right shoulder, digging deep into the muscle to muffle the kickback. He aimed just below one of the birds. He steadied his shot with his left hand and squeezed the trigger with his right.

Steve got his shot off last, so he knew the bird was his. The shotgun rammed back in his shoulder with bruising force. The shell fell to his feet as he reloaded the gun.

"Oooweee!" Dan cried out. "Got yourself a hit, Steve!"

It didn't take Sparky long to retrieve it after he got the command. He shot through the grass, mud flying up after him, and darted back seconds later, the bird in between his loose jaws. The Labrador dropped the dove at Steve's feet, wagging his tail, delighted at his own obedience. Steve gave him a pat on the head, running his hand through the dog's soft fur, fixing his flopped-over ear.

"Good boy," Steve cooed, his eyes locked on the bird. It twitched and flopped in a tiny circle, subtle signs of its agony.

"I'll get it," one of the hunters said when Steve didn't move. He picked the bird up by its head, walked a few feet away, then wrung the bird around a couple of times before slamming it down on the ground, feathers exploding up with the force.

"Wanna do the honors?" the hunter asked, opening the bag, pointing to the bird.

"'Course," Steve lied, walking over and scooping the lifeless body into his hand. It was so small. It bore so little weight. No wonder it could fly.

Steve had never had the stomach for this part of hunting, the corpse part. But it was the thing men around here had to do. You took care of what you shot. It was supposed to be a prize, part of the sport and competition and camaraderie. Steve liked the shooting but preferred the clay pigeons that got drawn out on the ranch when they'd shoot skeet. No blood, no death. Just cracked clay.

Steve looked down at the dove. That creature of innocence, the symbol of God's peace. What he sent to Noah at the flood's end: the promise of love. The acknowledgment that the world would start again, brand-new.

He thought about his daughter, about the Christmas Eve service the night before. How he'd just stood there. Let her get escorted out by Jan Oleander and Pastor Ben's wife. Didn't say a word. Not even when Lucy hissed at him, imploring him to be a father. He just stood there. In silence.

She was supposed to come over on Christmas. They'd made the whole plan when he called her after State. Have a couple drinks out on the porch. Redeem that last memory from the summer. Get her to see his point of view. Get her to feel his love—*God's* love—and bring her back into the light.

Steve dropped the bird in the bag. It landed with a muffled thump over the bodies of the other fourteen.

"Well, men," the hunter said, dumping the contents of the bag on the ground and counting them out. "That's the limit."

"Last shot, Steve!" Dan said, clapping him on the back. "I guess I'll have to buy you a beer."

"I'll never say no to that," Steve said, putting his shotgun away in the bed of his pickup.

When Dan walked away with the hunters to help them take down the decoys, Pastor Ben walked up to Steve.

"Sorry about Emmy," Pastor Ben said. "Not the cleanest way that could have happened."

"'Sfine," Steve grunted, avoiding eye contact.

"You're doing the right thing, you know," Pastor Ben said, putting his hand on Steve's shoulder. "You're obeying God."

"Yep," Steve said, shrugging off his hand, wanting to get away from him, almost daring to wish he'd never talked to Ben about any of this in the first place. That was wrong, he knew; Ben had helped him stay on the right path. But still. The constant checking in. The pushiness. It made Steve's skin crawl.

"Just," Pastor Ben said, as he walked toward his car, "keep fighting the good fight."

Steve grunted and waved and watched him drive away, grateful to be rid of him.

"So," Dan said, coming up behind Steve, dumping the decoys in the truck bed. He tipped his black cowboy hat back, clearing his throat with a loud grunt. "If you don't got anything going on for Christmas supper, the missus wanted me to say it'd be just fine if you joined us. We always got room at our table for a State Champion."

"Appreciate the offer," Steve said, looking out at the empty field, the land so flat he could see the curvature of the horizon. "But I've got somewhere I promised I'd be tonight."

"Missing out. She's making pot roast." Dan hopped into the driver's seat of his vehicle. "But more for me, then. Come on, now. Let's go get us that beer."

32

It had never taken much to make Emmy happy. A bowl of guacamole. A good Springsteen album. A football game on in the
living room on Sundays with the windows open. And an empty
sanctuary.

It started when she was young. She'd sneak off at the end of
her Sunday school class, under the guise of using the restroom,
and find her way down to the sanctuary, which had just emp-
tied out after the morning service, the parents headed to pick
up their kids from class. She never did anything. Just sat in the
front-right pew, the bathroom pass in her lap, looking up at the
ceiling, the organ pipes, the cross. She never moved. She just
sat. Whenever her Sunday school teacher finally came looking
for her, she never resisted leaving. But she always came back.

In high school, she was caught alone in the sanctuary so many
times Pastor Sherman sat her down for a talk with Steve and
Lucy. He asked her, "Are you trying to take something? What
are you looking for?"

And Emmy just looked back at him, her face a little flushed from the rush of the inquisition and responded in her steady, soft voice, "Same thing as you."

After that, Pastor Sherman just let her sit, asking her to lock up after she was done.

They never talked about it. Her sanctuary visits. It seemed like something that was wholly her own, and Lucy and Steve didn't see the need to stop it or step in. It wasn't like they were going to tell their kid to spend *less* time in church.

So after Steve finished up with Dan and the guys, got back home, and washed up, he wasn't surprised to see Emmy's car parked outside of the church that evening. Hers was the only car in the parking lot.

Steve pulled up next to it, parked his car, and sat for a moment before he cut the engine. He said a little prayer. For strength. For clarity.

The heavy oak door was unlocked and creaked open when he pulled on it, walking into the black-and-white-tiled receiving room, which smelled like lemon disinfectant spray. The extra Christmas Eve programs were scattered across the credenza on the far wall. The glass doors to the sanctuary were thrown open. Steve walked in.

Emmy was sitting by herself, as she had so many times before, in the front-right pew, her head thrown back as she looked at the high, unadorned ceiling of the church.

Steve cleared his throat. She jumped to her feet. He heard a harsh inhale of shock.

"Dad," Emmy said, her face ashen, her thin lips rounded to form an oval of surprise.

"Thought I might find you here," Steve said, walking down the middle aisle, running his hand along the smooth finished wood of the pews. "How'd you get in?"

"Michaela always hid a key to the sanctuary under the boxwood pot up front," she said, her hand clutching the pew beside her.

"Pastors' kids," Steve said, cracking his knuckles. "They get to have all the fun, huh?"

She looked taller, somehow, even though she'd stopped growing when she was in high school. Her cheeks were hollow, like that time her appendix ruptured and, after she got the surgery, was made nauseous by everything. She barely ate for two weeks.

It wasn't as drastic as it was then. But there was something gaunt about her. Caved-in. Like some kind of sickness was eating her up from the inside.

But when Steve got closer, he saw that her eyes were the same. Wide, like almonds, the same shape and color. Even in the darkness, he could tell they hadn't lost their shine.

"Thought you were gonna come over," Steve said, hoping to ease into the conversation, as if he could erase the events of last night by never acknowledging them.

"God had other plans for me," she said, cocking her head to the right and running her thumb along her jawline. Her nervous tick.

"Hear he's a busy guy."

"Always makes time for me."

"So you've got him on call."

"Something like that."

"Maybe I oughta get in good like that."

"State Championship not in good enough?"

"Folks always want more once they get what they want."

"I've never wanted much."

"That's why Johnson took that head-coaching position in Corpus."

"I've always wanted the simple stuff."

"But I can't blame him, really. He's gotta chase his dream."

"What dreams are you chasing?"

"I don't chase dreams."

"Do they chase you?" she asked, a little smile tugging at the corner of her lips. She tried to suppress it, putting a fist to her mouth, but that just made her smile more, and soon she let out a little laugh. *Her laugh.* Three notes, each one higher than the next, belted out from some deep place within her. Once she got started, it was hard for her to stop, and her laugh rang out in the silent sanctuary, amplified by the emptiness. And Steve couldn't help it: hearing those notes tickled something in him, and he had to laugh, too, and it was like he had never laughed before but had needed to for all of his life, his sides stitching, his abs contracting, his eyes watering as he let out little silent hiccups of laughter. Every time he thought he was done, he'd breathe himself back into calm, they'd look at one another, and, after a beat, start all over again, her peals of laughter trilling out from her, so easy, so natural. How had he created a person filled with so much light? How could he have let her go? How could he have forgotten...

Then he remembered. Like an answered prayer, the truth of the choice she had made slammed over him. And in the same breath of laughter, Steve felt his chest tighten. The room spun. His head throbbed. He reached for the pew to steady himself. The laughter was gone. Snuffed out like a candle.

"Dad," Emmy said, suddenly concerned as he stood, bent over the pew.

"I can't lose you," Steve said, sinking into the pew, burying his face in his hands.

"Dad," she said. He felt her hands on his shoulder. "I'm not going anywhere. I'm here. I'm still me."

"You..." His voice trailed off. He lifted his head to look at her.

Her thick, overgrown eyebrows came together in concern. Her hollow cheeks were flushed red. Her button nose was scrunched up, her nostrils flared in the fierce, determined resolve she'd had all her life.

"Got that job from the summer, it's gonna be in Houston,"

she said in a rush. "Marketing, you know. One of those cool corporate places. Wear jeans to work. Beer and wine served after five. Mom's moving there, and they had an opening with an office there. So I took it."

"Houston's big," Steve said, as the world came back into focus. "It might swallow you."

"If Jonah can survive the whale, I think I'll survive the city."

"But Jonah had God on his side."

She inhaled sharply, like he had slapped her.

He hadn't meant to say it.

It just came out.

But he *did* mean it.

Didn't he?

"Don't go," Steve said, his voice cracking, strained with the effort of barricading the emotions flooding his chest, pressing down on it, heavy and dense. "Don't go away."

"I can't stay here," Emmy said, her voice soft, gentle, honest. "There's nothing here for me."

"Everything is here. Your family is here."

"Mom's moving to Houston."

"We got places that need marketing. We got nice men that would—"

"Can't change my mind, Dad. There's not a magic man in the world who can change me."

"How do you know?"

"Because."

"That's not good enough."

"It has to be."

"It's not."

"Just love me."

"Loving you is all I do," Steve said, standing up. "Loving you is all I *have*."

"Then, don't stop."

She didn't get it. She didn't understand. He *needed* her to see. To come into the light.

"Your soul, Emmy," Steve said, reaching out for her hand. "I want to save you, protect you. This life you're leading, the road you're going down—"

"You can't take heaven away from me," she said, cutting him off, slapping his hand away. Her jaw was set, but her lips were quivering, pulled down at the corners. Tears welled in her eyes. "What if you're wrong? What if the life I lead isn't a sin? Can't you just try and imagine that?"

Steve looked at her. Wide eyes. Tired eyes. Eyes just like her mother's. Imploring him. Asking him. She looked like a kid. My kid, Steve thought.

And, because he loved her, he tried to imagine it. The kind of world she was convinced was true, good, and necessary.

Backyard barbecues in the summer. Sweat everywhere. Mosquitoes buzzing, always able to outlive any candle or spray. Her with an iced tea and lemonade. A girl by her side. Maybe holding her hand. Maybe dropping her hand because it was too hot. All of them together. Laughing.

Fall games at the stadium. Steve on the field, coaching. In some other town. A place far away from Steinbeck. Where no one would care about the right and wrong kind of love. Them in the stands. A kid on their lap. Could they have a kid? Was that a thing two women could do? But he imagined it all the same. A little boy in a football jersey, or a little girl, dressed the same.

Christmas Day. A pot roast on the table. Torn up wrapping paper scattered around the tree. Playing in the backyard with all the new toys. Giving them a break. Giving them a chance to be two people in love, without a kid, without a worry. Two women in love? He tried to imagine it, pressing through the seeming impossibility of that sort of thing.

And spring. Ice cream on the way home from an afternoon spent in a field filled with wildflowers. Taking family pictures in the bluebonnets. A sea of blue and white. The wind bringing that strong, warm breeze, all coolness, not punishing like it would be in a matter of weeks, summer always coming in too soon.

A lifetime together. A lifetime of memories. Building a family and making mistakes and coming back together after long periods away from one another. It would be full of so much love.

But after the lifetime ran out, when all was said and done, when the race had been run, then what?

It was the same problem. The issue of the afterlife.

So many Baptists are instilled with a fear of fire. The consequence of an unrepentant heart. An eternity engulfed in flames.

His baby girl. His heart. His light in life. He couldn't stand by and let her commit herself to that kind of fate. What kind of love was that? Opening the door to eternal suffering?

"Emmy," Steve said, tears leaking out of the corners of his eyes, running hot down his cheeks. "I can't let you live like that. I can't risk losing you."

There was a long pause. She stared at him. Her face was blank. No expression. No reaction. Almost like she'd expected to hear it.

"Then, I guess I'm already lost."

And she walked down the aisle, away from him, slamming the door shut.

33

EMMY

Emmy rushed out of the chapel, making her way to the car. She didn't cry. She didn't scream. She just started driving.

She wanted to see Cameron, feel proof of her love. That it was good. That it was enough. Even after all the changes, the memory of what they'd had before made Emmy race toward her.

The two-lane highway was empty. Just her, the headlights, and the flat road extending out, an unending darkness.

After half an hour of speeding, Emmy turned into the parking lot of their apartment complex. A loud bass beat was thrumming from somewhere. A Christmas party, maybe. As Emmy walked toward the door, though, the music got louder.

"It's Emmy!" Cameron screeched when she threw open the door, the sticky-sweet smell of spilled beer hitting her as soon as she stepped inside. The bass of some nineties punk song reverberated in her chest.

A group of people who Emmy recognized from Cameron's cohort were gathered around the kitchen, shouting over each other about something Emmy couldn't quite make out. It sounded like they were saying *Hemingway* and *asshole.*

"I need to talk to you," Emmy said, leaning in so only Cameron could hear her.

"No time for talking!" Cameron shouted back in her ear, her words slurred.

"I talked to my dad."

"Fuck your dad!" she screamed, and her friends roared back their approval, echoing, "Fuck your dad!" One pock-faced boy with blond dreads tied on top of his head let out a loud burp, and the crowd around him booed.

"Why are all these people here?" Emmy asked, trying to take in their faces. She had expected to find Cameron on the couch, reading a book, typing something out on her laptop, sitting quietly, peacefully, like she had seen her do a million times before when she walked through their door.

"You didn't answer your phone," Cameron said, shrugging, taking a long pull from her beer until it was empty. She grabbed another can from the table behind her.

"It was off."

"So I invited some people over."

"I was in a sanctuary."

"They're from my cohort."

"It's a sacred place."

"You're supposed to always have your phone on."

"I forgot."

"Well, while you found your God," Cameron said, turning away from Emmy, "I found some beer."

She cracked open a can and pulled on Emmy's arm, trying to drag her over to the kitchen, where the argument from before had turned into an overly competitive game of flip cup.

"Cameron, I really want to talk with you," Emmy said, digging her heels in so she couldn't pull her any farther. "Alone."

"It's a party, Emmy!" Cameron said, throwing up her hands.

"You're free to leave at any time. No one's forcing you to be here."

Where else could I go? Emmy wanted to ask, but she kept her mouth shut as Cameron bounded over to the kitchen, taking her place in line for flip cup.

Emmy watched the game without really seeing it. She thought of her father's face in the sanctuary. The way it seemed to crack just looking at her. His inability to accept her life, to take her back, to love her. And in her mind, that rejection flooded every street and every home in Steinbeck like the ten plagues that befell Egypt, the fodder for her recurring nightmares since childhood.

Breathing through the alarming wave of loneliness that nearly knocked her down, Emmy closed her eyes and imagined him sitting there in the sanctuary after she left, his hands folded in his lap. Emmy's chest tightened at the thought.

Cameron continued to ignore Emmy while drinking and arguing about books with the strangers flooding their apartment. Emmy didn't need to be there. Cameron didn't look at her once.

It seemed like everything had changed so suddenly. It was only yesterday that they had come together with some hope for the future, the promise of Big Bend hanging in the air. But her returning home had shifted something for Cameron, it seemed. Or maybe it had shifted something for Emmy.

Nothing was sudden, of course. Nothing shifted in an instant. Love gets lost over time, with a series of concessions.

Before, Emmy had never been able to picture the future. Life was the present—firmly rooted in reality. Fantasy, dreams, she had never had the benefit of that kind of longing. It had always been a risk, allowing herself to hope.

But after, with Cameron, there was the uncontrollable urge to picture it all. A surge of hope so strong it felt a little like panic. Emmy dreamed up a wedding day. A venue outside, white peonies and roses and baby's breath, a field in Texas in springtime. Blue skies stretched for miles and miles. It was easy to make herself forget the floods from April and May storms. Cameron had made what was once unthinkable completely tangible, real. What guarantee did Emmy have that she would ever find such a miracle again?

When Cameron left the game to get another beer, Emmy rushed toward her, pulling her away into the living room. She just wanted to feel heard, comforted. To erase her father's face and replace it with Cameron's hand in hers, the tenderness, excitement, rush of belonging that she'd felt on that first August night on top of the grain silo, when Emmy told Cameron everything she'd ever wanted anyone to know, and she listened and hummed her understanding, letting Emmy talk until the words ran out. And when all she had left was silence, Cameron had smiled and pulled Emmy's face into hers, and something broke apart and solidified in Emmy, and she called that feeling *healing* without ever assessing the damage that was still left behind.

In the living room, Emmy held Cameron's hand, hoping to feel some of that moment return. Cameron looked down at it. Rubbed her undercut.

"I just want to talk about what happened with my dad."

"I'm tired of talking about your dad, Emmy," Cameron said quietly, her face falling a little. "Aren't you?"

Emmy looked at the lips she had kissed so many times, perpetually chapped, always tugged up at the corners, bitten and pulled in moments of uncertainty, which Cameron was doing as they stood together, their hands still clasped. Cameron's face was flushed from the booze, and her eyes were slightly crossed, but narrowed. A sign of her conviction.

Emmy thought about the weeks spent in constant proximity, the location verification, the monitoring of all her technology. The break from that kind of vigilance, even for twenty-four hours, must have felt as much like freedom to Cameron as the open highways of Texas did for Emmy.

Some people don't have the heart to say *Leave*. So they make a place impossible to stay.

Emmy's throat throbbed with the realization. But she nodded. Squeezed Cameron's hand. Then let her go.

"Talk in the morning?" Cameron said, her voice mumbled, her eyes flitting to the table behind Emmy where they were setting up another game.

"Yeah," Emmy said, feeling like the wind was knocked out of her. "Sure."

Emmy slipped outside when they started playing beer pong. No one noticed.

The air was cool. A breeze picked up and blew through the leafless trees, their branches clacking together in a chaotic rhythm, like a line of spiders crawling up a concrete wall.

Emmy had never felt safe at night, especially in Walker, where the streetlights flickered a weak yellow fluorescent light. Nothing was illuminated. Everything was hidden. But, at that moment, Emmy felt comforted by the darkness. No one could see her coming.

The day of the Lord will come like a thief in the night.

Scripture embedded in Emmy so deep it often flooded her mind like one of her own thoughts. She looked behind her, paranoid suddenly that she was being watched. Something scurried across the street, big enough to be an opossum, but nothing else moved. She was alone.

A thief in the night. Maybe the Second Coming *was* at hand, Emmy thought. Her whole world was destroyed. Again. How many second comings do people get in a lifetime? How many times do they rebuild before they accept the end?

Ahead of Emmy, there was a white billboard with a black cross next to big black letters that read, *It's never too late to return Home!* She looked up at it for a long time.

Maybe the streets of Walker at night were like the Road to

Damascus, revelation waiting beyond every rusted, spray-painted billboard.

Emmy thought again of the parable of the Prodigal Son, his road back to his father's home. He didn't seek reconciliation with his father—only the safety of his home, the security of a roof over his head.

Was he really sorry? Or just desperate, starving? Did it matter, if, in the end, his father took him back anyway?

Reunion. Reconciliation. Retribution.

How could the father be certain the son wouldn't rob him blind once the sun went down, the celebration ended, and everyone had left, leaving all his valuables vulnerable to a man who had estranged himself from his own family? Was love always so open to attack? So weak in its defenses?

The second son... Did he feast with his brother, the one who was lost, then found? Did he hold out his hardened, calloused hands, the hands so dutiful in their obligation, and embrace the soft, delicate ones of his brother?

The father's love seemed so simple, so pure. And maybe that was how it was with God and his creation: always willing to take them back.

But Emmy thought the sons were more complicated, more compelling. Why didn't the sons interact? Biblical brothers competing for their father's affection never have a happy ending. So, what of the second son? Does he simply learn to stuff down his own feelings of betrayal and mimic the love of his father? Resentment never remains buried for long. It's always simmering, cooking love down to hate, admiration to jealousy, security to fear.

Emmy felt fear everywhere, in her chest, her fingers, the ringing in her head. It felt so loud that she imagined someone would hear it down the street and come running after her, saving her.

From what? Who was she afraid of? Why was she afraid of them?

The slamming of a door. The shouting of shame at the sky.

Every time love got in close enough to change her, it took away a chunk of who she was.

A car drove by, the headlights flashing as it passed Emmy, and a boy screamed something profane out of the window. Men never suppressed their urge for vulgarity, even on Christmas. Emmy walked on, with nowhere to go, not feeling fully safe but needing to keep her body in motion.

Emmy walked, cloaked in darkness, and wondered if she was born to love but never feel it returned. Maybe Sara was right and it had something to do with the stars, the way the planets aligned themselves when she was born. Her Leo sun, her Gemini moon, the fate of her life stretched across a universe wholly indifferent to its effects on her.

Or maybe the faith of her father was to blame. That her inability to conform and discipline her mind to choose the *right* kind of love had damned her to a lifetime of heartbreak.

Or maybe—and this, she feared, was most likely—maybe she loved Cameron and Cameron loved her back, and that still wasn't enough. Emmy wasn't the person Cameron wanted her to be: confident, brave, sophisticated. Emmy was too Texan, too friendly, too unwilling to give up the world in which she'd been raised.

It wasn't a sadness that Emmy felt so much as a hopelessness born from wanting. To heal, to be understood, to be loved: she longed for those delicacies of living like her great-great-grandfather must have longed for the cracked and severed landscape of his homeland when he arrived in the dry, landlocked desert of West Texas all those years ago.

The world as she had known it was this: love your parents, love your neighbors, love your God. Both her parents, at one point, had shut her out. Her friends had kicked her out. And God had...

What *had* God done, besides nothing? Emmy wondered. Sent a son to earth to create a collective obsession in humanity over redemption? Salvation? Heaven and Hell, us versus them?

Emmy looked up at the sky, looking for some kind of sign. An apology folded into the stars.

All she saw, though, was a flickering streetlamp and the Big Dipper, which her father had always taught her to find when they would stargaze in his backyard.

When Emmy looked back down, she saw the fluorescent sign for the Grizzly. She hadn't realized where she was going. It was still open for another two hours.

Emmy was sure that Jacob was home in Steinbeck, with Derek and Cora, but she went inside anyway. She didn't have any other place to go. There was an empty stool at the end of the bar where she and Sara had watched all those Cowboys games, and she slid on to it, trying not to take up too much room beside a group of fraternity boys drinking straight from their pitchers of beer like they were pints.

"Emmy!" David, Cameron's bartender friend, came over with a pint of her favorite already poured. He set it in front of her. "No Cameron tonight? She go home for Christmas?"

"Oh, she..." Emmy started, and then, not wanting to explain, said, "Yeah. She's home."

"Tell her to come by when she's back," he said, rapping his knuckles on the bar before walking away. "Finally finished that book she loaned me last summer."

Emmy nodded, feeling numb, feeling nothing, like her body was protecting her from feeling anything. Her father's face. Cameron's indifference. Her fractured heart.

She took a sip of the beer, an ice-cold Kölsch, trying not to think about where she was going to sleep that night.

"Heard you made a scene at that church of y'all's last night," whispered a voice Emmy knew well from behind her. She whipped around. Jacob dropped off two more pitchers to the fraternity boys beside Emmy, who screamed their gratitude, stuffing twenties into Jacob's shirt pocket.

"You gonna strip for them, or what?" Emmy asked, unable to resist.

"Ha ha."

"Seems like they want a Christmas show," Emmy said, giving a little hoot and holler for effect. "What are you doing here, anyway?"

"Picked up an extra shift," he said, a grin stretching across his face. "Rings ain't cheap, Quinn, let me tell you. You better start saving now."

Emmy opened her mouth to make some jab about how diamond-trading was usually unethical anyway and he could save his money by getting some other stone. But then she remembered all the imagined plans she'd made for a wedding she promised herself she'd never hope for, and it all erupted out from her. She told Jacob everything. The pain of seeing her father, the knowledge that she and Cameron were never going to make it, the fear that she'd never be able to make it work with anyone, the dread that she was destined for some divine punishment...

"Nope," Jacob said, doing his best to keep himself from looking horrified at Emmy's breakdown. He fixed his face, locked his jaw, and pulled her into his chest so that she sobbed into his flannel, the old familiar scent of Old Spice and spearmint calming her down. "Not that last one, Emmylou. You know better than that."

Jacob must have gestured something to David while he held Emmy because when she lifted her head, he ushered her up from the stool toward the door, while some of the frat boys behind them screamed, "I got something that'll make you feel better, darlin'!"

"Assholes," Jacob said under his breath as they walked toward his car. "But they tip well."

"There's nowhere for me to go," Emmy said, sniffling, once they were both in the car.

"Don't be stupid," he said, starting the ignition. "Remember what my mama used to say to you when we were little? With our sleepovers?"

"No," Emmy lied, wanting to hear it from him.

"Yeah, right," he said, rolling his eyes, knowing what she wanted. "'Love's an open home, baby. It's always been that way.'"

Emmy remembered the late nights at the Johnsons', s'mores out by the firepit, sleepovers in separate rooms, waffles in the morning, served with a small cup of coffee that was mostly cream and sugar that she always drank too fast, making her hands shake by the time her parents picked her up.

"You can stay at mine as long as you need," he said, driving toward his place. "I stay in Dallas most nights anyway, when I can. No sweat. You got stuff over there?"

"I don't have much," Emmy said, thinking of the small, borrowed suitcase she had stuffed underneath the bed, the five or so blouses she had in the closet, the underwear and socks and jeans and shorts in the drawer. "I could just leave it all behind."

"Yeah," Jacob said slowly, shaking his head. "But what you've got is still yours."

He kept his eyes on the road, but he reached over and grabbed her hand. They stayed like that until they reached home.

34

The next morning, Emmy walked into the apartment. Beer cans were scattered on the counter. A nearly empty handle of tequila rested on the floor under the table. Emmy thought she smelled pizza and looked down to find half an abandoned slice on the table where they put their keys. The whole place had collapsed into chaos.

Emmy breathed in the stale air, remembering mornings that were so opposite of this: lavender candles, fresh linens, the warm waft of dark roast brewing. Cameron's hand in Emmy's hair, lips on her neck, that timeless, endless breath of wanting and fulfillment.

Cameron stumbled into the living from the bathroom, wearing her oversize white T-shirt with no pants, her hair a mess, her eyes half-open and hungover. She squinted up at Emmy.

"You stayed at Jacob's," she said. And then, before Emmy could ask, "Still have your location tracked on my phone."

"Oh," Emmy said, the invasion of privacy a reminder of what had been lost.

"I turned it off," Cameron said, clocking her reaction. "Just wanted to make sure you were safe."

Emmy nodded. They stood in silence. Not moving closer. So much distance between them.

"You're mad," Cameron said. "I get that."

Emmy didn't say anything. It wasn't anger. It was a more exhausted feeling, a resignation. Mixed with a sort of longing as she looked at Cameron, which she hadn't expected to feel. So much of her had slipped away from Emmy in the past month, the mistrust and fear and control replacing all the comfort that she craved. But seeing Cameron so disheveled, so out of sorts, made all the affection in the world for her shoot through Emmy, making her smile.

Cameron cocked her head to the side.

"Place is a fucking mess," Cameron said, looking around, rubbing her undercut. "Why I hate throwing parties."

"Seemed more of a drunken gathering of literary nerds than a party," Emmy said, picking up the slice of pizza on the table and dangling it in front of her. "Messy literary nerds."

Cameron walked over and took the slice out of Emmy's hand, throwing it away in the kitchen.

"So," Cameron said, coming back over, taking Emmy's hands in hers. "Are you coming back?"

"Cameron," Emmy said, dropping her hand. "I can't...keep living like we were."

"I know," Cameron said, quickly. "I know. I can change. I can fix it. If you could just..."

Cameron paused, thinking it through. Emmy felt she could read her mind. If Emmy could just...

Accept her. Without conditions. Never need her to know Emmy's family. Never need her to hear about the way Emmy's family had treated her. If Emmy could forget about everything before and start over with her. If she could abandon Texas, move back east with Cameron, and see how much wider the world could be. If Emmy could live within the bounds of Cameron's love, life, perspective. If Emmy could grow up just a little bit, learn how to say *Fuck you* to all that had made her, if Emmy could live without fear, if Emmy could quickly mend the heart that her father broke and never give it or him a second thought. If Emmy could promise never to talk to anyone else. If Emmy could just…

"I don't know," Cameron said, finally, for once unable to find the right words. "I've been so crazy."

"Not crazy," Emmy said, bringing Cameron's hand to her lips, pressing them gently against her skin. "We just don't work anymore."

Cameron nodded, dropping her eyes, blinking fast, hard. She closed them and rubbed her temples, and Emmy thought she'd never known a more beautiful woman in her life, so she held her, then kissed her, then held her again. It was impossible to let her go.

An ending, Emmy felt, was a funny thing. It never came on its own. It had to be beckoned. And even then, it dragged its feet.

"I still love you," Emmy whispered into her neck, hoping it would get muffled there and seep into her skin, staying a part of her in perpetuity. "Why can't I stop?"

"Because it's real," Cameron said, a slight crack in her voice. She stroked Emmy's hair and rubbed her back, then sighed, deeply. "You're the only person from West Texas I could ever love," she said. "But that's the problem, isn't it?"

Emmy squeezed her tightly, knowing she was right, wishing she could expand Cameron, wishing she could give her just one more ounce of tolerance for her home and the people who raised her, so that she could love her just a little deeper, so that Cameron could see her just a little more clearly.

"I'm gonna be gone for a week," Cameron said, pulling herself away from Emmy, but still holding her shoulders. "Back up to Boston. My parents have some connections with PhD program directors up there."

"They're on board?"

"A PhD is enough prestige for them, it seems," Cameron said. "They want me back home. I was going to surprise you. With tickets. To meet them. But..."

She released her hands from Emmy's shoulders, sighing, looking down at her shoes. A pair of her jeans were slung on the back of the couch. She grabbed them and shimmied into them.

"I'm gonna run out and grab some coffee," Cameron said. "Suitcase is under the bed. You remember where you stuffed it. Take your time."

Emmy knew it was right, but it didn't make the blow any easier to bear. She watched her walk away, unsure of what to say, *needing* to say something.

"You changed my life," Emmy blurted out before Cameron walked through the open door. "I've changed because of you."

Cameron looked back at her, pausing in the doorway. The blinding sun outside reduced her to a silhouette.

"You always had that in you," Cameron said, her voice strong, confident. "Evolutionary Emmy."

She closed the door without another word.

PART FOUR: SPRING

And now these three remain: faith, hope and love.
But the greatest of these is love.

—1 Corinthians 13:13

EVEN WITH ALL THE BAPTISTS, Texans never stop dancing. A fiddle, a subwoofer, an abandoned acoustic—it doesn't matter where it comes from. If there's a beat, feet are moving. And there's no better excuse to do so than the spring.

Windows are thrown open, dance halls are filled, picnics and patios and pools start to open. There is an abundance in spring that is not taken for granted. It's almost an illusion. Summer comes on the heels of the season so quickly it's easy to believe that it doesn't exist. But Texans know better. They are conditioned in gratitude. When the warm breeze picks up and life returns to the state, they do not dread what is to come. They relish the moment, in the excuse to dance and sing and be fully alive and outside before the heat renders all of those things impossible.

Spring is a gift. It is temporary, fleeting. It gets washed away by May showers that bring in the summer heat too soon. But before that, the land gives way to life, the grass across highways filled with wildflowers and, across the state, dogwood trees and magnolias and crepe myrtles burst with color, the sweet warmth of their flowers blowing in the warm breeze, which picks up their pollen, carrying it across the land. Sowing new seeds. Preparing for new life.

35

STEVE

Before Johnson moved to Corpus, he and Steve sat together one last time at the diner. Johnson ordered bacon and eggs. Steve ordered a chicken fried steak.

"You see the article?" Johnson asked, sliding a printed page from the internet over the table. "Y'all made that list. The Super 25 high school rankings. For next season."

Steve took the paper and pulled out his glasses. At number twenty-five, there was a giant, blown-up picture of Miguel during the State Championship game, diving for that final catch, the one that made them win it all.

"Well, I'll be," Steve said. "Never thought we'd make it on any list outside of Texas."

"You did good work, Coach," Johnson said, taking a sip of his coffee. It was strange for Steve to see him without his bucket hat and gray, long-sleeved Steinbeck football T-shirt. He had on a black T-shirt and black jeans and fancy fifties-style glasses that

Steve never knew he needed. His head was shaved, like always, and he was smiling.

"Not good enough to keep you around."

"Gotta go try this head-coaching shit out for myself," he said. "But I'll miss it. Steinbeck's a special place."

"Bet our kids would make fun of us for this," Steve said, pointing at the paper. "Printing out stuff from the internet."

"Probably," Johnson said. He ran his hand up and down his smooth, bald head, and asked, "You seen your kid? Heard from her?"

"Not since Christmas," Steve said, folding up the paper and putting it in his back pocket. Miguel would get a kick out of it, a picture of him blown up so big in a national news article.

"Long time."

"Yep."

"Well," Johnson said, nodding. There wasn't much else to say. They lapsed into silence. It was comfortable. That old-friend sort of silence that never demanded to be filled. Steve took a long sip of his coffee and finished his steak.

"Gonna visit Houston?"

"Maybe," Steve said, looking down into his mug. "Not a lot of time to get on down there."

"It's always there," Johnson said, looking out of the window, squinting in the sunlight. "If you ever get too lonely."

"You worried about me, Johnson?" Steve asked, half-joking.

"Not as worried as you should be about that offense of yours," Johnson said, turning from the window to Steve, a wide smile on his face, all the seriousness of the moment before melted away with a little trash talk. "Without me calling plays out there, you really think that offense is gonna have any fire?"

"Miguel will just audible the hell out of the whole season," Steve said. "Be his own offensive coordinator."

"That's not a bad game plan right there," Johnson said, sticking out his hand. Steve shook it. "It's been an honor working with you, Coach."

"Same to you," Steve said, letting his hand go, feeling the heavy weight of loss sink into his chest.

Another person gone.

It was the last day of spring practices. The sun was getting closer. The heat would start back up soon enough. Boys would come back from their camps and summer leagues and conditioning plans. They'd get ready for the season in full pads. They would begin again.

The field felt empty without Johnson. A guy who could read Steve from across the field. Anticipate adjustments that needed to be made before he said anything. The coaches they had were good—excellent, even—but they didn't know Steve. Not their fault. That was the sort of thing that could only come with time.

It was a conditioning day, though, so there wasn't much to see. Just keeping the guys in shape. Making sure they didn't slack off. One successful season didn't guarantee anything. Never worked that way. Once spring ball started up, it was a whole new season, a whole new game.

The guys were running their timed mile. The linemen were always last, slower than the rest.

Miguel finished fast and came up to Steve afterward, still breathing heavy, wearing his classic, bright orange Astros baseball cap. He had a ball in his hands and a grin on his face.

"You think we can do it again, Coach?" he asked, tossing the ball to Steve. "Repeat the magic?"

"Sure as hell hope so," Steve said, gripping the football in his hands, running his index finger over the laces. "The way they started paying me, I figure we oughta make a habit of it."

"Got a meeting with a recruiter tomorrow," Miguel said, gesturing for the ball. Steve tossed it back to him. "Around five. At my abuela's. She's cooking. Want you there, if you can come."

"'Course," Steve said. "Got to get you ready for the dream.'"

Miguel tossed the ball back to Steve. Hard throw, tight spiral. Stung his hands when he caught it.

"Big summer plans?" Miguel asked, rolling his eyes when Steve shook his hands out from the sting.

"Same as always," Steve said, sending a dart back his way. He caught it with ease. "Getting ready for the season."

"Don't forget to have some fun, Coach," Miguel said. The other guys were finishing up their mile, starting the cooldowns on the other side of the field.

"I'll let you do the fun for me," Steve said. "Now, get down there and stretch. Can't have you pulling anything, give you an excuse to skip out on summer workouts."

Miguel gave him a grin and a salute and jogged over to his teammates, chucking the ball behind his back. It landed at Steve's feet and bounced forward, rolling around the grass until it lay motionless and abandoned.

When Steve got home from practice, he cracked open a beer and went out on the porch, trying to savor the silence.

All day, he was surrounded by noise. Most nights, too. Folks kept wanting to take him out, order him drinks, pick his brain, offer their own thoughts about the season. Steve was wined and dined all up and down the town. Never really a moment's rest. He stopped feeling like a person so much as a figure. People passed him around, night to night, trying to talk to him, get some sense of how his brain worked. It made them feel special, having the Coach over at their houses. And Steve learned to live with it, that feeling of being seen but never known. A sort of ghost.

There was no one left in town who he could relax around. Johnson had been the last. But he'd had to leave. Start over new. Build his own legacy, separate from Steve's.

Johnson was right, Steve knew. It'd be so easy. To pick up

the phone, to get in the car and drive. Texas was conducive to grand gestures. The highways stretched out for thousands of miles across the state. If you had a car and enough money for gas, you could go anywhere.

But Steinbeck needed Steve to stay put. Keep on planning for the season. Find out a way to repeat the magic. To make them a *program*, not just a one-season miracle. It was his priority. It had always been his priority.

Steve took a seat on one of the old red rocking chairs. The dusk was setting in. The cicadas were out and buzzing. Heat and noise.

Emmy always came over in May on the last day of practice. It was their little spring ritual. He'd cook steaks and potatoes and she'd bring the beer. They'd talk about the season, the semester, the varying threads of their lives that were separated but always managed to come back together. They'd poke fun at Lucy, her little quirks that only they knew. They'd wait until it got dark outside, and they'd go and look up at the stars. It never got old, a clear Texas sky at night, exploding with the brightness of the stars.

As he sat alone on the porch, listening to the cicadas drone on, Steve imagined her coming in, the crunch of gravel underneath her tires, the slam of her door as she jumped out of the car, the creak of the steps on the porch as she made her way up to the front door, and her laugh—those most magic three notes—reverberating in his house.

Steve would throw open his arms and hold her tight, then turn on the music real loud. Let Springsteen fill the silence. A housewarming of sound. He'd take his daughter's hand, twirl her around, and they'd dance like they used to when she was young and she was home and the world made sense.

Steve clung to it, that vision of his prodigal daughter. He couldn't let the image go. He sat out on the porch, alone, sipping his beer, thinking of her. Haunted by hope.

36

EMMY

On her last day in Walker, Emmy woke up from a dream.

Parts of it were fragmented in her mind, debris left from the shipwreck of her subconscious. It was an evening in summer at her father's house. Only he was still married to her mom, and they welcomed Emmy and Cameron and Sara into their home with open arms. It was the first time the three of them had seen one other since the incident.

Then the dream changed. It was Emmy and Cameron by the fields behind the church where Michaela and Emmy used to go at night, where they had kissed and then prayed in the back of the pickup truck.

In the dream, Cameron and Emmy were there at dusk, and the sky was pink and alive with clouds shifting away from the horizon like waves toward the shore. Emmy tried to be mad at her for her controlling behavior, but Cameron shoved her shoulder into Emmy's side, her playful way of saying sorry, and Emmy laughed and flicked her forehead, her way of saying *I forgive you.* They were in constant motion, their bodies getting closer together, until their foreheads were touching. She kissed Emmy's neck several times, and it was just as she remembered it: soft lips, full lips, pressure in the right place, pleasure shooting up her spine.

When Cameron finally kissed Emmy, it wasn't right. It felt like Michaela's lips, not Cameron's, and when she pulled away, she laughed and let out a sigh of relief.

"Oh, thank God," Cameron said. "I always worried about you. That you were my one weak spot. That I would always want you. But whatever we had is gone."

When Emmy woke up, she stayed in bed with her eyes closed for several minutes, holding on to the memory of Cameron before it went away completely. It had been nice, even if it had not been real, for Emmy to feel Cameron with her again.

In reality, it was clear: Emmy did *not* want her. Whatever good they'd had had been whittled away by dependency.

But in her dreams, Emmy still longed for her, a carbon copy of love that lived in her interior life. What happened to love, Emmy wondered, when it disappeared from the conscious mind? Especially first love? It couldn't evaporate, get sucked up into the clouds, and come back down again during the next storm.

If not into the air, then into the deep it must go. Beyond her waking mind, into the vault of memories—to be cursed with memories! Every second of Cameron cataloged with the desperate detail of someone who knows their object of observation cannot last forever.

Emmy wondered if she would always wait for Cameron in her dreams, those imagined moments where they could come together and be happy. Where they wouldn't have to separate. The mornings would be cruel and cold, but it would be a price she was willing to pay to hold her, touch her, feel her once again, even in the inscrutable form of a dream.

Sunlight streamed in through Emmy's half-closed blinds, and she knew she had to get up. She stretched and remembered the commencement ceremony for the business school was happening in a few hours. Emmy wasn't going. There was no point. It was just another reminder of what had been lost. If she had still been on good terms with her father, with Steinbeck, she knew there would have been a huge party at her father's house, filled with all the people who had watched her grow up and strive and study and work for what she was about to achieve: a degree and a steady salary, launched into the rest of her life. Her last semester had been uneventful. She went to class. She avoided the English building. She slept at either her mom's or Jacob's house. She stayed at her mother's house most weekends, and they ate and drank and talked in her backyard, never venturing out into the town, but repairing what had been temporarily lost between them, what had been broken in that year before.

Her mom had offered to host a little graduation get-together with the Johnsons for her and Jacob at the Grizzly, but Emmy hadn't been back there since she and Cameron broke up, and she didn't see the point in dragging out the year any longer.

It was time, she knew, to leave Walker: the people, the place, the memories.

"Jesus," Jacob said, when Emmy walked into the kitchen. She had to sidestep several moving boxes to get to it. "You look horrible."

"Yeah, well," she said, pouring herself a cup of coffee. "Didn't sleep well."

"Something came for you in the mail," Jacob said, hopping on the counter to sit in front of her, his long legs brushing against the cabinet. He held out a note.

The coffee was hot and strong and grounded Emmy, like it always did, in the firm realm of reality after a long night of sleep. It was necessary, because when she saw the handwriting on the front of the note, she could have sworn she was still dreaming.

She ripped it open. Threw the envelope on the ground. "Not in this house!" Jacob shouted. Emmy picked it up and threw it in the trash before opening the card.

There was a cartoon of a small wave crashing down on a beach, manufactured text that read *I'm SHORE the future is bright!* and a handwritten note underneath it.

Here's to you and all that your new life brings you.
Love,
Sara

Emmy's hands trembled slightly as she read the note over and over again.

"Graduation card?" Jacob asked.

"Yeah," Emmy said, clearing her throat. She read it one last time before she closed it and stuck it in her back pocket.

"Some kind of aunt? Family friend? Long-lost relative?"

"Something like that."

"They give you any cash?"

"Words have their own value, don't they?" Emmy asked absentmindedly, thinking about Sara, wondering where she was. Probably back home in the Panhandle. Her niece's birthday was in May. Strange, Emmy thought, what information the brain retains.

"Since when?" Jacob asked. "We're small-town gold diggers, remember? Why you should've stuck with Trust Fund for a little longer."

"Cameron didn't have a trust fund," Emmy lied, picking at one of her cuticles. "How am I ever going to pay you back for all of this?"

"Just promise to visit Kiera and me in Dallas," Jacob said, kicking his feet against the cabinet. "'Cause business school's gonna be a bitch, and I'll need a little dose of your crazy to keep me sane."

Emmy stuck out her hand, and he shook it, their old sign of

a binding promise. Then they lapsed into a conversation about nothing, giving each other a hard time, enjoying the ease of a slow Sunday morning together, one last time.

37

Later that afternoon, Emmy left Walker and drove east toward Waco. Her mom was already in Houston, and she didn't like the idea of Emmy making the ten-hour drive alone, without any breaks, so she reached out to the Shermans, and they agreed to let her stay the night. Before Emmy could even ask, her mom said, "Michaela's not there. She's in Austin."

Emmy wasn't sure if the sinking feeling she felt was relief or disappointment. Maybe a little bit of both.

Out on the open highway, the sun was high in the sky, burning hot and bright. In a week or two, it would become unbearable, summer swooping in a month too soon, as always. On the side of the road, wildflowers started to bloom. Bluebonnets, their base a deep, dark blue, layered with cerulean, giving way to white at the top, stood stalk straight and swayed in the wind. It looked like a slow-moving ocean on land. Tangled in the weeds, there were patches of coral and red and yellow flowers, the Texas Paintbrushes.

Life was returning to Texas.

Emmy arrived in Waco with an hour to kill before she was supposed to be at the Shermans'. So she made her way through town, stopping at the university, walking through the campus, admiring the old oak trees. Their thick trunks, gnarled and twisted from decades of growth, cast wide nets of shade over the pavement and impeccably kept lawns. Water ran through immaculate fountains. Bench swings creaked back and forth in the breeze.

She drove through a coffee shop near campus, picking a drink they called a Cowboy Coffee—yeehaw, Emmy thought as she took her first sip—and drove through the overpopulated streets of downtown, passed the two old grain silos that had been re-purposed into a home-goods supercenter, with a fake grass lawn that had dozens of food trucks surrounding it and thousands of people packed on it, running around, taking pictures, laughing, waiting in lines that wrapped around the block to gain entry.

It was strange, seeing so many people find so much joy in artifice, when a mile down the road, the land cracked open to make way for the mighty Brazos River, its wide, muddy waters running strong, southeast, toward the Gulf of Mexico. Emmy drove along the road parallel to the river, a slight scenic detour, and along the western bank saw small limestone cliffs, the sur-face white and cragged and obscured in most places by trees, their leaves different shades of green. The colors reflected on the water, pastels blurred and distorted by the current, like a Monet painting left in the rain.

It was the same road Emmy had taken when she drove through the town with her dad, heading for one of her many summer softball tournaments across the state.

"Why are those rocks there?" Emmy had asked him, awe-struck by the limestone cliffs. "I thought all of Texas was flat."

"It's a fault line, you know," he said, looking over at the limestone. "The Balcones Escarpment. Spanish settlers saw the tiers on the rock and thought they looked like balconies."

"Fault line? In Texas?"

"Used to be mountains all over," he said, leaning over the wheel to get a better look at the rocks. "The Ouachitas. But they eroded. Their roots are still around, deep in the ground. The invisible mountain range."

"Why do you know so much about rocks?" Emmy asked, trying to see if they would reveal themselves, those invisible mountains, the unseen frontier of Texas.

"They're God's fingerprint," he said. "The only way of seeing how long it took to create all this."

It was hard—almost impossible—to ignore the contradiction of his belief. That he could buy into evolution, but he couldn't wrap his head around the concept that love may be more boundless than how it was described in the same book that asserted the world's creation had happened in six days.

Emmy's anger often ping-ponged between Cameron and her father. Cameron for giving up on their love. Her dad for not believing in it.

As she drove, Emmy took deep inhales, trying to breathe through her anger, expel it out into the open, not let it lie dormant, invisible, like the Ouachita Mountains under Texas soil.

The Shermans' house was a little outside of Waco, in a small suburb with well-paved sidewalks, impeccably kept lawns, and streets filled with long one-story ranch-style houses. Emmy pulled in front of theirs, which was painted bright red with a white door, like an elongated barn. Before she even reached the door, Pastor Sherman and his wife were outside, walking up to greet Emmy.

Mrs. Sherman was a waif of a woman, with slender arms and a shock of long white plaited hair that she threw over her right shoulder. She wore no makeup and an old pair of overalls with a white T-shirt underneath.

"Emmy Quinn," Mrs. Sherman said, pulling her in for a hug, "we are so happy to see you."

"Emilia," Pastor Sherman said, coming up beside Mrs. Sherman. He was a tall man and towered over his wife, built much more like Michaela—broad shoulders, long legs, a long crooked nose, and warm wide gray-green eyes. "We have so much to catch up on."

They ushered Emmy into their home, which smelled like fried chicken, sautéed garlic and onions, and some kind of fruit crumble. The table was set, and Pastor Sherman took Emmy's bag to the guest room while Mrs. Sherman sat her down at the table, pouring her glasses of water and wine, refusing to let her help with anything, gushing over how much she'd grown up, how much she looked like her mother, how exciting it was that they would both be in Houston together.

They said grace before they ate, and Pastor Sherman blessed the food and the people, and as soon as he said *Amen*, Emmy took a bite of the best fried chicken she'd ever had in her life: tender and spicy and breaded just right.

Emmy asked about their kids, and when they got to Michaela, they told her everything, without hesitation or shame or awkwardness. She'd come out to them two years into college, and it had been hard, but they knew it would be worth it to work through it with her. She'd told them about Emmy and her and the back of the pickup truck, how that had solidified everything for her, but she wanted to make sure there was no other way around, wanted to make sure it wasn't a choice. When she was certain it wasn't, she told them. They'd all cried. It broke their hearts. But they stuck with her. Through the first bad girlfriend who loved Michaela so much she couldn't let her go to the most recent one, a law student at UT who was smart and funny. They lived together in Austin.

They asked about Emmy, about how her parents had handled it, and she told them the whole thing, every painful detail, and they held her hands and told her that they were sorry it had worked out the way it had. But that they were proud of her. That they were there for her. And that she wasn't wrong or damned or strange. She was just wholly herself, and she was loved.

When they were finished eating, Mrs. Sherman insisted on doing the dishes, leaving Emmy and Pastor Sherman alone at the table.

Once she heard the rush of sink water and the clatter of dishes from the kitchen, Emmy leaned in to ask one last question. The only one she'd really needed an answer to.

"How'd you get to be so on board with Michaela?"

"Oh, it was simple really," Pastor Sherman said, taking a sip of wine, then twisting the liquid around in his glass. "I just remembered what mattered most."

"My dad says he loves me," Emmy said, speaking slowly, making sure she got all the words right. "Loves me so much that he can't stand to see my soul get damned. And so he can't support me. So how did you do it? With Michaela? What makes your love different?"

Pastor Sherman leaned forward in his chair and clasped his hands together underneath his chin. He stayed silent for a long time. Then, finally, when he had his answer, he let out a long sigh.

"It was," he said, "the most profound realization of my life."

Since they were little, in Sunday school, they were taught that salvation was the entire point of Christianity. A person derives their meaning in life from the promise of their entrance into the next one, the price of admission being the belief that a carpenter's son from Nazareth was also the Son of God.

After hearing out Michaela, though, Pastor Sherman had started to think about the notion of salvation and what it meant to live a good Christian life. And then it occurred to him: if a person's love were motivated by the concept of salvation, then their love had inherent limitations. It was a performance on earth to get into heaven. All their actions were then motivated by that unknowable place. *The afterlife*, as it was called.

Love, Pastor Sherman explained, was the moral code of Christianity. But would a person still act in accordance with this moral code if they knew there was nothing waiting for them? No ostensible prize at the end of everything? Or, worse, that they might be *denied* entry into that very place they clung to?

At its heart, at its essence, the message of Jesus was *Love your neighbor as yourself and love your God with everything you've got.* He demanded that it come from people's hearts, their minds, their souls. Total focus—not on salvation but on love.

"If it all turned out to be fake, if Christianity was all just smoke and mirrors, if God really was dead and an illusion like so many have speculated," Pastor Sherman said, his voice deepening with each sentiment, the way it did when he used to preach his sermons, "it wouldn't change anything for me. Because my faith, my purpose, what propels me forward every day is not the notion of salvation. That at the end of this life, I'll be permitted entrance into the next one." He paused and took an enormous gulp of wine, wiping his mouth with the back of his hand. "It's love. It's not us versus them. We aren't 'running the race' for the prize at the end after all. We're running because we've got the legs to do it, the lungs to support us, and something embedded deep within us, driving us forward."

"So," Emmy asked, trying to keep up with him, "the point isn't to get into heaven, it's to do things well on earth?"

"It's not so much doing things *well* as committing yourself to love, which, according to Jesus, is supposed to be boundless. Radical. Transformative. But often, we get distracted by our desire to be right."

Emmy rubbed her jawline with her thumb, listening, trying to understand. *Needing* to understand. Pastor Sherman breathed out a little laugh and took off his glasses, cleaning the lenses with his shirt sleeve.

"I think it comes down to two things, Emmy, really," he said, putting his glasses back on. "The desire to be *right*. And the desire to be *true*."

He let the silence wrap around his words. An old pastor's trick. Hooking someone in with the promise of expansion.

Right and *true*. Emmy turned the two words over in her mind. She nodded a little once she understood their distinction.

"When we focus on salvation—who gets saved and who gets damned—what we're really prioritizing is who is right and who is wrong," Pastor Sherman continued, taking her cue. "But we ignore what it means to be *true*. So instead of loving folks, we try to get them to see why they're *wrong* and why we're right.

"We've fought wars because of this. We've justified stealing humans and their lands with this logic. And in our crusade—and I do not use that word lightly—to make the world right, we've lost the truth. Which is, simply, to love one another without condition, to the best of our conditional ability."

Pastor Sherman clasped his hands together when he was finished and gave a satisfied sort of sigh, smiling at Emmy.

Emmy thought about her father. His commitment to her soul. His inability to see her clearly, love her clearly, because he couldn't guarantee her safety in the afterlife. It sort of broke her heart that he was so blinded by righteousness that he had lost sight of love. But it also set Emmy free, the idea that his inability to accept her was not because she was unworthy of his love; it was because he was unwilling to give it. He was the one making a choice with his love. Not her.

"Could have used that kind of sermon when we were in Steinbeck," Emmy said, wiping her eyes.

"I wish I could have given it then," he said, shaking his head. "But I didn't understand. I was still learning. We're *always* still learning, Emmy, and growing. Changing our minds and seeing the world in a new way."

"I wish my dad would see that," Emmy said, glancing up at the clock. It was getting late.

"You're young," he said, checking the time, too, and getting up from his chair. "So a year feels like forever. But it's not really so much time."

"You really think he could change?" she asked.

"As long as the sun rises in the east," he said, smiling, walking toward the kitchen to help his wife, "there's time for him to come around."

Just before dawn, Emmy left a note on the counter, thanking the Shermans for their hospitality. She wondered if her mom had known how much she needed to talk with them, to see what acceptance in a family could look like. Her mom was probably just worried about her driving at night. But still. A part of her hoped that her mother had known a conversation like that would happen.

By the time Emmy made her way through Marlin, out of Waco, the sun had started to rise, a steady inch of light that forced the black sky to ombré into a deep red that sat on the horizon, putting the telephone wires and farm fences and trees in silhouette.

Stratus clouds sprawled across the sky, white wisps that took on the varying colors of the sun as it rose, red to pink to orange to gold. The cattle ranches on the side of the road were massive, pocked with cows and longhorns and horses running free. The fields were lush, green, filled with life. In such contrast to the dust, the brown, the dead emptiness that surrounded every home Emmy had ever had.

There was fog over the fields that started to clear away as the morning came in. But before it lifted completely, the semicircle sun on the horizon illuminated its density with light. Flecks of gold stood suspended in the early-morning haze.

It was a feeling she used to get in church. It filled her up as she looked at the sky, the landscape, all the space Texas had to offer. It was enough for Emmy; she was enough for it. It felt like a sort of gift, an olive branch from the infinite, and her heart swelled with gratitude at the thought that such a thing could still exist for her. She had never seen a vision of redemption, that value so instilled in her during her decades in the Baptist Church, but that drive—with the cattle ranches and the sunrise and all the space of an empty two-lane highway—seemed pretty close to it.

Something rose up in Emmy as she drove toward her new home. That unshakable feeling that she was staring down the barrel of an eternal promise, that people like her were created, that they were beautiful, and maybe, possibly, in spite of everything she had ever been told about them, that they were loved.

★ ★ ★ ★ ★

ACKNOWLEDGEMENTS

Writing is an isolated act that is always made better in collaboration. To that end, I have so many people to thank for helping this story fall into your hands.

Thank you to my wonderful agent, Amy Elizabeth Bishop, for understanding this story's heart and for all the nuanced notes that made it stronger. You are the best in the biz, and I'm so happy we get to work together. To Brittany Lavery, for the passionate insights, the patience in the revision process, and the deep, genuine enthusiasm for this story throughout the editing process. To the entire team at Graydon House Books, my sincerest thanks for all the work you've done to help bring this book into the world.

To my teachers: you've made me the student I am today. To Jennifer Loupe, for the separate summer reading lists, which included the life-altering *East of Eden*. To Susan Perry, for making me a conventionally sound writer and critical thinker. To Diane Creekmore, for helping me fall in love with the rhythm

and language of Shakespeare. To Edward Carson, for radical-
izing me with your lectures, empathy, and clarity of vision. To
Christine Metoyer, for teaching me historical perspective and
for becoming a great friend. To Stephen Hebert, for giving me
room to question and doubt and grow. To Natalie Hebert, for
growing alongside me.

To the English department at Baylor University for teaching
me even when I was shy and silent in class discussions. Thank
you to Mark Andrew Olsen, who taught me to ease up and *earn*
moments of sentimentality. To Arna Bontemps Hemenway, who
pushed my writing and critical thinking about craft in ways that
changed my stories and my life. To Dr. Coretta Pittman, for in-
troducing me to the personal essay form and for the open discourse provided in her classroom. To Dr. Jerrie Callan, whose
class discussions were so invigorating I decided to go all in on
an English Literature degree. And to Dr. Sarah Gilbreath Ford,
for the class discussions on haunted places, which greatly influ-
enced the way that I write about Texas.

To the WLP Graduate Department at Emerson College for
helping me hone my craft. To Steve Yarbrough, Yu-jin Chang,
Maria Koundoura, Richard Hoffman, and Amy Hoffman for
the intellectual leaps your classes made me take. To Rick Reiken
and Kim McLarin, who saw the earliest versions of this novel
and helped make it better by gently prying the un-working bits
of the manuscript out of my stubborn hands. To Julia Glass, who
saw the first iteration of this novel in the form of a short story,
and who always encouraged me, supported me, and laughed with
me on the twelfth floor of Ansin. And finally, and most especially, thank you to Mako Yoshikawa, who has been my greatest mentor and confidant in this writing process, who believed
in these characters and their stories, and who taught me from
my first class at Emerson through my thesis defense. I owe you
a great debt of gratitude for all the life you've helped breathe
into this novel.

To my darling, beloved Boston buds: my heart bursts with joy at the thought of you. Getting to learn from and read the writing of Nihal Mubarak, David Coco, Christina Montana, Prerna Somani, Ciera Burch, Jose Martinez, Brooke Knisley, Raina K. Puels, and so many others has made me a better human and writer, and helped quell that pesky, creeping sense of doom from rising up, reminding me of why it's such a beautiful thing to be alive. This sentiment is of course extended to the Tam Team, Khánh San Pham, Will Gibbons, Laura Rosenthal, Jessica Klein, and Devon Capizzi. The beers, venting, and laughter we've all had together has kept me sane and warm and inspired. And Capizzi, I'm sorry I talked to you about this novel for two years straight and refused to let you read it until the end. Next beer is on me.

To my heart in Texas, my friends who have seen me through it all: Kelsey Taylor, Brooke Fader, Clara Cooke, Katy Craft, Meredith Richter, Leigh Cummings, Tyler Segura, Kate Mathalone, Haley Barton, Kate Warren, and Noel Webb. And to Reghan Gillman, my second sibling, my sister, I love you with all the depths of my being and am grateful, as always, for the gift of your gorgeous soul.

To my family, every last member of it: your love has made me who I am today. To Anastasia, for all the long phone calls about craft and plot and story. To Hayden, for being the best big brother, and my favorite reader. To Payton, for your love and endless support and enthusiasm. To Dave, my West Texas expert, for all the notes and encouragement and close reading. And to Diantha, my first teacher, my greatest friend, my spiritual guide: everything I am, I owe to you. Your love made me strong, Ma.

Finally, to anyone who has ever been told that they are not enough, that they must change, that they have not measured up to the standard set out by one religious figure or the other: you are so wonderful, you are so loved, and your radical sense of identity will make the weight of this world so much easier to bear. In short, you are golden lightness, necessary to keep this plane of existence illuminated. Love is all I've got for y'all.